NO SAFE HAVEN

KIMBERLEY AND KAYLA R. WOODHOUSE

NASHVILLE, TENNESSEE

S0-AJV-156

Hudson Public Library
555 Main St.
PO Box 188
Hudson, CO 80642

Copyright © 2011 by Kimberley Woodhouse and
Kayla R. Woodhouse
All rights reserved.
Printed in the United States of America

978-1-4336-7116-6

Published by B&H Publishing Group,
Nashville, Tennessee

Dewey Decimal Classification: F
Subject Heading: MYSTERY FICTION \
MOTHER-DAUGHTER RELATIONSHIPS—FICTION
\ SURVIVAL AFTER AIRPLANE ACCIDENTS,
SHIPWRECKS, ETC.—FICTION

Authors represented by the literary agency
of Alive Communications, Inc., 7680 Goddard Street,
Suite 200, Colorado Springs, Colorado, 80920,
www.alivecommunications.com.

Scripture quotations or paraphrases are taken from the New American Standard Bible®, Copyright © 1960, 1962, 1963, 1968, 1971, 1972, 1973, 1975, 1977, 1995 by The Lockman Foundation. Used by permission. (www.Lockman.org). All rights reserved.

Publisher's Note: The characters and events in
this book are fictional, and any resemblance to actual
persons or events is coincidental.

1 2 3 4 5 6 7 8 • 15 14 13 12 11

DEDICATION

This book is dedicated:

From Kim:

To Dr. Gary Greene, for taking a little music major and encouraging me to write. He went home to be with the Lord during the final edits of this book, but his encouragement and love for his students will always be remembered.

And to Kayla—may we continue to grow in love and craft as we travel this writing journey together. I love writing with you, Squirt.

From Kayla:

My very first published book.

Dedicated to Jesus, My Lord and Savior, and to Ms. Karen, for her fantabulous idea.

And for Mama, for making me laugh and putting up with me even when I'm grumpy or sarcastic. I love writing with you.

ACKNOWLEDGMENTS

As most of you know, it takes an enormous number of people to bring a book to the point where it is now—in your hands. And so, Kayla and I wish to thank:

First and foremost—Thank You, God. Without You, none of this would be possible.

Our Readers—for your support, encouragement, notes, and excitement. What fun it is to have you along on this journey!

Jeremy and Josh—the Woodhouse "boys" who put up with deadlines, edits, brainstorming, and plain ol' craziness. We love you.

Tracie, Colleen, Donita, and Karen—for your mentorship, guidance, love, and prayers.

Our brilliant and amazing editor, Karen Ball—Wow. You are the best of the best. Where would we be without you? You've taught us so much and made our writing sing. Thank you. Thank you. Thank you.

Julie Gwinn—you are a marketing genius. What fun to work with you! Thanks for all you do.

Diana Lawrence—Thank you so much for your outstanding work on the most incredible cover ever. Wow. You are so gifted. Thank you for bringing Andie's face to life so beautifully and for the accuracy in all the details.

Everyone at B&H—we love and appreciate you all. What an honor to be with such an incredible publishing house.

Missy Smothers with the Talkeetna Rangers—you, my dear, are a gem. I thought for sure the day would come when you'd tell me I'd asked my quota of questions, but you didn't. Thank you—I will miss our chats! Thanks also to rangers Joe Reichert and John Loomis for their expertise.

Phil Lee—a true Denali/Sultana climber. Thank you so much for your willingness (and patience) to help with all the minute details, providing pictures and mountaineering expertise. Thanks too, to your sweet wife, Diane. What a privilege it was to meet you.

Wendy Callis—of Callis Kennels in North Pole, Alaska. You are a wealth of information. Can't wait for all the excitement to come in the next book as well.

Bill Zink—our genius pilot source. Thank you so much for taking the time to answer a bazillion phone calls and questions about planes, flying planes, crashing planes, etc. You never once said I (Kim) was crazy. (Even though I'm sure you thought it more than once!) And a huge thanks to you and Pam for all your support and prayers!

Our agent, Andrea Heinecke, of Alive Communications—you have been our champion and friend. Thank you.

Our crit/early readers—Darcie, Mary, Ronie, Keighley, Carrie, Evangeline, Lori, Casey, Tammy, Katie, and Eryn. Thank you.

Snow City Café—the managers and chefs who took such good care of us, and of course, our server, Ezra, who made the experience even more enjoyable. We love your food!

The amazing folks at NASA who graciously answered our questions about missile interceptors and thought our imagined defense/weapon was pretty cool. And to the wonderful people and producers with *EMHE (Extreme Makeover: Home Edition).* Thank you for everything you have done to support our family.

With appreciation and love,

Kimberley and Kayla

PROLOGUE

MARCUS
March 31
Fairbanks, Alaska
3:02 p.m.

The passenger door slammed, the vibration rippling through his bones, like a skeleton rattled by the wind. He shook his head. Dark thoughts and a sense of foreboding. Things had to happen. Fast.

Before that foreboding became reality.

He smacked his palms on the steering wheel and fought the urge to curse his circumstances. But they were of his own doing. No turning back now.

A glance to the rearview mirror, and he watched the retreating form of his fellow soldier—his best special ops man. The man's rigid back. His quick and hard steps. They told the tale.

It was too late.

Regret washed over him in waves of heat and pain. As the knot in his gut intensified, thoughts of his family rushed to the forefront of his mind. Vivid pictures. But the smiling faces, instead of bringing relief, made him nauseous.

He looked again at the rearview mirror. His friend was already around a corner, out of sight. But that wasn't what grabbed his attention—what put all his senses on alert.

His eyes widened. A car barreled toward him at an alarming speed . . . a car with no driver. That meant only one thing. Remote-control delivery system.

For explosives.

Was that why Maddox got out of the car?

In that instant, pictures flashed in his mind, like a movie before his eyes.

Rich black hair, a silky halo around the beauty that was his wife. Startling blue eyes, a mirror of his own, shining in the face of his precious daughter. Both, ever and always, filled with love . . . with trust . . .

He'd been such a fool.

Jenna . . . Andie . . . I'm so sorr—

Sound was blotted out—and then exploded around him. Screaming, crushing metal compressed reality as his body jerked from the impact of the other vehicle.

A rush of air filled his lungs as adrenaline surged through him.

He knew what was coming next.

CHAPTER ONE

JENNA
One Year Later
April 6
Anchorage, Alaska
5:02 p.m.

The plane dropped like a 3,000-pound stone.

Jenna Tikaani-Gray braced herself with one hand, and held a warm, foam cup away from her body with the other as they jostled along. These pockets of air were turning the flight into a wild ride at the fair. Good thing she loved the fair almost as much as she loved flying, because they were dropping again. Down, then up, then down again, until the sky turned to silk and the plane sailed along.

At least the turbulent takeoff hadn't spilled the coffee.

After a long, slow sip, Jenna released a sigh as their small de Havilland DHC-2 Beaver left the bowl of Anchorage, Alaska, and lifted high into the clear blue sky above. The mountains around Anchorage always produced a bumpy ride, but she'd managed to pass coffee to Hank and their other passenger without mishap.

Only one more leg of the journey and they'd be home.

A beautiful hand reached across the seat, welcoming her embrace, and she smiled at her twelve-year-old daughter, Andrea. Such a sweet kid. Jenna had been blessed from above with her only child. Andie had been through such trial and heartache, yet faced the world with pure joy.

Jenna squeezed her daughter's fingers as the radio buzzed and crackled.

"Juliet Kilo 3-2-6 November," Departure Control came through the channel loud and clear. "I'm getting no mode C on your transponder. Squawk 2-3-7-5 i-dent."

Hank, the pilot, replied, "Roger. 3-2-6 November, squawking 2-3-7-5 i-dent . . ."

"Negative radar contact. Maintain VFR. Do you have another transponder?"

"Roger. I'll switch to backup."

Jenna leaned over the side of her seat, watching Hank flip the switch from transponder A to B. She waited for word from Departure Control.

"Still negative radar contact. Can you maintain VFR?"

"Roger that, Control. No problem."

Hmmm. Very strange. How could both transponders be malfunctioning? She furrowed her brow. When they returned to North Pole, she'd have to get it checked out. Good thing Hank was an experienced pilot. Since Marc's death, Jenna hired him to pilot their plane, and knew he could handle whatever might happen.

Andie pulled on her arm, bringing Jenna's attention from the cockpit back to her daughter.

"Mom?"

"Yeah, sweetie?"

"What does VFR mean?" Andie's fascination with flying rivaled her own.

Jenna let the tension ease from her own features as she leaned close to Andie, a little thrill rippling through her body. How she loved talking about flying. "Visual Flight Rules. Hank filed an IFR flight plan—Instrument Flight Rules—but the transponders must be malfunctioning, so the tower is instructing him to fly VFR, meaning visually. If we didn't have a clear day, that would make flying VFR trickier, sometimes impossible."

"Is it safe to fly VFR?"

Andie must've noted her reaction earlier. Jenna had never been good at hiding things from her inquisitive child.

Jenna noticed the other passenger glance back at them from his seat next to the pilot, and she held back a frown. The rough flight could explain the man's lack of a smile, but what caused the fierce look he shot them? Jenna cocked her head, questioning the man with her silent stare. A poke from Andie brought her back to the question.

"Yes, it's safe."

"Just checkin'." Andie giggled, the dimples indenting her cheeks so like her father's. As she squeezed Jenna's hand she turned to look out the tiny window next to her seat.

The man watched Jenna as she faced forward once again. Something in his intense gaze pulled at her, but she couldn't discern what. She'd been so excited about going home that she hadn't paid much attention when they were introduced. His name was . . . Cole? *Ugh. Good job remembering the details, Jenna.* Marc had taught her better than that.

Well, whether she could remember his name or not, something about this guy bothered her. Then again, the power of his gaze pulled her like a magnet. She forced herself to break the connection and focused on the scenery beneath them. Greens and blues melded with the white of melting snow. This was her favorite part of flying. Watching the beauty of God's handiwork skim beneath her.

The two men up front spoke in hushed tones, bringing her attention back to their puzzling guest. Hank approached her before the flight, asking if they could take another passenger, and she didn't mind. The added income would be nice. But who was this guy? And why, if he were just another tourist, was he so serious?

Jenna closed her eyes. Never mind about him. She had other, more amazing things to focus on. Namely, the news from Andie's neurosurgeon. The results were far beyond her expectations and, for the first time in many years, Jenna allowed herself to dream big for her precious child. Tragedy and hurt could now be replaced with hope. The future was, at long last, bright.

She reached for the dog tags around her neck. If only Marc could be there. He'd been distraught when, as a toddler, their daughter was first diagnosed. As if that first news weren't bad enough, the additional diagnosis two years ago just about broke the man. He'd never quite recovered, and his demeanor forever changed. The once crazy adventurer—a man full of life and laughter—closed himself behind a stone wall of protection.

She'd fought long and hard to penetrate his defenses, but taking care of Andie had become their focus, taken all their energy. When their daughter went in for brain surgery a year ago, the walls between them fell as they cried and held one another in the surgical waiting room. But Jenna never had the chance to discover what drove her husband to such emotional extremes. The accident took him before Andie was released from the hospital.

Opening her eyes, she blinked back the tears threatening to spill down her cheeks. *Stop it! This is no time for tears. It's a happy day.*

They would move on from here.

She turned to gaze out the window. How long had she been lost in her memories? And, for that matter . . . she leaned closer to the glass, searched for familiar landmarks . . .

The scenery wasn't right.

Jenna frowned. Where *were* they?

She opened her mouth to ask Hank, but brisk movement in the cockpit drew her attention to the two men up front. All she saw was a sight that shoved her heart into her throat.

Hank and the man beside him were fighting! The man grabbed Hank's arm and—

A gun! Hank had a gun!

Before she could move, Hank jerked his arm free, took aim, and shot the radio. Jenna glanced at Andie, then ripped open her seatbelt. Andie's mouth hung open, her eyes wide. Jenna yanked the belt off her and shoved her over the seat toward the rear of the plane. She climbed after her frightened child, signaled her to crouch in the floor, then hunched over Andie, hugging her tight, whispering calming words to shield her from the horror of the scene unfolding in front of them.

The plane plunged and veered to the west.

Heart thundering, Jenna monitored the scuffle through a crack between the seats and prayed for wisdom and safety. What was happening?

Arms wrestled and tangled—the passenger pushed upward, almost hovering over Hank. What if he *killed* Hank?

The thought of losing their pilot had her straightening, ready to clamber over the seats. Someone had to fly the plane or none of them would survive. The plane teetered and shuddered. Jenna felt the panic rise in her throat. *God, no! You can't do this. You can't let Andie die! Not like this. Not when she's survived so much. She's all I've got left.*

The passenger rammed a fist into Hank's face. Though Hank fought back, he soon crumpled under the intense blows. But that wasn't what shocked Jenna. What sent a jolt of confused terror through her was the evil smirk on Hank's face as he croaked out five awful words: "You'll . . . never make . . . it . . . alive!"

What did he mean? Was that a threat to the man hovering over him? Or . . . to them all?

A sickening sound pulled her attention back to the men. Bone on bone. Apparently the passenger had delivered one last blow, rendering Hank unconscious. Determination stretched taut over the man's features as he shoved Hank to the floor behind him and climbed into the pilot's seat. He tossed a small cord to Jenna. "Tie his hands!"

He fought to level off the plane, then glanced back in her direction. His breaths were ragged and his eyes bore a glassy sheen. He looked different . . . unfocused. Dare she depend on him? Jenna wasn't sure about anything. It was all happening too fast.

Grabbing Andie, she hauled herself back over the seat and fumbled with the cording. It was a good thing Hank was unconscious, as her knots needed work. She darted a glance toward the cockpit, and decided to strap Hank back in. Their landing could be really rough if this guy didn't know what he was doing, and she wanted their former pilot to be in good enough condition to go to jail.

"Leave him!" Even though the man's upper lip was sweaty and his skin's hue resembled mashed peas, his glare could burn a hole through steel. "You two buckle up!" He turned back to the controls.

Jenna bowed her head. *God . . . help us . . .*

"This may be bumpy, I don't know . . . what they did to . . . your plane . . ." The man's words grew alarmingly slurred. "I'm not feeling . . . so . . . hhhoo . . ."

In a matter of seconds, he slid down his seat and slumped over the yoke, arms limp at his sides.

Time stood still. Jenna could hear her lungs taking in air, could see Andie's eyes widen, could feel the plane dive forward—but she couldn't move. *God, help me! Spare my daughter, please!*

Andie screamed.

In that split second, Jenna's survival instinct kicked in full force. Bolting up, she grabbed Andie. "It's going to be okay, baby."

She slid a hand down Andie's cheek, shooting a quick glance to the plane's air speed and altimeter. They'd dropped 3,000 feet since the last time she'd noticed. No time to panic. "I need you to help me move this guy, and then I want you to grab Hank's headset and buckle up in the copilot's seat. Can you do that?"

Without waiting for an answer, she squeezed Andie's shoulder and climbed over seats into the cockpit. Adrenaline pumped pure strength through Jenna's veins as she moved the bulk that was the man who had tried to save them.

Or kill them.

She shoved his solid, muscled frame over the seat, then into the seat behind hers. She motioned for Andie to help strap him as she tugged on the yoke to lift the nose. Hank was sprawled, his legs at an odd angle, but she had bigger concerns at the moment.

Like landing the plane.

As soon as the man was strapped in, Andie grabbed Hank's headset, dashed back to the front, and climbed into the seat next to Jenna.

Jenna took a deep breath and turned to the controls as Andie buckled in. Their brief nose dive had increased the air speed. She pulled back on the throttle, then looked through the windshield—and gasped.

Denali, "the high one," the tallest mountain in North America, loomed before her. They shouldn't be anywhere *near* the Alaska Range, and yet here they were—flying straight into the South Face.

"Your seatbelt, Mom!"

Jenna's hands gripped the yoke tighter. No time for a seatbelt. She needed control of this plane.

"Mom!"

"It's okay, honey. Calm down."

"But, Mom—" Andie gripped the headset—"can you save us?"

"I'm gonna try, sweetie." For all the confidence she forced into those words, she knew all too well that two weeks of flight ground school and one lesson didn't quite give her the know-how to get out of this alive. *Oh, God! Show me what to do!*

Pulling up on the yoke, she worked to level out the small aircraft. The Beaver's response didn't feel right. Her gut told her something was very wrong.

Calm. She needed to stay calm. For Andie.

A glance down at the gauges confirmed her suspicions. The fuel gauge was low. Too low. And still dropping. *Lord! What do we do?*

Stay calm. Stay. Calm. "Honey, I need you to set those four dials on the radio controls to 1-2-1-5. That's the emergency frequency. 1-2-1-5. Okay?"

Andie nodded and obeyed. The kid had been through brain surgery and a lifetime dealing with a rare physical condition. She knew when to do what she was told without asking questions. Her hands shook as she sucked in a deep breath and started turning the knobs. "Okay, Mom." Nervous blue eyes met hers as she handed over the headset. "It's set."

Slamming the headset onto her head, Jenna winced. *Careful. Breathe. Andie's relying on you.* "Mayday! Mayday! Juliet Kilo 3-2-6 November needs emergency assistance. We have no pilot aboard capable of flying this plane. Mayday! Mayday!"

Crackling, hissing, static, and then silence.

"Mayday, mayday! Juliet Kilo 3-2-6 November requesting emergency assistance!"

Nothing.

"Mom, the radio's dead. Hank shot it. Why would he do that, Mom?"

Andie's sweet voice filled the cabin as reality set in. Tears quietly streamed down her daughter's face.

"Baby, I don't know, but I have to try to land this plane. Put your head between your knees right now and cover your head with your arms."

Her brave little trooper obeyed, and Jenna prayed for guidance. Taking a firm grip on the yoke, she tried to turn the plane. The rudder gave a brief response and then locked. Something was wrong with the ailerons. What had she forgotten? Why wasn't it responding?

Okay, Jenna, think. Cut your descent. Flaps down. What else can I do? Oh, God, help me remember! Help me think. The fuel gauge flashed at her now, only fumes were left. There was no avoiding it: they were going to crash. She needed to strap herself in. Fumbling with one hand made it all the more difficult. "Andie, help me with the buckle."

Taking in the treacherous view in front of her, she made a decision for their lives. She had to steer away from Denali. Sultana stood to her left, towering in all her glory. If she could just get close to Kahiltna glacier, she might be able to land there. Tourist planes did it all the time. Right?

But they were too high. The controls were almost useless.

She'd have to find a different place to land and soon. With all her might she worked the yoke to turn west, away from the 20,320-foot Denali, but the mountain face of Sultana rushed toward her at a terrifying pace. The yoke locked and the plane jolted on a pocket of air, engines sputtering with the last drops of fuel.

Not much time left.

No radio.

No controls.

No fuel.

Nowhere to go.

Bracing her feet in the floor, she pulled on the yoke with all her weight—hoping she could lift the nose even an inch or two—but the plane no longer responded. At all.

As they raced toward the steep mountainside, Jenna did the only thing left to her: prayed for snow to be deep enough to cushion their landing.

With one last cry for help, Jenna let go of the useless yoke and flung her arms over her daughter's body, inhaling Andie's scent: Citrus shampoo and a sweetness all her daughter. But she couldn't tear her eyes away from the scene.

Metal crunched. Glass shattered and peppered her arms. The plane creaked and groaned as they slammed into Sultana's unyielding side. Metal screamed, and Jenna understood. The mountain had ripped the wings from the fuselage.

Her breaths seemed hours apart as the plane pummeled the snow-packed earth underneath them. *God—!*

But the desperate prayer was blotted out when everything went from the brilliant white of the snow to deep, deep black of unconsciousness.

ANDIE

April 6
Sultana, Denali National Park
7:23 p.m.

Air crossed my face.

What's that? Was someone breathing beside me?

Something rustled next to my hand.

Wind . . . Is that the wind? As if a curtain lifted, my thoughts began to clear. *Why would I feel the wind inside an airplane?*

Something wasn't right.

Placing a hand on my head, I put slight pressure to it. Why—how—was my head hurting? I lifted my sore eyelids.

Oh! Bright light.

How long had I been unconscious? Where was I?

Again I opened my eyes, this time with caution.

Blurry images floated around me. A spinning sensation flip-flopped my stomach. *Why am I spinning?*

Sunlight streamed through small, cracked windows and red polka dots spotted otherwise blank walls. *Where am I?*

The spinning stopped.

Weird.

I wiggled within the tight confines of my seatbelt, trying to escape its grip, but conked my head on a lumpy thing hanging in the air above me. *That's gonna leave a bruise.*

Why wouldn't these straps budge?

I unlatched them—then fell.

Ouch.

I rubbed my shoulder where I'd landed. Was it bruised too? *Perfect, just what I need right now.*

I looked up. I was on the *ceiling* of the plane? I'd been hanging . . . upside down? As if on cue, I could feel all the blood draining out of my head. Letting out a groan, I rubbed my cheeks and forehead. *Why is my body aching so much?*

And where was Mom? She wasn't hurt, was she?

I climbed out on my hands and knees through what must have been the windshield, but moving only made the dizziness worse.

"Ouchy!" My head started to hurt. Really hurt. What was the weird, zinging pain?

Pain? Emotions swirled through me, like a hurricane of confusion and fear. The last time I felt pain, they told me I needed brain surgery.

Tears slid down my icy cold cheeks.

God, what's happening?

I shook my head and continued crawling out of the broken-down airplane. *Do* not *let it irritate you, Andie.* As I wiped at the tiny droplets, a gritty, dirty feeling coated my fingers. I looked down at my upturned palms. They were smothered in dirt. And blood.

Lots of blood.

Oh, great.

Spots danced in front of me like Mexican jumping beans . . .

Then there was nothing.

- -

My eyes popped open. The clear blue sky loomed above and blurry, lazy white clouds floated by.

It took a second to remember where I was . . . what had happened? I glanced around. *How am I all the way outside?* How long was I unconscious? Pain still shot throughout my body, unfamiliar electrical waves.

Okay . . . Deep breath. *Andrea Tikaani-Gray,* do *something.* I grunted and pushed myself to a sitting position. Why did it take so much effort just to sit up?

One more deep breath.

Reaching my left hand underneath my long, black hair, I gently touched the scar on the back of my neck. The familiar bumpy groove greeted my fingers—it was intact. The sticky feeling of blood didn't cling to my fingers . . . on that hand. So there was no blood or wounds on my scar, right?

My surroundings came into focus. Snow, more snow, boulders, more snow, glass, more snow, the airplane . . .

Uh-oh. The airplane. Hadn't I been in the airplane? Or did I dream that?

I glanced around, then wished I hadn't.

Some sort of big, metal, whatchamacallit was smashed against a rock and the tail-rudder-thingamabob had fallen off and lay on the other side of the crash. There was no sign of the wings, and the windshield lay shattered in a million pieces sparkling on the snow as they reflected the sun's light. Lying in the middle was a lump.

Mom?

My body protested as I jumped up and ran over to her. Blood covered her pale body. *Blood* . . . Pulling in air, I jerked away before my stomach decided to rebel again.

"Mom! Wake up!" I shook her shoulder, but it didn't help. I looked around for somebody . . . anybody . . .

Another figure lay on the ground.

I clenched my eyes. This couldn't really be happening.

I trudged through the snow and fell on the ground. Tears spilled down my face turning into ice as a scratchy voice inside my head stated the most awful truth:

They're all dead. You're alone.

CHAPTER TWO

ANDIE
April 6
Sultana, Denali National Park
8:13 p.m.

Alone.

The word slammed into me, like a brick smashing into my noggin. But even as I felt panic starting to crawl through me, another voice whispered . . .

God wouldn't leave me alone.

I closed my eyes. I wasn't alone. God was there. *Think about it, Andie.* If I was going to die, wouldn't He have made me die in the crash?

Okay, maybe not, but still.

Words flowed through my mind. Words I knew and loved.

> *The* Lord *is my light and my salvation; whom shall I fear? The* Lord *is the defense of my life; whom shall I dread? When evildoers came upon me to devour my flesh, my adversaries and my enemies, they stumbled and fell. Though a host encamp against me, my heart will not fear; Though war arise against me, in spite of this I shall be confident.*

I released my breath in a long sigh. *Okay, I'm not alone. Maybe I'm jumping to conclusions. Just because they're not moving doesn't mean they're. . . . But even if they are—*

I didn't even want to think about that it hurt so bad. But I had to think about it. What would happen if nobody did wake up? *Even if they are*—I straightened my back and clenched my fists—*with God, I don't need to be afraid.*

I wiped my tears, sniffed, then nodded.

I will be strong!

I took a deep breath and hiccupped. Searing pain shot through my chest as the cold air rushed in. I remembered where we were.

Crashed on the side of a mountain.

Wonderful.

It was cold outside. *I need to be careful.* All those years of Mom reminding me to wear a coat and warning me about frostbite, yet I still sat there ignoring the fact that I was surrounded, sitting, and *covered* in snow.

Brave, brave, I have to be brave.

A drop of blood made its way down my hand and onto the pure white, sinking into snowflakes and reminding me that my hand needed to be cleaned up. And fast.

I closed my eyes, then shoved it into the cold snow. Would it wipe the blood off? Peeking with one eye, I pulled my hand out. The blood was gone. But a glance at the snow showed me where it went.

Ugh.

Andie, get over it. It's just a little bit, you'll be fine . . .

I examined my hand. Three long cuts sliced across the top and one on my palm. I winced. The one on my palm looked like it needed stitches.

Deep, red, with blood oozing out.

Rats.

I covered the red patch with clean, white snow, then trudged over to Mom.

My stomach clenched as I fell to the ground beside her, slamming my knee into something hard.

Ow! What was that?

I sucked in air between my clenched teeth, then closed my eyes and counted to ten. *That's gonna leave another nasty bruise.*

Swinging my leg out from beneath me, I rotated it, then sighed as the feeling came back. *Okay. You're fine.*

Mom needs you now.

I picked off some of the glass pieces and huge, sharp, shards lying on Mom's chest. If one had stabbed her . . .

Thank God they hadn't. But a big gash on her leg proved disturbing, as well as the multiple cuts and bruises. She had to wake up. I couldn't do this . . . God knew that, didn't He?

I touched her face. "Mom, don't leave me. I can't lose you, too."

She didn't move.

God, please! Wasn't it enough to lose my dad? *How am I supposed to do this alone?*

The answer was there. In my mind. In my heart. I didn't have to go on alone. She'd wake up. She had to. I just needed to be brave for her. To think.

What would Mom do in this situation?

Another tear slid down my cheek. I stared at her face as if she would give me an answer. I could hear her voice in my head: *Check to see if anything's wrong with you.*

Okay, sure. I could do that, right? I checked myself the way she did when I got hurt. First my arms, then my ankles, then my legs. Nothing was broken—that I could tell—but I did have some pretty mean bruises.

What else does Mom do? What does she check? Think, Andie. If she were here, what would she do?

I smiled. She'd play my favorite song, "End of the Beginning" to calm me. Make me smile. I closed my eyes and let the song start.

Remembering all the times Mom let me sit in front of our CD player listening to David Phelps sing, then pressing rewind over and over and over again made laugh. But . . .

There would be no more sweet sound of Mom's voice, no more comforting touch, no more welcoming embrace. Not if we didn't get off of this mountain.

Soon.

I stood up and trudged through the knee-high snow. Facing the possibility that everyone else might be dead, or die, was not my idea of "good news, new life."

But you've got to keep going for Mom. That way, when she wakes up—if she does—she won't have as much to do. Come on, Andie, night's darkness will be here soon.

It was up to me to get my mom off the mountain. To get her to safety. To do it now.

I stared up at the sky.

God, I am all alone, aren't I?

LEAPER

April 6
8:20 p.m.

Leaper's last conversation with his boss, Viper, and the rest of the group swam through his head. The constant buzzing annoyed him, like a mosquito on a mission, intensifying his headache. If only he could wipe the memories out as easily as he smashed one of the bloodsuckers. For that matter, it'd be nice to get rid of the pounding in his head as well.

"I don't care what you have to do! Just get rid of Gray's family, and get me AMI!"

"But, sir? What if they have the information we need?"

Viper's dark eyes narrowed. "I'm tired of waiting. They had their chance."

Leaper's rookie jumped into the conversation. "We don't know that Mrs. Gray and the kid know anything. The little girl has special needs. Killing them will only raise suspicion—"

Viper's reply was stone cold. "Not if it's an accident. Small planes go down all the time."

Leaper nodded. His orders were clear. "Yes, sir. An accident."

"Good. See to it and report back to me."

"Yes, sir." He stiffened his shoulders and turned to follow the rest of the group as they exited. This job would be the death of him.

"And Leaper?"

Possibly sooner than later. "Sir?"

"Don't ever question me again." The words dropped like a sledge hammer, their meaning clear. The next time would be the last time.

For anything.

He straightened. Met Viper's glacial gaze. "Yes, sir."

Pain ripped through his skull, washing the memory away, returning him to reality. Death would be welcome if not for one simple fact.

He'd sold his soul to the devil.

ANDIE
8:32 p.m.

Maybe if I look for stuff in the cargo bay, I'll find something to do.

I nodded. *Occupy yourself . . .*

As I neared the plane I saw how smashed and ugly it was. Scrapes and dents covered it. Poor little thing.

Yes, it was an inanimate object, but still!

Large pieces of metal lay implanted in the squishy snow. Water bottles, big metal thingies, bags of cargo, some of Mom's "necessities" . . .

Another step—and I sank into waist-deep snow. Clenching my eyes I let out an aggravated sigh.

Now I was freezing.

I climbed out of the hole, shivering. Sad day. Getting too cold was just as bad as getting too hot, since my body couldn't regulate either one.

I need to put on heavier clothes. And a bandage for my hand would be nice.

I spotted one of our suitcases jammed underneath the cargo door. *Maybe I can find some in there.* I pulled it out with my good hand and popped it open, clutching my scratched hand to my chest. A throb seemed to run alongside the scratches.

Is that normal?

An old night shirt lay smashed in the corner of the suitcase. *How do I tear this thing? My multipurpose tool . . . where is it?*

I felt my pocket, and sure enough, it was there. I pulled it out—and memories of Dad came flooding back. He'd been so excited to give it to me, I could still hear him as if he was standing there, talking to me in his deep, gravelly voice . . .

"I got it from a special shop out of town. The owner would have charged extra to engrave someone's name on it, but he gave me a discount when I told him it was for your birthday."

"Daddy, it's so beautiful!"

He smiled. "I thought you would like it." He pointed to the delicately carved wolf. "He says the tikaani on the front means good luck. I made sure it didn't have a knife so you wouldn't hurt yourself." He winked. "But it does have scissors, just in case."

I'd smiled back at his use of the Ahtna name for wolf. Even though he wasn't Ahtna-Athabaskan like Mom and me, he respected our heritage and used the fun-to-say native words frequently.

I missed him so much.

A cold blast of wind chased the memories away, but the sadness remained. I swallowed back more tears and rubbed my hand over the smooth wooden case.

Get a grip, Andie. Concentrate on what you need to do.

By the time I finished bandaging my hand and Mom's wounds, my hand—and the new bandage on it—were coated in blood once again.

"Wonderful."

How much time would I have before the temperature really dropped? Last week, when we'd left home, the sun had been coming up after 7:00 a.m. and going down before 9:00 p.m. That meant this week it would be coming up after 6:30 a.m. and setting after 9:00 p.m., right?

I need to hurry if I'm going to get Mom in a sleeping bag. I should probably put the other dude in one too.

Crawling back into the plane, I found two of our expensive sleeping bags. And the tent.

Unfortunately it was ripped.

"Snap!"

I'd always wondered why Dad bought $900 sleeping bags. They were supposed to keep you warm in 40-below temps. I guess we'd see if that was true.

I found our winter gear and put on my purple coat, ski mask, and a pair of goggles, then grabbed two other masks and goggles for Mom and the Other Dude.

After covering up everyone's exposed skin, I sat down with a huff. *Daddy, I wish you were here. You'd know what to do. Why did you have to leave? I miss you so much. I didn't even get to say good-bye.* I closed my eyes, and pictures of the fight on the plane came to me.

Hank was a friend of yours, right? Then who's the good guy here—? My eyes popped open. *Hey, where is Hank?*

I stood up faster than a bolt of lightning. Was he spying on me? Was he hurt? *I hope not. He may be my only hope of getting out of here. But if he's the bad guy . . .*

I marched toward the plane. *He better not be spyin' on me. If I find out that he's alive and can—*

A brown object caught my attention.

I glanced around. No one was watching so it couldn't be one of those remote-controlled bombs, could it? I crept closer to the bag.

Hank disappeared from thought as I sighed and put my hands on my hips. *And why didn't I find this before?* Mom's emergency bag. *Figures.*

I dragged it over to my new makeshift "camp." It was a good thing Mom always packed enough food, clothes, and emergency supplies for forty-five people.

I'll have to thank her when she wakes up.

Dad used to tease her, saying she packed the whole house. His voice still rang in my ears: "Be it car, plane, or dogsled, your mom always travels prepared for anything and everything."

I smiled, covered my mouth, and with sarcasm gasped, "We forgot the kitchen sink!"

I pulled Mom out of the sleeping bag, wrapped her in some blankets, then wrestled her back into it. By then I was exhausted. But I couldn't rest yet.

Time to build a fire.

Thankfully I knew how. *But can I?* I scanned my surroundings. *No, not enough oxygen, not enough wood.*

Not any wood.

I was sure Mom brought a camp stove. But had it survived the crash?

My stomach growled.

Maybe I should look for berries so there's food for everyone. That is, if anyone else wakes up.

I went to dig in the snow around the plane, remembering how Mom and I used to pick berries and one time had a berry fight.

Okay, so maybe more than once.

As the memories flooded over me, I realized I was just trying to latch onto something happy. There were no berries up on this glaciated, tree-less, vegetation-less peak.

No berries, and no people.

So, no one can come to save us?

My head shot up and I scanned the area around me.

Someone groaned. And it wasn't Mom.

I jumped. Then, turning around, I listened for the sound again.

Another groan. This one louder.

I crept toward the plane looking all around to make sure it wasn't an ambush of bears or something. *Okay, Lassie. Time to come save the day.* Where was that dog? *Oh wait*! This wasn't TV. I was alone, on Sultana, in Alaska, in April, before tourist season.

Wonderful.

Maybe I should have called Balto.

I approached the hole I'd crawled through earlier. Glass was sprinkled everywhere. The smell of blood made my stomach churn.

Something, or someone, lay sprawled on the "floor" in the middle-ish, covered in dark, red blood.

Hank.

CHAPTER THREE

COLE
April 6
Sultana, Denali National Park
9:19 p.m.

The scent of plane fuel filled his nose. Reaching for his throbbing head, Cole Maddox forced his eyes open. Where was he? Memories tumbled over one another, like rapid fire from a machine gun, but he couldn't put the pieces together.

A plane. A sense of urgency. The need to rescue—who?

A spasm of shivers gripped him.

Cold. So cold.

As his senses took in his surroundings, his mind slowly cleared away the fog. The stars overhead were brilliant. Bright moonlight shone on the snow, giving it an ethereal glow.

He lay at an odd angle . . . he was on a steep slope. The snow underneath reminded him of the treachery of bush Alaska. The aches and pains humming throughout his body reminded him he was alive.

Then the pieces fell into place.

He'd found them.

He'd been drugged.

He didn't save them.

The rest of the picture unfolded as he looked around him. Clearly, they'd crashed. So who flew the plane? Last thing he remembered, he'd been in the cockpit. And where had they crashed? And how did Hank manage to drug him? He hadn't eaten anything and the only thing he drank—

The coffee!

But why would Jenna Gray drug him? He shook his head. Couldn't have been her. Hank was the only logical explanation. But how?

A vague memory nudged him. He'd awakened earlier to that same smell of fuel, knew he had to get Marc's wife and daughter out of the plane. But thanks to whatever narcotic Hank used, he'd only been able to drag one of them through the windshield before he collapsed.

A child's voice singing a tune he didn't recognize brought his attention back to the present. His body tensed as he lifted himself to a sitting position, where his gaze collided with a pair of brilliant blue eyes. Marcus's little girl.

Bundled up in a sleeping bag next to her mom, she stared at him. Her ski goggles rested up on her forehead. All he could see were those penetrating eyes.

He swore under his breath. If he guessed correctly, she was just as smart and intense as her father. How much did she know?

She tilted her head, seeming to study him in the silence.

He held her stare. Kid looked scared and confident all at the same time.

Another lapse of time passed.

She raised her eyebrows. "Who are you?"

Child or not, he answered to no one. Especially when the facts weren't straight in his mind yet. Cole forced himself to focus. His mind felt like meat that had gone through the grinder one too many times.

"Well? Aren't you going to answer?" She wiggled out of her cocoon and crossed her arms over her chest. Oh joy. Drama queen.

He was in charge here. And he needed a new plan.

"Hello? Are you deaf? Why are you ignoring me?"

Cole huffed, bringing the zinging pain in his ribcage to the forefront of his mind. No time for broken bones. He looked down at his legs. Maybe if he pretended to check his own injuries, she'd leave him alone.

"Excuse me, mister, but I asked you a question. And considering you were a passenger on *our* plane, I think I have the right to know."

Her voice quivered, but only slightly. And the set of her chin—just like her father's—was anything but frightened. Would knowing his name satisfy her? Probably not. "Cole."

"So you *were* ignoring me." She chucked a bottle of water at him. "Just Cole?"

"Cole Maddox."

"Well, Mr. Cole Maddox, should I trust you?"

He stilled. Looked up again. The question caught him off guard. Must've been the drugs. She'd never taken her narrowed eyes off him. *Brave kid. Like her dad.*

He schooled his features to indifference. "What do *you* think, Andie?"

That gaze of hers could be a weapon. Innocence and wisdom. Terrifying combination.

"Well . . . *Cole*," her eyes narrowed to thin slits as she spoke, "I'm not quite sure. You know my name, but that wouldn't be so hard since we were in a small plane together, and I'm sure my mom must've used it at some point. You fought with Hank, who we've known for a long time, but then he shot the radio, so what do we really know about him? I realize you *tried* to save us, but you could've just been saving your own neck since we were gonna crash anyway. I don't know how or why the fight started, so again, I'm not so sure. So with all due respect, I'd like to hear from *your* mouth if I should trust you. And why."

Cole stared. She didn't look older than ten or eleven, but there she was, in control, sounding like a skilled, unyielding interrogator. Maybe she wasn't a kid at all, but a midget operative in disguise.

He shook his head. Obviously an only child. A highly intelligent, wise-beyond-her-years only child. And clearly, Marc had trained her well.

"Look, kid—"

"My name's not *kid,* and you are avoiding the question. Again."

"Okay, Andie. I'd like for you to trust me. But trust has to be earned." Every muscle and bone in his body ached. He looked off into the distance, at the moonlight illuminating the mountains in the sky above. "As to why you should do so"—he brought his gaze back to hers—"well, *I'm* not trying to kill you."

Her eyes widened at that. So she could be shaken. Somehow that made him feel better.

"Okay then, Mr. Cole Maddox. I think we're gonna have to work together."

He shivered again.

"Ya know, if you would've stayed in the sleeping bag where I put you, you wouldn't be so cold."

She'd managed to get him into a sleeping bag? And he'd moved? Why?

"You also need to cover your face. We were lucky it was warm earlier." She laughed. "Well, warm for up here. But seriously, you gotta watch out for frostbite. You've been exposed a while since your little Houdini stunt."

Shock hit him hard. This kid was good. He was supposed to be the rescuer, and here this little girl was taking care of *him*. Whatever drug Hank used must've really done a number on his faculties. Stupid to drink or eat anything when he knew what Hank was up to. Couldn't afford any more mistakes like that. Not if he wanted to stay alive.

Not if he wanted to fulfill his promise.

"Here." Andie stood in front of him holding up a cocoon-shaped bag. "You might need this."

"Thanks." He slid his legs into the bag, pulled it up and around him. Once he was zipped in, he watched his little caretaker climb back into hers and cuddle close to her mom. "How long has she been out?"

"She hasn't woken up yet."

Some serious emotion in those stiff words. With good reason. "Do you have any idea how long ago we crashed?"

"I don't know. I think it's been a couple hours."

He checked his watch. Four hours since they took off. That would add up. "Are you hurt?" Should have asked that sooner. Brain still needed to clear some. The cold had penetrated his mind, and all he wanted was sleep. But this was bad. He had to think, make a plan to get these two off the mountain safely.

"Not really." Her voice, so calm just a few minutes earlier, shook. "A cut on my hand. But I'm worried about my mom."

He unzipped the bag. "Let me see that cut."

"It's fine."

Slipping out of the needed warmth, Cole breathed the cold air. He rubbed his arms and legs and moved over to Andie. "Let me see it." Too gruff. "I'll be careful." That was nicer. Wasn't it?

"I already bandaged it." She avoided eye contact.

Stubborn kid. "Just let me look at it!" Way too gruff. Not good.

Her bottom lip quivered, but when she looked at him, her eyes shot daggers. "Fine." She escaped her own cocoon and plopped in front of him, a brown bag in her grasp.

Andie threw her glove down and thrust her arm in his direction. As he unwrapped her hand, he drew in a sharp breath. "Wow. That's a cut."

"It's fine."

"Look, kid, you don't have to be brave in front of me—"

"Hello? My name's not *kid* and I'm not being brave. It's fine." She pulled a box out with a huff.

Cole raised his eyebrows. "Okay then. It's fine. But we need to bandage it differently. Got any butterfly bandages in there?" He indicated the box—a first aid kit of massive proportions—sitting in her lap.

"I'm not sure." She looked away again. At her mom.

The emotions playing across her face weren't lost on him. He took the kit. "This won't take long, let me get this cut closed up and then I'll check her injuries." At her quick glare, he inclined his head. *"Then* I'll leave you alone and get warmed up, okay? Why don't you try to get some rest?"

Andie just shook her head.

He taped up her hand with swift movements.

She continued to stare at her mom. A single tear made a trail down her cheek.

"You're set. Would you like to help me with your mom?"

"Sure." She moved to squat beside him. "Her leg's hurt. I bandaged it, but we'll need to change the bandages soon."

They worked in silence for several minutes. Jenna's leg seemed to be the worst of her injuries, but she had a knot on her head too. Could be a concussion. With luck, it wouldn't be too severe. His lip curled. Yeah. When had luck ever been on his side? Tiny cuts—likely from glass fragments—covered her. He glanced up at

Andie. "She's okay for now. Get back in your bag. We won't be any help to her if we don't stay warm."

Andie nodded, but something was obviously bothering her. "What's the problem, kid?" It came out more gruff than he intended, but she just stared at him.

"My name's not *kid.*"

He met her stare. If she wanted to answer, fine. If not, he would get some sleep. He was about to shrug and roll over, when she tilted her head.

"I have one more question."

He arched a brow. "Which is?"

"Why were you on our plane today?"

ZOYA

April 6
North Pole, Alaska
9:27 p.m.

Dasha and Sasha stood at my side as we searched the sea of people for Andie and Auntie Jenna. Where could they be? And what was going wrong that they were delayed so much? "Where do you think they are, Mom?"

She shook her head and sighed, then glanced down at her watch again. "I don't know. Jenna wanted us to be here ninety minutes after they were supposed to land. And we're late." She looked at the landing strip in the distance. "That should've given them plenty of time to take care of the plane and whatever else needed to be done."

"Well, what should we do?" The dogs whined, sending a chill up my spine. *God, where are they?*

"I'll call Jenna's cell in case there was an emergency and they took a cab home or something."

Yes, be patient. Be patient . . . Be patient. You know how to wait, Zoya. The chant didn't help to ease my anxiousness.

Mom dialed, then frowned. "That's odd. It's going straight to voicemail." She patted my shoulder. "I'm sure they're fine. Don't worry."

But, she was worried, it was written on her face.

I buried my face in Sasha's fur as Dasha nudged me with her nose. They were worried too. I could tell.

So we waited . . . And waited.

It was almost midnight when we left. Without Andie and Auntie Jenna.

JENNA

April 7
Sultana, Denali National Park
12:21 a.m.

Unforgiving rocks pressed into her back. Pain jolted up through her legs. The cold of the air chilled her lungs. The cocoon around her kept her from moving.

Andie! Where was she?

Voices drifted through the night air. Two voices. One wonderfully familiar. Breathing out a sigh of relief, Jenna latched onto Andie's voice. *Thank You, God!* Her daughter was alive, speaking, moving around. The sounds became crisp and clean as the haze wrapping her mind cleared. Andie was talking to someone. Well, questioning someone. Jenna smiled. *That's my girl.*

With a moan louder than she intended, she struggled to pry a hand loose of its confines and lift it to her face. The headache was intense, but it meant she was alive. Now if she could just open her eyes and see for herself that Andie was really there, in one piece, and out of danger—

"Mom!"

That one word was enough to lift the two-ton weights resting on her eyelids. She managed to flutter them open. Andie hovered over her. What a beautiful sight. "Hi, baby." She reached for her daughter's face. "You okay? Are you hurt?"

Andie's teary giggles melted her heart. "I'm okay. A little blood here and there, but I'm okay."

Jenna loved her daughter's laugh. The sense of humor that couldn't be crushed. Chuckling along with her daughter, she thought about Andie's statement—her twelve-year-old and blood were an interesting combination. Poor kid. She could only imagine what had transpired while she was unconscious.

"You need some water, Mom. Can't let you get dehydrated." Andie reached into her sleeping bag and pulled out Jenna's emergency bag. Rummaging around, she lifted out a bottle of water. "Just a few sips."

The cool water slid down her throat. Wow. She was so tired. "Thanks," the word came out raspy, "I needed that."

"Mom, you look exhausted. Are you okay? Does anything hurt really bad?"

"I'm okay." *Please, God, let that be true.* "Just needed to see my girl."

Andie climbed back into the sleeping bag next to her. "I love you, Mom."

"Love you too, sweetie. Thanks. I *am* really tired." She struggled to keep her eyes open, but they wouldn't obey. Their predicament sent chills through her core. What would they do? They'd crashed in Denali National Park, but it wasn't tourist season yet and the park didn't allow vehicles past the welcome center. It was remote. And treacherous.

If only they could have made it down to the Kahiltna. *Stop the "if onlys"! You can't do anything about it. You've got to get out of here. That's the only thing that matters.*

But, she was so tired. Opening her eyes again, she looked at Andie. She had to find a way to take care of Andie. Would anyone be able to find them?

Fear gripped her, so deep and powerful it clamped the breath in her lungs. They didn't have much of a chance. Her heart raced and her breathing quickened. They would die on this mountain. Her eyes shut of their own accord. Such hard work to keep them open.

"Mom?" Andie's voice penetrated the cloud hovering over her mind.

She had to keep trying. Her daughter needed her. But before she could respond, her body shut down all thought as she drifted back into the deep black calling her.

CHAPTER FOUR

COLE

April 7
Sultana, Denali National Park
12:34 a.m.

Cole sighed. At least Jenna's waking up had turned his interrogator's attention away from him. Now if those two would just go to sleep and stay asleep. He had work to do.

Too many unanswered questions ping-ponged around in his head. What did Hank use to drug him? Why would Hank want to kill him too? Unless . . .

Hank and the others knew.

The realization dropped like a bomb. That meant he had less time.

Glancing over at mother and daughter, he watched their breathing patterns. Interrogator Andie kept opening her eyes. *The kid is scared.*

Warmth seeped into his limbs. Maybe he should take a power nap. It was cold and dark, and his body needed to rid itself of whatever toxin Hank had slipped him.

3:04 a.m.

He woke with a start. The night sky was cloudy now. A storm must be coming. He could feel it in his knees.

Cole inched his way out of the warm sleeping bag and watched the girls for any sign of movement. Confident they were asleep, he crept toward the plane.

The flashing light caught his attention immediately. He'd have to dismantle it, but it was already too late. They probably had the grid of their location within minutes after the crash. They would come. Soon. And there was nowhere to hide.

He ripped open the parachute, located the homing device, and pulled out his Leatherman. It took less than ten seconds to dismantle the beacon. He used the side of his boot to drag snow, burying the fragments beneath the pristine whiteness.

Another mound of material lay outside the crumpled plane's door. As he reached for it, he recognized a tent. At least, what used to be a tent. No wonder the kid had bundled them in the sleeping bags. The tent was useless. A moan inside the plane made him scowl.

Hank.

A new wave of anger surged in his gut.

Cole climbed through the wreckage and approached the prostrate form. He knelt beside him, whispering as loud as he dared. "Hank." He shook his shoulder. "Hank, can you hear me?"

Another moan.

"Hank. I don't have time to mess around. Open your eyes."

A bloody eye slid open halfway. "Co—"

"Don't try to speak." Cole's hands balled into fists and then grabbed the man's collar. "I didn't come in here to listen to anything you had to say. You're going to listen to *me*. Blink once for yes, twice for no."

Hank blinked once. And struggled to pull in air past the constricted collar.

Cole threw him down. "They're coming for you, aren't they?"

A single blink.

Cole ran his hand through his hair and let out his frustrations in a huff. "They knew about me? That I would be on board?"

A jagged breath preceded Hank's single blink.

"Do they know where it is? Is that why you tried to kill Jenna and Andie?"

No response, only a blank stare.

Cole yanked up Hank's collar again. How easy it would be to kill him. "Answer me! Do they know where it is?"

Pain contorted the man's face, and then a double blink.

Cole dropped him back to the ground as relief rushed through him. At least he had one thing going for him right now. If he could keep them all alive long enough.

With a last look at his one-time friend, he knew he had little time to search. The plane was in shambles. It had rolled after the crash and landed upside-down. Bags and equipment lay strewn across the ceiling-now-floor. He found his duffel, grabbed it, then looked around for anything else he could use.

A small case caught his attention. Jenna's briefcase or laptop bag? Time to find out if Marc's pretty wife knew anything.

He took a moment to do quick surveillance. The girls continued to sleep. Good.

With quick hands, he yanked at the zipper on the bag. It caught on something. He pulled a small flashlight out of his boot.

As the beam of the light lit up the complication, he inhaled and threw the bag down. It was locked.

Smart lady. Grudging admiration stirred, then shifted. To suspicion.

What was she hiding?

ANDIE

April 7
Sultana, Denali National Park
3:17 a.m.

I stared through the gigantic hole at Cole as the clatter of Mom's briefcase echoed in the small plane. What was he doing, going through our stuff like that?

"What are you doing?"

He jumped up and glared.

I glared back. *Don't you look at me like that. You're the one who was snooping around in our stuff.* If he wanted to play "who-can-be-meanest-the-longest" I was ready.

"I'm figuring out how to keep us alive out here. Taking inventory of what food we have." He gave a small nod and scanned me from head to toe.

Was he always this grumpy? *Like I believe you were prying open Mom's briefcase to protect us.* He knew I didn't trust him. This would be interesting.

"*That* isn't where you're supposed to get food." Pointing at the emergency bag outside the plane, my jaw clenched. "That's where the food is."

He sighed.

I stared.

Time slithered by.

Have fun getting yourself out of this one.

"Look, it's really late. Let's get back to sleep." He worked his way out of the plane.

Our gazes collided once again. Mine harsh and penetrating. His grouchy and tired. I crossed my arms and shifted my weight to one leg. "Well, should I trust you?"

"You asked that earlier."

"Earlier I didn't see you looking through our stuff and trying to open Mom's briefcase. *Earlier* it was different."

He frowned and rubbed his forehead. "Look, let's just go outside."

"Why? What are you hiding in here?"

His eyes squinted, and I tried not to smile. Clearly, he wasn't sure what to do with me. Which was fine. Dad always said the best place for an enemy was off-balance. 'Course, I wasn't sure if Cole was an enemy or not.

"All right, little interrogator. The truth is I couldn't see because it was too dark. I thought that was some sort of lunch bag or the emergency kit."

"Then what's that in your hand?"

He looked down at the flashlight.

"Plus, I could see fine when I came in here a second ago." *Ouch! Didn't see that one coming, did you?*

He fixed me with a hard look, but I couldn't tell if he was mad or just . . . kind of impressed. "You asked. I answered."

Okay. Mad, it was.

I rolled my eyes. *Fine then, Mr. Grump.*

With that, he moved past me and made his way outside and away from the plane.

I followed him. My eyes slid over to Mom. She would live and everything would be all right. Period.

"Andie."

I turned back to Cole. His face was still hard, but he looked tired, too.

"I know it's hard for you to trust me. I can't explain things right now, but I need you to get some sleep. Tomorrow's . . . going to be tough. On all of us."

"Will Mom be okay?" I turned to look at him. What was it about him that made me feel queasy?

"Just get some sleep."

I swallowed back the tears that threatened to escape. Was she really that bad?

"She'll be fine."

But what would happen now? What if Mom *didn't* wake up?

"Cole?"

"Yeah?" He grunted and lay down.

I watched him closely. *Better not get his temper goin' again.* "Nothing."

CHAPTER FIVE

JENNA

April 7
Sultana, Denali National Park
5:03 a.m.

Soft snores woke Jenna with a start. She hadn't heard snoring since Marc died. It took a moment for her realize where she was.

Oh. Right. Plane crash. Snow.

As her brain came to life, she began to wiggle her fingers and toes, testing out the feeling in her body. Her right leg ached, but everything else seemed to just be bruised and sore.

Wrangling her arms up through the confines of the sleeping bag proved to take all her effort. After breathing hard for several moments, she lifted her foggy, iced-over goggles. Andie must've done this. Every inch of her skin had been covered, protected as much as possible from the elements around her. She'd have to praise her daughter later. She probably saved their lives.

Jenna unzipped her sleeping bag and a swirl of bitter-cold air nipped at her still-warm flesh. Her skin immediately responded to the chill, prickling and stinging. Head pounding, she ran a hand down her face and forced her eyes to focus.

The sky was still bathed in dark; sunrise wouldn't be for a little while. She scanned the area. White as far as the eye could see, broken up by craggly mountain ridges. The clouds hovered below, making Jenna feel like she was floating. Away from the world. And so very alone.

Each movement took great effort, but she was thankful the fog in her head had lifted. What would've happened to Andie if—?

"Mom?" Andie broke through her train of thought. "Mom, you're moving around. Are you okay?"

"Yeah, I think I'm okay, but help me with this leg, all right? I think it's pretty messed up." The pain intensified as she moved, but she fought to not let it show.

"Okay." Andie slipped from her sleeping bag and brought the emergency bag to her.

Jenna nodded in the direction of the snores. "Is that our passenger?"

"Yeah. He helped me with your leg."

As she pulled up her pant leg and checked the wound, she discovered someone had indeed bandaged it already. Blood soaked through the cloth. She clenched her teeth. The wound would need a closer look if they were going to get off this mountain.

Jenna eased off one layer of gauze after another, stealing glances at her daughter. A lot of blood had saturated the strips, and she knew what the sight of blood did to her hemophobic preteen. But Andie was taking it pretty well. So far.

When Jenna reached the wound, she knew the best thing was distraction. "Hey, could you get me some alcohol swabs, the Bactroban, and some fresh gauze?"

"Sure thing, Mom."

"And after you bring me those, could you scrounge us up something to eat? There should be plenty of granola bars and trail mix in the emergency bag."

Andie sighed, her clear eyes reflecting a deep relief. "I can definitely do that."

"Thanks, sweetie." Jenna kept the wound covered with the blood-soaked bandages until Andie handed her the items she requested.

She watched her daughter sit cross-legged a few feet away to dig through their emergency food. Facing the other direction. Smart girl.

Jenna lifted the gauze. The gash on her lower calf went deep into the flesh and muscle. Much deeper than she originally thought, but she couldn't do anything about that. She wiped it down, sucking in a deep breath and holding it. She cleaned the injury the best she could, filled the gaping slash with antibiotic cream, and wrapped it tight. Air whooshed out of her lungs as she released the pent-up breath. She prayed she could keep infection at bay until they were rescued.

If rescue was even possible.

Well, if it wasn't, she'd need all her mobility to fight her way off this mountain. What she knew of the Alaska Range brought little comfort. The base camp for Denali climbers was located on the upper Kahiltna, but not many people signed up for the climb this time of year, so there wouldn't be any rangers stationed at the camp yet. They didn't start bringing in supplies and keeping rangers there round the clock until the end of April. Tourist season didn't start until the middle of May, so the chance of rescue by a tourist plane was slim, too. And Sultana wasn't climbed often because it was steeper than Denali and endured horrendous weather.

Talkeetna rangers used Sultana as a barometer for climbers of The High One. At over 17,000 feet, the mountain, known among Native Alaskans as Denali's Wife, took the brunt of the storms that swept in from the West.

Once again, Jenna took in the area around them. Denali National Park was a beautiful, treacherous, and extremely remote preserve, boasting some of the tallest mountains in North America and close to the Arctic Circle. The very things that drew tourists were what worked against Jenna and Andie now.

Chances for survival did not look good.

She glanced over at the sleeping man. More snores emanated from him. Who was he? Why had he fought Hank? To be some kind of hero? Shaking her head, she looked back to her daughter. "Andie, did you find some protein bars?"

"Yeah, Mom. Right here." She tossed one to her.

"Thanks, honey." Opening the foil wrapper, she relished the rich strawberry scent. Amazing how a little snack bar could smell so good and make her mouth water. She must be really hungry. She took a bite. "Hey, you did a good job yesterday. I'm so proud of you. Wouldn't have made it without your help."

Andie beamed under her praise, but moments later burst into tears.

"Oh, baby, come here." Jenna pulled her daughter into her arms. "I'm sorry. I know this is scary."

"It's not your fault, Mom." She choked between sobs. "I just wasn't sure what to do when I woke up all alone. You've always been there, ya know?"

"I know—"

"And with Daddy gone, and then that horrible crash . . . and then you were so still . . . you didn't even move! I thought— I thought—"

Jenna placed her hands on either side of her daughter's face. "Andrea, look at me. I'm still here. We're going to get through this, okay?"

"Okay." Andie sat up, swiping at the tears turning to ice on her cheeks. "But this is really scary, Mom. What're we gonna do?"

Jenna smiled down at her daughter. "Well, for starters, I'm going to finish eating this and get some energy. You need to eat something, too. And then, we're going to find our extra gear and dress properly for these temperatures."

"And then?"

"Well . . ." Jenna looked at the vast wilderness around her. "Then, we'll make a plan."

"A plan? Mom, wait a minute, when you say make a plan that means . . ." Andie took a deep breath.

Seconds passed.

Her daughter's shoulders slumped. "You mean, you don't think we'll be rescued?"

Jenna wanted to reassure her daughter. To tell her everything would be okay.

But she couldn't.

COLE

April 7
Sultana, Denali National Park
6:01 a.m.

"Mom, I don't know what it is, but I think we should trust him."

"Andie, honey, we don't even know *who* he is or why he's here. Now lower your voice, we don't want to wake him."

The debate over his trustworthiness had been going on for several minutes. Cole faked a few snores and kept his breathing steady.

"Okay, Mom. I just know we could use his help."

So his little interrogator had turned into his champion.

"I know, Andie. But right now, he looks like he needs more help than we do, and *I* need to concentrate on making sure we survive."

The comment stung his pride. Yeah, he probably looked pretty rough. And he'd slept hard. No doubt thanks to the drugs in his system. But he'd sworn to Marcus he would protect his family.

Problem was, so far he'd done a lousy job. He didn't protect them from Hank. From the crash.

And they didn't trust him.

The danger had just begun. Only they didn't know that. And they weren't prepared for it.

Well, things were about to change. As their voices trailed off, Cole listened to their footsteps as they navigated through the snow. They were headed to the plane, most likely looking for supplies. He unzipped his bag and climbed out of the warmth.

Temperature's dropped. A lot.

Not a good sign.

He stood and stretched, assessing all the aches throughout his body. No time for pain. It was time to take control. It wouldn't be easy, but he'd have to convince Jenna he was there to help them. He didn't trust that woman. She probably knew more than Marc had believed, and she was definitely hiding something. He just didn't know what. But he would find out.

Cole trudged through the snow to the wreckage and cleared his throat to give them fair warning of his approach.

"Cole! You're awake." Andie's dimples beamed a smile up at him.

Wow. No arguments this morning. Her warm greeting sent a jolt through his cold heart. But the feeling didn't linger as he glanced from daughter to mother.

Jenna's forehead furrowed. So much for convincing her he wasn't the big, bad wolf. "Yeah, I'm awake. How are you feeling this morning, Jenna?" See? He could be Mr. Nice Guy.

"Fine." Her answer was curt as she went right back to digging around in the plane. "Andie can bring you something to eat and drink if you're hungry."

So far, so not-so-good. "Thank you, but I'm fine. Do you feel up to hiking and climbing?"

Her head popped up out of the cargo hold. "Excuse me?"

"We need to move. It's not safe here. Are you up to it?" He knew his tone was condescending, but this woman infuriated him. And for no apparent reason—other than the fact that she didn't trust him. *Well, the feeling's mutual, lady.*

She climbed out of the hold and moved toward him with a limp. Placing her hands on her hips, she stood to her full height, barely up to his chest. "It doesn't matter if I'm up to it or not, Mr. Cole whoever-you-are. Which brings me to another point. Who are you? I don't know why you were on our plane, but in case you haven't noticed—we crashed. I have to protect my daughter." She dismissed him with a wave of her hand. "There's a storm coming, and we need to prepare to survive it."

"Um, *no*." He wouldn't let his exasperation show. "We need to get to higher ground before the storm hits."

"Higher ground? You want to climb *up* this mountain?" Moving forward, she laughed. Toe to toe with him now. "Are you an idiot?"

Cole clenched his teeth. He would not. Let. His. Exasperation. Show. "You heard me. Higher ground."

Her face held an expression he couldn't decipher. Like the calm before the storm. "The safest thing to do is stay with the plane. It could be days before they find us, but the ELT should alert them we are here. So for your information, there is *no* way we are going up this mountain." She crossed her arms.

"Yes, you will. And we're going to get ready. Now."

"Who do you think you are? This is my plane, my supplies, and my daughter's *life* you're playing with. And another thing, this mountain we're stranded on is Sultana." She stormed back to the hold. "It's not exactly the easiest mountain to climb and, in fact, very few people even attempt it each year. Going up is out of the question."

Andie stared up at him wide-eyed.

"Sultana? We're on Foraker."

"I know exactly where we are. Sultana. Just because white men came in and renamed mountains that had been named by my people for generations, doesn't mean I will use them."

Andie tugged on his jacket. "Um, don't think you want to start an argument about the mountain names." Her little voice held a hint of warning.

"Oh really?" He leaned closer to her. "Why's that?"

"People've been known to get into huge fights over it. Even fist fights." She held her hands out like she was holding a scale. She tipped one hand then the other. "Denali, McKinley. Sultana, Foraker. Begguya, Hunter."

"Okay, I've heard Denali and McKinley, but the others, not so much."

"It's the original Athabaskan names versus the new names. Denali means 'The High One.' Sultana means 'The Wife.' And Begguya means 'The Child.' That's why they changed the national park's name back to Denali National Park, out of respect for the Native people and our heritage. Most real Alaskans will always use the name Denali rather than McKinley."

"But what about the other two? The wife and child?"

"People still fight about it. Native Alaskans want to stay true to the original names, but a lot of people don't even know them."

He sighed. Great. Jenna probably thought he wanted to argue about everything. "Andie, would you mind rolling up our sleeping bags? I need to talk to your mom."

"Why?" She shifted her weight and crossed her arms over her chest.

There. That untrusting look again. "I need to apologize."

She softened just a little. "Good. You better." She patted his arm as she walked away. "Good luck." The kid perplexed him to no end.

"Thanks." Cole didn't try to hide his sarcasm. He yanked the warm hat off his head so he could run his hands through his hair. What a mess. How was he supposed to fulfill his promise when the stubborn woman wouldn't even listen?

He approached the cramped opening of the cargo hold. The only way to accomplish his goal would be to strike at her weakness. And Jenna only had one weakness that he could find. Andie.

"Jenna?"

She turned toward him, anger shooting sparks out of her eyes.

"Look, I'm sorry." He gritted the words out and shoved his hands into his pockets. Uh oh. The keychain was gone.

"Oh yeah?" She wasn't budging an inch.

Just get to the point, Maddox. "You and I both know that crash was no accident." The sudden tremble in her chin told him his words had the desired effect. He dug around in his pockets. Oh well, he'd have to look for it later.

She glanced to where Hank lay.

"Hank meant to kill you, Jenna." Short. Succinct.

Tears glistened in her eyes. She slumped to the floor. "How do you know that?"

"Didn't you see him pull a gun?"

She nodded.

Here was his opening. "We can't stay anywhere near this crash site. We've got to protect Andie. They'll be coming after us and soon. Hank had a parachute with a homing beacon. I'm pretty sure he sabotaged the plane. Then he planned to aim the plane to crash into the mountains while he parachuted to safety. They'll be coming to the coordinates of that beacon. And that beacon will lead them directly to us."

Terror gripped the features of her face. "Who?"

"The people who want you dead."

"Someone wants me dead?" Her voice squeaked. "What? How . . . ? Who . . ." She cleared her throat and narrowed her eyes. "How do I know you're not one of them?"

"Not just you, Jenna. Both of you. And you know because I promised Marcus I would protect you." There. He'd told her the truth.

A quick inhale and she brought a hand to her throat. "You knew Marc?"

"Yes. I'm very sorry for your loss."

"I need some air." She moved past him to the fresh air and snow outside.

He followed her. "Look, I know you don't trust me."

"That's an understatement."

Cole ignored her comment and grabbed her arm. "We have to get away from the wreckage. Our best bet is to climb up and away from the plane. I promised to protect you, and that is what I'm going to do." His voice commanding, he gripped harder, willing her to turn around.

She turned to face him once again, but yanked her arm free and glared at him. "What about the ELT?"

"Hank disabled it . . . Just like the ailerons, the radio, and who knows what else."

Her shoulders slumped. Finally a chink in her armor. "The fuel tank . . ." Her whisper barely reached him.

"What?"

"The tank began to lose fuel at an alarming rate after you collapsed." She dropped to the snow, winced, and grabbed her injured leg.

"You know how to fly?" That surprised him.

"Not really. I've gone through flight ground school, and one lesson." She lifted her pant leg.

He couldn't help but notice the blood had soaked through the bandages again. "That needs stitches."

"So what? You're a doctor now, too?" She pulled herself up to stand. The fire in her eyes could not be missed.

He ignored the barb. "All right. We know that the plan was well thought out. A backup plan for each backup plan."

"What are you talking about?" Hands flew to her hips.

"Jenna. They want you dead. Isn't that clear?"

Her head flew side to side. "No. There's got to be a mistake. What about the flight plan? I heard Departure Control. They knew we were in the air. Good grief, we've known Hank for years, I—"

"If I know these guys—"

"What guys? Who are these—"

"If I know these guys, they found a way to erase it." He disliked giving her one blow after another, but the stubborn woman wouldn't shut up.

"What about the rangers?"

"They have no idea we're here."

Jenna began to pace. Her face a mask of determination. "Okay. So we need to get away from the wreckage. But why can't we go *down* the mountain? The Kahiltna glacier is down there, and there's a better chance to be seen or rescued."

"No. They'll be expecting us to do that. And right now, we don't want to be seen. It's too dangerous. We need them to believe that you died in that crash."

"Well then, let's go down another way." She just wouldn't give up. Pacing around him, her voice calm, she refused the truth. "Going up is too dangerous. I need your help to *protect* Andie, not kill us all making a trek we have no business taking on a good day."

Enough of this. He grabbed her shoulders, stopping her in her tracks. Maybe he could shake some sense into her. "The only ones who know we are here are the people who want you dead. They will be coming. Soon. When they find the plane, if they take the time to check it, they'll know we are alive, and they will search . . . no take that back—they will *scour* this mountain below the crash site. They won't stop until they find us. And kill us." He shook her with the emphasis of his words. "The only chance we have is to go up and hide for as long as we can."

Her eyes were wide orbs. Maybe he'd gone a little too far.

"How do you know so much about whoever it is that's doing this?"

Cole let his hands drop as he gazed off down the mountain. "I've seen firsthand what they're capable of. They won't stop. Ever."

Silence surrounded them. As they stood there, Cole listened to her breathing. A heavy sigh, then a couple of quick breaths. He turned to watch her, afraid she would collapse in the snow.

But instead, she set her shoulders, lifted her chin in a defiant gesture, and pointed her finger into his chest. "Let's get one thing straight right now."

There was no way to mask his surprise at her strength. "All right . . ."

"You hurt one hair on my daughter's head," she poked him hard in the chest, "and I will rip you to shreds."

Cole sighed. This was going to be harder than he ever thought possible. At least she was willing to leave. "Deal." He'd tackle the rest of the argument later. And time was running out. "We need supplies. Let's go through the plane and see what we've got. We may be stranded up here a while."

"Fine." She sniffed.

Pulling a bag from the wreckage, he watched Andie approach. "The sun will be up within the hour, and we need to be moving by then."

CHAPTER SIX

JENNA
April 7
Sultana, Denali National Park
6:27 a.m.

Jenna stood up and surveyed the piles around her. Marc always teased her about being prepared for nuclear fallout, but she was thankful she had insisted on keeping the plane stocked with equipment in case of an emergency. The inflatable raft wouldn't do them any good right now, but the mountaineering gear would. For the hundredth time that morning she wished she had paid more attention to her husband's instructions about climbing, but Cole seemed to be at ease with the ropes and harnesses. She'd have to learn fast. That or trust him, and she wasn't quite sure she could do that yet.

Cole worked on a camp stove that had seen better days before the crash. They didn't have a lot of gas for it, but at least they'd be able to heat water. There were three backpacks, two hauling sleds, five sleeping bags plus the one Hank had, ice axes, crampons, a shovel, stakes, ropes, and various other survival items. Her emergency bag had plenty of water and food for several days, and she always kept a couple flats of water in the plane, but what if it wasn't enough?

Shaking her head, she went back to search for the snowshoes and skis. Marc had welded special holders into the back of the plane for them, but as soon as she reached the tail cone, she realized they were long gone. The crash had torn off the end of the tail with the rudder. The skis and snowshoes were stored in that narrow slot—so they were now buried somewhere on the mountain with the rest of the wreckage. With a sigh, she turned to take another look at what was left.

What if Marc had stashed things in the seats? As Cole went back into the hold to search, she decided to follow her hunch and check the rest of the plane. Crawling through the mangled fuselage, she yanked on the seat cushions above her head and ducked as the contents of the compartments tumbled out.

A small black case engraved with Marc's initials caught her attention. As she turned the shiny box over in her hands, she noticed the lock. With no way to open it without a key, she shrugged and tucked it into her pocket. She would save it because it was Marc's. And that made it important to her.

"Jenna? Do you really need all this duct tape?" Cole's voice drifted over to her.

She ignored the question and shook her head. He had no clue.

Life vests and flotation devices filled the floor, but when she opened the next seat, her breath caught in her throat.

"Cole! Come here!"

As he approached, she heard his intake of breath. He'd seen them as well.

"Jenna, where did you find these?"

"In the seat. Isn't it wonderful? We can call for help!" Her excitement bubbled up. They would be saved.

Cole picked up the small, handheld radios. "No, we can't."

"What do you mean?" She yanked one of the radios from his hands. "Of course we can."

"No. Jenna, we can't." He closed the narrow space between them and lowered his voice to a whisper. "Don't you see? Anyone can listen in. And it's naïve to think that if we called for help only the 'good guys' would hear us."

"But—"

"Jenna. Listen to me. We'll use it if we have to, but right now, someone wants you dead. And they'll stop at nothing to accomplish their goal."

"I don't understand! If we called for help, couldn't the rangers protect us? Get us out of here?"

He pried the radio from her fingers. "I'm counting on them helping us, yes. But right now, no one knows we are here—*except* the ones who tried to kill you. Hank dismantled the battery on the emergency beacon and somehow changed your flight plan. No one knows to come rescue us. No one knows where we were headed."

"What? How do you know all this?" This couldn't be happening.

"I watched Hank during the preflight check. And realized he could've done much worse. Which he obviously did." He raked his hand through his hair.

"So, we really don't have any hope?" Her breaths came quicker. "Are you sure we can't hail the rangers?"

"These things only have about a five-mile radius. From what you said, there's probably not a soul within thirty miles. The rangers are in Talkeetna. So who do you think is most likely to hear if we were to make a call for help?"

The weight of his statement sat like a polar bear on her chest. She knew all too well he was right, but she'd pushed anyway. Always looking for a way out, for some small glimmer of hope. As much as she hated it, he'd made his point. Defeat filled all the tiny little crevices of her heart that had begun to dream of a safe and easy escape from this nightmare. "I guess we should finish going through all this stuff." As she picked her way through the remaining bags, Jenna wondered if Cole was trying to save them or get rid of them.

― ―

In less than thirty minutes, they'd found a goldmine of supplies, but Jenna's heart sank every time they pulled out something new. Marc had teased her, yes, but he'd also put a lot of thought into these supplies. He spared no expense, only the best for his family. So why did she still doubt him?

She pushed the traitorous thoughts back. Marc had been a wonderful husband. He loved her. She knew that. Closing her eyes, she brought a fist up to her chest. Yes, she *knew* that—but what about that conversation she'd overheard? Who was Amy? And why did he spend so much time with her? Now she would never know and the memories she had of their fifteen years together would always have a shadow over them.

"Hey, Jenna." Cole called to her from deep inside the hold pulling her out of her depressing train of thought. "Check this out."

The man had volunteered to climb into the tiny cargo hold—and that was no easy feat since he was well over six feet tall—but it unnerved her to have him digging around in their personal things.

Jenna stuck her head into the opening, schooling the expression on her face. "What's up?"

"I thought you might want to see this." Cole pointed to the corner.

As she made her way over to where his finger directed, her heart did a flip-flop. There—taped to what would have been the upper corner had the plane remained upright—was her list.

The list she'd made with Marc at the kitchen table the night he insisted they all take a trip into the mountains. Before Andie's dangerous episodes. Before brain surgery. Before Marc shut her out. Jenna remembered arguing with him . . .

"Marc, she's just a baby, and with her diagnosis, we'd have to be really careful in case of an emergency."

"Jenna, honestly," Marc teased her, "you always want to be prepared for everything, but we can't possibly protect her from *every* little thing that could possibly happen every minute of *every* day."

"Oh, honey, I know that. But what if we got stranded in the mountains, or what if we had to make an emergency landing over water, or the weather turned bad and we crashed somewhere?" She knew her dramatics were overkill, but she needed him to see that she was right.

Hands up, signaling surrender, Marc chuckled. "Okay, okay. You win. Let's make your emergency list, and I'll make sure the plane is always supplied." Reaching for her, he drew her into his embrace. "You know I love you."

"Mm-hmmm." She relished his strong arms around her.

"And even though I tease you, I love your lists."

She swatted his arm.

"I do, hon. It's a good thing. And I know it."

- -

Jenna's hand slid over the plastic-encased paper as the memory faded. Tears slid down her cheeks. Every year since, he'd ordered new gear, teasing her about the list. She'd had no idea it was here. No idea he'd kept it, posted it, used it as a guide.

"He loved you very much, Jenna." Cole's hand on her shoulder invaded her private moment.

Sobs shook her as she crouched in the corner, tracing the smiley faces and "I love yous" scribbled around the edge of the paper. They'd continued to banter as they'd worked on the list. The last "I love you" she'd scribbled, he'd immediately tried to outdo her and wrote, "I love you more." Like he had the final word.

"Jenna?"

He just wouldn't leave her alone. Was it so hard to let her have a moment or two of grief? Good heavens, she had a daughter with a rare nerve disorder, she'd lost her husband only a year before, and now she'd been in a plane crash. It would be nice to just go back to bed and wake up from the nightmare of it all. If she had a bed.

"Jenna, we really need to get moving. It's already light. They'll come. Searching." His tone impatient and worried.

"Okay." She wiped the tears from her face.

"I'm going to pack these flats of water on the sleds with some other supplies for later. We'll hide them away from the crash site."

"Won't we need the water?" Her mind wanted to engage, but her heart hurt.

"We can't carry the weight." He placed a hand on her shoulder again. "We need to go up. We'll melt snow if we need to."

What was the use of arguing? She needed to put all her energy into protecting Andie. "What about . . . him?" She didn't want to look at Hank's injured body.

"We'll send someone back for him. He's injured pretty severely, one, possibly both of his legs are broken, but he's got protection from the wind, and someone covered him up." Cole looked at her, his gaze determined. "You understand that we can't risk bringing him, don't you?"

"What if we pulled him on one of the sleds?" The man had tried to kill them. The reasoning behind it eluded her. But leaving him seemed inhumane.

"It's too dangerous and I don't think he'd survive. Besides, like I said, we need to hide the sleds with extra supplies for when we come back down." His gaze softened. "I promise we'll send someone back for him, and we'll try to make him as comfortable as possible."

While she couldn't bring herself to admit that leaving Hank seemed like sweet revenge after what he'd done, she did feel guilty. All she could do was nod. She needed to think of Andie and do everything in her power to keep them alive.

ANDIE

April 7
Sultana, Denali National Park
7:19 a.m.

"What are you talking about? We don't need an ice chest with packets, it will just slow us down. And if you haven't noticed, we are surrounded with *ice*." Cole threw the ice chest onto the ground and glared at Mom. "Be reasonable, Jenna!"

She is being reasonable.

"You don't understand. Those are Andie's medical packets for her vest. They keep her cold, so of course we need them!"

See? I told you. I smiled on the inside. *Men.*

Mom stormed over and picked the packets back up. She shook a finger at him. "I'm trying to protect my daughter, and in order to do that we *have to* take them."

Time seemed to creep by as I waited for their arguing to stop.

"Never mind!" Mom crossed her arms and stomped over to our stuff. She started packing.

I looked heavenward with a sigh. *Please help Mom not burst a blood vessel.* Or kill Cole.

Cole watched her vent, then shook his head.

Ya did it to yourself, dude.

- -

No! I stared at Cole. "But, he has to come with us, we can't leave him here!"

Cole stared at the plane as Mom hobbled over.

"What's going on?" She glared at him and put her hands on her hips.

Cole ignored her and turned back to me.

"Andie, there won't be enough time or energy to bring him with us." Cole shook his head. "I'm sorry. But we'll have to send someone back for him. He'll be all right."

"No!" I kicked the snow and clenched my fists. Why couldn't they see that Hank didn't have that much time left? Tears fell again.

"Andie, I promise we'll send someone back for him." Cole kneeled down in front of me and grabbed my fist. "But you need to let this go."

"Why? Hank will die if he doesn't come."

"Andie." Mom walked over. "We need to leave him in God's hands. There's nothing we can do about it."

"Jenna, this isn't helping." Cole stood and again looked toward the plane.

God, please, I can't leave him here!

"What are you talking about? She's my daughter, let me handle this." Mom followed Cole over to some packs.

I snuck back to the plane.

Hank lay on the floor/ceiling. His gaze held confusion.

Did he hear our conversation? Tears spilled out of my eyes and into my goggles, but I couldn't stop them.

I grabbed four water bottles and some granola bars then put them next to Hank's left arm. My stomach growled. I needed to eat something. But who could at a time like that?

"Why . . . are you . . . helping . . . me?" Scratchy and yet sweet, his voice seemed to float in the sad little plane.

"Hank." I grabbed his hand and squeezed, not even thinking about the blood that coated it. If we were leaving him—if he was going to die—he needed to know something. "God loves you, just like He loves me. Just like He loves everyone." I gazed into his eyes, searching for a sign as more tears escaped. "Jesus died for you and me so that we can have eternal life with Him. All you have to do is believe in Him, Hank. Please, just believe."

He just stared. After a long pause, he nodded.

"Andie."

I turned and saw Mom standing at the entrance, eyeing Hank. "We need to go."

Giving his hand one last squeeze, I tucked his arms into the sleeping bag, and covered him with an old army blanket Dad used to use.

Hank gave a firm look. "Go."

I stopped and stared.

"No time . . . Go!"

- -

I barely noticed as Mom put the climbing harness on me. She talked, but her words seemed to bounce off walls in my head, echoing.

Yet, I still didn't understand them because they were slurred. I thought I was passing out. But I wasn't dizzy. No blackness came.

I heard faint voices. Someone pushed me down.

I sat in the snow.

How did I get on the ground?

Cole. Cole was pushing me back telling me to lie down. My stomach growled. That was it. I hadn't eaten anything all morning. I needed food.

"Andie . . . Andie, can you hear me?"

I shook my head and blinked trying to clear the fog.

Cole sat, digging in the emergency bag. Something about him sparked inside of me. But what was it?

Kind brown eyes shot up and met mine as he passed me a granola bar. Was he concerned about me?

"Eat. Now." He turned back around.

I shook my head and opened the bar's crinkled wrapper.

Cole Maddox, are you hiding something?

Cole checked and made sure our harnesses were secure, then we started climbing.

I slipped a couple of times but regained my balance. The ropes and harnesses were uncomfortable, the straps of the pack pulling at my shoulders, but I didn't complain.

Mom's and Cole's were uncomfy as well, and they weren't complaining.

But my muscles ached and it hurt to breathe. *Ugh, this is awkward.*

Stop it, Andie. You've climbed up hills and steep inclines before. Then again, none of them were even close to this steep.

After climbing for what seemed like hours, Mom and Cole slowed down.

It's me, I'm slowing them down. I always make everything harder for everyone. *Stupid nerve disorder.*

We kept climbing, but the longer we climbed, the shorter the distance we seemed to go.

Why is this taking so long?

My face scrunched as my back began to itch.

Then my face.

But, it wasn't a normal itch. It was more of a static-y, tingling itch.

My cheeks and back began to burn and my legs weakened as things seemed to swirl around me.

Was I overheating?

Mom. I've got to tell Mom. Dizziness began to take over and my goggles started fogging up.

"Mom? I—"

My foot slipped.

Air rushed all around me as the rope slid through my hands and the harness. I felt the rope's pressure on the butterfly bandages. My chest closed up. I couldn't breathe. Blurry images flew by as I sailed downward.

Everything disappeared.

CHAPTER SEVEN

COLE

April 7
Sultana, Denali National Park
10:51 a.m.

"Andie!"

Jenna's scream echoed around Cole, and it was all he could do to keep them steady as she strained at the ropes to go after her daughter.

"Jenna, stop! Hold still!"

She wasn't listening. "Andie!" She looked up at him, terror in her eyes.

Before she could say another word, he moved down the line to Jenna and yanked off his head gear.

"I told you not to put her last! Do something! Please—"

The wind whipped around them, making it difficult to hear. Standard climbing procedure was heaviest to lightest when skills were equal, or strongest people first and last. With Jenna's injury, he'd done the logical thing: made a decision. So many things could go wrong and with this unfamiliar terrain, he had no desire to put them all at risk by weighing them down. But that didn't matter to this terrified mom. He lifted her a few feet up the rock face to a ledge. "I'm going to anchor you here," he yelled. "Stay put. I'll go down after her." Sinking two of their ice axes deep into the snow-crusted terrain, he wrapped and anchored their ropes. "I need you to watch these, make sure they hold, and be ready to help, understand?"

Jenna nodded, removed her own hat and goggles, and grabbed at his coat while he secured their lines. "Something's wrong, Cole. Please hurry." The anger in her voice had dissipated, replaced with desperation.

That got to him.

Before he could put up his guard, feelings surged through him. Things he hadn't felt in years. Hadn't allowed to surface. Because he couldn't afford to do so. Caring always led to pain.

Stop. Focus.

He lowered himself down the rope. Andie had fallen about twenty-five feet below Jenna, as far as the ropes would allow. But that wasn't what bothered him. She hung upside down, completely limp. He knew that she had some kind of rare disorder, but he hadn't had time to find out all the details. He hadn't expected to find a vibrant, functioning, normal kid.

A new question plagued him. What if he'd put them all in danger by pushing too hard?

It wasn't long before he reached her still form. "Andie." *Keep your voice calm.* He pulled her upright. "Andie, talk to me. What's happening?"

"Uhhhhhnnn . . . mmmomm . . ."

Cole yanked off her goggles and checked her pupils. Eyes were glassy. "Andie, I need you to stay awake."

"Uhh . . . kay . . ."

He pulled off her ski mask. Bright red cheeks, skin hot to the touch. He yelled as loud as he could up to Jenna, careful not to let his alarm come through in his voice. "She's burning up. And she's bright red."

"Take off her coat! She's overheating!" Jenna's words fought the fierce wind as they floated down to him, but he didn't miss the panic in her voice.

That's right. Marc's words registered again. The kid couldn't sweat or feel pain.

"Andie, stay with me. Stay awake." He lifted off her pack, unzipped her jacket, and gently pulled her arms out one at a time. Grabbing some snow from the side of the cliff, he wet down her face and neck. Surely it wouldn't take long for her to cool off in these temps. "Andie, look at me."

No response. All her symptoms pointed to heatstroke, but could it really be that? On the side of a mountain? In frigid temps?

"Andie"—he made the words forceful—"wake up."

Jenna's shout echoed down to him, "Cole? Cole? Andie?"

Cole rubbed Andie's face again.

Her eyes opened and worked to focus on him. She blinked. "Cole . . ."

He released a sigh. "Hey, you back with us?"

She glanced around. Each moment that passed, her eyes gained clarity.

"Did you hurt anything? Can you talk to me?" He continued questioning her, hoping the lethargy would clear. He removed his own ski goggles and placed a hand to her forehead. At least her skin wasn't burning any longer. He unclipped a water bottle from a carabiner at his waist and positioned it at her lips. "Drink."

He looked up at Jenna and waved an arm, hoping she understood that Andie was alert and okay. That was too close. His heart thumped. Time to squelch these feelings.

After chugging the entire water bottle, Andie smiled. "Cole?"

"Yeah?"

"You have icicles on your eyebrows." She reached up, tentatively touching his face, and smiled again. "It's kinda warm today, huh?"

He allowed a small laugh to escape. "I'm glad you inherited your dad's wit. Guess you're feeling better?"

"Well, I don't know. Everything's not so fuzzy anymore." She shrugged her shoulders. "Thanks, Cole. Guess I overexerted. I'm sorry I slowed you down."

Cole winced. It was his fault, pushing them to extremes to prove he could protect them. "Andie, no. You didn't do anything wrong." He checked her harness. Avoided eye contact. "Sometimes . . . well sometimes, I get too focused on the mission."

"The mission?" Andie giggled. "Oh, Cole. You are *way* too serious. Now you sound just like my dad."

He allowed himself another brief chuckle as he clipped the water bottle back into place and prepared to climb. "Well, your dad and I were friends. I should have told you earlier. And yes, we had many missions together."

"I know."

"Oh? How did you know?"

"I overheard you talking to Mom. It's okay, it reminds me of my dad."

He cocked an eyebrow and checked their ropes.

"But that doesn't mean I trust you."

"Of course not."

"So, are you ready to get me up this mountain?"

The kid had spunk. "Sure thing. Let's get you up to your mom. I'm sure she's pretty worried."

"All right, Mr. Mission. I'm ready."

After repositioning himself in his harness, he tied Andie's coat around her waist and shoved her hat and mask into the pockets.

"You can't stay exposed to these temps too long, so once we get up there, you need to cover your skin, okay?"

"Yes, sir!" She gave him a mock salute.

"Safe to say you don't have to wear your heavy coat while we're climbing."

"Good guess." She giggled again.

Cole had forgotten the beauty of a child's laughter. Andie was almost a teen, but she touched something deep. Just like his—

He shook his head. Couldn't let his thoughts go there. "All right, I came down here without my ice axe, so you are going to have to hold onto me while I get us up over that ledge. I need you to carry your pack though. I'll do all the work, but there's no other way to get it up there. Then you can have your mom check you out, get you geared up properly, and we'll move some more. Sound good?"

"Yep." She was already grabbing hold of him, positioning her legs and arms to be out of the way as he climbed.

"Need more water?"

"I'm good. At least until we get the next twenty or so feet."

Man, she reminded him of her dad. Especially in the early years. "Smart aleck. Since you're so brilliant, your call name will be Einstein."

"Awesome! I've always wanted one of those! Now let's get movin,' tough guy. We're wasting daylight." She hugged him tight.

One step, two. Each slow and calculated as he pulled them up the rope. Almost past the sheer vertical climb. Cole held the girl pressed to his chest. Careful not to grip too hard. She was so small . . . he could crush her without even thinking. Concentrate on the pressure. The progress. The fact that this was what mattered—getting out. Not that this child had done something no one else had been able to do. For a long time.

Made him feel.

His teeth clamped together. Focus. Focus on what was important. On getting her up to her mom. Safe. Analyze the mountain. Each step. Don't think about the interactions with these two since the crash.

Wait a minute. Interactions since the crash . . .

He frowned. Why had Andie rushed back to Hank's side before they left? "Tell me about your conversation with Hank."

Her face scrunched up, frowning from her hairline down to her chin. "I don't know why he did what he did. But, he deserved to know that God loves him no matter what."

"Oh really." Cole couldn't help the cynicism that washed out the words.

"Yeah, really." Those demanding eyes grabbed his attention.

No, he wouldn't get suckered into this one. He looked away.

"No matter who we are, or what we've done, God loves each one of us. Don't you believe that, Cole?"

Such innocence. Such faith. Totally blind. "Look, I don't want to burst your bubble, kid. And I don't want to belittle what you believe in, but no. I don't."

She sighed. Then shook her head. "It's a good thing God doesn't give up on us as easily as we give up on Him."

"I didn't say I gave up on Him."

"But you never gave Him a chance, did you?"

"Let's just say I've never needed to."

She laughed at him. This tiny preteen, who struggled for her own life—was laughing at him. "Oh, you've needed to. You're just too stinkin' stubborn to admit it. And for your information, Hank listened. He needed to be taken care of. Maybe you do too."

He didn't like the way this conversation was going. "Well, maybe you should *pray* for him. That would take care of him."

His sarcasm wasn't well received. Andie shot him a glare. "I *have* been praying for him. And I'm gonna *keep* praying for him.

And you know what? I'm gonna pray for you too. 'Cause *you* obviously need it."

"Let's table this discussion for later."

"Why?"

"Because I need to know more about your . . . disease."

"Yeah, good excuse. And it's not a disease."

He cocked an eyebrow at her irritated tone. "Okay then, it's not a disease. But since you have me as your captive audience, why don't you explain your . . . *problem* with me."

She studied his face. "As long as you promise we'll talk about God later."

"Fine. Whatever." Tenacious kid. "Now tell me about . . ."

"HSAN? Sure, okay. It stands for Hereditary Sensory Autonomic Neuropathy."

"Wow. That's a mouthful." His words were clipped as the thin air pressed his lungs.

"Yeah, you should try to spell it."

He *humph*ed.

"Anyway, I can't sweat, I don't feel pain, and I also had brain surgery last year. But it was for something else, because I couldn't feel the pain of the problem, so they had to do surgery. But I'm better now."

Did all preteen girls dump information this fast? "So, you could have . . ."

"What?" Andie scrunched her eyebrows. "Just say it. I'm not a baby."

"I know that. I just realized you could have died back there and I didn't like that thought." The exertion of climbing, carrying extra weight, and talking began to make him light-headed.

They were almost over the ledge. Andie waved her hand at her mom, smiled, and then looked back at him. "You know what, Cole?"

"Hmm?" He concentrated on his grip, securing each foothold before the next.

"I think you're the first person to actually understand the depth of my disorder on the first try. Seriously, people—even family members—don't always get it until they've been around us for a long time. Thanks. For understanding."

Heaving them over the ledge onto easier terrain, his heart hammered in his chest. And not just from the exertion. How could this be happening? A carefully guarded space inside him begged to be unlocked.

No. Not again.

Never.

He unfastened Andie and collapsed in the snow as mother and daughter united. They must've made some good progress today, the air was thinner. Definitely higher altitude. Breathing deep, he took a minute to take off his pack and compose himself. *Keep your mind on the mission.*

His traitorous mind had other plans.

Not one soul had penetrated his heart in more than nine years. And that was how he wanted it. His promise was costing him more by the minute.

The girls' voices drifted over him.

"Oh, Mom, I was so scared! I tried to call your name, but it was already too late. I just wish I could feel it sooner."

"Honey, I'm so sorry. I should've checked your temperature earlier. I'm just glad you're okay." Jenna touched noses with her daughter. "You'd think in two-degree weather, we wouldn't have to worry about it, huh?"

Andie's giggles floated in the air around him. "Mom, you crack me up. I'm so glad you're my mom. I don't know what I'd do without you."

"Same here, kiddo. Thank God He saw fit to give you to me."

Cole turned away from the scene. *Then why does He take people away?*

Clouds continued to swirl and gather around the peaks of Denali and Sultana. The weather wouldn't hold much longer. They had to move.

"Jenna, Andie," he barked. "Time to go."

Jenna turned and approached him slowly. "Cole. Thank you." Placing one hand over her chest and another on his arm, she continued, "I can't tell you what it means—"

"Not a problem. But we need to get moving." His words impaled her smile, but this was solid ground. The mission. "There's a storm coming. I can feel it."

Hurt shone in her eyes. "Okay." She went back to Andie. "Honey, we need to go."

In silence, they replaced packs and adjusted ropes.

"We're ready, Cole." Andie gave him a thumbs-up and lifted her ski mask over her head. A smile shaped her lips, but her complexion was pale.

"You all right?"

"I'm tired. But if I don't keep moving, my body will just quit."

Cole turned to Jenna for help. What did that mean?

Jenna's eyes were guarded. "Don't push too hard."

He could read between the lines. If something happened, she'd blame him. Well, that wasn't going to happen. He pasted on a smile and looked to Andie. "All right, Einstein. I want you right behind me this time, and I mean *directly* behind me, okay?" He attached another shorter rope between just the two of them. "If you need anything, tug on this rope, and if you slip or misstep, I'll feel the tug. Keep your coat around your waist for right now, but keep your skin covered. Got it?"

"Got it."

"Let's go."

Snow began to fall. He kept their pace slower and more cautious. Snow crunched beneath his boots as his crampons took hold each icy step. If the situation wasn't so dire, he'd be enjoying this trek. Sultana was a steep climb, but she was beautiful. Every time the sun broke through the clouds, the snow turned into a million, brilliant prisms.

An all-too-familiar sound broke through his reverie. He put up his hand and looked down at the girls. "Stop. Quiet."

Tearing off his goggles and hat, he strained his ears, listening to every sound. The clouds partially below them now cut off his line of sight, so he focused all his energy on his hearing.

Then it came . . . the steady thump. Like an airborne heartbeat.

A chopper.

"Cole!" Excitement filled Jenna's voice. "Cole! They're here! They're here to rescue us! Go down, let's go down!"

"No!" He knew that helo. It wasn't rangers.

The girls stopped in their tracks.

Jenna stared him down. "Why?" She yanked at her goggles and mask, eyes fixed on his face. She must have read the answer there, because horror filled her eyes and her face drained of color. "No. You mean . . . ?"

"We need cover, and fast. If they spot us up here, they won't hesitate to kill us."

Andie and Jenna drew close. Cole checked out the surroundings. About twenty yards east a rock outcropping might provide cover. He prayed the ledge would be enough. His gut told him they were in for more than the girls could handle.

Pointing to the area, he waited for Jenna's nod. He grabbed the girls' hands. "Okay, dig your crampons in with each step so you have a grip, we're going to move as fast as we can."

With a deep breath, he charged forward, dragging them along.

The *thwump-thwump* of the helo's blades grew closer.

Each step took great effort. Clunky boots sinking into the deep snow. His arms stretched behind as he pulled and tugged the girls, leaning all his weight forward, the ropes were taut. Just a few more feet. His muscles burned, his lungs starving for air. Just . . . a few . . . more . . .

Diving for the small area under the rocky ledge, he pulled Jenna and Andie with him. They collapsed in the snow, chests heaving, gasping for oxygen.

He glanced below. Clouds moved in and out. The helicopter shifted with the wind and snow, but clearly hovered over the crash site. Minutes dragged by. Ten, then fifteen . . . If only he could see!

A break in the clouds gave him a brief view. Ropes swung below the helo. They must be checking the plane. A curse blew out his lips. It would give away the one card he had left—that Andie and Jenna were still alive.

A huge blast of Arctic air hit them, throwing them back against the rocks. At least the bad weather was working in their favor. Cole leaned back out to check the chopper. The ropes were being pulled back up as it rocked and swayed in the wind. But it continued to hover.

Too much time had passed. His brain grasped for escape options. But then, another break in the clouds opened a full view to him. "Oh, no." All the air in his lungs left him in a great *whoosh* as he anticipated the next move from the enemy below.

"Cover your ears!" Looking back at the girls, he yanked the ropes closer to him, pulling them in from the edge.

The short whistle of the missile barreling toward its target preceded a deafening explosion.

Both girls screamed, their gazes glued to the blast.

Cole glanced down. A giant fireball exploded and then grew in huge waves of flame and smoke, like an angry beast devouring everything in its path.

CRACK!!

The mountain rumbled around them and Cole threw himself over Andie, shoving her as far under the rock as possible. "Jenna!" He grabbed for her, even as his head collided with the massive ledge—and light disappeared.

CHAPTER EIGHT

ANDIE
April 7
Sultana, Denali National Park
1:59 p.m.

The snow roared and thundered around us.

Hank was dead.

God, why?

"*We'll send someone back for him. He'll be fine.*"

Fine? *This is what you call fine? He's dead!* I balled my hands into fists. If we had taken him with us, he could still be alive.

But then we *wouldn't have been.*

No sooner had we gotten under the hanging-rock-cliff-thing than the snow pummeled down. If it hadn't been for Cole, we would have been dead.

I couldn't believe it. Didn't want to believe it. Someone was really after us, and wanted to *kill* us. My body trembled.

Hank was dead; we could have been dead.

We could die . . . We probably would die.

What was happening? All I knew at the moment was we were safe under a gigantic rock with an avalanche in action.

And I was cold.

But I felt safe.

My head rested against something that heaved up and down in a slow pattern.

Cole.

His arms wrapped around me, protecting me from the powerful cascade of snow.

He was cold, unconscious, and had a huge bump on his forehead.

He had risked *his* life for me.

He had saved me.

But why? Was he really a good guy, or the bad guy? Could I really trust him with our *lives*?

Flashbacks and memories flooded over warming my heart.

In many ways Cole was just like Daddy.

Strong, protective, gruff but lovable . . .

And secretive.

Dad always had secrets. Did men always have them?

"North Korea is anxious to get the prototype" . . . What was he saying? What did he mean? And why did *I* need to keep it a secret?

I shook my head.

Daddy was dead, so I didn't need to remember it any longer. *You just need to forget about it, Andie.*

The ground shuddered. Or was that me?

I wanted to trust Cole. But why was he still not awake?

Where's Mom? Why can't I see her?

I tried to see past Cole's massive shoulder.

What if Cole dies? What if his head injury is worse than it seems?

I shook him, but with his muscular frame he didn't feel a thing.

Ugh. God, what do I do now? Am I supposed to sit here while we run out of oxygen?

Cole began to stir.

Wow, that was a fast reply!

Whether he was good or bad, he was alive.

And that's what matters. He's trying to keep us safe. Right?

"North Korea . . . prototype . . . North Korea . . ."

I shook my head, ridding it of the annoying chant. Why did it keep popping up in my mind?

God, please get rid of that memory, it's driving me crazy! Please help Mom and Cole be okay.

Cole began to wiggle within my grip.

Thanks, God.

LEAPER

2:01 p.m.

It was done.

No one needed to know anything else.

Regret washed over him as a memory of Gray talking about his family surfaced.

What was wrong with him? Had he gone completely soft? Or had the stress of Viper breathing down his neck finally snapped every fiber of what little sanity he had left?

He shook his head to clear the questions, and sat a little straighter in the small, metal seat. Even in his discomfort, the facts were there. He did his job. End of story.

He turned his thoughts to the task at hand. Once AMI was acquired, they would all be very rich. A sardonic chuckle started in his gut. Ah, yes, money was a powerful thing. A trusted ally, a best friend, a companion—that didn't talk back or give orders.

The end result would be worth it. And nothing would get in his way.

Nothing.

JENNA
April 7
Sultana, Denali National Park
2:03 p.m.

Fingers of fear crawled their way across Jenna's back. She pushed the swell of claustrophobia back down her throat. She just needed to see Andie.

Pawing her way through the snow, Jenna finally opened a hole to see the small area where Cole and Andie lay. Only a few feet separated them. Relief swept over her. Once again, her daughter was safe. She could almost reach out and touch her.

Thanks to that infuriating man.

Snow continued to pour from above. He'd been right. Again. Had they climbed down like she'd suggested, they would be buried right now. *Lord, thank You for saving me from my own foolishness.*

She attempted to free her legs, but with the snow still tumbling down the mountain, it was no use.

Stuck. Under half a mountain of snow.

Glancing up through the small hole, she checked the forms of her daughter and rescuer. Thankfully, Cole had covered Andie with his large frame and used the rock overhang as a shield from the onslaught of ice and snow. But Jenna had been curious, drawn to the horror of the sight below her and she'd ventured a little too far away from the cover. Ignoring the tugging of Cole's protectiveness. Her defiance and rebellion had gotten her stuck. Again.

How stupid could she have been? What was she thinking to get so close to the edge? The moment had been so surreal—her eyes drawn to the destruction below her—but still, she should've known better. Once again, Jenna was grateful her actions hadn't taken her life. She might be buried, but at least she could breathe. And she could see her daughter. Plenty to be thankful for.

But poor Hank. She'd known him all these years, never suspecting the evil that lurked inside. If she had been a better example to him, could she have changed this outcome? Could she have saved Hank's life? The stark emptiness of her own lack of effort made the guilt inside her grow, eating at the sensitive places of her heart. *Lord, what have I done?*

The roar of the avalanche continued and made her ears ache. How long could these things last? She and Marc had many friends who climbed these mountains in their younger days. And she remembered the pictures of beautiful avalanches. Listened to the guys tell the stories of several they witnessed during one climb. So how much *more* snow would come down with an explosion?

Her neck ached from holding her head up. She laid her head back down in the snow and covered her head with her arms. It still sounded like a deafening train rushing past at breakneck speed. The snow began to lose its clean smell, instead it reminded her of clothes packed away too long. If they weren't careful, they'd run out of fresh air in the few cubic feet of safety they shared.

Voices pulled her head back up as the thunderous noise dwindled into a dull rumble and then disappeared. Jenna watched her daughter hug Cole. Tears streamed down her baby's cheeks as they both pulled gear off their heads.

"Cole, thanks. That was so scary." Andie wiped her cheeks. "Have you seen Mom?"

Jenna lifted her hand through the hole in the snow. "I'm here. Just buried."

"Mom!" Her daughter shifted with stiff, awkward movements. "How do we get out of here? There's barely enough room to move—do we even have air to breathe?"

Cole looked down at Andie. "We're going to have to dig." He turned his attention toward Jenna. "You okay?"

"Yeah, but you better start digging. The air already feels stuffy." Jenna didn't want to voice her real thoughts. No one needed to be reminded they could suffocate.

"Okay then." He moved a few inches. "Andie, you're going to have to reach for my axe behind me. You and I will work on ventilation holes, then dig space to move in so we can try to get your mom out."

Andie nodded and reached for the ice axe. "Got it." She looked scared. "Cole?"

"Yeah?"

"Thanks again."

"No problem. You would've done the same for me, right?" He winked at her daughter. Jenna could have hugged him for helping to lighten the moment.

"Um, sure. 'Cause I'm so big and strong and protective." The twinkle in Andie's eyes was back.

Cole reached toward Andie's hair, but quickly withdrew his hand.

"Cole, you really gotta stop stuffing all your emotions down. It's not good for you."

Good ol' therapist Andie.

Their rescuer just stared down at her. Then he shook his head. "You make me smile, Squirt."

Jenna's heart thundered in her chest. How would Andie react to that nickname? Breath in her throat, she silently watched and waited.

Tears began to glisten on Andie's pink cheeks.

Cole frowned. "What's wrong?"

"My dad . . . he used to call me that when I was little." Andie swiped at her face. "I just miss him."

"Hey, I'm sorry." Cole inched farther away. "I won't use it."

Andie grabbed his hand. "No, I like it. It's a good reminder to keep moving forward, and it brings me special memories. Besides,

I think he would like it that you're here protecting us, helping us."

Jenna wasn't sure how she felt about that. Some days it seemed Marc had been gone forever, other days, it rushed back as if it'd happened yesterday. She had given Marc her whole heart, and full trust. Her world seemed to tilt off-kilter with the thought. How could she possibly trust someone else that she'd only known a day? She glanced back at Cole, who carefully poked holes through the snow.

He didn't appear to know how to take Andie either. Always so honest, forthright, and yet innocent and sweet. His fidgeting proved to Jenna that her daughter had struck a nerve.

"I promised your dad, Andie. And I intend to keep that promise."

"Is that all? Just because you promised my dad?"

Something akin to gentleness crossed his features. "No. That's not all."

"Good, because I need to tell you something."

Jenna waited. What could make Andie sound so serious?

"I really do trust you, Cole. God brought you here, I'm sure of it. And I wanted you to know how I feel."

He didn't respond. In fact, Jenna thought he looked a little shell-shocked.

"Cole? Did you hear me? You told me that trust had to be earned. And you've definitely earned mine . . ."

Jenna shut the rest of the conversation out. Should she trust this man, too? *Could* she? How had things spun so far out of control? *God, what am I doing? I feel so lost. I have no idea what to do, and I don't know if I should trust this man. Is Andie right? Did You send him to us?*

There was no audible answer. No shining light from above, telling her it would all be okay. But in her heart, she knew to trust her daughter's instincts. Trusting didn't come easy to her anymore, but for Andie's sake, she needed to try.

She laid her head down again, her mind reviewing the incidents of the past few days, like a silent film replaying over and over. Could all of this be happening? Really?

Her eyes closed. She was tired. And cold. And buried.

"Jenna?" Cole's hand on her shoulder roused her. Had she fallen asleep?

She looked up into his eyes. They were a deep brown. Chocolate brown. So strong. So deep. "I'm okay."

"Let's get you out of here, all right?" The shovel in his right hand had been put to use. The area under the ledge had already been expanded.

Wow. How long had she slept? She tried to move forward, but the crushing weight on her back and legs prohibited any movement. "Good. I feel like I've got half a dozen moose sitting on my back side."

Cole's deep laughter filled the small space. And did funny things to her heart. "Ah, so I see Andie not only inherited her father's wit, but your humor and charm as well."

She eyeballed the intense man crouched in front of her. Good grief, when he smiled . . . Why hadn't she noticed how attractive he was before now? She shook her head. "*Ha ha.* Now if you don't mind, I'd like to restore feeling to my legs."

His chuckle drifted over her as she watched him scoot back over to his pack. Pulling out his ice axe again, he glanced back at her. "We need more air. Every time I punch through, more snow falls down."

He poked the axe through the snow wall several times until she saw light burst into their tiny shelter. Soon the air held that clean, sweet smell of freshly fallen snow.

As he approached her again, he instructed Andie to eat a snack and drink plenty of water. He really wasn't so bad. Strong, capable, and just a little bit ruggedly-too-handsome-for-his-own-good. And it helped that he was looking out for her precious daughter.

Cole crouched in front of her again. "We really need to get moving again. Do you think you're up for it?"

She furrowed her brow. "Are we still going up? I thought since they blew up the plane, that maybe they'd leave us alone now."

He shook his head and continued to dig in the snow around her.

But she wouldn't let him speak, she barreled on ahead, "And wasn't it snowing before the avalanche? What about the explosion? Couldn't anyone have seen that? Is it safe to climb in this weather? What about Andie—"

His large hand covered her mouth. "Jenna, you need to be calm." He glanced back at Andie. "And cooperative."

Oooohh, he made her so mad. Attractive or not, he was impossible.

He removed his hand.

Good choice. She just might've bit him.

Cole held up a hand and brushed the hair from his face. "Now look. I can see the steam getting ready to billow out of your ears, but just remember, we're doing this for Andie, okay?"

Why did he always have to do that? "Fine."

"And yes, it's still snowing. But I think we've got time before the big storm hits. We need to make as much progress as we can—get as far away from the crash site as possible." He took a deep breath. "Now, is that enough explanation for you?"

"No. As a matter of fact, it's not." *She* was the mom here. "What—do you have Spidey-sense or something? How could you possibly know about storms in the Alaska Range? These mountains create their own weather. And you didn't bother to answer my questions."

His chiseled face froze. Then he frowned. Then his jaw did that little twitching thing in the cheek, like Marc's when he was really mad. At her.

Ugh. She couldn't for the life of her figure out why this man brought out the worst in her—how he could get under her skin like a tick burrowing for blood.

She sighed. Yes, she *was* the parent. She needed to start acting like it. "Look, I'm sorry. Marc was the high-octane-military-mission-lives-on-the-line kind of guy. While I was the stay-at-home-take-care-of-the-baby type. It was all fine and dandy to hear about his stories, but I never had to live it."

"Jenna." Her name came out on a sigh as he wiped a hand down his face. "I'm not used to having to explain myself. But don't worry about it. You and I both know the rangers are too far away to have seen anything. Had the explosion not triggered the avalanche, eventually, someone would've seen the wreckage and smoke. But being that we are so *lucky* right now, not only was there an avalanche, but we've got a major snowstorm brewing. It's like all the powers that be are against us." His jaw continued to twitch. "Look, you've had to deal with a lot, and you're injured. Just let me help, okay?"

Her heart performed a little backflip.

Dare she allow someone access to her carefully protected world?

CHAPTER NINE

ANDIE

April 7
Sultana, Denali National Park
3:19 p.m.

Cole tried as hard as he could to pull Mom out, but this was taking longer than I'd expected. *God, please give Cole strength. Please.*

"Andie? I need you to help me dig your mom out. I want you to loosen the snow, then I'll pull it off her."

I hesitated, then nodded and started digging. *Why am I so stiff? This should be easy . . .*

"It's okay, baby." Mom's rough smile eased some tension, but didn't help the impatience taking over.

This is taking way too long, we should've gotten her out awhile ago.

"Do you think anything's broken, Jenna?"

Mom winced and peeked down at her leg. "I don't think so, but I'm going to need a new bandage."

Cole nodded and removed the last of the snow.

Mom sat up. I threw my arms around her neck and squeezed hard. Perhaps too hard.

She grunted and patted my back. "Andie?"

"Whoops! Sorry." Pulling away, I smiled. "I guess I don't know my own strength."

"It's fine." Mom leaned down and gave me an Eskimo kiss. "Your *sentsiis* is cold!"

I rubbed my nose. *Wow, it is cold.* "Oh well. Guess that's what happens up here."

Cole turned to us. "We should start digging out from underneath this ledge."

"All right." Mom tried to stand, but her leg gave away.

"Mom, are you okay?" I could feel my heart beating in my chest. *Calm down . . . Calm down . . . Calm down . . .*

"Yeah. I need to get used to the altitude, that's all." She stood again.

"Oh, right. You're a whopping five feet higher, wow, that's some altitude!" I giggled, easing the tension that wanted to take over.

"Okay, little-miss-smarty-pants." Mom reached over and tweaked my frozen nose.

"Let's get out of here." Cole pointed to the hole he had dug and then climbed through.

I followed close behind. Rubbed my arms. *Brrr . . . it's cold.*

Cole started to mess with our harnesses. "We need to start climbing."

Mom's smile faded. She didn't look too happy.

"Jenna, my gut tells me they'll be back."

I shuddered. *They'll be back?*

"We have to climb up. It's our only option. If we go down, they may find us."

Hmm. So he's Mr. Grumpy-pants and Mr. Drill Sergeant.

"Okay . . . but for how long? And that storm's coming. We really don't know how much time we have." Mom's gaze shifted to the sky.

Yeah, I'm cold enough already, I don't want to be caught in a storm.

"We've already been over all this. Twice. We'll climb for as long as we can." Cole clenched his fists.

"What about shelter?"

"Jenna—"

I jumped as Cole swung around to face us.

He frowned at Mom. "I've got it, okay?"

My eyes widened. *Uh-oh. You've done it now.*

Mom slammed her hands on her hips. "*Excuse* me?" Her eyes narrowed. "For your information *Cole*, this is my daughter's life we're dealing with. I'm just being cautious."

"And for your information, *Jenna, I* am trying to protect you!"

Wowzer, he's mad.

"Cole Maddox, you—"

"Jenna, I know what I'm doing!"

I stared at Cole. What was wrong with him?

"I know Andie is in danger, I know you're upset, and I know there's a storm coming!"

"Cole!" Mom glared at him with such heat I thought the glaciers would melt. "You are by far—"

"No!" Cole's voice boomed and echoed. With each word his voice rose. "You are going to set your little injured self on the snow and stay right there while *I* take care of this!"

"While I *take care of this . . . While* I *take care of this . . . While* I *take care of this . . ."* I looked at the peaks surrounding us as his words echoed.

"Wow!" I clapped and jumped up and down in a circle. "Do that again, do that again!" I laughed as Cole's words continued to echo.

"While I *take care of this . . ."*

Mom and Cole turned to me.

"I found your nickname." I couldn't hold back a grin. "I hereby name you Echo!"

Cole's eyes narrowed. His jaw clenched. "What did you just say?"

"I said I hereby name you Echo! I think it fits perfectly. Einstein and Echo, sounds nice . . ." My smile faded at his expression, and a shiver raced up my spine.

"Why?" He glared.

"Um, duh! Did you not just hear your voice?" Was he mad at *me* now? I stopped jumping and stood there. What did I say wrong?

Mom sighed, her glare deepening. "Look, Cole—"

Cole held up a hand. When he spoke, his voice was quiet. "No, I'm sorry. I shouldn't have yelled at you like that."

Mom nodded, gave a small "you're forgiven," and turned around mumbling to herself.

I stared at them.

Was it something I said?

Cole walked over, secured our harnesses and packs, then started climbing. Within the first ten minutes, I ran out of breath and the snow got bigger.

And fell faster.

My mind was distracted, I could barely keep track of where I put my feet. A chill ran up and down my spine. *Last time I couldn't keep cool, now I can't keep warm . . .*

My fingers started to go numb.

Don't slip, don't slip, don't slip. Whatever you do, don't slip.

I took another step, then paused.

I couldn't feel Cole tugging the rope as he climbed.

I jerked my head up. Walls of white surrounded me each direction I looked. I could barely see my own hands on the rope.

My eyes widened.

"Cole!"

COLE

April 7
Sultana, Denali National Park
4:35 p.m.

A whiteout.

Just what he needed.

Huffing and puffing inside his ski mask, Cole scolded himself. *I've put us all in danger.* And that tenacious kid had put her trust in him.

He failed. Again.

To make matters worse, the little snit had to go and give him a nickname. And it hit just a little too close to home. He clamped his jaw, grinding his teeth.

His legs felt like Jell-O, his lungs burned from the brutal cold. Wind whipped around him trying to steal the pack from him. There was nowhere to go.

Blinking his eyes, he rubbed the front of his goggles with his gloves. Still nothing. Too much snow. Too much wind. And he'd pushed too far, too long.

Kneeling in the snow, he heaved the pack from his back. Time to seek shelter.

Past time.

Cole turned around and sat in the snow. He couldn't see any trace of the girls behind him and the rope between him and Andie was only ten feet long. Anchoring his crampons in the snow beneath him, he tugged on the line. The rope became taut as he dragged the two girls up the side of the mountain. Each pull took an enormous amount of effort and air. For each six inches of rope he tugged closer, it took thirty seconds to catch his breath and start again.

Taking too long. They worked their way up as well, the rope would slack, he'd gain more ground, but not fast enough for his liking. Fear and exhaustion were probably taking their toll on the girls. They couldn't take this.

The storm churned around him.

The wind deafened him.

His heart hammered harder in his chest, beating out the rhythm . . . *you've killed them, you've killed them, you've killed them* . . .

No! He'd made a promise. And he cared . . .

Images floated into his mind, and he was too tired to stop them.

The hospital.

The gurneys.

The white sheets.

The police officer offering his stilted condolences . . .

He lost his grip and the rope slipped through his fingers. *No!*

Cole shook his head, clenched his teeth, and uttered a guttural cry into the wind as he caught the rope. He couldn't lose Jenna and Andie. Not now. With everything in him, he pulled on that rope. Inch by solitary inch, he dragged the girls to him.

His girls.

They needed him. And he needed them.

A weight the size of Denali dropped into his gut.

His heart had been opened, and there was no stopping it now.

CHAPTER TEN

JENNA
April 7
Sultana, Denali National Park
5:00 p.m.

Jenna's leg, shocked with pain, went numb and gave out. Again. Falling to the snow-covered mountainside, she cried. She couldn't see anything, hear anything, and her leg throbbed in time to the gusts of wind pelting her body. The hard tugging on the rope attached to her brought her head back up. *Pull it together, girl. Andie needs you.*

She struggled to her feet and forced the fear to the back of her mind. Each step took extraordinary effort and she'd run out of water fifteen minutes before. Nothing to see but the rope in her hands and the cloud of white. Everywhere. A strange sensation prickled her skin. The white closed in. Claustrophobic feelings overwhelmed her common sense.

She felt blind.

Her breaths were short. There was no way to get enough air, and her muscles burned with the lack of oxygen. *Suck it up,*

Jenna. Keep going. One step at a time. She would not abandon her daughter.

It seemed an eternity had passed.

One small step, a few more inches of rope. Another small step.

And then a small, gloved hand grabbed onto hers. *Andie!* Giant arms wrapped them both in a fierce hug.

She'd made it.

Exhaustion made her body weak. If Cole hadn't been holding them up, she would've collapsed in the snow. Relief flooded through her at holding Andie close, but the horrific pain from her leg throbbed into her brain. Her breaths came faster.

How would they survive in this storm?

Cole's intimate presence swallowed her before she saw what he was doing. His hand was on her ski mask-covered face as he pulled back her hood. Warm breath seeped through the material protecting her skin, until she felt his lips pressed against her ear. She sucked in her breath as tingles shot through her body.

"Jenna." His warm breath skated along her earlobe and neck.

He'd come this close so she could hear. Nothing more. She needed to remind herself of that fact.

"I'm going to build a snow cave for us, and I might need your help. Are you okay?"

She nodded, unable to speak with him so near. He wouldn't have heard her anyway.

"Hold onto Andie, stay tethered. I'm going to get it started, and you two will at least have a little cover while I dig out the rest."

Her head bobbed.

His mouth lingered against her ear like he had more to say, but after a moment he drew away.

The rope pulled and tugged at her as he worked a few feet away. She brought Andie close and hugged her tight. There was nothing like having her daughter near.

Andie pulled away slightly and reached for her water bottle under her coat. After taking a sip, she offered it to Jenna.

Blessed water. There couldn't be a better gift than that. She was so thirsty. Before she realized it, she'd drunk the whole bottle, the excess on her lips turning to ice before it could even dribble down into her ski mask.

She covered her face, turned Andie around, and tucked the empty bottle inside her pack. Grabbing her daughter's hand, she tugged her to the ground where they sat huddled together.

Squinting, she attempted to see through the snow to Cole. But the blizzard didn't allow her to see him working—working to save their lives. Once again.

She'd been so hard on him. That wasn't her intention, but he brought out the worst in her. At least when it came to being in charge and protecting Andie. Something else stirred in the pit of her stomach. Marc had been gone a year, and she promised herself she could never love again. But she was lonely. And had to admit that always having to take care of things weighed her down. Even though he exasperated her, it was nice to have a strong, protective, hunky guy watching out for them.

A harsh realization slammed into her: Cole needed prayer. No matter what happened between them, she needed to pray for him. Especially now as he was risking his life to save theirs.

Bowing her head, she reached for both of Andie's hands. The wind would keep them from hearing each other, but Jenna knew that her daughter would be praying as well.

She prayed aloud, letting the wind and snow whip her words up to the heavens. "Lord, I feel so small right now. We're lost and in danger, I've never been more scared in my life, but I know You are still in control. I don't understand why people are after us, but please keep us safe."

A hand on her shoulder brought her head up. Cole lifted her out of the snow. When her leg gave out and she stumbled forward, he caught her in his arms. She straightened and for a brief moment relished the comfort of those strong arms around her. How long had it been since someone had held her? Protected her?

Cole kept one arm around her waist as he reached out for Andie and hauled them both a few feet to the right. In a matter of seconds, he lowered himself to his hands and knees and brought them with him to the opening of a snow cave.

Guiding them inside, he motioned for them to stay, then he went back into the swirling white of the storm.

Jenna unattached her harness and yanked all the gear off her head. Oh, how wonderful it was to breathe without all the cloth over her face. She helped Andie get out of her harness, and smiled at her daughter, watching her remove all the layers from her face. "Sweetie, it is so good to see your pretty eyes."

They hugged again.

Andie sighed.

Enjoying the warmth without a wind chill, Jenna looked around. Where they sat was barely big enough for all of them to sit huddled together, but it was secure. The opening had to be crawled through, but she knew enough about snow caves to understand the basics. They would put their packs in the opening when they were all done to protect them from the elements.

She observed three ventilation holes that he'd made above their heads, but they'd have to keep punching their ice axes through if the weather continued like this. They'd need fresh air, but with it still snowing, the holes could fill up fast.

A small battery lantern lit up the space, casting a yellowish glow onto the snow.

Cole crawled back through the opening and shoved all their gear into the hole he'd vacated.

The space shrank with his large presence.

"Hi." He took off his hat, goggles, and ski mask.

"Hi." She and Andie spoke at the same time.

"Well," he grinned at them, "I know it's kind of small, but I'm about to remedy that."

Jenna nodded her agreement.

"Can I help?"

Cole smiled at Andie. "Sure thing, Einstein. But you and your mom need to scoot over to the entrance by the packs. Get as close together as you can because I've got to stretch out to do this, okay?"

"Okey dokey." Andie did as she was told.

His light brown hair stuck to his head all matted down from the mask and hat. It was kinda cute. Jenna watched this giant of a man try to maneuver in the tiny space. He must have sensed her scrutiny because he looked at her with those chocolate-brown eyes as the edges of his mouth lifted. Jenna froze as his gaze captured hers.

"Jenna, I'm gonna need you to man the bucket. As I dig out each tunnel, you'll need to get the snow outside." He turned his attention to Andie. "When I'm done with each tunnel, you need to come behind me with that smaller shovel and pack it all in, smooth it over. Make sense?"

"Yep. My dad and I used to make forts when I was little. He always talked about how to make snow caves in case we ever got stranded."

Cole took the larger hand-shovel and began on the first sleeping tunnel. He looked back at Jenna. "Hey, you might want to pray I don't hit any rock." Turning his head back to the task at hand, he chuckled.

Jenna laughed along, but took his suggestion to heart. In a blizzard, no one can be sure about the terrain around them. Any large rocks in this area could make it difficult for all of them to be able to stretch out and sleep. So she prayed and waited until he'd accumulated a good pile of snow behind him before she moved the packs and hauled it out the entrance. The wind took her breath away. A stake marking the entrance with rope tied to it leading out into the blizzard caught her attention. Unsure where the rope led, she understood that he had given them a small way to find the cave if they needed to venture out.

Bucket after bucket, she threw the snow to the right of their "doorway," down the mountainside. She crawled back inside.

Stopping for water, she noted the progress they'd made. Cole was already digging the last of the three tunnels, while Andie worked in the middle one smoothing and packing the snow. Marc had told her that people could survive long periods of time in snow caves, but she hoped they wouldn't have to personally prove those facts.

Water slid down her throat as she took another sip. Exhaustion set in again. Her limbs ached, her lungs burned.

Cole scooted out of the last tunnel with a big grin on his face. "All done. Andie can finish packing it out." He patted her arm. "You look done in, Jenna. Let me haul out the rest of the snow. There's not much left."

It took all her energy to nod. She really should help finish getting things set up, they all needed food, water, and rest. Plenty of rest.

Andie finished smoothing out the last tunnel as Cole hauled out the snow.

Jenna grabbed the sleeping bags and laid one out in each tunnel. He'd made the middle one longer. Probably to accommodate his tall frame.

"Hey, Mom, I'm hungry. Can we eat something?" Andie bounced up and down on her knees.

"You bet." Jenna pulled her pack toward her. "As soon as Cole is back in—"

Cole's head appeared in the opening at that moment. "Who's hungry? 'Cause I'm starved."

Andie smiled at him, and helped him stow some of their gear back into the hole, blocking out all the nasty weather outside. She brushed the snow off his head and shoulders as he rubbed his gloved hands together.

Jenna brought out beef jerky, trail mix, and a few protein bars. They were all so close together, it was a tad bit awkward. As they sat crisscross-applesauce, their knees touched. She wasn't used to sharing space like this with anyone other than her daughter since Marc died. The closeness of Cole made her flush. No, maybe it was just the heat from her leg. With her leg bent, the throbbing and heat became more prominent.

"I'll pray," Andie announced as Jenna redirected her focus on passing out the food.

Cole's eyes widened but he didn't say anything.

"Go for it." Jenna smiled at her daughter.

"Dear God, thank You for this food and for Mom and Cole and this really cool snow cave. Please keep us from any more crashes . . ." she took a deep breath, "explosions, avalanches, bad guys, and injuries. And we could really use some help getting home. In Jesus' name, Amen."

Jenna watched Andie tear into the food, and Cole stare at her daughter with his mouth half open. He obviously wasn't used to the bubbly, unashamed-of-her-faith, tell-it-like-it-is Andie. Or, he wasn't used to prayer. Either way the man was in for an adventure.

Their food quickly consumed, Jenna passed out water bottles, and collected the trash. She really needed some sleep. Certainly she could feel 100 percent tomorrow if she could just get some sleep.

"Hey, Mom?"

"Hmm?"

"I need to use the little girl's room."

They both looked to Cole for direction.

"There's a container in my bag for that." His words were nonchalant.

"Ewww!"

"No. I don't think so." Jenna spoke at the same time as her daughter. "And please remember, we are *not* of the male species." She crossed her arms for effect.

Cole looked up this time and laughed. "Yeah, thought you'd say that." He raked his hand through his hair and nailed Jenna with his firm stare. "You do realize there's a blizzard going on outside?"

"Yes."

"And you realize how cold it is? And how fast things . . . um . . . freeze at these temperatures?"

Andie threw a glove at him. "That's just gross." But she giggled as she said it.

Jenna felt the heat creep up her neck, flooding her cheeks. "I think we are very aware. We *are* native Alaskans, Mr. Maddox. Ahtna-Athabaskan, to be precise. Our ancestors have been on this land for generations." She forced herself to look him in the eye, even though she had to admit she was embarrassed by the situation and her little tirade. "But you must understand that there is *no* way we could possibly . . . well, you know . . . in front of a . . . a *man*!"

Cole opened and then closed his mouth. Then opened it again. "I do understand. That's why I staked out the entrance and roped it to another stake several yards away. There's a tiny snow cave at the end of that stake. And I do mean tiny. So, one of you will have to stand guard outside. I dug a hole for, well . . . you know, but at least you'll be protected from the elements."

"Okay, okay!" Jenna held up her hands to cut him off. "We don't need to discuss it in detail. Andie and I understand survival in the bush."

He chuckled again. "Just stay together. You wouldn't want me to have to come get you."

"Oh, you are so bad." Andie retrieved her glove. "Better watch it, she might do something to you in your sleep."

Jenna enjoyed the banter, even if it was about bathroom usage. She and Andie geared up and crawled out.

When they returned, Cole helped them brush off all the snow, and they prepared to go to sleep.

All the remaining water bottles and food were tucked into their sleeping bags to prevent freezing, and Cole waited to turn off the lamp until she nodded at him.

In the dark, she could hear the wind's howl, Andie's shuffling in her bag—that one always was a wiggle worm—and Cole's deep breaths as he settled in.

"Will you pray for us, Cole?" Her daughter's voice seemed more childlike in the chilly darkness.

"Why don't you handle it for me this time?" His husky voice sounded strangely uneasy.

"Okay." Andie wiggled again in her sleeping bag. "God, it's us again. You know what's going on. You know how scary all this is. And You know where we are and how long the storm will last. Thank You for the food we have, and for a safe place out of the blizzard. Thanks for sending Cole. Show him how to help us. And keep him from driving Mom nuts—"

Jenna couldn't help it, she laughed.

Cole grunted.

"I'm not finished." Andie directed at them.

"By all means, continue," Cole grumped out.

She shuffled and her sweet voice changed directions again. "And God, help us all to sleep and not be scared. In Jesus' name, Amen."

Quiet hovered over them for several moments.

"Good night, Mom. 'Night, Cole."

"Sleep well, Squirt."

"Good night." Jenna pulled the sleeping bag closer to her chin and rolled to her side. She needed sleep. Tomorrow, they could tackle everything else.

Tomorrow they'd get out of this.

She hoped.

CHAPTER ELEVEN

LEAPER

April 7
Fairbank Memorial Hospital
Fairbanks, Alaska
9:34 p.m.

"They're dead."

Leaper's best operative, Shadow, stood at-ease, his hands clasped behind his back, and looked toward their boss. "Blew up the plane. Avalanche covered the site, and now there's a storm on the mountains."

The black suit stretched taut across Viper's shoulders. The man was massive. News of the deaths didn't even make him flinch. "Are we positive?"

"Leaper said they were taken care of. I'm sure the explosion and avalanche took care of any bodies. They'll be buried for years."

Leaper nodded as he watched the exchange. "As long as there is no evidence of the crash. It's in a national park."

Viper glanced at him and then walked to the window. "Leaper is correct. So we'll send out one more search team. After the storm. Make sure there's no evidence, and no chance they survived." He pulled out a small black box and rubbed it between his fingers. "Now there's the rest of the mission. I gave them plenty of time to cooperate and hand it over. It's a shame it had to end this way but we're behind on deadline, and North Korea will not wait forever. I want Gray's research, files, programs, prototypes—everything."

"Yes, sir."

"I want to know what else Gray was working on. And why things fell apart. Maddox had something to do with it. But he's been eliminated." He leveled those dark eyes on him for a heartbeat and then turned back to Shadow. "Make sure no one else was involved."

"Yes, sir." Shadow stood straighter.

Viper looked back at him. "You've been awfully quiet, Leaper. Is there a problem?"

"No, sir."

"Good. I'll give you two weeks. No one should even know they're dead for quite a while. I want you to find AMI."

"Yes, sir."

Shadow glanced at him and nodded as Viper left the room. The air around him crushed his lungs. What had he done?

ANDIE

April 8
Sultana, Denali National Park
2:02 a.m.

Flop!

Ouch.

The impact of my stomach hitting the ground forced a groan from my lips. Even though the sleeping bag offered slight cushioning, the ice floor was still extremely uncomfortable.

I rolled onto my side. Why couldn't I just lie there and make myself fall asleep like everybody else?

Another sigh escaped. *Well, counting sheep isn't going to work.*

I rolled onto my other side, hip bone bruising at the *thunk* of landing. *You've got to be kidding.* Hadn't I hurt myself enough?

Daddy always called me a wiggle worm, but I wiggled for good reasons. Besides, Daddy had snored, so why couldn't I move a little?

Okay, more than a little.

I rolled onto my back, remembering all the times we camped out in the living room with the Princess tent and Barbie sleeping bags.

I really missed him.

Cole snored in his tunnel across from me.

I wrinkled my nose. Why was he so loud?

Daddy snored loud too.

Why do I keep comparing Cole with Daddy?

I frowned. How many times had I exaggerated the likeness? Why couldn't I love Cole for who he was?

Because he's not Daddy . . .

My frown deepened.

He's not supposed to be like Daddy.

I glanced at Cole's sleeping form, then rolled back onto my stomach.

What about the guys chasing us? What was happening that they wanted us dead?

I looked over at Mom. Sleeping peacefully. Would she get hurt?

Not with Cole around. I smiled. *Whether they want to admit it or not, they like each other.*

Again my gaze drifted to Snoring Beauty. Could I let him replace my dad? Could I allow him to take his place? I shook my head. Cole was there to protect us. End of story.

But then again, I couldn't imagine life without him. What would I do if he got hurt? Or worse . . . died?

I let out a shaky breath.

Okay, God. Let's talk . . .

JENNA

April 8
Sultana, Denali National Park
2:13 a.m.

A wiggling, warm body next to hers forced her eyes open.

"Hi, Mom," Andie whispered.

"Hey, sweetheart. What brings you over here in the middle of the night?"

"I missed you, and I can't sleep very well when I'm not in my waterbed." Andie licked her lips. "That's not all of it. I guess I just wanted to talk."

Jenna reached her arms out of the sleeping bag to pull her baby close. She kissed the top of Andie's head. "I love that. What do you want to talk about?"

"Well, things are a little crazy. It's scary." She sighed dramatically. "But I'm glad Cole's here."

"Me too, kiddo." Jenna stole a glance at Cole's sleeping form. "I wasn't sure about him at first, I mean, we hardly know him. But he has helped us a lot."

"Mom?" Andie fiddled with the zipper on Jenna's sleeping bag. "Why are people trying to kill us?"

Wow. That was a loaded question. "I'm not sure, honey. But I'm afraid it has something to do with your dad. Maybe all his years in the military. You know he worked on some amazing things."

"I thought this kinda stuff only happened in the movies."

Jenna chuckled. "I wish that were true. But how about we concentrate on happier things, okay?"

"Are you avoiding the issue, Mom?"

"Yes. Most definitely."

Andie smiled up at her. "I figured as much. You're a mom and you have to protect me."

Jenna touched noses with her daughter. "Yes, I do. And as scary and weird and crazy as all this is, we need sleep. So that tomorrow, we can face another day."

"I know." Andie gripped her tighter.

"Andie? Look at me."

Those beautiful blue eyes met hers. Eyes so much like her father's.

"I love you. And I will do everything in my power to make sure we get out of this. I know it's scary, but we've got to think positive. And we've got to have faith."

"Okey dokey. I will. Love you, Mom." Andie yawned. "I think I'll go back to my sleeping bag."

"Good idea. Let's get some sleep. And I love you more . . ."

"No, you don't."

"Yes, I do."

"I love you more . . ."

"No, I love *you* more . . ." Jenna drifted off, content that the love of her twelve-year-old was enough to get her through another day.

COLE

April 8
Sultana, Denali National Park
7:38 a.m.

Cole rolled over and found himself face to face with a snow wall. Plopping back onto his back, he groaned. He wanted his ComforPedic bed. The crash had done a number on his back and every muscle in his body was tied in knots. The cold just tightened him up more.

Turning over to his stomach, he stretched and began the crawl to escape his sleeping quarters. He glanced over at Jenna. She lay on her side, her ski mask in one hand, cheek cradled in the other. The chill in the air chapped her cheeks and lips. Dark hair escaped the hood of the cocoon-shaped sleeping bag, and cascaded onto the white snow beneath her. She was beautiful.

That's enough, Maddox.

Forcing himself to look away, he stretched his arms behind him. He should check on the weather. Yeah, check the weather.

He glanced over to Andie's sleeping bag. It lay limp and flat. He checked Jenna's tunnel again.

No Andie.

His gaze flew back to his tunnel. And then to Andie's again.

She wasn't there.

Alarm seized his gut.

He crammed his feet into his boots and grabbed his coat. Packs and gear went flying as he worked his way out the entrance. Punching through fresh snow, he enlarged the hole so his large frame could fit.

Just a few more feet.

A blast of snow greeted him as he escaped their shelter. The blizzard had intensified during the night and was worse than anything he'd ever seen. The wind knocked him off his feet. He hadn't taken time to cover his head, face, or eyes, so he used his arm as a shield. He had to find Andie.

A shrill scream ripped through the air.

Andie!

He grabbed the rope and followed the line, stumbling every few steps through the deep and blowing snow. Each time he stood up, the wind knocked him back down.

Cold. So cold. Air so bitter it froze his insides with each inhale. He lost feeling in his cheeks, nose, lips, but forced himself to keep going. Crawling, clinging to the rope.

In a matter of minutes that passed like hours, the other stake greeted him. The end of the rope.

But no Andie.

Cole tried to stand again, squinting into the wind, eyelashes frozen. There was no way she could survive in this. He had to find her. And soon. He cupped his hands around his mouth and yelled into the hurricane-force winds, "Andie!"

Nothing.

"Andie!"

Something grabbed his boot.

He bent down, searching with his hands. He found an arm, a shoulder, and then her head. Tightening his grip, he lifted her up and pulled her into a hug.

They stood there for several seconds, just holding on to one another. Andie shivered and trembled, her fear apparent in the tight grip around his waist. The wind ripped at his face, forcing his eyes to water. As if Mother Nature herself was throwing everything at him to break down his barriers.

So much for not getting attached.

Taking hold of the rope once again, Cole dragged Andie back to their shelter. He shoved her in ahead of him, and they crawled to safety, scarcely able to breathe.

"What happened?" Jenna leveled an accusatory glare at him.

"Why don't we ask Andie?"

Andie shivered again, a single tear leaving an icy trail as it dripped onto her coat.

"Well?" Cole fixed his gaze on her face. "Why were you out there all alone?"

"I woke up." She sniffled. "And I had to go, really bad."

"Didn't I tell you to only go out in pairs?"

Jenna shot him a glare. Mother scooted closer to daughter. "Why didn't you wake me up, honey?"

"You were so tired, Mom, I just wanted to let you sleep." She glanced up at Cole, those blue eyes seeking forgiveness. "I held onto the rope, I promise. But then the wind knocked me over and I fell down, and couldn't find the rope."

"I bet that was scary." Jenna soothed her child.

Oh, great. A Hallmark moment. Please.

"Yeah. But then I heard Cole calling my name and I knew everything would be okay."

Another prickly piece of his heart melted. Along with his anger.

Jenna stroked Andie's hair. "Well, you should've seen him tear out of here when he couldn't find you. He threw my pack into my head!"

Cole flicked his gaze to Jenna. "Did I hurt you?"

"I'm fine, Cole. But it was nice to see how protective you are of my daughter." Her dark eyes searched his, and then she broke the connection and looked back at Andie. "Now, both of you seemed to wander off without anything covering your faces and you look like you have a bad case of sunburn. Let's take care of that and get something to eat, okay?"

Andie clung to her mom.

"Squirt, you all right?"

"I'm fine. I just scared myself when I fell." She nodded as if trying to convince herself.

But there was more to it. And he intended to find out what it was.

— —

April 8
Sultana, Denali National Park
10:43 a.m.

Cole pulled cards out of his pack. Years in special ops and long missions of waiting taught him to pack light, but pack prepared. He was thankful he'd found his duffel before they headed away from the plane—at least he'd grabbed a couple of crucial items. It didn't take long for the walls of the snow cave to close in on its occupants. Jenna seemed lethargic after breakfast, and Andie fidgeted.

"Okay, you two. How about a game?"

Andie sighed dramatically. "That would be awesome, Cole, I'm soooooo bored."

He laughed. Only a preteen like Andie could make a one syllable word into six. "Jenna, you want to join us?"

Her knees were pulled up to her chest, head leaning against the wall with her eyes closed. "Hmmm?" She cleared her throat. "Actually, I think I'm going to take a nap. I must not have slept so good last night." She turned to Andie. "You gonna be okay?"

"Sure, Mom. It's not like we can go anywhere."

"Okay. Save a game for me later."

He watched her crawl into her sleeping bag and close her eyes. In five seconds, her breathing signified she was out.

"She always fall asleep so fast?"

"Only when she's really tired." Andie shrugged her shoulders. "So what game have you got?"

"Ever heard of Phase 10?"

"Nope."

"Good. 'Cause it's fun and it takes a long time to play."

Andie's giggles filled the cave as he shuffled and dealt the cards.

It took a little while for her to get into the game, but by their third round, she was cutthroat. Talk about competitive spirit. This kid could give some grown men a run for their money.

After several snacks, five times all the way through Phase 10—and covering every topic from her husky named Dasha to her favorite fingernail polish—Cole's back was killing him from sitting so long, but he noticed Jenna stirring. "Hey, sleepyhead, how you doin' over there?"

Jenna crinkled her brow and scrunched up her nose. She probably had no idea how cute that was.

"Watch out. She can be pretty grumpy when she first wakes up." Andie gave him a conspiratorial grin.

He placed a hand in front of his mouth, pretending to be secretive, and whispered loudly, "And her hair's a mess, too."

Gloves, socks, and her ski mask became airborne and flew at them. Cole pretended to crouch behind Andie. "Take cover, we're under fire!"

Andie's laughter filled the tight space as she attempted to shield him with her tiny body. She offered as much protection as if he stood behind a flagpole.

"Hey, she must like me. She didn't throw her boots."

Jenna scooted closer and laughed along. "That's because I didn't want them to be damaged by your hard head." She pulled out her water bottle. "Anybody else thirsty? Hungry? I think I slept too long, I've got a headache."

Cole wanted the atmosphere to stay light. "Sleeping Beauty has spoken. Why don't we eat, play a couple more rounds, and then hit the hay for the night. Sound like a plan?"

"Yes!" Andie pumped her fist up and down. "Mom, you should see me clobber this guy at cards."

"I can't wait, sweetie."

"Neither can I, Squirt." Cole loved the softness in Jenna's expression. He'd definitely like to see that more often. "Neither can I."

CHAPTER TWELVE

ANDIE
April 8
Sultana, Denali National Park
9:07 p.m.

I snuggled in my nook trying to fall asleep. The events of that morning played through my mind, swirling around, bonking into one another as if they all wanted to haunt me at the same time.

The snow, the cold.

A potty break, a patch of ice.

Did I hurt myself? I reached down to rub my puffy ankle. *No, I tripped and fell. That's all. No harm done. It might be a little bruised, but nothing to worry about.*

Andie, you're gonna be fine. No. Harm. Done.

Cole snored in his hole across from me. His chest heaved up and down as he took deep breaths. He looked calm and disturbed all at the same time.

What's he dreaming about?

I shrugged the question off and a shiver raced up my spine. Tugging on my coat I wrapped it around me. *Just remember, it's better to be cold than hot. Better. Better . . . But colder.*

My teeth began to chatter. Curling up into a tighter ball, I tried not to think about the coldness.

Cole shifted.

I shivered again, causing my ankle to wiggle and hang limp at a strange angle. I took in a fast breath and squeezed my eyes shut.

Don't look at it, Andie.

Once the odd feeling in my stomach disappeared, I opened my eyes.

Cole turned around and looked at me with sleepy eyes. I tried to turn facing his direction. My ankle didn't move like it should have. I winced.

"Hey, Squirt, you okay?" Cole got out of his sleeping bag and crawled over.

"I . . . just hit a rough patch of snow, that's all."

His face softened but I could see that he wasn't entirely moved. "Can't sleep?"

"Yeah."

"Bad dream?"

"Kinda."

"Do you want to talk about it?"

I shrugged, trying not to let my amazement show.

Did you really just ask me if I wanted to talk about it? Wowzer, you must have taken some sort of non-Cole medication. Are you *okay?*

"It's okay, Andie, if something's wrong you can tell me about it."

"Okay. Thanks." *Daddy used to say those same words.*

"Here"— he grabbed an extra blanket and handed it to me— "just don't get too hot."

"Okay."

He crawled back into his nook, shaking his head.

Should I tell him about my fall? "Hey, Cole?"

"Yeah?" He turned around, his chocolate-brown eyes swirling with something I couldn't interpret.

"Um, nothing."

It'll only make him worry. I've caused enough delay already.

April 9
6:15 a.m.

Something like metal clinking against metal rang in my ears . . .

Cole's awake.

I stretched and yawned, feeling my muscles gain strength with every movement.

My eyes slid open. Cole sat in the middle of the cave lighting the camp stove.

I giggled. His hair was a mess.

He looked over at me, his brow furrowed. I pointed to his head. "Is that a new style?"

His mouth curved into a "don't-you-dare-make-fun-of-me" smile. "Sure."

He went back to lighting his new little friend. I looked around. Why was Mom still asleep? Did she let Cole take over? That would be a first.

"Andie, would you grab my black bag and wake your mom up?"

"Sure." I crawled over to the bags that sat next to Mom's tunnel. "Hey, Mom, wake-y, wake-y."

I rummaged around in the giant packs looking for Cole's. *Ah ha! Come here little bag!* I yanked and it fell onto Mom's sleeping bag.

"Whoops, sorry about—"

Mom didn't even move.

"Mom?" I crawled over and shook her shoulder. My gaze jerked to Cole.

He crawled over, then grabbed her wrist and checked her pulse. His eyes clouded over and he felt her forehead.

Cole stuck his hand in the snow and started to wet her face down.

She began to stir, then opened her eyes. "Andie?" Grogginess seeped through her words and her eyes squinted from the lantern's light.

"Mom." I grabbed her hand. "You're all right!"

She put a hand to her head. "Yeah, but I have a killer headache. I need some *tuu*."

Cole quirked an eyebrow and turned to me.

"Water."

He nodded and crawled over to the emergency bag.

"How are you this morning, sweetie?"

"Mom, I'm fine. But you're not. I may not be able to feel pain but I can see yours just fine."

"Okay. But it's just a bad headache."

"You mean *killer* headache." I brushed her hair behind her ear.

"Right."

Cole passed her a water bottle. "Drink. You're starting to get a fever. We don't want you getting elevation sickness."

She took a sip but choked and started coughing. "Cole . . . the bucket!"

He grabbed the bucket and she lost her dinner. Her coughing got harder.

"Mom?"

"Andie, I need you to go to your tunnel." Cole didn't look at me but kept his attention on Mom.

"I . . . is she okay?"

"She has elevation sickness, that's all. Now scoot. She needs her rest, then she'll be fine."

"Okay, yeah." *She'll be fine. Just needs some sleep. She'll be fine.*

COLE

April 9
Sultana, Denali National Park
7:11 a.m.

"Jenna?" Cole whispered as loud as he dared. "Stay awake for now."

She nodded, her eyes glued to his.

Their faces were only inches apart, the cave didn't offer a lot of room. He wanted to stay with her, but the smell from the bucket would make them all sick if he didn't dispose of it.

"I'm going to dump this and clean it up a bit. I'll be right back."

He crawled out of the cave, and dumped the bucket, convincing his own stomach that it was made of steel. Why couldn't guys handle a little puke?

His wife had always nagged him about helping more, and now he had a small taste of it. A new respect for mothers rushed through him. The diapers they changed, the messes they cleaned up—he hadn't done any of it.

Next time, he resolved to do more.

Wait a minute. Next time? What was he thinking? There could be no next time.

But as he inched his way back into their shelter, he had to admit that he wanted another chance. Needed another chance.

He made his way back to Jenna's side. "It finally stopped snowing."

"Good." Her response was weak.

"You need water. And lots of it. It's the only way to get you out of here."

"Okay."

He tucked his arm up under her head. "I'm going to gently lift you every few minutes so you can take a few sips."

She nodded.

Andie's voice floated over to him. Humming a soft tune.

Jenna closed her eyes.

He lifted her and she drank.

The day passed quietly.

Jenna drinking, Andie humming, Cole trying not to lose his heart completely to two dark-haired native girls in a tiny snow cave near the top of Sultana. It all seemed so simple with the rest of the world shut out.

He allowed a few thoughts about having a family again. It couldn't actually happen, but desperate circumstances called for desperate daydreams.

Andie stopped her humming and broke through his silent reverie. "Cole?"

"Yeah?"

"How's Mom doin'?"

"She's doing better. She's got some color back, and she's had a lot of fluids."

All was quiet for several moments.

"Cole?"

"Yeah?"

"I don't mean to be nosy, but I saw your altimeter and I'm curious. What altitude are we at?"

No way to get anything past this kid. "About 14,000 feet."

"So that means we have a long ways to get down." No emotion in her voice, just direct statement. Processing every detail of their situation.

"Yeah." He sighed again. He'd pushed too hard, gone too far.

"Cole, you did the right thing." She had some radar on her. "It's not your fault." A sniffle followed. "I just want to go home."

"I know, Einstein. Me too."

"You know, I think you're the only one I'd allow to call me that. I like it."

"Good." He glanced down at Jenna as the silence descended again. Her eyes were open looking at him.

"Hi."

"Hi back. How're you feeling?"

She slid her arms out of the sleeping bag. "Much better. Headache's gone."

"Do you want to try to sit up and eat with us? If you can keep food down, we should probably try to start hiking down tomorrow."

"Yeah, that'd be nice. I'm hungry. I'd like to *c'eyan*."

He moved out of the way so she could ease out. "Huh? I couldn't make that sound if I tried."

"Eat, Cole. I'd like to *eat*."

"Oh. Gotcha. More Athabaskan?" Keep her talking. See if she's really thinking straight again. "How many people speak it?"

"A lot of the native languages are dying off. A few dozen people speak Ahtna fluently, but my grandmother and mother made sure that we used some of it at home. I want to pass that on to Andie as well."

"So, teach me some."

Andie piped up, "Cole, you are a *ciił*."

"Oka-ay. I hope that's not a cuss word."

Andie smacked his arm. "No, you goof, it means 'man.' *Ciił*."

"What's that breathy thing you're doing at the end? I can get the *kee* part, but I don't think I can copy that end sound."

Andie shrugged. "You're hopeless. You can't be an expert on your first try. It takes practice."

Jenna sighed and rubbed her stomach.

"You're right, Einstein. But first, I'd better make some broth. Before your mother wastes away." He winked at them. "Then see what else you're hungry for." He reached into the bag for the powdered broth base, and checked the ventilation hole in the cave.

Andie slid out of her space and scooted up to her mom. Jenna reached down and kissed her head, stroking her daughter's hair with her hand.

A beautiful sight.

The water took a while to heat in the thin air and he dissolved a packet to make the steaming chicken broth. At the rate they all devoured it, he knew the warm liquid had done its job.

Jenna spoke up out of the blue. "I'm in the mood for peanut butter."

"Peanut butter?"

Andie laughed. "Your face is priceless, Cole." Much to his surprise, she pulled little containers of peanut butter out of a bag. "Mom loves peanut butter. And it's a good source of protein. You should try her peanut butter mud bars," Andie leaned back, dramatically smacking her lips. "They're to die for."

Cole grabbed the bag. "Let me see what else is in this Mary Poppins bag of yours."

Peanuts, cashews, almonds, beef jerky, granola bars, fruit leather, power bars, trail mix, more powdered broth, packets of powdered hot chocolate, more peanut butter, and microwave popcorn.

He held up a shrink-wrapped package of popcorn. "Now how exactly are you supposed to cook this?"

Jenna gave him a sheepish look. "In a microwave."

Cole shook his head. "Well, that's obvious, but—"

"I know you think it's weird, and Marc always teased me about being overly prepared for everything, but I never really thought I'd be stranded on a mountain. I just made sure there was plenty of food with us that wouldn't perish." She shrugged.

Andie came to sit beside Cole. "We normally have string cheese with us too, but we ate all that on the flight to Anchorage."

The two laughed together as if sharing a private joke.

Another chink in his armor fell.

These two really were amazing. Their relationship, their depth of character, their resilience . . . he could stand to learn a thing or two from them.

Of course, he'd never admit that to them. They'd be impossible to live with.

Not that you're planning to live with them.

He frowned. No. Of course no—

"Cole?"

"Yeah, Squirt?"

"Can we play Phase 10 with Mom?"

"Sure thing. But I need to change your mom's bandage first."

"Yuck. Do I have to help?"

The squeamish look on Andie's face reminded him of the bucket incident. "No, I'll take care of it." Throw-up was one thing, blood and guts were right up his alley.

"Here's the first aid kit." Andie turned away as Jenna scooted toward him.

"Let's get this over with." Jenna gave him a tight-lipped smile. "I'm not too fond of blood myself."

Cole worked on Jenna's leg as she lay back on her sleeping bag. The wound was swelling, the skin all puffy and red. And it still oozed blood. Cole's lips tightened. He'd have to get them off this mountain before infection took over.

"How is it?" Jenna's voice was quiet.

He considered lying, but knew better. She'd see through that in a heartbeat. "Not great, but it has a fresh bandage." Andie's concern showed in her eyes. Time to shift focus. "Hey, why don't we get all the stuff repacked so we're ready to head out in the morning. We'll play a game or two and then get some sleep, okay?"

When they finally crawled into their sleeping bags, Cole lay on his back, staring at the snow ceiling. Here's hoping the weather cooperated come morning. Jenna's leg upped the urgency that needled him.

He had to get them off this mountain.

April 10
Sultana, Denali National Park
6:42 a.m.

Movement above his head jolted his mind awake. He jerked himself up, smashing foreheads with Andie. "Ow!" Cole rubbed the collision spot.

She leaned back on her knees as if nothing happened.

"Guess not feeling pain can be a good thing, huh?" He groaned as he slid out of his bag.

"Sure." Andie had a twinkle in her eye. A mischievous one. "Just means I'm tougher than you."

"Or have a harder head."

"Good one, Echo." She bounced on her knees.

"Anxious to get moving?" He laced up his boots.

Another dramatic sigh. "You have *no* idea."

"Oh, I think I have a pretty good inkling." He ruffled her hair with his hand and crawled out the opening.

Looking over his shoulder, he tossed out, "Wake up your mom and you guys get ready to go."

Brilliant blue sky met him as he stood outside their shelter of three nights. The air was crisp and clean, the wind light; there wasn't a cloud in the sky. Perfect.

Within minutes, the girls were beside him, harnesses attached, gear all packed.

"Are you feeling up to this, Jenna?"

"Yeah, not perfect, but all right. The warmth of the *saa* on my face feels amazing."

"Sun, right?"

Jenna smiled back at him. "Not bad. You learn quick."

"Andie, why don't you check the cave one more time for anything we might have left." After she was out of earshot, he took Jenna by the shoulders. "Are you sure you're okay?"

She tucked her head as if their closeness made her shy. "Yeah. I'm weak, but we've gotta move, right?"

"No crazy stunts, okay?"

She laughed.

He tightened his hold. Then on impulse pulled her into his arms. "Seriously, let me take care of you. Let someone else take the reins for once."

His words must've hit their mark. She pulled back, gaze darting down, around, and then finally met his eyes. She took a deep breath and patted his chest. "That's easier said than done, Cole."

His feet were glued to the spot, his arms tightened their hold again. He licked his lips. "Try."

Her mouth dropped open and then closed as she wiggled in his arms. Not quite pulling away, but clearly skittish, scared. Jenna looked up at him again and stilled, her hands resting on his chest. "O-Okay."

This woman did strange things to his heart. Guiding her head to his shoulder, he drew her to him and hugged her. She felt entirely too good in his arms.

Focus. He needed focus.

Andie returned and they rigged up in silence. Cole took the lead again, with Andie close behind, and then Jenna. The first couple hundred feet down didn't take too long, and Cole was thankful for the crampons and ice axes that helped anchor them.

They ate and drank as they descended, not wanting to waste any time, but after a couple of hours, he noticed Jenna slow down. He found a good spot to rest, and allowed them all a few minutes to catch their breath.

Andie, who had chattered all day in the snow cave, was suspiciously quiet. "Einstein, you haven't said a word since we left this morning. What's up?"

Her eyes shot to her mom and then back to him. "The snow cave was safe. The blizzard kept the bad guys away." She leaned closer and clung to her mom. "Now that we're back out here, it's scary."

Jenna hugged her daughter close.

He had no words to offer. The kid was right. He gave her a simple nod and turned to her mom. "How are you holding up?"

"I'm tired, and my leg aches, but I can do it." Her breaths were short, like she'd just run a marathon.

Patting her shoulder, he turned around, squelching the emotions pounding through him. He couldn't fix this. But he desperately wanted to.

The unmistakable rhythm of chopper blades shattered the quiet of the mountain around them.

Reflexes kicked in. His eyes darted, checking their surroundings, and waited for the helicopter to show itself. The *thwump-thwump-thwump* still beat a pattern far away, carried by the wind to their place high up on the mountainside. His only hope: that his instincts were correct and they had been expected to stay lower and head down.

They stood like statues. He held his breath—and then the chopper rounded the mountain, thousands of feet below them, performing a slow search back and forth.

Time for action.

Cole grabbed the girls and raced them to some nearby boulders. The drifts were high enough here.

Jenna and Andie looked to him for direction, fear apparent in their eyes. No questions asked this time. Just pure trust.

He pulled their heads toward his so they could hear him. "I'm going to bury you in the snow. I need you to jump into the drifts behind these rocks and cover up as much as you can. I'll bury the gear, and then check to make sure you're covered."

Andie nodded. Jenna yanked off her ski mask and bit her lip.

"What is it, Jenna?"

"I . . . I . . . don't think I can do that . . . be buried, I mean . . . I—"

He grabbed her shoulders. "You don't have a choice. This isn't a game." He didn't temper the sharp edge to his words. This was no time for fear. "Just remember to breathe slowly, and don't move. We *cannot* let them see us."

Andie tugged on his arm. "But what about you, Cole?"

"I'm a little less conspicuous than you two." He pointed to Jenna's red ski jacket and Andie's bright purple one. "Now move! Then stay still."

Within seconds, the girls were digging in and hauling snow on top of themselves. He buried the gear, and then finished covering them, making sure they couldn't be seen.

The sound of the helicopter was still far below them, and he worked fast, hoping they wouldn't spot his movement. The blizzard that had almost taken their lives three days ago had provided the snow that would hopefully save their lives today.

Tucked into his own cocoon of snow, he listened.

And waited.

CHAPTER THIRTEEN

JENNA
April 10
Sultana, Denali National Park
9:14 a.m.

Cold penetrated Jenna's layers, but that didn't stop her body from sweating.

Fear oozed out of every pore and wiggled its way into her insides, tightening like a vise on her organs.

Breathe. Just breathe.

Now was not the time to panic. The childhood nightmare resurfaced—one where she was buried alive. *No!* She needed to stay calm and quiet to protect her daughter. To protect Cole. It'd been a long time since tight spaces had caused a reaction, mainly because she hadn't been alone in a small space since before Andie was born. The need to protect her daughter had always over-powered her fear.

Until now.

God! Help us! Protect us . . . Please . . .

She prayed for the snow to be deep enough. She prayed for the chopper to not get too close. She prayed for enough air for all of them to breathe.

"'What time I am afraid, I will trust in Thee . . .'" The words slipped past her lips in a bare whisper.

The roar of the helicopter grew, the mountain beneath her vibrating with the rumble.

It must be right on top of them.

What if it blew all the snow off them? What if they found Andie before Jenna and she never had the chance to tell her daughter good-bye? Just like Marc.

Please, God! Don't let them find my baby.

The roar continued. Was it hovering?

Sweat trickled down her back, sending chills up and down her spine. She tuned her ears in to all the sounds around her.

There! Snow crunched. Steps. Getting closer.

They're coming!

If only she could see. The walls of her snow tomb closed in. Where were they?

The rhythmic sound of the chopper blades faded. But the footsteps surrounded her. How many were searching?

Calm down. Calm down. *They can't see us, we're covered in snow. "'What time I am afraid, I will trust in Thee . . .'"* Peace flowed through her.

"'What time I am afraid, I will trust in Thee—'"

"Over there!" The muffled shout reached her ears.

Oh, no! She'd said it out loud!

The crunching drew closer. More muffled shouts.

"'What time I am afraid . . .'" God, now would be a good time to intervene.

"What's that? Rook! Check your nine."

Rapid gunfire resonated through the snowy layers.

Jenna's heart seized so hard pain shot through her. Had they just shot Cole? Andie? *What was happening*?

She couldn't breathe. It was as though the enemy grasped her throat with prickly fingers.

I. Will. Trust. In. Thee! God! Do something!

Too late, she realized she was hyperventilating. "'I . . . will . . . trust . . .'"

Spots danced in front of her eyes, and as her body relaxed of its own will, blessed peace took over, covering her in a blanket of quiet.

LEAPER

9:16 a.m.

He hated helicopters. The radio crackled in his headset.

"Sir! Sir!"

Leaper rolled his eyes, gritting his teeth against the pain. "What is it, Rookie?"

"Didn't you hear me? I repeat, there are footprints."

He exhaled a frosty breath. "Yes, I heard you. There are *no* footprints but our guys'. Did you check to the west like I asked?"

"But, sir, I beg to differ, there are definitely footprints."

"Shut up, Rook! I've already checked it out. We are returning. Be at rendezvous in sixty seconds."

"Leaper! I think you need to hear me out—"

"That was an order! Get back here before I decide to leave you on this mountain!"

"Yes, sir."

The ache in his head continued. He had to remain in control, could show no sign of weakness.

As the rookie climbed up the ladder, he made a decision.

The kid was no longer a valued member of the team.

ANDIE

April 10
Sultana, Denali National Park
9:51 a.m.

Brilliant white surrounded me as I waited. I couldn't hear the chopper floating above us. It must have left. I didn't hear the footsteps anymore. But what comfort did that really give?

What was happening?

If the bad guys won, it'd be over. If we didn't get off the mountain, it'd be over. If we didn't get out of these holes and get more oxygen soon, it'd be over . . .

A small hole appeared above my head and snow fell onto my face. I saw a gloved hand pulling the snow back.

Oh, no, they've found me!

As the hole got bigger sunlight streamed through—what sunlight there was—but it was enough to make me close my eyes.

No wait, that's because I was scared.

"Andie?" Cole's voice drifted through the hole.

Cole?

No, that must have been my imagination. He wouldn't uncover us so soon, would he? Maybe the bad guys are holding him hostage and he's worried about me.

Almost all the snow was off me and someone's huffing sounded above my head.

Go away, you evil-chopper-flyin'-devil!

"Andie, Einstein, talk to me . . . Andie, wake up!" Chilly hands held my head.

I opened my eyes, forcing them to focus. Brown hair, brown eyes, broad shoulders, and relief etched on a hasn't-been-shaved-in-a-while face.

"Cole? . . . *Cole!*" I threw my arms around his neck and squeezed. *Thank You, God!* "We're alive! They didn't find us!"

"Squirt, you really had me worried." His strong arms squeezed me.

A smile crept onto my face. "Cole?"

"Yeah?"

I tilted my head and nestled against his shoulder. "Thanks."

"No, thank you, Einstein." He pulled back and smiled at me.

"For what?"

He turned his head sideways, brow scrunched.

I followed his gaze. Mom!

His eyes clouded as he crawled over to her. "We need to get your mom out. Crawl around to the other side and start digging."

We dug, side-by-side.

Cole pulled Mom's limp form out.

Uh-oh . . .

Cole's arms moved swiftly as he laid her head by his knee and again tried to awaken her.

"Mom?" Moments slurred by as we watched her deep breathing.

"She's asleep." Cole shook her shoulder again.

She stirred.

I sighed. *Thanks, God.*

"Jenna?" Cole placed his hand on her head. "Jenna? Can you hear me?"

Her eyes slid open. "Cole . . . Where's Andie?"

Mothers.

"Mom, I'm right here." I grabbed her hand and squeezed.

She sat up, her face scrunching as if each and every muscle was refusing to cooperate.

"Jenna, you're sick. Lie back down." Cole tugged her back toward the ground.

Anger reflected on her face as she jerked her arm away. "Excuse me, Mr. Maddox, I'm capable of sitting up. A little pain won't do me any harm."

Cole raised his eyebrows and held his hands up. "Oh. Well, pardon me."

Mom nodded and sat up. "Better."

"You two are hysterical. You should fight like this more often just for the fun of it." I poked Cole on the shoulder. "You could win *America's Funniest Home Videos.*"

Mom blushed and Cole stared.

"I guess that was kind of silly of me. I'm sorry, Cole."

"No need to be."

I smiled and took a deep breath. Although the air burned my chest, it felt good to be in the fresh air again.

"I think it's safe to say that we can start climbing down now." Cole stood up and wiped snow from his pants.

"Okay, I'm ready." I jumped up.

Mom stared at me.

I smiled back. *You're gonna have to trust him sooner or later. After all, we're stranded on a mountain together.*

Cole unburied our packs and handed them to us. "Okay. Let's get started. And Andie, you might want to retie your shoes."

I looked down. *Oh.*

The thick shoelaces looked dejected and sad.

I retied my right, but paused while tying the left. It was bigger than the right one. My shoe felt tighter—much tighter.

I loosened the laces and started tying it again. It hurt. Was it from my fall?

No, I must've had the laces too tight.

"You guys ready? We should start moving." Cole did a quick glance-check at where our packs had been.

Always being careful. Just like Dad.

"I'm . . ." Mom stood up and grunted. "I'm ready."

"Me too."

We hooked back up to our harnesses, Cole going first, me second, and Mom in the back. Then we started climbing down.

My lungs still hurt as we climbed, but knowing that the air would get thicker comforted me. And I assumed Mom and Cole too.

Within the first ten crampon-jabbing steps my ankle started to feel funny. Three steps after that it twisted weird. Then it moved so I stood on the side on my foot.

I looked down at my shoe. *When we stop I'll check it.*

Each time I stabbed my crampon into the ice it twisted weirder, it was heavier and I wished more that we could stop so I could check it.

Then it started to hurt. Really bad.

Just a little bit farther, a few more steps. I distracted my mind by thinking of Dasha, my black-and-white husky with amazing blue eyes that always got her what she wanted. Like treats and attention.

Again, I jammed my crampon into the snow but the movement pushed my ankle back in the wrong direction. I tripped and started doing a somersault down toward Cole, pulling Mom with me.

"Eeeek!"

The rope stiffened as Cole yanked it toward him and grunted. Mom scrambled to get her crampons into the ice and I followed.

I screeched again as my foot slipped, making it harder to stab my crampon into the ice. My breaths came in huffs as Cole started climbing up toward us.

"Are you two okay? Did you hurt anything?" He huffed and puffed as he stared at my eyes through the goggles.

"Andie? Baby, are you okay?" Mom scooted closer and rubbed my shoulder.

Was I? "I . . . I'm fine. Just a little shocked, that's all." I nodded and looked at Cole. Did he know something was wrong?

If he did, I hoped he'd explain it to me. All I knew was that I couldn't think clear enough to figure it out for myself.

CHAPTER FOURTEEN

COLE
April 10
Sultana, Denali National Park
4:58 p.m.

They'd made good progress today, but Cole wanted to make it back to the crash site. The sleds were there, and he needed to check for a working radio.

The events of the day had taken their toll. Andie was skittish, jumping every time she heard a different noise, and she kept falling down. A lot. Jenna seemed to be in a daze, kept pulling her ski mask up as if she couldn't breathe, and biting her bottom lip. They both looked like they could collapse at any moment.

Forging ahead, he hoped that at the next drop-off he'd be able to see where they had crashed. He pulled out the altimeter—they were about 1,000 feet above it.

A few more yards and he reached the ledge. There it was. The plane wasn't visible under all the snow, but he saw the debris field the avalanche created. He'd be able to find it. He stopped and waited for the girls, wanting to share the good news.

As he looked back, Andie tumbled toward him. Jenna not far behind.

The buckles of his pack came apart with a flick of his fingers, and he threw it down. "Andie?"

She looked up at him with those big, blue puppy-dog eyes.

"Andie, what happened?"

"I just fell, Cole. I'm all right."

Cole glanced at Jenna. Exhaustion covered every inch of her.

"Andie," he jerked off his head gear and raked his hand through his hair, "there's something you're not telling me."

Tears filled her little-girl eyes. "I just fell. I'm sorry."

Cole hated to push it, but his gut told him that wasn't the whole story. "You need to shoot straight with me."

"Cole!" Jenna's shout wrenched him back around.

His eyebrows shot up.

"Let me take care of this. You've done enough." She limped toward Andie, her complexion a nasty gray, but her eyes steel determination.

"Jenna, look at you! You're exhausted and sick. You can't see that there's something else going on here." He turned his attention back to Andie. "Something happened up there during the blizzard—"

"Cole, I said . . . let me handle this." Jenna clenched her teeth and grabbed the front of his jacket.

Andie shook her head, tears ready to spill.

Cole ignored Jenna and spoke to Andie. "If you're hurt, let me check it out. You've been falling down—"

"Cole—"

"—and you always used to shift your weight from one leg to the other, and now you don't. You subconsciously try, but end up putting all the weight on the one leg."

Andie's tears flowed now. "I didn't want to be a bother. I kept slowing you down. I'm sorry. I didn't know I was really hurt—"

"Co—" The hand on his jacket went limp. Jenna plummeted to the ground.

ANDIE

April 10
Sultana, Denali National Park
5:16 p.m.

"Mom!" Things seemed to run in slow motion. Cole caught Mom just before she hit the ground.

"Jenna!" Cole laid her on the ground and took off his mask. "Andie, get the emergency bag!"

I ran as fast as my legs would carry me over to the brown bag, and scooped it up. My ankle kept giving away and slowed me down. *What's going on with this thing?*

I made it over to Cole and passed him the heavy pack.

His jaw clenched as he worked to push her pant leg up. It wouldn't budge. Her leg was too swollen. He pulled something out of his pocket and started cutting and ripping her pant leg.

I sucked in air.

Blood seeped out of the bandages.

"Andie, don't look."

As Cole unrolled the wrappings, the smell drifted up my nose and I turned around. *God, please don't let it be infected.* "Cole, is she okay?"

There was no reply.

"Cole?"

"I don't know."

"No . . . she has to be okay!" I stood up and started pacing. "I've had enough of all this pain, I've had enough of all this danger, and I've had enough of all this fear! I want to go home with you and Mom and stay locked up forever, and be happy and alone and not have to worry about danger and mountains and bad guys and—"

"Andie!"

My foot gave away again and I fell onto my rear end. My brain stopped its tirade as I recovered from the stun.

"Andie?"

I knew he didn't want to leave Mom's side, but I couldn't move. Every bone in my body ached along with my emotions. "Cole, this is just too much." I laid down with my back to him and closed my eyes.

Cole's stern voice made them pop back open.

"Now you listen here, young lady, we're not giving up. Your Mom needs us, now more than ever. You have to be strong."

I didn't want to answer, I didn't want to move. But I knew he was right.

"Andie?"

"Okay. If you promise to help me."

"Squirt, we're in this together, remember?"

"Okay."

He rebandaged mom's leg and covered her up. "I need you to come here."

I stood up and walked over, head hanging.

"I'm going down to the crash site."

My head shot up. "What? Why?" *You promised not to leave!*

"When we left we packed emergency supplies onto the sleds and buried them for when we made our way back down. I need to go and find those supplies so we can put your mom on one of the sleds. Can you stay here and watch over her?"

"But, Cole—" Emotions swirled through me.

"I need you to be brave, Andie. Your mom needs our help. This is the only way. Look"—he patted my shoulder, then pointed off to a ridge that was near the blown up, snow covered, plane crash—"I'll climb down that ridge so that you can see me the entire time."

"How will you find the supplies under all of that snow?"

"I have to try."

"Wouldn't it have been destroyed in the explosion?"

"Andie, I don't know. I buried them away from the plane, but I don't know."

But Cole, I don't want you to go. I stared at him.

"Squirt, this is the only way."

I knew he was right. But it still hurt to think of him leaving us. Alone. "Be careful."

"I will. Don't worry."

Tears threatened to spill out. *Andie, be brave.* No matter how many times I said it, the fear remained.

He unattached us from the harness.

I sniffed as the strange emotions grew bigger, stronger.

Was I betraying Dad? Was it wrong to feel this way about Cole?

God?

As if an answer to prayer, two words echoed in my mind:

Tell him . . .

Daddy would still be my hero. I didn't have to move him to second place.

I smiled. *Okay, God.*

"Hey, Cole?"

"Yeah, Einstein?" Cole turned and grabbed his pack.

"I love you."

He jerked to a stop and stared at me.

Yes, I really mean that.

A strange faraway look glimmered in his eyes. "I'll be back before you know it." He started climbing down.

Sitting down beside Mom, I watched his every move. *God? I'm sorry. I haven't been handling things the way I should have. Please, please, keep Cole safe.*

I grabbed mom's gloved hand. Why was he so surprised when I told him I loved him? He may have been hard to like, but not *that* hard!

After awhile, I saw Cole looking around near the crash site. *God, please help him find it.*

He uncovered a sled. After about ten minutes he was climbing again, dragging the sled behind him.

It's getting colder. I shivered and wrapped my arms around my stomach. *Cole, get up here soon.*

I peeked again at the ridge and gasped.

Cole was gone.

CHAPTER FIFTEEN

COLE
April 10
Sultana, Denali National Park
8:08 PM

The cold, icy floor of the crevasse greeted him with the impact of a three-hundred-pound football player slamming into his side and forcing all the air from his body.

Stunned from the fall, Cole struggled to suck air back into his lungs. He blinked rapidly. One short breath. Then another. And another, until he could finally breathe normally again. It'd been a long time since the wind had been knocked out of him. The painful reminder was not a welcome one.

With a grunt, he flopped onto his back, but the pack was cumbersome and awkward. And not a very good pillow. Pain radiated up and down his right side as the numbness from the impact disappeared.

Great. Just great.

He inhaled deeply, testing his lungs. The cold air burned through him as he forced them to expand. No ribs seemed to be broken.

But he was in a hole.

Alone.

Studying the walls of sheer ice and snow that towered above him, he worried about Andie. Probably getting a little anxious right now. Did she see what happened? Hopefully not. The snow-covered ridge had hidden the sliver of an opening into this dangerous drop. He hadn't seen it until it was too late. If Andie had been watching, he'd probably just slipped from her view.

Cole shook his head and stretched each of his limbs and sat up. *Focus, Maddox.*

This was a mission. A minor setback. He just needed a plan.

He removed his pack and outer coat. Where was the sled? It hadn't fallen into the crevasse with him, so hopefully it was still up there, and hadn't slid farther down the mountain. They needed the supplies, and they needed the sled to be able to get Jenna to safety.

Another wave of worry passed over him. How had he let himself get so attached to those two? Feelings and worry had no place during an assignment. He needed to shake it off.

Focusing his gaze on the hole he fell through, he envisioned successfully climbing out. It wouldn't be easy scaling the slick ice. Examining the ravine-like walls, he realized it reminded him of a slot canyon. Only this wasn't rock. And it was narrower than any slot canyon he'd ever hiked or climbed. Pulling back the layers of sleeves covering his watch, he glanced down to check the time.

A heavy sigh slumped his shoulders as the facts sunk in to his brain.

Only a couple hours of daylight left.

He had to climb out of this crevasse and hike all the way back up to the girls.

He wouldn't make it before dark.

But he had to make it. He'd made a promise.

New determination spread throughout his body. No time to waste. Cole crouched down by his pack and dug out another bottle of water and a protein bar. He downed the nourishment quickly, keeping his gaze above him on the climb ahead.

He didn't have all the right gear for this, but still had an ice axe and crampons. If he could climb the first ten feet on the north side, he should be able to turn sideways and climb the rest of the way shimmying between the two ice walls.

Dangerous, but doable.

"All right, God. I'm not convinced you're there, but Andie sure is. Jenna needs a hospital, and many lives are in danger. So for their sakes, how about a little help?" He shoved his outer coat into his pack, lifted it up, and settled it onto his shoulders. Buckling the straps at his chest and waist, he took one last, long glance upward. From here on out, he would have to concentrate on one step—one grip—at a time.

ANDIE

April 10
Sultana, Denali National Park
9:00 p.m.

Cole was nowhere in sight.

Cole!

Memories of my dad's death flooded back.

Mom crying, someone apologizing, my brain refusing to function as I listened to Mom tell me the bad news. Mom's pain, my anger.

Lost hope.

In the hospital, I wouldn't eat anything. Wouldn't talk to anyone but Mom and Zoya. The only thing I did was read my Bible. And pray.

I prayed a lot waiting for Cole too. I couldn't lose him. Not after all he had done for us.

As I sat there realization settled in that he had protected me every step of the way. He had been there the whole time. Just like my dad.

He could never replace my dad, but I loved him more than words could express.

He had to live, he just had to. I'd already said good-bye as much as I could, I didn't want to say it again.

Mom couldn't die, I wouldn't let her.

Cole couldn't die; if he did, I'd have to kill him.

The tears wouldn't stop, they just decided to invade my "moment."

A gentle prodding, not as interpretable as words, filled my mind and I jumped.

This isn't over yet, Andie . . . have patience.

The "Have Patience" song popped into my head.

There was a snail called Herbert, who was so very slow . . .

"Okay. I'll wait."

So I did. And waited. And waited. And waited. And waited a little bit more while eating a power bar. Then waited. And waited. And waited.

I couldn't occupy my mind from the fear of it all. Looking over at Mom, I sighed. "Okay, Lord, time for some action and a pep talk."

After putting Mom in a sleeping bag, I lifted her head up and gave her some water, then checked her temp with our TemporalScanner thermometer.

102 degrees. *Great.*

"Okay. Time for the pep talk." Grabbing my pink and green mini Bible from one of the packs, I sat down beside Mom and started reading.

"'This I recall to my mind, therefore I have hope. The LORD's lovingkindnesses indeed never cease, for His compassions never fail. They are new every morning; Great is Your faithfulness. "The LORD is my portion," says my soul, "Therefore I have hope in Him." The LORD is good to those who wait for Him, to the person who seeks Him. It is good that he waits silently for the salvation of the LORD. It is good for a man that he should bear the yoke in his youth.'"

Okay, Lord. You're letting me grow in You.

"'I called on Your name, O LORD, out of the lowest pit. You have heard my voice, "Do not hide Your ear from my prayer for relief, from my cry for help." You drew near when I called to You; You said, "Do not fear!" O LORD, You have pleaded my soul's cause; You have redeemed my life.'"

True . . . but it's so scary. I'm only twelve!

I closed the Bible and held it close. "God, we've already been through a lot. But I know that Cole isn't dead, unless he met an angel who miraculously told him about You. You wouldn't let him die after we've come all this way, would You?"

There was no response but the wind whistling and swirling the snow around Mom and me. I closed my eyes. Why was this so hard?

"I know I've done a lot of bad things in my life, but could You please help us out of this mess? I know it's a lot to ask, but could You at least save Cole and Mom? They deserve to live, they deserve each other."

No thunderous voice answered. No lightning flashed. Only a gentle whisper rang in a mind covered in darkness and weakness: *Trust Me.*

We would make it. I didn't know how, I didn't know when . . .

I just knew we would.

God was still in control and always would be, no matter what.

I glanced at the ridge line. All I could see were bumpy white clumps of snow and the faint outline of the ridge.

Cole still wasn't there.

He'll come, Andie.

Mom was lying on the ground, her chest rose and fell.

Brilliant shades of orange and pink blended together in the sky as the sun set. I shivered and hugged my middle.

It's getting cold and dark. I should do something to keep Mom out of the wind.

Well, thanks to the last few days, I knew how to make a snow cave. I scanned the area around me. *That snowy, deep, clumpy area looks good.*

"God, help me do this correctly." I planned out each of the steps, making sure Mom was as much out of the wind as possible.

"Please, Cole. Come back." I glanced one last time at the ridge. "He's in Your hands now, God."

I turned and started digging.

He'll come, Andie . . . He'll come.

COLE

April 10
Sultana, Denali National Park
9:46 p.m.

Third time would have to be the charm. Cole studied the walls once more. What'd he miss? His aching muscles and bruised body screamed at him from the two unsuccessful attempts. Fatigue was setting in, and he couldn't—*wouldn't* allow it.

Hands on his hips, he looked down at the floor. Emotions churned inside him. That was the problem. Or was it?

Clarity seemed to settle over his mind as he let a new thought take root. By holding himself back, pretending to *not* feel anything, and attempting to make this just another mission—had he set himself up for failure?

And just this once, could caring actually give him the drive to make it?

Andie's words replayed in his mind. *"I love you."*

"No!" His voice vibrated against the ice. Rage bubbled up inside him. He'd lost everyone he'd ever cared about. And for what purpose? Why?

Andie and Jenna believed in God. But look at where that got them? Marc was gone, and now their lives were in danger. What if their faith was all a cover? What if they were involved?

Cole paced the floor of the narrow crevasse. Seven steps one way, seven steps back. Back and forth.

In his mind, he pictured Jenna. Her beautiful eyes haunted him. She lay up there unconscious. Needing help.

"I trust you, Cole."

That sweet voice. Andie had managed to wrap her little-girl fingers around his heart and squeeze it back to life. Sure the numbness had been a protective measure for a long time, but that little girl up there had opened his eyes again. To love. Family. The longing to be needed.

And she did need him.

Right here. Right now.

He slammed a glove-covered fist against the ice. He didn't care what it took. They wouldn't make it without him.

Adrenaline rushed through his veins as he allowed himself to truly feel for the first time in many years. A tidal wave of emotion tumbled throughout his body, but instead of the weakness that always followed—a surge of energy jolted through him.

Empowered by it, he thrust his ice axe into the wall and attacked the task of climbing.

With each step, the spikes of his crampons dug deeper as his drive toward the top could not be stopped. *Hold on, girls. I'm coming.* His chest threatened to explode as he pushed himself harder, faster, farther. Ignoring the burning in his muscles, he lifted his weight to each new hold. Jenna's beautiful face flashed in his mind. Then Andie's piercing blue eyes. She trusted him. He had to save her.

The space was tight at the opening of the crevasse. Every cell inside him begged for oxygen, but only a few more feet.

Another step.

Then one more.

His axe breached the top and he slammed it down a couple feet in front of him and dragged himself the rest of the way out.

Rolling onto his back, he sucked air in deep, fast breaths.

It didn't matter that his pack was cutting into his kidneys, or that the straps sliced into his shoulders. It didn't matter that the air froze his lungs.

He'd made it.

Brilliant stars glittered in the midnight sky above. Taking the time to catch his breath, he enjoyed the limitless expanse. What an amazing sight. Maybe Andie's God existed after all.

The air was bitter with cold, each puff of air from his mouth making a tinkling sound as the moisture turned to ice. He better move fast if he was going to make it up the mountain to the girls. Especially if they didn't have any shelter. They could freeze to death.

Cole stood up and searched for the sled. He planted a stake by the opening of the crevasse so they wouldn't stumble upon this one again. Need to be more careful.

About twenty feet down the ridge, he found the sled. Grabbing the ropes, he attached them to his harness on each hip.

Now he just needed to get up to his girls.

The thought froze him in his steps. *His girls*? Yes, he'd made a promise. And he would let it drive him forward.

Two hours later, Cole trudged over what he hoped was the last ledge. But as he crested it, the snowy terrain stood barren. No sign of them. Where could they be? He thought for sure this was the area he'd left them. Turning around, he looked down below. No. He *knew* this was it. The spot he showed Andie to watch for him.

It didn't add up. Jenna was unconscious. Andie couldn't carry her mom, there was no way. But all the gear and the girls were . . . gone. His gaze scanned the snowy mountainside.

Wait. What?

A small stake with something attached to it about fifty feet away.

He plowed his way toward it. Each agonizing step brought him closer, until he recognized the colors on the stake. Someone had made a checkerboard flag out of red and pink duct tape, clearly marking the entrance to a snow cave.

Cole pulled the sled up behind him and collapsed to his knees. "Way to go, Andie. Way to go."

CHAPTER SIXTEEN

ANDIE
April 11
Sultana, Denali National Park
1:32 a.m.

Thud . . . crunch. Grunt . . . thud.

My head shot up at sounds coming from outside.

Cole? No other sound came.

I sighed. I guess it was just the wind.

But the creepy sense that someone waited on the other side of the packs haunted me. I left my pile of thirteen duct tape wallets, crawled over to Mom and her bag, and pulled out our Maglite.

Turning the lantern to its dimmest setting, I held my breath. What if it's not Cole? He would call out if it were him. *God, what do I do? Please protect us.* Let this just be my imagination.

Something bumped into the packs, making one slide off its perch. I stared at the hole, but all I could hear was the wind, all I could see was darkness.

It's just the wind. Just the wind. Just the wind.

After a few moments, I crawled over to the fallen pack and placed it back where it came from. I crawled away.

It slid back to the ground. Then another one fell. The packs disappeared and all I could do was sit there, unable to move.

What if it was one of the guys trying to kill us? Did my duct tape flag alert them to where we were?

The outline of someone's figure appeared in the entryway, huffing and puffing. My imagination went into overdrive. *It can't be Cole. He'd tell me if he were here, right?*

My heart pounded in my chest as I lunged forward, pushing the creeper back outside. As our bodies collided, the stranger grunted, and I bounced backward.

As soon I hit the ground I grabbed the Maglite. My head throbbed, but I lifted the huge flashlight to strike. My arm felt like lead as I let it fall to hammer the intruder.

"Andie!" The stranger gripped my arm and stopped the flashlight mere inches away from his head.

Tears flowed from my eyes and ran down my cheeks.

Cole?

Had he not seen my blow coming, I would have cracked his head open. Maybe even killed him. My body started to tremble. The wind whistled as it blew through the opening, causing my bare face to freeze as the tears fell.

"Cole." I could feel my eyes widening and my body got weaker by the second.

"Andie, come here." His voice sounded hoarse and he pulled me close. His breaths came in gasps. The journey back up the mountain had taken its toll.

Oh, God, I'm so sorry! Sobs started to shake my body, I was cold, tired, in total misery.

"Shh . . . It's okay, Squirt, I'm here." Cole stroked my hair as I cried, clinging to his huge frame.

"Cole, I'm so sorry! I didn't know it was you. I'm so scared, I didn't know what to do!" The tears turned into sniffs as I snuggled closer to him. I didn't want to let him go. I couldn't.

"Andie, you're fine. I'm here now. We need to put the packs back."

I nodded. *Pull yourself together, Andie.*

Cole pointed at Mom. "How's she been?"

"Uh"— I sniffed and wiped my nose—"okay . . . I think."

"Well. That's better than nothing." He paused and stared at me.

I blinked and cocked my head.

"You've got ice all over your cheeks." He chuckled and wiped at them.

I puffed them out to emphasize the cold fact.

"You're a goofball."

"Hey! Only a true goofball can make thirteen duct tape wallets, a duct tape flag, and two duct tape checkerboards—*including* pieces—in only a few hours."

"Seriously?"

"Well, I had to do something to occupy my time while you were gone. After I took care of Mom, I still had a lot of time on my hands. She's been sleeping the whole time." I took a deep breath and closed my eyes. "So I put my hands to work creating something, then I'd go check her temp and try to cool her down. If you hadn't come back, I don't know—"

"And you built the snow cave?" he interrupted. "All by yourself? You didn't overheat?"

"Yep, yep, and nope. I took off my coat and rubbed snow on my neck to keep cool. It kept my mind off worrying about Mom—knowing I could help protect her. Although, it's not as pretty as the one you made. The walls aren't as smooth, and the tunnels aren't straight and— "

"Andie." He smiled. "It's wonderful, Einstein. I'm proud."

Tears fell down my cheeks *again.* Then I punched his shoulder. "You should be. It's not easy, I can tell you that much!"

"I know." He stretched his back and looked around at my piles of creations. "What's with all the duct tape?"

"Oh, we always have it with us. Duct tape and peanut butter, the two necessities of life." I smiled.

"I see. And how's your ankle?

Uh . . . Better to keep the subject off my ankle. *He doesn't need more to worry about. It doesn't hurt anymore, so that must mean it's better, right?*

"It's kinda funny 'cause when Mom and Dad went on their first date, he wore a pink shirt and red tie. Mom teased him about it, saying he shouldn't wear pink and red together. So every year since then, on Valentine's Day, he would wear the same conglomeration. So that's why the flag is pink and red. Plus you can see it well against the snow."

Cole laughed. "And your ankle?"

"It's fine."

It wasn't a lie. Well, not really. Okay, it was. But he had more important things to worry about.

Like Mom.

And getting us off the mountain.

And keeping the bad guys away.

ANDIE

1:46 a.m.

A small tingling feeling raced up my back. I pulled off one of my layers and sighed. *If only Dasha were here.*

Cole's eyes met mine.

"I'm fine."

"You sure?"

"Yeah."

Cole still showed concern but he dropped the subject.

"I do miss Dasha."

"Remind me who Dasha is."

"My *li'uudzi* and *lggeyi* husky *łic'ae.*" I giggled. *See if you can figure that one out!*

Cole's brow furrowed. "Your what?"

"My black-and-white husky dog."

"Oh, right." Cole nodded. "And why did she all of a sudden come to mind?"

"Well . . ." I sighed. "Dasha's special. It's almost like she can sense when I'm getting too hot or cold."

"Are you hot?"

"I'm fine."

Was he still worried? Even though he was a man—an *army* man at that—he seemed to worry about me a lot. "Anyway, she's really smart. One time we were playing outside and I started to get hot but didn't know, so Dasha pulled me down and ran to grab my water bottle. Once she was sure I was drinking she ran inside to get Mom. It was really close. I almost had to go to the hospital."

"Wow."

"Yep. We also started training her with hand signals. She's really good at it." Why was I blabbering so much? *Must be from the lack of company.* I smiled on the inside. *Or, in other words, lack of interesting company.*

"What kind of hand signals?"

"Well, I can tell her to get the newspaper, to roll over, shake hands, speak, jump up, spin in a circle, grab my favorite stuffed animal, lick somebody, etc." My mind started to fog and things started to spin. *Uh oh.*

"Cool."

If I told him I was hot, he'd worry. If I didn't, I would pass out and he would be even more worried. Harsh. "Uh, Cole?"

"Yeah?"

"Maybe I am getting a little too hot."

Cole spun around to face me. He yanked off my jacket.

Everything went black.

- -

My eyes slid open and slowly focused. "Oh . . . hi."

Cole sat at my side hovering above me. "Hey. I'm glad you're okay, Squirt."

"Yep." I sat up, making sure I wasn't still hot. "I'm fit as a fiddle."

"You sure you're not hot?"

"I'm pretty cold now."

"Leave your jacket off for a few minutes just to make sure."

"Okay . . ." I watched as he hesitated then turned back to the small camp stove thing. He kept looking back over his shoulder.

I rolled my eyes. "Cole, I'm fine. Stop worrying so much." *Men.* I sighed. *Maybe I should have told him sooner.* I nodded. That must be it.

Just so long as he didn't tell Mom, we would be good. In her condition she couldn't handle having to take care of me on top of having enough strength to take care of herself.

And Cole. Couldn't forget the huge, lovable, worried Cole. He was part of the mountain climbing circus too.

Oh, brother. I was in the company of an injured mother who needed to take care of herself instead of others and an obnoxiously large and mysteriously weird army man. Of course I was going insane.

It was only natural under the circumstances.

JENNA
April 11
Sultana, Denali National Park
3:56 a.m.

The quiet surrounded her like the cozy sleeping bag that held her. Jenna blinked, then pulled herself from the sleep that wanted to pull her back. Her leg was like a portable heater inside the bag. And the throbbing pain in it pounded out a steady rhythm that radiated all the way up to her head.

Good. Maybe it would keep her awake enough to talk to Cole. There was so much to tell him. Her leg must be infected. The pain, the heat . . . clear signs. Antibiotic cream could only go so far, and with the elevation . . . well, she knew the statistics. Injuries couldn't heal up here. They only got worse.

How long would she survive? And how long would she have clarity of mind to be able to explain things to him? She let out a huge sigh. Someone had to take care of Andie.

A rustling close by sounded like someone rolling over. Jenna turned her head and found Cole watching her.

"Jenna?" Cole whispered. "You awake?"

She nodded.

Cole worked his way out of his sleeping bag and brought her some water. "Here. Drink."

Water was an amazing thing. As it slid down her throat, she felt like new life was breathed inside her body. It soothed. It quenched. It cooled. "Thank you."

Inches away from her own, his face conveyed a tenderness she didn't think she'd see from this hard military man. He lay down next to her, propped up on an elbow. "How're you feeling?"

"Warm."

He reached a hand to her forehead and touched her skin lightly, then frowned. He scooted closer and helped her unzip the sleeping bag. "Let's get you uncovered, and see if we can cool you down."

"Okay. But Cole?"

"Yeah?" He continued working, not looking at her.

"I have a lot I need to tell you."

His gaze jerked back to hers. Uncertainty, fear, and a little distrust flashed across his features. Anger sparked—then died as quick as it started. Who was she kidding? She'd given him every reason not to trust her, just by being unwilling to trust *him*. On top of that, she questioned him constantly, demanding to be in control all the time. He may never understand, but it was high time she did some explaining.

What if the fever worsened? What if she became delirious? She may not get another chance. "Cole, I really need to talk to you. While my thoughts are still straight."

"Okay." He slid back into position with his head propped up on his hand. "Talk. As long as you keep drinking."

Someone was taking care of her for a change. Bossing her around. The thought brought a small smile to her lips. "First, I want to thank you. For everything."

Cole started to shake his head.

"Nope. Don't interrupt, and don't shake your head." She gave a feeble laugh. "Second, I want to apologize for making life difficult for you the past few days."

He let out a chuckle, but quickly covered it with a straight face. "Sorry."

"Smart aleck. Anyway, I've always had to be in control where Andie is concerned, and after Marc died, well . . . let's just say, it was my way of dealing with things."

"Okay." Those deep brown eyes searched her face, and the connection between them was palpable. He listened with intent now, not just with his ears.

"Andie has always had special needs. But we wanted her to have the most normal life she could. Wait, let me back up. She has a rare nerve disorder. Did you know that?"

Cole nodded. "She told me a little about it. But I probably don't fully understand it."

Jenna leaned her head back and stared at the snow cave ceiling. "Can you help prop me up? I want to be able to drink and talk. This is going to take a while."

"Sure." He rolled up his bulky coat and positioned it under her head. "You probably need to drink some more anyway. We need to get some Tylenol in you as well. Might help bring the fever down."

Rolling over to her side, Jenna lifted her head and sipped. Laying her head back down on the coat, she looked at Cole. "No. No Tylenol yet. The pain will keep me awake and alert for now."

He looked as though he was going to argue, then he nodded.

"Andie was diagnosed at eighteen months. She was a tough cookie, but most Alaska natives are. When the doctor came in to explain the problem to us, I wanted to know how to fix it. But there wasn't a way to slap a Band-Aid on it and make it heal."

He nodded again, his eyes begging her to continue.

"What she has is called HSAN—"

"Hereditary Sensory Autonomic Neuropathy."

Jenna stared at him, mouth open. Cole just grinned. "Andie told me."

"So did she explain it?"

He nodded. "But go ahead. You may give me more info than she did."

"Andie doesn't feel pain until it's twenty to thirty times the intensity you or I would feel. The nerves don't signal the brain because they're missing fibers. She also can't regulate her own body temperature, and that's why overheating can kill her. The nerves can't get the message to the brain that she's too hot, so she doesn't sweat."

Cole held up a hand. "Okay, so let me ask a question."

"Go ahead."

"She's never sweat? Never?"

"No."

"Wow."

"Yeah. They told me if she ever got hot enough to sweat, using their twenty to thirty multiplication scenario, she would be dead. It was crazy, we had to control the temperature everywhere we went. You'd think in Alaska it would be easy, but it wasn't. Most places had their heat too high in the cold months, so we'd have to drag her out into the subzero temperatures to cool her off. Going to friends' houses became an impossibility. Traveling even more difficult. So we bought our own plane, and Marc flew us everywhere we needed to go."

Cole raised his hand again.

Jenna grinned at this big man acting like a schoolboy. "Go ahead."

"What about playing outside?"

"Well, in the summer months, we had to watch the temperature closely, and since we're tilted so close to the sun during that time, the sun could heat her up fast. Even if the air temp was only forty degrees. In the winter months, well . . . that's another story."

Cole tilted his head. "How so?"

"Andie would come running up to me with the digital readout for the outside temp and say, 'Mama, look! It's cold, I go outside!' and she would barrel out the door without socks, boots, gloves, coat, or hat. Marc and I would haul her back in and tell her that she still had to be careful. We didn't want her getting frostbite."

"A real daredevil, huh?"

"Oh, you have no idea. Take a stubborn child, and remove the fear factor. Think about it. If you have no fear of consequences—mainly pain—you'd try just about anything."

Jenna watched as Andie's reality sunk in. "Yep, she tried to fly. Would climb anything and everything. And would insist that her daddy catch her as she dove toward the concrete—which, as you can guess, scared Marc out of his wits." Jenna couldn't help a laugh. "The funniest thing happened when she was about three and a half. She went through this phase—you know watching all the other toddlers run around and fall down. Well, Andie discovered that other kids would fall down and cry and someone would pick them up, kiss them, dote on them . . . you get the picture."

"Oh boy."

"Yeah. 'Oh boy' is right. Because she started falling down on purpose. She'd cry at the top of her lungs, but as soon as someone picked her up, she would clap her hands and smile. Like it was all a big game."

"Sounds like you guys had your hands full."

"Yeah, well, let's just be honest. I don't think Marc or I ever slept with both eyes closed until she was at least five years old."

"Okay." Cole's face took on a quizzical expression, like he was stumped by something. "So explain this—the other night, she was shivering. Said she was really cold in the snow cave. I don't understand."

Jenna liked this guy. He paid attention, and he really seemed to care. "Well, it goes both ways."

"What do you mean?"

"Her body can't regulate her temperature if she gets too hot, but her body also cannot regulate itself if she's too cold. Once her temperature starts to rise, you better watch out, because it's extremely difficult to bring it down. Fevers can be life-threatening to her. She can't sweat, so her body can't help itself out. The same thing with cold—once her body gets too cold, it continues to plummet. Doesn't know how to warm itself back up."

Cole absorbed this information, his expression so like Marc's when he prepared for a mission that Jenna caught her breath.

"Andie told me she had to have brain surgery."

Seems like her daughter had confided quite a lot in Cole. "A couple of years ago, Andie got sick. Really sick. She curled up in a little ball, her eyes glazed over, and she wouldn't eat, drink, or even talk unless you forced her."

"What happened?"

Jenna breathed deeply. "We didn't know. All we knew is that our child who had never complained of pain—*ever*, in all her life—now said her head hurt."

Memories of that terrible time flooded her, all the worry and fear, the struggle to understand . . . The worst journey she'd endured as a parent: watching her child suffer—lay so still and unresponsive—without answers or a way to help. She choked back the emotion and forced herself to go on. "The doctors couldn't figure out what was wrong until they did an MRI of her brain." Jenna blinked back tears. Even now, all this time later, it still shook her. "They discovered another rare condition."

"What did they find?"

"Her brain was being squished by her skull. It's called a Chiari malformation of the brain. Basically, her brain didn't have enough room, so it was oozing down into the spinal cavity, putting pressure on her spinal cord."

The somber expression in his eyes said it all: it was too much for one kid to endure.

"Anyway, a large fluid-filled cyst had developed on her spinal cord because of the pressure, and she began to have worse problems. She'd fall down the stairs, run into the wall, miss the chair when she was sitting down. It was horrible. And it took an awful toll on Marc to watch his baby struggle."

Jenna glanced over to where Andie slept. "She kept a smile on her face through most of it, but every once in a while, it really got to her." Jenna shook the memories away. "Andie had brain decompression surgery a little over a year ago."

"I'm sorry."

Those two, quiet words, so full of compassion, almost undid her. "But as awful as that was—"

Jenna swallowed back the grief threatening to overwhelm her. "There's more. While she was still in the hospital . . ."

Cole's eyes widened, understanding dawning. "Marc."

Jenna nodded. "While my little girl lay in that hospital bed, I had to tell her the worst news of all—"

Emotion clogged her throat, choking off the words. Tears dripped off her chin as the memory and grief resurfaced. When she could finally speak again, it was in a whisper.

"I had to tell her . . . that her daddy was dead."

CHAPTER SEVENTEEN

JENNA

April 11
Sultana, Denali National Park
4:23 a.m.

"Jenna, I'm so sorry."

She waved him off, swiping at the tears on her cheeks. "I know. It's okay. Just a really, *really* hard time for us." Jenna turned her head away for a moment, composing herself. "But things are better now. We're still dealing with the loss, and we still miss Marc . . . so much. But that day we all got on the plane, Andie and I were on our way home from her one-year checkup with the neurosurgeon. He'd given us such good news. I thought . . . I thought . . ."

"What?"

The tenderness in that word did her in. The dam broke. Sobs shook her as she forced out grief-filled words. "I thought things were finally changing . . . for the better. That we'd finally come out of the darkness."

Silence engulfed her as her tears were spent. Cole sat watching her, his eyes a shimmery mirror of emotion. His jaw clenching and unclenching.

"That's why you have to promise me, Cole."

He frowned. "Promise you what?"

"Promise that you'll take care of Andie if something happens to me."

"Jenna, nothing is going to happen to you." He reached out and took her chin in his hands, so her eyes met his determined gaze. "I'm going to get you off this mountain. Both of you. I promise."

She placed her hand over his. "Promise me, Cole. Please."

Their gazes locked. Something sparked to life in his eyes, and Jenna started. If she hadn't known better, she'd think it was . . . passion.

"I promise you, Jenna. I will take care of both of you."

Searching his eyes, Jenna was stunned by a powerful realization. She believed him. Trusted him. But more than that . . .

She wanted this man. For herself. And more than anything in that moment, she wanted to be held by him. To know she was safe and secure. "Cole, I—"

His lips covered hers. The kiss was brief, but so intense Jenna thought she might be consumed by it. When Cole pulled back, she struggled to think straight.

He pressed his forehead to hers. "I promise, Jenna."

She searched his eyes. "Thank you." Jenna tried to catch her breath, but it was no use. This man stirred up her heart.

A part of her deep inside, a part she thought had died forever when Marc was killed, screamed to come back to life. But instead, she broke the connection and turned her head away.

Cole moved back, and cleared his throat. "Let's slide you all the way out, so I can redress your leg."

Before she could reply, he scooted up to her head, grabbed hold of her sleeping bag, and slid her out into the open area. "Go ahead. Tell me more about Andie. It'll keep your mind off the pain while I take care of this."

His hands probed her leg and pain shot through her. She gasped, then clenched her teeth and did as he suggested.

"You know Marc was a brilliant computer programmer."

Cole gave a slight nod, but kept his focus on her wound.

She looked away and went on. "He could make a program for just about anything. And after he got out of the military, he was hired by the government to do some really secretive stuff. I don't know anything about it, but after his death, they contacted me for his research and the work he'd done. And they've been . . . insistent. Trouble is, I don't know where any of it is."

Cole's hands stopped moving and he raised his head.

"The phone calls and visits have been more frequent recently, and I'm tired of it. Marc made a lot of money, so he was obviously good at what he did. But that doesn't mean anyone has the right to hound us. And if he was working for them, shouldn't they know where his work is? Shouldn't they have his research? My husband is gone and Andie and I need to move on. We don't need to be harassed."

He studied her for a moment, looked like he was going to say something, then nodded and went back to work on her leg.

Jenna fell silent for a moment. What else should she tell him? "My best friend, Anesia, is the only other person who knows all the ins and outs of Andie's condition. She has copies of all the medical files and has been with me through all of this. In case something happens, she'll know what to do."

"Jenna, you're going to be fine—"

"Don't start with me, Cole. Just let me finish—" She bit her tongue. There she went. Getting all irritated with him again. And he was just trying to help.

"Yes, ma'am." His eyes held a slight twinkle.

"Oh, I'm sorry." Jenna laughed behind her hand. "I go overboard, I know. Just bear with me. My brain's getting fuzzy again."

Her protective instinct as a mom must have given her a surge of adrenaline to make it this far. But the effort took its toll.

"Go on."

"This is important: Andie doesn't trust easily. Her best friend—Anesia's daughter, Zoya—means the world to her. And until *you* flew into our lives, Zoya was the only one besides me that Andie has let in since her father died."

"But Andie seems like she would have lots of friends." It was more a statement than a question.

"You're right. She has lots of friends. But she keeps most of them at a distance. Not in an unkind way, she just doesn't let too many people close. Does that make sense?"

He shrugged his shoulders and looked away.

"The point, Cole, is that Zoya and Andie have a special bond. It goes beyond anything I've ever seen."

"What do you mean?"

"Well, before we knew about Andie's brain condition, Zoya had what she described as a nightmare, but I think it was more a kind of premonition. Because she and Andie are so connected. She *knew* her best friend was about to go through a terrible time. From then on, she stuck to Andie like glue. Anesia wasn't sure what to make of it, so she told us about it saying Zoya was insistent. The bond between the two girls grew, and then a few days later, when we received Andie's diagnosis, we were shocked. We couldn't take it in, that a kid's nightmare could reflect real life."

Tears threatened as all the grief of losing Marc washed over her again. But she needed to finish. Needed to go on. "Zoya didn't make a big deal of it. She didn't even want anyone to know, but she was so confident God had given her Andie as a friend that she thought He must've allowed her to have the dream so she could be a better friend to Andie in her time of need."

"So what are you asking me? Not to make fun of Andie's friend? Or what?" Cole scratched his head.

"I'm asking you to try to understand the bond between these girls. Because there's more."

"Okay. Shoot."

"The end of Zoya's dream was that Andie would lose someone close to her." She inhaled sharply, preparing for the stab of pain she knew would come after the next words. "And then Marc died."

LEAPER

April 11
Fairbanks Memorial Hospital
Fairbanks, Alaska
5:13 a.m.

"Nothing, sir." Shadow stood at the foot of the bed. Face grim, jaw tight.

Leaper narrowed his eyes. "Where did you look?"

"The entire house. All the computers."

"Gray wouldn't have had anything so easily accessible."

"Yes, sir. But the wife's friend kept coming to check on the place."

"No one saw you?"

"No, sir."

He ran a hand over his whiskered face. "We'll need to do a complete sweep of the entire property, but for that, we'll need to . . . *occupy* any suspicious friends."

"Yes, sir. That may be a problem, sir. The friend, Anesia Naltsiine, has contacted the media. They've already discovered that the flight plan was canceled, and the controller at the tower caved when questioned about the flight taking off from Anchorage. He's in custody."

He slammed his hand on his leg. "North Korea is getting agitated. We need to deliver, and soon."

"Agreed, sir." Shadow approached him. "So when can you leave?"

"They won't say. But I plan on getting out of here tomorrow. Did you get everything I requested?"

"Yes, sir. Your little stunt in the helo the other day cost you, didn't it?"

"Just come get me tomorrow. 0900 sharp." With a wave of his hand, he dismissed the man.

Staring at the beige walls, he imagined something different than this life he'd chosen. No covert activity. No sinister plots, weapons, or selling to the highest bidder.

Yes, those beige walls were beginning to drive him mad. The sparse décor reminded him of a fresh start. Clean slate.

Leaper shook his head and shifted to stare out the window. He'd been involved too many years to grow a conscience now. But why would his mind keep drifting in that direction if he was a hardened, greedy, self-serving . . . criminal?

A new presence filled the room, and without even looking, he knew.

Viper.

The darkness of the man's heart poured out like his shadow. And as Leaper turned to give his boss his attention, the last glimmer of hope escaped and slipped through his fingers, like water trickling down the drain.

ZOYA

April 11
North Pole, Alaska
5:16 a.m.

An ear-splitting scream pierced the air.

I ran in that direction. Large snowflakes fell, blocking my view. A loud roar thundered around me and the ground began to shake.

A gunshot echoed on the ice walls that instantly shot out of the ground and surrounded me.

Andie!

Jumping up, I started running again. A chopper flew overhead, circling in the sky, looking for prey.

Dark clouds emerged from the middle of the night sky, swirling in an unusual way. Fire spilled forth like a huge tornado just waiting for its chance at destruction.

I looked over and saw Andie struggling in the arms of a man in black. They both stood still. The man shot up into the sky as if he had supernatural powers and then disappeared.

Andie fell to the ground. I raced toward her.

Dasha barked and the fiery tornado came closer. We ran for our lives.

A wicked laugh echoed from the dark cloud and a face with red eyes and a snickering smile appeared. "You'll never make it alive."

Something bumped into us, shoving us toward the ground.

The strange being grabbed Andie, and I jumped forward to reach her. My face met something hard and I lay there unable to move from the force of the blow.

Fire raced across the ground, heading right in her direction.

Someone jumped and pushed her out of the way just before it hit.

The ground shook and the evil laugh rang in my ears again. A giant hand reached toward me.

"AHHHH!"

I jerked up in my bed, heart hammering in my chest and face burning. The door to my room flew open as Mom rushed in.

"Zoya, what's wrong?"

Sweat trickled down my forehead. I was unable to speak.

The dream replayed through my mind.

"Zoya, Zoya!" Mom shook my shoulder and put a hand to my forehead.

Tears spilled down my cheeks as realization set in.

"Mom, something's happening to Andie! She's in trouble, we have to do something!" My face dripped with sweat and tears.

Mom's worried expression met my eyes. My whole body trembled. The threatening words rang through my mind.

You'll never make it alive.

"Honey, shhh. It's okay. Just tell me what happened."

I closed my eyes, not wanting to retell the awful dream.

Okay . . . okay, you can do this, Zoya.

As I retold the haunting scenes they became even more vivid. Once finished, another dream which I had promised to forget crept back into my already agitated mind.

A hospital . . . pain. An endless wait.

Death of someone dear.

Before I knew what happened, Mom had her strong arms wrapped around me. "It's okay."

"But what if—"

"Shh. I know. I know. And I believe you."

"They should've been home six days ago."

"Yes, but we've done all we can." Mom pulled back. "We'll keep trying, but let's get some sleep and we'll figure this thing out tomorrow, okay?"

I nodded.

She kissed the top of my head. "Everything will work out."

"Can we pray?"

Mom nodded.

We bowed our heads and asked God to help us find our friends and to keep them safe.

"Get some sleep." Mom pushed me down to the bed. "It'll be okay, you'll see."

As she exited the room, she flicked off the lights and the room darkened. The door creaked closed and I heard the *thump thump thump* of her steps as she walked away. The hall light stayed on.

"You'll never make it alive . . ."

CHAPTER EIGHTEEN

COLE
April 11
Sultana, Denali National Park
5:18 a.m.

He studied her profile. Jet black hair, smooth skin, perfect lips. Her native Athabaskan heritage evident, and he'd never seen anyone more beautiful. Not even Amanda. Thoughts of his wife flooded him. Once again, he'd betrayed her memory. What kind of fool was he?

"Cole?"

"Uh huh?"

"What are you staring at?"

He blinked several times. Good night, she caught him. "Sorry. What were you saying?"

"I was telling you about Andie's friend Zoya."

"Uh huh."

"Cole!"

"What? I'm listening. The kid had a dream. "

Jenna reached a hand toward him. "I can see I've overwhelmed you, and frankly, I'm too tired to go on."

He looked into her eyes. She must be in an incredible amount of pain. "I'm sorry, Jenna. I'll get something for the pain." He needed the distraction.

She gripped his hand with a strength he wasn't expecting. And she wouldn't let go. "Cole, tell me."

"Tell you what?" Did she know how he felt? How could she read him so well?

"How bad is my leg?"

Relief washed over him at her question, but quickly faded as the answer sank in. He raked his other hand through his hair as she squeezed the hand she held. She deserved the truth. But it hurt to think of the complications. "It's infected. Not gangrenous, but we need to be careful."

She closed her eyes and nodded.

"I cleaned it, applied more antibiotic cream, and rebandaged it, but . . ."

Her gaze locked with his. "But what?"

"It can't heal at this elevation. I've got to get you off this mountain. And soon." He reached into the bag and pulled out the Tylenol. "Here. Take this, and then get some sleep. You need rest."

"Okay." She nodded again, as if accepting an unavoidable fate. After a few sips of water and swallowing the pills, she lay back down. "Did you find the sleds?"

"Only one. There's a little food and water, but at least it was the one with the radios."

Jenna's eyes flashed at him and she attempted to sit up. "But I thought you said it wasn't safe to use the radio?"

"It's not. We don't know who could be listening in. But once I get you down to the glacier, we might just have to."

"What if they come back?"

"I'm hoping they've given up. At least for now."

She leaned her head back and sighed. "Okay. You've gotten us this far."

"Jenna, I will do everything in my power to get you guys to safety and protect you. You know that, don't you?"

"Yeah. Just don't forget your promise . . ." Her eyes closed, the grip on his hand went limp.

"I won't forget," Cole whispered and touched her forehead.

The woman confused him on so many levels.

He slid his hand over to her silky hair. So black it held a hint of blue. Running his hand down a lock, he rubbed the soft strands between his fingers.

Get a grip, Maddox!

Cole leaned back against the icy wall and reined in his thoughts. She made him promise. Begged him. But what if it was all a lie? Could she know more than she let on?

And what about her faith? Andie was outspoken with hers. But Jenna . . . she held everything close. Quietly watching and guarding . . .

He turned away from Jenna. How did they do it? How had this one woman and one young girl peeled back his carefully constructed layers in such a short time? Now all he wanted was to know more about them.

Marc had shared pictures and stories of his family, but his own pain prevented him from paying close attention. There never seemed to be a way to heal. Until now.

Memories assaulted him again. He shut his eyes. Nine long years.

But it seemed like yesterday . . .

It was good to be home.

Hard to believe he'd been in Pakistan the night before. Amanda urged him to sleep in, but his body's clock was off. As his beautiful wife glided into the room, a steaming breakfast plate in her hand, he watched with a smile, then pulled her into the bed beside him.

"I'll share." He winked, enjoying her warmth. Man, he missed her when he was called away.

Their toddler—hair sticking straight out of her head, with teddy bear in tow—appeared in the doorway. "Me too! Me too!" She jumped on the bed.

"Careful, you little wiggle worm," Amanda chided. "We don't want to spill Daddy's breakfast."

"'Kay, Mommy. I be careful."

Chloe sidled up next to him, molding her little three-year-old frame to his side and placing her hand on his chest. It never ceased to amaze him how that one tiny touch could heal so many sore spots inside his heart. The missions became harder and harder to distance himself from.

"Daddy, we pwayed for you evwy night." Her small hand patted him as she leaned her head on his arm.

"Did you now?" He smiled at Amanda.

Her blue eyes shimmered. "We sure did. Chloe had special requests for you every day. Like, 'help Daddy eat his brussel sprouts,' and 'keep Daddy strong,' and my favorite, 'let Daddy come home today.'"

Cole squeezed his daughter, kissing the top of her head. "Thanks for praying such good prayers for me." He turned to Amanda. "But you don't have to worry about me, sweetheart."

"I know." Amanda reached up and touched his face. "I don't. You're in God's hands, and I trust Him."

Her faith was unshakable. And it made him uncomfortable. "So, what have you got planned for the day?"

Chloe popped up on her knees, eyes lit up. "We go to the park, and I get to wear my new wubber boots!"

"Really? That sounds like fun."

"I'm gonna spwash in mud puddles." She slid off the side of the bed. "I show you my boots, Daddy."

"Okay." He pulled Amanda close again.

"I figured you needed some debriefing time, and she's dying to wear those new boots."

Her curly hair tickled his neck. "Thanks, you know me well. Although, at the moment, I don't want you to move."

She tipped her head back to look at him, and then leaned in for a kiss. "So you missed me, huh?" Her fingers ran along his jaw.

"More than you know—"

"Look, Daddy!" Chloe jumped up and down at the foot of the bed.

"Wow." Cole cleared his throat. "That's some outfit."

Chloe twirled in her red rubber boots, pink-and-black striped skirt, purple T-shirt, and yellow raincoat.

Amanda giggled beside him. "She obviously gets her fashion sense from you." She poked his chest and scooted off the bed before he could retaliate.

Chloe grabbed her hand. "Let's go, Mommy. I'm all weady."

"Let me get dressed, Munchkin." Amanda blew him a kiss as they headed to the bathroom. "And then we'll give Daddy some man-time."

Their voices trailed off down the hallway.

Cole slid out of bed and pulled a T-shirt over his head. At least he didn't have to go anywhere. But he would be required to file his reports online.

A grunt preceded his drop to the floor and he put in his quota of push-ups for the morning. Every muscle in his body ached from this last mission, but he had to stay in shape. After the set of 200, he hopped to his feet and headed to the weight machine.

"Cole?" Amanda's voice drifted up the stairs. "We'll be back in an hour or so."

"Okay." He shouted down.

"Love you!"

"Wuv you!"

The door slammed as he finished a set of fifteen bench presses. Around the station he worked, faithfully putting in each set. Sweat dripped from him when he finished and grabbed a towel. A hot shower should kick his brain into gear. Then he'd have just enough time to e-mail a few brief reports before the girls returned.

Exiting the steamy bathroom, Cole headed for the computer desk. The phone rang before he could even sit down.

Too much to do. Besides, he hated answering the phone, he'd just let the machine get it.

Beep. "Mr. Maddox, there's been an accident. Please call—"

He lunged for the phone. "Hello?" The handset slipped in his sweaty palm. "Hello?"

"Mr. Maddox?"

"Yes?"

"Mr. Maddox, this is Doctor Wilson from Providence Emergency Room. I'm sorry, sir, but you need to come down here."

"What happened?"

"There's been an accident. Your wife and daughter—"

"Are they all right? Tell me what happened."

Silence.

"Are you there?"

"Sir, you need to come here. To the Emergency Room. Now. There's . . . sir, I'm sorry. There's not much time."

He threw the phone down and grabbed his keys. How could this happen? Why didn't he go with them? Were those few minutes of laughter and smiles just an hour before . . . the last he'd spend with his family?

Anger boiled to the surface as his truck tires squealed on the driveway. "God, she trusted You! Where were You?"

— —

The angry question rang in Cole's memory, even as the kink in his neck sent a sharp throb to his brain that brought him fully awake. The vision of three-year-old Chloe remained in his mind.

Oh, how he missed them.

A shiver gripped him, he needed to warm up his aching body. Cole crawled over to his tunnel and climbed into the sleeping bag. As he wrapped himself in the cocoon and zipped it up, his thoughts returned to the dark-haired beauty and her daughter.

Could they really not know? Was it possible they had no idea what Marc really did? What programs he'd created? The prototypes he helped construct?

That kind of money didn't grow on trees—and it sure didn't come from the government. Jenna was too smart. She had to know. The perks of her lifestyle no doubt helped her turn her conscience off.

He rolled onto his side. No. They couldn't know. If they'd suspected anything at all, those two would have interrogated Marc until he succumbed to the pressure of their united force.

The battle raged within his mind. If Jenna was telling the truth, if she didn't know anything, then should he tell her? His teeth clenched at the thought. Finding out what her husband really did . . . it would be ugly. He could imagine the fire shooting out of her eyes. She'd hate Cole for keeping the truth from her—almost as much as she'd hate him for telling her. And he could forget her ever trusting him again.

He jerked onto his other side. What an idiot. He'd sat there while she opened her heart. Trusting him. And when she'd talked about Marc's death, he wanted to rip his own heart out of his chest. What would she do when she discovered Marc's death was no accident?

That her husband had been murdered?

What would Andie think? *She* trusted him. How would she see him after hearing the truth?

With a groan, Cole flopped onto his back. This was ridiculous! And exhausting. *Go to sleep, Maddox. Forget all this and just go to sleep.* He let his eyes drift shut . . .

How was he going to explain to a twelve-year-old that her dad had been killed for a program? A program for missile defense—*war.*

A program her dad had sold to the highest bidder.

CHAPTER NINETEEN

JENNA
April 11
Sultana, Denali National Park
6:30 a.m.

Too hot. The fever raged inside her. She struggled to open her eyes. Images swirled around. A soft rustling sound. Hopefully it was Cole who was awake.

"Cole?" It took every ounce of energy to push out the whisper.

More rustling. "I'm here."

"W-water. Please."

She strained to watch him move around and reach for the water. His outline rimmed with a haze. How long did she have? The infection was getting worse.

After a sip, she grabbed the front of his jacket and pulled him close so he could hear her words. "This is bigger than you or me, Cole."

"What are you talking about?"

"I asked you to promise me to take care of Andie." A chill rushed through her as sweat beaded on her forehead from the effort. "But that wasn't completely fair. Yes, I need you to get us out of this, to make sure my daughter is protected and safe, but the only way you can accomplish that is with God's help. You've got to trust Him, Cole."

He leaned back, but she tugged at him, keeping her grip.

"Jenna, I've seen what trusting God can do. And I don't buy it."

Another chill racked her body and she felt the heat rise in her cheeks. She already cared too much . . . *God, what made him so bitter?*

His eyes narrowed, filled with anger. "My wife trusted God. She prayed for me. For years. And you know where her trust got her?"

Jenna shook her head. He'd been married? "W-where?"

"Dead."

A soft gasp rose out of her throat.

"And not just her. But our daughter as well. All those prayers. All that trust. And *He* allowed them to be run down by some drunken fool while they were on their way to the park."

Such loss. This explained so much. "Cole, God didn't run down your family."

"Believe whatever you want, Jenna. But He and I aren't on any kind of speaking or *trusting* terms. I don't need His help. I've got it under control. I just wish the circumstances were different."

"Of course you do, I do too—but circumstances don't change who God is. Any more than they change our need for Him." Her body shook from another chill that seemed to ravage all her insides. Jenna closed her eyes and lay back.

"Jenna?" Cole's concern was evident as his gentle hands gripped her face.

She lifted her lids a brief moment and licked her lips. "No matter what happens, Cole. I will still trust Him."

As the haze engulfed her again, she heard his soft words. "Amanda would've said the same thing . . ."

COLE
7:21 a.m.

"Cole?" A voice penetrated his deep sleep. "Cole? Wake up."

Something kept pushing on his shoulder. He opened his eyes. "Huh?"

"Wake up." Andie's face hovered over his, but it was the fear in her voice that had him fully awake. "I'm worried about Mom." She rubbed her eyes.

He had his bag unzipped and was at Jenna's side in a heartbeat. "Okay, let me check her."

Andie watched him, eyes wide. "Thanks. She feels awfully hot to me, but I'm not the best judge. Is she gonna be all right? Isn't there anything else we can do to help her?"

"She needs more water." Cole touched his hand to her forehead. *She's burning up.* Their last conversation still burned in his mind. Her simple words echoing a haunting harmony with the memory of Amanda's voice.

Andie scooted closer in the cramped space. "What do you want me to do?"

"Here, hold her head up a little, and I'll try to get some water down her throat."

Working together, they managed to get Jenna to swallow some water, but as the night wore on, Cole grew more concerned.

"I'm worried, Cole."

"Me too, Squirt." He unzipped Jenna's sleeping bag again. She must have covered back up last night. We've got to bring her temperature down. Bring in some clean snow, we'll melt and refill the water bottles. And you can keep trickling small amounts into her mouth."

Andie nodded at him, biting her lip. Tears stood on her lashes, ready to spill down her cheeks.

He patted her arm. "It'll be okay. We're getting off this mountain. Just watch."

Her eyes seemed to search his soul. The heartache he saw there bolstered his resolve to do everything in his power to protect them.

As she turned to leave, he squeezed her shoulder. "I promised, Andie. And I don't go back on my promises."

Another slight nod, the faint glimmer of hope in her eyes.

"Go on, when you get back I want to check out your ankle."

She ducked her head.

That, more than anything else, told him he'd allowed her to avoid it way too long. He'd been distracted when Jenna collapsed, back when he first asked Andie about the ankle. But now that Andie would have to hike again, it was time to pull rank. "We've got a long way to go, and I need to make sure you're okay. The sled is only big enough for your mom and her pack. So we'll give your mom some more water, try to get her to swallow some Tylenol, and then head out."

"Okay."

Jenna's fever seemed worse every time he touched her skin. They managed a few more sips of water down her throat, but she needed an IV, and fast.

He turned to Andie, softening his next words. "Andie, I need you to shoot straight with me about your ankle. What happened?"

She brushed her hands over her mom's forehead and kissed it. Taking a deep breath, she straightened her shoulders before looking up at him. "I fell down."

"That's obvious, Einstein. But did you feel anything? See anything?"

"Feel? You've got to be kidding me! I don't feel things like normal people, remember?"

"Fair enough, but did you see anything? Did your ankle start doing anything strange?"

"Yeah, it kept buckling."

"And you kept this from me because . . . ?"

"You had enough to worry about! And I didn't want to be the cause of slowing everyone down."

Cole grit his teeth. "You can be as infuriating as your mother." He stopped the frustrated words. Last thing the kid needed was for him to heap guilt on her. "Andie, listen. I just want to take care of you, but I can't do that if you don't tell me what's going on."

"I'm sorry."

"Don't worry about it. Just don't do it again"—he tweaked her nose, drawing a smile from her—"and give me your leg so I can check it out."

She stuck her leg out in his direction.

The laces on her left boot were stretched taut over the swollen limb. He worked the boot off, stealing glances at Andie's face. She never flinched, but seemed captivated by her injury. As he pulled off three layers of socks, he grimaced at the purple, green, and yellow skin that greeted him. "You did a number on it, all right." He probed the bones under the skin. "It doesn't seem broken, but it's definitely sprained."

"Just a sprain?"

He glanced at her face and almost burst out laughing on the disappointment there. Crazy kid. Ever the daredevil. "A bad sprain."

That perked her up. "How bad?"

"On a scale of one to ten? Fifteen."

"Cool!" She touched her swollen skin and it squished under the pressure.

He inspected the injury, lips twitching as she continued to stare and poke. Now if only she hadn't done any permanent damage walking and falling on it. "Tell me about your heritage. What does your last name mean?"

"We're Ahtna-Athabaskan, but *you* already know that." She poked his arm. "At least, if you were paying attention when you were supposed to, Mr. Mission. Mom's maiden name was Tikaani—that means *wolf* in Athabaskan—and she wanted to pass on our heritage to me, so she kept the name and hyphenated it."

"Makes sense." Cole continued to work on her ankle and then chuckled to himself. "So, in essence, your last name means wolf . . . gray . . . gray wolf."

Andie rolled her eyes. "Wow. I'm amazed. You figured that one out all by yourself."

Laughter echoed in the tiny space, filling every crack and crevice and warming his heart.

ANDIE

7:28 a.m.

"Cole, why were you on our plane?"

Cole's eyes shot up and met mine as he sat in front of me, wrapping my ankle.

I raised an eyebrow and crossed my arms. "Well?" he would answer me whether he liked it or not.

"I bet you're pretty scared, huh?"

"Maybe. But you're changing the subject." I leaned back against the snow/ice wall of my tunnel. My stomach flip-flopped.

God? I need some answers. "So? Why were you on our plane?" *And if you change the subject, so help me I will throw you outside in the snow!*

"Andie—"

"No! Don't you dare change the subject." I was shaking and didn't even know why. "You told me to shoot straight with you, so now *you* have to shoot straight with *me.*"

He glared.

"If you won't answer that question, then answer this one." I sat up and tucked my legs underneath me. "Did you know what was going to happen to us, to the plane?"

He still didn't answer.

"*Why* were *you* on *our* plane?"

Cole sighed and tipped his head, looking at me. "Andie the Interrogator strikes again."

I blinked back tears. Now he was just trying to get me scared. It wouldn't work. "I have every right to question you."

"Yes, but you won't give me time to collect my thoughts to answer your questions."

I turned away. Several moments slid by. "Okay then, I'll give you two minutes. By then you'd better have a good answer. A *true* answer."

He leaned back, closing his eyes. I could almost see the wheels inside his head turning.

My throat was all tight and choked. What kind of story would he come up with? Would it be true or made up? I tried to focus on something else.

"Okay. Here it is."

- -

"Go right ahead. I can't wait to see what you've come up with." My eyes narrowed to slits. *It'd better be the truth.*

His jaw clenched. "Fine. I was on your plane because I made a promise to your dad."

I searched his eyes. Then nodded. "Okay. And?"

"And that's all I can tell you right now."

I just stared at him. He was lying. But then again, Dad used to say he couldn't talk about some things too. Did they really know each other?

He sighed. "I'll tell you more when your mom wakes up. For now, let's just clean up this mess."

"Fine. Whatever."

I started cleaning. "Men. This is why I'll never get married."

Cole's brow lifted, and a little smile pulled at his mouth. But he didn't say anything.

I kept going. "Boys are clueless. They can't answer simple questions, and they want to control everything." I blinked back more tears. *Just like Daddy.*

We cleaned up the little area.

"So what do you want to do now?" I crossed my arms over my chest and leaned back.

"You won't interrogate me further?"

"Fine. Let's just talk." A smile crept onto my lips. "Did you hear about what happened at the football game last night?"

It didn't work, my voice squeaked. Cole chuckled. "It's not even football season."

"Oh. Well, then . . ." I grabbed the sleeping bag and pulled it over my lap to use as a blanket. "Wanna come sit?"

Cole shrugged and crawled over.

As he sat down, I tucked the sleeping bag around his lap. He wrapped his arm around my shoulder and I snuggled up against his side, welcoming the warmth. My dad used to sit with me like that. A stray tear worked its way out from under my lashes.

"You okay? Worried about getting off this mountain?"

I did *not* want to talk about dying up here. I guess he could tell, because he changed the topic.

"Why don't you tell me about that vest of yours."

I took a deep breath. No. I would not let our circumstances push me down to the depths of despair. *Just don't think about it.* "Well, the phase-changing cooling stuff inside the packets was originally designed by NASA, they have some sort of special formula or . . . something in them. Anyway, you put them in the freezer or in ice cold water and they freeze kinda like ice. Although, they last longer than ice cubes. And only stay about fifty-seven degrees."

"So, do they cool you down?"

"Yep. The packets absorb my body heat. As they melt they go from a foggy white solid to a clear liquid. Once they're clear and mushy, they have to be changed out and 'recharged.'"

"How long does it last?"

"Depends on how hot I am. If it's not too hot, it can last a couple hours. But if it is really hot, then sometimes we have to change them out every fifteen to thirty minutes."

"Wow."

"Yeah, I'm really thankful for it."

"I can see why. And I can also see why your mom insisted on taking them with us."

"Yeah. She's great like that."

Cole nodded.

"Mom's really protective. She doesn't let anyone see what she's feeling inside. Ever since Dad . . ." Memories crashed in like a tsunami attacking my brain. I swallowed back tears. *It's no fun being a girl.* "Well, ever since then, she hasn't been the same." I just sat there, fiddling with my thumbs.

"Squirt, you okay?"

What would he do if I told him how scared I was?

I shrugged. "I guess."

He looked down at me. I could tell he wanted to say something. Wanted to have a serious talk. "Don't worry, Squirt. I'm gonna protect you and your mom."

I sniffed and wrapped my arms around his middle.

Silence stretched between us.

Cole squeezed my shoulder. I snuggled closer. "Your mom and I were talking earlier, and she explained your disorder in more detail."

I nodded. "Okay."

"She also told me more about your brain surgery."

"Yep."

"I had surgery when I was a kid too."

"Really? How come?" Pulling away, I pushed hair from my face and stared at him.

"I hurt my arm."

"Do you have a scar?"

"Yes."

I wonder if it's as big as mine . . . "Can I see?"

"Sure, we can compare."

"Okay." I grabbed my hair and threw it over the top of my head, then turned around so he could see the back of my neck.

"That's quite a scar."

I turned back around and dropped my long hair.

"Do you have a MedicAlert bracelet so the doctors will have all your info?"

I smiled. *Always worrying about every little detail . . .* "Yes. It's got my info and ID number."

Cole nodded. "Can I see?"

Was he curious to see what it said or to see if I was telling the truth? I shrugged and flipped the bracelet over.

UNABLE TO
SWEAT, HIGH PAIN
TOLERANCE, CHIARI
DECOMPRESSION.
SUBJECT TO HEAT
STROKE. NKDA

Again he nodded. "Cool."

"Can I see your scar now?"

Cole pulled up his sleeve. A small scar ran across his right forearm. Something else caught my attention. I pushed his shirt up farther.

Huh?

"What is it?" He tugged his sleeve back down.

"This tattoo." I tapped his arm.

"What about it?"

I studied his eyes. "My dad had the same one on his arm."

He turned his face toward Mom.

Should I push it? I had to know, so I plunged ahead.

"Cole, Hank had this tattoo on his forearm too."

CHAPTER TWENTY

JENNA
April 11
8:17 a.m.

Jenna held her breath. When had Andie seen Hank's tattoo? Was it really the same one that Cole—and Marc—had?

"You're right."

She closed her eyes at Cole's answer. What did that mean? Were Cole and Hank in this whole thing together?

"Andie, we all had the same tattoo because we worked together. For a long time."

So Cole wasn't the only one who'd worked with Marc. Hank had, too? How much more hadn't Cole told her? He probably knew all the details and secrets that Marc had kept from her. Deep in the recesses of her mind, she'd known there was more going on with Marc's work than he'd say. But she was too afraid to admit she suspected Marc hadn't been honest with her.

"What?" Andie's agitation was quite clear. "How could you all work together, and then Hank try to kill us? None of this makes sense."

"Andie—"

"What does the tattoo mean?"

Another sigh from Cole. Jenna knew, but understood that Cole would never tell. Marc had sworn her to secrecy. She wiggled to roll over to her side. She needed to diffuse this situation, and now. "Andie?"

"Mom! You're awake!" Her daughter crushed her in an awkward, upside-down hug. "How are you feeling?"

"Not so great. But I'm okay." She squeezed her daughter's hand. "Cole?"

"Yeah, I'm here."

"Can we get out of here?" Their eyes met, and something almost electrical passed between them. But then it was gone, and Cole was all business.

"I'd like nothing more."

Jenna sat up, then coughed so hard she thought she'd bruise a rib. If only she could beat this blasted infection. Her leg throbbed, and moments of clarity seemed few and far between.

"Jenna?"

She looked at Cole. Saw the concern in his eyes. "My leg is getting worse. And I feel the haze closing in again."

"Jenna, please—"

"Mom—"

She held up a hand to stop them. "Don't worry about me." Spots danced in front of her eyes. But she blinked hard, fighting the darkness. "Andie, just remember that I love you. Listen to Cole. And Cole, you remember your promise." Each word took energy she didn't have. *God, help me, please.* "Now, Cole, please get us off this mountain."

Andie's eyes and Cole's brief nod were the last things she saw as the black engulfed her again.

LEAPER

Fairbanks, Alaska
10:24 a.m.

"So, I hear you called the rangers?"

The rookie squirmed under his intense scrutiny. "Yes, sir."

He narrowed his eyes. "I see."

"I know what I saw, Leaper. Footprints. So since you insisted on ignoring it, I called the rangers to find out if anyone was climbing Sultana."

"And?"

The man seemed to gain confidence and leaned on the desk in front of him. "I think you already know, *sir.* There was no one climbing that mountain. Hardly anyone climbs it. The targets are alive."

His temper flared as he threw his bourbon glass across the room. "Rookie, when are you going to learn to be part of this team?"

"What are you trying to hide?"

"I'm not hiding anything, you sorry piece—"

"You've known all along they were alive, didn't you?" The kid's nostrils flared. *"Didn't* you?" Clarity settled in his eyes. "So you just covered up the fact that you didn't complete your assignment." Rookie stood up straight. His eyes wide. "And—you—"

Rookie's words stopped abruptly as his gaze landed on the gun in Leaper's hand.

"Intend to kill you? Yes."

The report echoed off the walls as the bullet hit its mark. Leaper leaned back in his chair. "It's a good thing you've got no ties, kid. No one will ever know."

Shadow burst through the door, then jerked to a halt when he saw Rookie's slumped form on the floor. "Leaper?"

"He was a rat." His popped the safety and threw the gun on the desk. "About to doublecross us."

"Yes, sir."

"Clean up the mess, will you? I need some fresh air." He could only hope Shadow didn't see how forced his air of authority was. As he wheeled himself out of the room, two grim thoughts escaped. First, he should be the one lying in his own blood.

Second . . .

He hated himself.

COLE

April 11
Sultana Ridge, Denali National Park
12:05 p.m.

The wind whipped around his shoulders. Andie was tethered to him with a short, four-foot length of rope, but still she held his hand in a tight grip as they worked their way down the threatening terrain. Jenna and her pack were strapped to the sled he pulled behind them. He didn't think she had much time before the infection raged through her blood stream and killed her.

He wasn't going to let that happen. Andie and Jenna's bond was amazing. No way was he going to see Andie go through another loss.

No way was he going through it himself.

That's why he *had* to get them off this mountain.

Not because of a promise, or because they were in danger, or even because they might know something about Marc's work. It was because he cared.

Plain and simple.

Andie tugged on his arm.

He pulled down his mask. "You okay?"

She stopped in front of him. "Yeah, but can we rest?"

"Sure thing. Need to get more Tylenol in your mom."

Andie plopped down onto the snow. "Good. I'm so tired, Cole. And that's normally a bad thing—one of the clues Mom uses. 'Cause I never feel tired unless something's wrong."

"Hey, Squirt," he tilted her chin up so she'd look at him, "it's okay to be honest. You need to drink and eat, and then we'll keep moving. Just make sure you let me know if it feels worse, all right?"

She nodded and stared at her mom.

They ate and drank in silence, and Cole checked their dwindling supplies. Plenty of nuts and granola bars, but only two water bottles remained. No time to stop and melt more snow. He needed to get them rescued. *Now.*

"Andie," he motioned her closer, "come help me with your mom."

She seemed more lethargic than before. Did that mean something more dire than just fatigue? *Maybe I should keep her talking as we hike.*

"Lift her head up, let's try to wake her enough to swallow these pills." Cole patted Jenna's face, while Andie talked to her.

Jenna moaned.

"Okay, this is going to taste nasty, but I'm going to grind up this Tylenol and mix it with the last few swigs in this bottle. Jenna, you need to swallow it." He continued talking as if she were awake, more for Andie than anything.

"Andie, lift your mom even higher. Try climbing onto the sled behind her and lifting her shoulders and head up onto your knees. I'll coax this into her mouth."

Andie positioned herself under her mom and kept patting her shoulders and talking to her.

With a glance at Andie, Cole nodded and brought the liquefied medicine up to her mom's mouth. "Jenna, listen to me. You need to swallow this quickly. I'll give you some fresh water as soon as you have it down."

She moaned again.

Cole took that as an affirmative answer. Working Jenna's jaw with his left hand, he gently poured the contents of the first bottle into her mouth. As she swallowed, she sputtered and grimaced.

"Blechhh . . . wha . . . ?"

Cole gave her some fresh water to drink. "Good job. Maybe that Tylenol will help bring your temp down." He grinned at her puckered expression. "Keep drinking. You need it."

Jenna never opened her eyes, but at least she responded. Andie sat there with her mother's head in her lap, stroking her hair.

"We need to keep moving, so get your mom's headgear back on, all right?"

With a nod, Andie did as she was asked and prepared to go. Within minutes, her small hand gripped his again.

As they trudged along, Cole had dangerous decisions to make. Sultana was steep. Very steep. They could continue straight down and try to hit the Kahiltna glacier, then follow it back up to where the base camp for Denali climbers was located, or they could cut across the ridge to Mt. Crosson and climb down from there.

Either way, they wouldn't make it before sundown.

He chose the ridge, hoping it would be easier with the sled and Andie. As the afternoon wore on, he shoved her hand into the pocket of his coat so he could use his ice axe to help him navigate the narrow ridge. Andie's grip was tight as they trudged through the deep snow.

Conversation lagged as the wind stole most of their words, but he continued to ask questions about her home and her dog. After hours of hiking against the elements, Cole noticed the kid slow considerably.

"Andie, let's stop."

His jerky halt brought her attention to him. She stood in front of him, as if waiting for direction.

"Squirt, I think I need to try to call for help. It's not storming, and the other helicopter hasn't been back."

Her eyes widened. "But Mom said it wasn't safe to use the radio."

He knelt in front of her. "I know, sweetheart, but I don't know what else to do. We haven't seen anyone else, and your mom's getting worse."

"Do you think it'll work?" Her voice seemed so small.

"I don't know. But I think we should at least try."

"Okay." Such complete trust.

He pulled the radio out from under his shirt. Hopefully his body heat had kept the batteries warm enough. "Let's keep moving. And see if we get any response."

As he flipped the channel of the small radio to channel one, he looked back to Jenna. They really needed some good luck.

"Hey, Andie?"

"Yeah?"

"Now would be a good time to pray."

She stopped in her tracks and grabbed his hand. "God? You know where we are, even though we don't. Please don't let any bad guys hear us on the radio, and please help us to be rescued. And please help Mom . . ." Her voice choked with sobs. "Please let her live."

New resolve surged through Cole. He pressed the talk button on the radio. "Is anyone monitoring this channel?"

No response.

He changed to another channel.

Nothing.

And another.

Twenty minutes passed as Cole continued to try the radio. Settling back on channel one, he tried again. "Is there anyone on this channel? Can anyone hear me?" Static trickled through the tiny speaker. His heart sagged.

"We hear you," a voice squawked. "We're climbers on Denali. Identify please."

A sigh of relief—the voice wasn't one he knew. Definitely a good thing. Maybe they actually had a chance. "Party of three, stranded for a week. Need emergency assistance."

"What is your location?"

"We just crossed the ridge from Sultana to Crosson. Can you assist?"

"Will get in touch with the rangers. Anyone injured?"

"Yes, we have one unconscious, severe infection in the leg."

"Stay on this channel. We'll let them know at base camp."

The radio came to life as Cole listened to the interchange between climbers, base camp, and the ranger station in Talkeetna.

Help was on the way.

Hopefully they were the *only* ones on the way.

ANDIE

April 11
Mt. Crosson, Denali National Park
9:31 p.m.

We sat there waiting, tense moments ticking by. Cole crouched beside me, trying in every possible way to get Mom's fever to go down. I tried shaking her shoulder, but all of my attempts just made things worse.

She trembled all over and kept moaning.

All my energy drained into the snow underneath my feet as I sank down next to Mom.

Cole decided we couldn't go any farther since it was dark and he'd told the rangers where we were. I didn't know if I agreed or not. I couldn't stand waiting for the helicopter to come and rescue us. I needed to do something. Something helpful.

But all I could do was pray—pray and hope that by some miracle God would make Mom's leg better and just make the bad guys vanish. That He would get us off the mountain to safety.

"God, You've taken us this far. Please, get us the rest of the way through." The wind howled in my ears and I barely heard my own words.

God, please.

My heart ached. A thousand words wanted to jump out of my mouth, but none came. I needed to ask Cole questions, but they wouldn't form. I didn't know what to do. I didn't know what was going to happen.

"Andie?"

Cole's voice drifted through my foggy mind. His hand lay on my coat-covered, sore shoulder.

"Andie, I can see them, they're almost here."

I nodded. The sound of helicopter blades echoed in my head.

Shouting.

Someone's strong arms picking me up.

Heat.

Everything was a blur.

God, are You picking me up? Are You bringing me to heaven? Do I get to see Daddy again? Daddy . . .

Mom? Where's Mom?

Fuzziness was taking over, and sense was no match for its overpowering pull. A white light shone bright in front of me.

I'm dying.

Something soothing was poured into my mouth. After a few moments, my blurry eyes focused.

We were in a helicopter, Mom was attached to machines, and I leaned against someone.

Cole. What's going on? I thought I was going to heaven to see Dad.

I sat up straight.

Cole turned to face me. "Hey, Squirt. You okay?"

Searching his eyes was like looking into a brown hurricane of emotions. First he appeared sad, then concerned, then gentle.

"Cole?" My throat didn't cooperate and my words came out in a croak. Why was I still there? *I'd rather be with Daddy than here!*

"I'm here, Squirt." Cole's eyes seemed to search my soul.

Though thankful to be alive, I couldn't help the niggling feeling of disappointment that I didn't get to see Dad again. *God? What are You doing?*

Someone had taken off my goggles and ski mask and wrapped me in a blanket.

"Andie?"

My tears started falling and the sobs came again. Cole pulled me back in his strong arms.

Why couldn't the arms be Dad's? What stopped me from going to heaven? What was God planning?

I glanced over at Mom. She wouldn't want me to die. *But if I'm not going to die, she can't die.*

My heart exploded with mixed emotions. Relief and disappointment. Thankfulness and anger. *God, I can't live without my mom. What are You doing?*

I knew I just had to believe. *But, what if I can't?*

I squeezed Cole.

His gentle squeeze back calmed my riled-up heart.

I sighed. *Okay God, it's up to You now. Take us and do what You want. Even . . .* I swallowed hard. *Even if it means death.*

As I drifted into sleep, familiar, gentle words rang in my mind:

Do not fear, for I am with you; Do not anxiously look about you, for I am your God. I will strengthen you, surely I will help you, surely I will uphold you with My righteous right hand.

CHAPTER TWENTY-ONE

ZOYA
April 11
North Pole, Alaska
10:45 p.m.

I sat on our couch as Mom made yet another phone call. Night and day she'd kept at it.

It's okay, Zoya. They're fine.

I couldn't stop thinking about my dream. Every part of it terrified me. Every image haunted and lingered in my mind as the scenes replayed over and over.

Dasha and Sasha sat at my feet. Even though they were dogs, I could tell they understood something was wrong. How could they not?

What a week. After the first day and no word from Auntie Jenna and Andie, Mom contacted the police. Nobody knew anything. Then she called the press. The phone rang off the hook from friends and family calling. But there was still nothing.

At least they were digging.

Andie was in trouble. Big trouble. My stomach's rolling told me that was true. But I didn't want to believe it.

God, what's going on?

"Honey?"

I stood up. Mom's face answered my unasked question.

"Anything? Anything at all?" My voice quivered. The dogs whined.

"I'm sorry. Nobody knows what's happened. They have no record of the plane landing. Not anywhere."

I fell back onto the couch with a huff.

The phone rang for the forty gazillionth time and Mom walked back into the kitchen.

God? Let them be okay.

"Hello?" Mom's voice drifted out to the living room. "Yes." There was a pause. "What happened?"

I jumped up. *Did they find Andie? Or is this another emergency? What else could go wrong?*

"Yes, we're on our way. . . Thank you."

I ran into the kitchen. "Who was it?"

Mom turned to me with tears sliding down her face. "Go pack a bag and then get Sasha and Dasha. We've got more than an eight-hour drive ahead of us." She put the phone on the charger and turned her back to me.

"We're going to Providence Hospital."

LEAPER

April 11
Fairbanks, Alaska
11:01 p.m.

"Sir?"

Leaper jerked his head to the doorway. Shadow had a knack for sneaking up on him. "What is it?"

"We have a problem."

"What *kind* of a problem?"

"A radio transmission was intercepted in the Alaska Range between climbers and the Talkeetna rangers. About a rescue."

Leaper felt the blood drain from his face.

"A party of three. Stranded for a week." Shadow's face was a stiff mask.

He shoved the chair back as his fist slammed against his desk. They just had to survive, didn't they? "Are they on their way?"

"Yes, sir. The transmissions started over FRS, that's why we didn't hear it first."

He cursed under his breath.

"Sir—" His best operative faltered, seeming to search for the right words. "Is there something you're not telling me?"

Leaper ignored the question. "Have you informed Viper?"

"No, sir."

"I'll need to call him immediately." He wheeled his chair closer to the phone and picked it up.

"Sir." Shadow leaned his thick arms onto the desk in front of him. "You told me they were taken care of. How can they be alive?"

"What's done is done."

"Sir! When you were in the hospital, I was the one who reported to Viper, and now you're telling me you *knew* they were alive?" Shadow ripped the phone from his hands.

Deep breath. Stay calm. Through clenched teeth he ordered, "Sit down, Shadow."

Rage filled the man's eyes, but he sat. They both knew the consequences of this mistake.

"I will inform Viper. And *I* will take the blame."

Shadow narrowed his eyes and nodded.

"And we'll have to change strategies to get AMI. I'm sure the press will be all over the place."

JENNA

April 12
Providence Hospital
Anchorage, Alaska
6:29 a.m.

Beep.

Beep.

Beep.

The monotonous sound greeted her as she opened her eyes to the shadowy room.

Where was she? Looking down at her hand, she noticed the needle and tubes attached to her arm. The muscles in her back and neck growled at her in protest as she glanced around at her surroundings. Machines, plain walls, a TV hanging from the ceiling.

A hospital.

She let out a deep sigh of relief. They'd been rescued.

Jenna tried to reach a hand up to her head, but the effort proved too great. Concrete would be easier to lift. At least it felt that way.

She blinked rapidly to bring the rest of the room into focus. Man, she was groggy. How long had she been out? Her tongue stuck to the roof of her mouth, and the constant hum in her ears seemed locked in by cotton balls shoved deep into the canals.

To her right, she saw Andie asleep, curled up in the bed next to her. Her heart clenched at the beautiful sight. She didn't know what she would've done if—

Thank You, God. Thank You for taking care of her and getting us off that mountain.

The room held a bit of a chill. She'd have to thank the doctor or the hospital personnel later for watching out for her little girl. Hospitals were a warm nightmare for a child who couldn't sweat. The hospital maintenance in Philadelphia had worked round the clock to keep Andie's ICU room the correct temp after her brain surgery. Most patients in the ICU needed warmth to recover. Not Andie.

Looking to her left, she spotted Cole asleep in a chair. His head lay back on top of the chair and his long legs stretched out in front of him. Poor guy. That couldn't be comfortable.

Jenna took a moment to drink in his features. His hair appeared darker in the dim light, a week's worth of whiskers covering his jawline and chin. Even in sleep, the man exuded strength and confidence. Just like Marc.

But that's where the similarities ended. Marc had been a solid man, of average height, with dark hair and brilliant blue eyes. Andie inherited those eyes. Jenna smiled at the thought. Andie—her baby—so full of life and spunk and curiosity. She couldn't resist another peek at her amazing daughter. What a gift. No one could compare with her spirit—that unbridled joy that seemed to ooze out of every pore.

She turned her gaze back to Cole. Another solid, strong man, but a good deal taller than Marc. He towered over her five-foot-three frame. His light brown hair reminded her of a little boy's—always tousled. Thoughts of him in such a peaceful state brought a flutter to her stomach.

But then he shifted in his sleep and scratched his arm. The faint edge of the tattoo showed beneath his rolled-up sleeve.

Her mind dove into the place her heart didn't want it to go. What did he know about Marc? And why were she and Andie in danger? Why would Marc trust a man like Hank? And why would Hank betray her husband?

Jenna lifted her gaze to the ceiling. *Lord, why is this happening? And why do I feel . . . things for Cole?*

Oh, why couldn't life be simple?

The beeping of the monitor sped up.

Cole stretched and stood over her. "Jenna?"

"Hi." His presence did funny things to her insides. "I'm awake."

"I can see that. You okay? Your heart rate jumped."

Good thing it was night. The heat of a blush raced up her neck. "Just thinking."

"Yeah? About what?"

"Well, about this crazy mess we're in. About Andie. And . . ." she paused and got lost in his intense gaze. "Well . . . about you."

He grabbed her hand and squeezed it. His smile diminished as he looked away. "I don't think I'm worthy of your thoughts, Jenna."

"Cole, that's ridiculous." She tugged at his hand, but he wouldn't budge.

"No, it's not." He lifted her hand to his lips and then laid it back down, releasing it.

Jenna watched him pace the small area at the front of the room. He had something on his mind. Was he waiting for her to give him the green light?

He ran both hands through his hair, and turned back to her. "We've been through a lot in a few days. I just don't want you to regret anything."

"What are you so afraid of?"

Her words hit their mark. Standing stiff at the end of her bed, he didn't move for several minutes.

"Well?"

"Everything." He rested his arms on the end of the bed and looked down. "Of caring. And then losing everything. All over again."

His honesty and apparent grief shook her to the core. "Cole—"

"Jenna. Don't."

"Cole, please. Don't shut me out. Not now." Tears sprang to her eyes. There were days she really hated being female. This was one of them. The last thing she wanted him to think was that she intended to manipulate him with her emotions.

He walked back around to her and placed a hand on each side of her shoulders on the bed, pinning her with his gaze.

For several long seconds, their eyes locked. If only she could convey everything in her heart through her eyes. She had opened her heart to him. She trusted him.

But who was this man? And how did he hold such power over her?

He leaned closer and hesitated, just above her nose. "Jenna, I . . ." Clamping his mouth shut, he looked down, leaning his forehead against hers.

"You what?"

Pulling back a few inches, Cole lifted a hand to her face. As his thumb trailed down her cheek, Jenna saw the depth of emotion in his eyes. For one brief moment, all the walls were gone. All the hesitation. All the doubt.

"I think you're amazing." He closed the space between them.

With a gentle brush of his lips against hers, electricity shot through Jenna's body.

He slid his hand to the top of her head, swept the hair away, then kissed her on the forehead.

Before she could open her eyes, he stood and walked away.

"But I can't handle this now." The firm set to his jaw was back. "Jenna, we really don't have a lot of time. The media has already picked up the story and aired the first details."

How dare he change gears like that! Her heart pounded, the machine echoing the sound for everyone to hear. Infuriating man. "And?" She didn't mean for her tone to be so clipped, but he deserved it.

"I'm concerned about you and Andie." His arms crossed over his broad chest, muscles rippling. It was totally distracting.

Whatever. Two could play at this game. She jerked her head back up to meet his gaze. "Cole, I'm thankful you were there, and I'm glad you're here now. But I think we need to cut to the chase."

"Cut to the chase?" He walked toward her, anger shooting out of his eyes, hands clenching and unclenching at his sides. "This isn't a game, Jenna. It's real. And I know those guys. They can't afford for you to be alive."

Her hands fidgeted with the thin hospital blanket. She searched his eyes. Something powerful lurked behind his anger. Something that begged her soul to move closer, grab on, and never let go.

Cole knew more than he'd let on. That much was clear. And if she wasn't mistaken . . .

It scared him.

Narrowing her eyes, she steeled her heart, and plunged ahead. "Okay then. Why don't you just tell me, Cole."

He narrowed his eyes. "Tell you what?"

"What you've been keeping from me about my husband."

CHAPTER TWENTY-TWO

COLE
April 12
Providence Hospital
Anchorage, Alaska
6:49 a.m.

It had come. The moment of truth. How had he let it come this far?

He shook his head. A twelve-year-old inspiring, inquisitive interrogator. That's how.

Andie's thirst for life, her overwhelming joy despite her hardships, her love and admiration and . . . her trust opened his heart. One little girl had demolished every barrier he'd erected.

And that little girl's mom . . .

Jenna.

She made him want to fight.

With her.

And *for* her. Made him feel everything a man *needed* to feel.

For cryin' out loud, he'd kissed the woman! What was he thinking? Now she'd never trust him again. Not after she knew the truth.

As he gazed out the window of the hospital room into the predawn sky, he raked his hands through his hair. The wee hours of the morning were not a good time for this. His heart ached. It was his own fault. He never should've let them in. Caring always led to pain. The proof was inside of him—the twisting and turning in his gut like a knife slicing through him.

He walked back to Jenna's bed. Better to just get this over with. "We all met at Fort Richardson. About fourteen years ago."

"Who's 'we all'?" Jenna pushed the controls on the bed lifting her up. Her eyes narrowed.

"Marcus, me, Hank, Lee, Austin, and several others." He sat down in the chair, leaning his elbows on his knees. Clasping his hands, he bowed his head and stared at the floor. He couldn't look into her eyes right now. Couldn't bear to see the pain he was about to inflict.

"So, about the time Marc was getting out?" Her voice now held an edge to it.

"Yeah. About a year before we all supposedly got out."

"*Supposedly*? Exactly what are you saying?"

Staring down at his hands, the words churned inside. Like a volcano erupting within him, he couldn't stop it.

He looked at Jenna. Pleaded with her to understand. "Lee was a genius. He knew we all had unique skills and that we could form a team to do jobs for the government. Our intention from the beginning was to make the world a better place. Make our country stronger, less vulnerable. And for a long time, that's what we did. We were still part of the army. Albeit secretly. And then 9/11 happened. It hit us like a ton of bricks, changed us all in ways we never imagined. But we resolved to work harder. And we remained a team."

Memories of those years pushed to the front of his mind. He'd felt whole, complete, when they were on a mission. Like he could conquer anything. And then he'd lost Amanda and Chloe. Nothing was ever the same again.

"So you're saying my husband lied to me? He didn't actually get out of the army?" The stiff set of her shoulders made him want to run. Now. First time he'd ever wanted to run from a fight. But she didn't want to believe him. He was ruining the memory of a man she'd loved for a long time.

One look at her face told him the truth.

She still loved Marc.

Cole walked to the end of Jenna's hospital bed and dared a look into her eyes. "It was top secret, Jenna. None of us could talk about it."

"But I don't understand." Her shoulders drooped. "We were so close . . ." Jenna's voice drifted off as she turned away.

"It's not what you think—"

"Don't bother telling me what I think, Cole. You have no idea . . ." A single tear slipped down her cheek. "Just don't bother. Please, go on."

He watched her for several moments. The firm set of her jaw told him to back off, even though her words contradicted. The urgency of their situation won out and made him press forward. "Eventually, Lee's focus started to change. We excelled at what we did, each man with his own unique abilities and specialties. Each mission became more dangerous. The stakes constantly raised. But it soon became evident that Lee had become disgruntled with our superiors. Decided it was better for us to be a separate entity. Decided he wanted to make more money. Those of us who were lower in rank didn't know the extent of the changes he put in place. Our military service was important to us. We took pride in it. But questions started popping up in my mind. The people we came in contact with were not cut from the same cloth as before. It all seemed a bit too . . . shady."

Jenna's eyes popped open and bore into his. "What are you trying to say, Cole?" She sat motionless, her brow furrowed, knuckles white as they gripped the edges of the bed.

"Only Lee, Hank, and Marc knew the truth about our new operations. But several of us began to speculate. The money rolled in, and our Army brothers looked at us differently." His hands clenched into fists. "All those years wasted! Years of honorable service to our country. Years of upholding freedom. Years of doing what was right—gone. Do you hear me? Gone!"

"What do you mean Marc knew? What are you trying to say? That my husband was doing something illegal?" She threw him a murderous glare. "Well, I'm not going to let you defame him! Marc was a good man. He was a Christian! How dare you accuse him of underhanded . . . whatever it is you're saying. What does this have to do with the guys trying to kill us? What about the *bad guys*, Cole?" Her lips formed one single, grim line. Defense mode.

But her eyes betrayed her. Jenna had been suspicious of Marc's work as well.

Cole hated what he was about to do. To all of them. But it had to be done.

Moment of truth.

"Jenna, I know this is hard to understand. Like you said, your husband was a genius with computers. I don't know when or how things changed, but . . ."

She was shaking her head. Denying it. Like she knew what was coming.

"Marc worked *with* those 'bad guys,' as you call them." He faced her, head on. "We all did."

ANDIE
April 12
Providence Hospital
Anchorage, Alaska
7:10 a.m.

What?

Cole's voice pierced the curtain between Mom's bed and mine like a lion pouncing on its prey.

Cole Maddox, you did not *just call my dad a criminal!*

I slammed my fist onto the bed, pushing myself up into a sitting position. I threw back the curtains and two sets of eyes darted toward me.

"What did you just say?" My voice cracked.

"Andie, we didn't know you were—"

"I can't believe you just called my dad a criminal!" No amount of changing the subject could get him out of this one.

Cole's lips thinned. He didn't take it back.

"My dad was the greatest man on earth. I can't believe you, who *knew* him, would even think such a thing!"

"Andie, Cole didn't mean—"

"No." I threw back the covers and glared at him. "Cole Maddox, you take those words back, and you take them back right now! My dad was the best man to ever live!"

Cole looked hurt, and I could feel my eyes burn. I wanted to strangle him . . . and to strangle him good.

My hand flew down to my IV, I ripped it off and jumped up.

"Andie!"

I ran over to Cole. Standing face to face with him I clenched my fist. "I can't believe I ever trusted you!"

Cole reached for my arm but I jerked back. "Get away . . . you monster!" The room began to spin, I staggered, lost my balance, and then fell onto the floor, smacking my forehead against the cold tile.

Mom yelled something, but I couldn't hear or see anything but Cole. And my rage.

He rushed over.

"I . . . I've been so blind to trust you." Tears ran down my cheeks. I tried to hold them back. Nothing in my body seemed to work. "You made me trust you! You made me think you would always be there!" The sobs got quicker, worse.

I jumped up. I couldn't see where I was going. *Why is everything spinning?* My head felt like a ton of bricks and then a feather. Why wouldn't it stay attached properly? Something gooey ran down the side of my head.

I'm bleeding?

Cole stood in front of me holding my shoulders in a firm grip. He was talking to me. Saying something important.

But I didn't—couldn't—listen.

"Andie, calm down!"

No, I won't!

"Get away from me!" My brain went fuzzy again. All I could see was Cole, and all that registered was the urge to strike him for harming my family.

Before I knew what was happening, my arms and legs were aimed at him.

I took a swing, but slipped on the floor and fell, crashing into machinery. A sharp feeling shot through my head. Sliding to the floor I no longer tried to restrain the tears. My hair was plastered to my face and something liquidy dripped down my chin.

Cole's warm hand rested on my back. "Squirt, shh . . . Calm down. It's okay. You're hurt, let me check your head."

The warmth of his hand on my cheek calmed my racing mind. A glance into his eyes showed concern . . . I couldn't let him deceive me again.

I sniffed and my back tensed as I shoved him away.

He leaned closer and caressed my shoulder. "Andie, I wasn't insulting your dad." His hand returned to rubbing my back. "Look at me. I need to check you."

I shrugged his hand off. "No . . ." My breaths came in gasps. "I don't care what excuses you make. You betrayed us, Cole!" My voice rose with every word.

"Andie—"

"Just get *away* from me!" I jumped up and tried to run around him, but still not able to see.

He grabbed my arm.

"Let me go . . ." The plea was followed by gut-wrenching sobs. My tears fell faster and I jerked my arm away.

"Andie, stop!"

I screamed and pulled away from Cole's grip. Fuzziness and floating objects surrounded me. Pain shot through my head.

Something slammed against the wall.

"What's going on?" Familiar and stern, the voice echoed off the walls.

Auntie Anesia?

Was I swerving or was that the room?

"Andie!" Someone ran over and yanked me away from Cole. "What do you think you're doing, mister?"

Zoya?

"Anesia, go get the doctor, the call button's not working." Mom's voice quivered.

Zoya's arms wrapped around me. *What's going on? What's wrong with me?* Machines and alarms blared. Or were my ears just ringing?

Soon Auntie Anesia came back with the doctor at her heels. Why was my vision getting blurry again? Was there fog in the room?

Cole stood against the back wall. Shock filled his face.

God?

The tingles started to race up my back and my cheeks began to burn.

"Andie?" Mom's voice floated over to me but I couldn't focus. "She's overheating, we need to get her cool!"

"What happened?" I could feel the doctor checking my head as his gruff voice demanded an answer. People started talking, but I couldn't hear the words.

My heart still raced and my soul cried out in pain.

Spots and that crazy tunnel hearing.

Darkness.

JENNA

April 12
Providence Hospital
Anchorage, Alaska
7:18 a.m.

The nurse replaced the IV in her unconscious daughter's arm.

Jenna's hands shook and her heart raced. Andie had smashed her head twice while raging against Cole. There'd been no warning. No slow simmer of her feelings until they boiled to the surface.

Jenna had no clue that Andie could lose it like that. Her beautiful, sweet, laughing child had turned into a raging ball of fury in defense of her dad. Jenna wanted to react the same way, but that niggling doubt at the back of her mind told her there might be truth to Cole's words. Hadn't she seen Marc slipping away? Seen his love for money? His constant drive to be the best?

The nurse wiped down Andie's face. The gash in her eyebrow was long and bleeding. Poor kid. Nobody should have to deal with all this at twelve years old. Jenna's heart ached for her beautiful child.

Andie only wanted to defend her father. The memories they had of Marc were good. If only Marc hadn't gotten himself involved in this mess.

No. Marc was a good and honest man. He'd poured himself into their family. Sure, they'd undergone some horrific trials. That could change anyone, couldn't it? And he really didn't care about the money, he just wanted to provide for them. He always wanted the best for his family.

What about Amy? What about the phone calls? The long trips? She gripped her head. The taunting always came at the worst time. That nasty voice wanted her to believe that Marc wasn't faithful to her. That he was an awful man. Who deserted his family.

No. No. No.

No! Marc couldn't have been involved with any evil, greedy men. Andie had a right to defend her dad. And Jenna really needed to focus her energy on her daughter right now.

But what if they were wrong? What if Marc really *was* responsible for what had happened in the plane, on the mountain?

"Jenna, we're going to take Andie down to the ER for cleanup and stitches." Dr. Baker stood over her, interrupting her swarming thoughts. "You all look like you need some space to sort things out." She didn't miss the look he shot toward Cole.

Jenna nodded at him, noting the worry etched in his wrinkled brow. "But—"

The doctor leaned a little closer. He'd known them since Andie was born, and didn't hesitate to cut her off. "Might I suggest a psych consult? You all have been through an enormous amount of stress."

"I really don't think that's necessary, Dr. Baker."

"What if I bring someone up to the room tomorrow? Just to talk things through? It won't be official, I promise."

"Fine. Whatever. But I reserve the right to ask him or her to leave, all right?" No matter how well the man thought he knew them, he really didn't have a clue. No way would she allow anyone to grill her daughter for a stinkin' psycho evaluation.

The doctor nodded. "Agreed."

"I'd also like you to be present."

The doctor quirked an eyebrow at her. "You aren't going to make this easy, are you, Jenna?"

"Not if I can help it." She stared down at the blankets, pretending to smooth out the wrinkles. "Now, I would like to go with my daughter."

"I'm afraid that's not possible this time. There's not enough room for the two beds, and it would be too much trouble to move you and all the equipment."

The ever-faithful, ever-quiet Zoya spoke up. "Can I go with her?"

The doctor glanced back at Jenna. "I think we can make an allowance this once."

"Sure, hon. She'll need you." Jenna pasted on a smile. Jenna loved Zoya as if she were her own flesh and blood, and knew Zoya's heart hurt for her friend. "Please, don't let anyone else near her, okay?"

Zoya grabbed Andie's limp hand. "I won't, Auntie Jenna. I've never seen her so angry. Will she be okay?"

Anesia laid her hand on her daughter's shoulder. "I'm sure it's been a traumatic few days. She'll be fine."

Two nurses prepared the bed for moving, and then whisked her child out the door.

The doctor hesitated a moment before he spoke. "Whatever it is that just happened? Let's make sure it doesn't happen again. Andie needs to heal. I haven't even begun to tell you the extent of her ankle injury. She needs to stay off of it. Completely. We'll get her stitched up and run a CT scan while we're at it, but things need to be calm by the time we get back. Understood?"

Jenna glanced around the room. Cole stood stiff as a statue. That muscle twitching in his jaw. Anesia's eyes narrowed, studying him. The doctor seemed exasperated with the whole situation.

"I understand." She forced her words out. "It's been a harrowing experience for all of us. I had no idea she would ever react that way. But she's all right?"

"I believe so. Her eyebrow is split open. A lot of blood, but head wounds always bleed profusely. I'll take a look at her medications. Maybe the dosage of steroids triggered her temper. But please remember, she needs to stay off that ankle until we can discuss the injury further and talk about her physical therapy."

"Is there someone down there to protect her?" Jenna couldn't bear the thought of Andie being in danger.

"I'll make sure a nurse stays with her until we bring her back up. The hospital is safe, Jenna. We have lots of security, twenty-four hours a day."

"Thank you, Doctor." Jenna squeezed her eyes shut as he left the room. What a nightmare. Andie had never reacted so violently to anything. Ever. Poor kid. Jenna hoped her daughter's ankle wasn't damaged permanently, but understood the doctor needed to take care of one thing at a time. How much more could they take?

A familiar hand touched hers, bringing her eyes open. She gazed into her friend's eyes. "Anesia. Thanks for coming."

"Girl, you know I would do anything for you. Now *please* tell me what's going on." The dart of her eyes to Cole showed Jenna her friend's suspicion of the man.

"Actually, I think Cole and I need to finish before they bring Andie back." Anger returned as she looked over at her handsome, one-time rescuer. Conflicting emotions surged through her. How could she care so much and yet loathe him at the same time? The temptation to hate him and his stupid accusations almost won the battle over her Christian beliefs to love her neighbor as herself.

That muscle in Cole's jaw worked into overtime. "Anesia," he held out his hand in greeting. "I'm Cole Maddox. I've heard a lot about you."

Her longtime friend shook his hand, but didn't respond.

"Don't guess there's any way I could ask you to leave?"

Anesia's shoulders were rigid, arms crossed over her chest. "Not a chance."

"Even though you understand that this will put you in danger?"

"I'm the closest person in Jenna's life, Mr. Maddox. I think I'm already in danger. So just get on with it."

"Fair enough. Do you have a laptop with you?"

Anesia nodded, her expression quizzical.

"I think it's time I clear up this mess." Cole took the chair beside Jenna's bed again and looked at Anesia. "Do you mind if I use it?"

She looked to Jenna for approval and then grabbed her laptop bag from the doorway where she'd left it. Handing it over to Cole, she turned back to Jenna. "You okay? We were so worried. What happened? The news on the radio said there was suspicion surrounding your crash and they were investigating."

"Really? Suspicion?"

"Uh huh, something about the flight plan being erased, and garbled flight transmissions."

"Oh good grief. This just won't end, will it?"

"What won't end? Are you okay?"

Jenna gave her a weak smile. "Yeah, it was horrible, but I'm okay, I think. This infection in my leg is pretty severe." Jenna darted a glance at Cole. "I'll tell you everything in a little bit, but I need to understand what I'm up against."

Her friend's expression told her she didn't agree. "Who do I need to go beat up? 'Cause you know I will."

Jenna let out a feeble laugh. Feisty Anesia. Smaller than Jenna's own petite frame, Anesia didn't look like much of a threat, but Jenna knew otherwise. They'd been through so much together. Her trusted friend would go to battle for her with bare hands if needed. "Who's watching the house? And what about your kennel?"

"Peter said he would keep an eye on your property, and Joe is taking care of the dogs."

Cole's gaze shot up from the computer. "Who's Peter? And Joe?"

"Peter's been a friend of our family for a long time. Anesia and I both hire him to do odd jobs for us. And Joe is Anesia's friend. They're both safe."

A brief nod and he was immersed again in the computer.

"I brought the twins with me." Anesia's eyes held a familiar twinkle.

"You're going to sneak them in, aren't you?"

"Well, I'm going to try to do it legally first." Anesia's eyes turned serious and she whispered, "Are you okay? Really okay?"

"I don't know. This whole thing with Marc has driven me crazy for too long. I really need to know. Before I lose every good memory I have of him."

"*Ts'akae*! Are you sure you should be worried about that right now? Your plane crashed, you almost died—"

"I need to know about my marriage first, Anesia. I really need to know." Tears were unwelcome at this point, but her eyes didn't want to cooperate. How to ask? She didn't even know where to start.

She took a deep breath. Better to just blurt it out. "Cole, I need to know if this has anything to do with some woman named Amy." Jenna bit her cheek after she choked out the words. How embarrassing to say it out loud. What would he think of her now? That she'd failed as a wife?

Anesia's hand gripped hers tighter.

Cole's focus stayed on the computer screen for several seconds. But finally, he cocked his head, furrowed his brow deeper, and lifted his eyes to meet hers. "A woman named Amy?"

She really didn't want to hear his answer. Oh, why did she ever ask that question? It'd be better not to know. Not to bear the humiliation of seeing the pity in Cole's eyes. Her own eyes stung. Stinking tears! Biting her lip, she attempted to swallow her anguish.

Cole brought the computer to her lap, and brushed her arm with the back of his hand.

Anesia stood like a sentinel on her other side, holding onto her hand with a grip that threatened to break her fingers. Her friend would stick with her. No matter what. But this man? This man she dared to believe in? Dared to open her heart to? No. He would leave. She prepared her heart for the worst.

"Jenna," those brown eyes captured hers, "this won't be easy. Read it. It'll explain. AMI isn't a woman." As if reading her thoughts, he added, "And I'm not going anywhere."

Jenna sucked air through her lips and prayed for strength. She could do this. The laptop displayed an e-mail server. And a thread of e-mail conversation. Waiting to be read.

As the words formed sentences, and those sentences came together in her mind, Jenna gasped. No. It couldn't be. Page after page she read. Scrolling down, down until she reached the end.

She stared at the computer screen. In black and white, the screen taunted her.

"Marc . . . he was a good man. But something inside him changed. He did something I never thought he'd do." Cole stroked her arm. "He sold out to the highest bidder. Yes, our group started out thinking that we could change the world. But greed and selfishness and the appeal of power took over."

"How dare you tell me what kind of man my husband was." Jenna spit through clenched teeth, breaking from his grasp. "It's all a fabrication. Marc would never do anything like that." Her heart sank. She could defend her husband all she wanted, but the facts glared at her.

Cole gripped her shoulders, hurt evident in his eyes. "Believe what you want, Jenna. But those e-mails are real. AMI is real." He turned away, the planes of his face hardening. "And you have a little girl whose life is in danger because of your husband's choices."

"Why didn't you tell me? Or are you not really who you say you are?" She knew it wasn't fair, but her heart ached. How could she have been so stupid? So blind? Cole played a part, just like Marc.

"I'm sorry, Jenna. I should've told you. But I didn't know if I could trust you."

Tears streamed down her cheeks. Marc never trusted her with the really important stuff either. Otherwise, he wouldn't have gotten involved with such a greedy group of men. She might've stopped it.

Anesia held the laptop, the compassion in her eyes telling Jenna she'd read the thread. Her friend knew. It was true. All of it. How could Marc do this to her? And why? Just for the money? Could her husband really have changed that much?

"Jenna?"

She couldn't bear to look at Cole.

"Jenna. Look at me." His voice softened. Not a command, but a plea.

Closing her eyes, she shook her head. No. She wouldn't give him the satisfaction of knowing—

But Cole continued on anyway. The bed creaked as he lowered the side rail. The mattress sank as he sat next to her. "Jenna. Marc *was* a good man. I'm here because of him." His warmth seeped over to her. His breath tickled her face. "I know you hate me right now. I know you're mad at Marc. But listen to me. Please." His forehead touched her cheek for a brief moment.

Then he pulled back with a jerk and walked across the room.

She dared to look at him.

"Jenna, I confronted Marc near the end. He told me the truth about what our operations were doing. And then he realized what a crazy mess he'd gotten himself into. He tried to fix it, Jenna. He wanted to set things straight. To hand over the systems to the U.S. government, and tell you the truth. I promise."

Tears streamed down her cheeks. How could Marc have done that? How could she not have known what he was involved in? Was Cole telling the truth? What if he created the e-mails to cover up for himself?

"Jenna. There's more."

Those beautiful brown eyes no longer begged her to drown herself in them. They were hard. Just like his expression.

She looked away. "I'm listening."

"Marc contacted the FBI. I don't know all the details, he didn't get a chance to tell me, but they were working with him to bring down the whole enterprise. That's what he was doing . . . when he was murdered."

CHAPTER TWENTY-THREE

ANDIE
April 12
ER—Providence Hospital
Anchorage, Alaska
8:55 a. m.

My head throbbed.

Pain was such a strange sensation.

Something beeped next to me. A few hushed voices whispered in the distance. Babies cried.

What's going on? Memories flashed through my head.

Cole, Mom, Zoya, anger, fear. Broken-hearted pain.

I shuddered as the anger gripped my heart.

Where's Cole?

I was in some curtained-off little room somewhere in the hospital. And I was mad?

I was sorry for what I did, but then again, I wouldn't have minded landing a blow or two on Cole.

God, what am I thinking? What's going on? I was sure that if God hadn't been holding my heart together, it would have ripped in two.

And then it came again. That memory I'd tried to forget . . .

"We have to hurry, North Korea is anxious to get the prototype . . . All right, I'll see what I can do." Dad hung up the phone and I took a step forward.

"Daddy, whatsa prototype? Where is North Korea? And why do they want it?"

Dad spun around. "Oh, boy." Rubbing his forehead, he sat down in his office chair. "Come here, Squirt." He patted his lap and I ran over. Pulling me up onto his muscular leg, he kissed my cheek. "Squirt, I need you to do me a favor."

I started messing with his buttons and smiled up at him. "I'll do anything for you, Daddy."

He smiled back and tugged my braid. "I knew you would. But, I need you to keep a secret for me."

"What kind of secret?"

"Well . . ." He frowned. "A very, very, very important secret."

"Like what you're getting Mommy for Christmas?"

"Even more important than that."

"Well, okay, Daddy. I guess if it's that important I can keep this secret." I leaned against his shoulder and smoothed out his shirt.

"I need you to . . ." He pulled me closer. "You can't tell anyone, not even Mommy, about what you just heard, okay?"

"Why not?"

"Because"—He took a deep breath—"because it's important that nobody knows. Nobody can hear about it. All right?"

"Okay, Daddy, I guess I can keep it for you . . ."

The memory faded.

I'd kept his secret. But what did that mean, now? *Time to figure it out.*

I slid my eyes open but they fell shut. A warm hand held mine and squeezed. Again, I tried to open my stubborn eyelids.

"Hey, you're awake."

Squinting, I tried to make my eyes focus. "Zoya?"

"It's me."

"Thank God." I sighed. "Will you help me sit up?"

"I guess . . . but if you get dizzy or anything, tell me, okay?"

I nodded as the back of the bed started moving up. "I'm glad you're here. I don't think I would make it without you."

Her eyes clouded over. "Oh, Andie! I've been so worried, I didn't think we'd ever find you! When you didn't show up at the airport I didn't know what to do and—"

"Hey! Calm down, it's okay, I'm right here, I'm not going anywhere." I patted her hand and smiled.

"I'm sorry. But I couldn't help but worry, Andie. You know that. You were missing for *six days*."

"I know." I shuddered. "But, I'm here now, so let's not worry about it, okay?"

"Okay. But what happened?"

"Brace yourself, this is going to take awhile."

Zoya nodded and leaned back in her chair. I told the whole crazy story, Zoya asking questions here and there.

". . . the helicopter came and took us here, then . . ." I spaced out, staring at the white curtain surrounding my bed.

"Andie?"

"Cole and Mom were talking. I overheard the last part of their conversation. Cole accused my dad of being one of the bad guys. That's why I was so mad. But . . ."

"But?"

"I don't know. I mean, he could have been telling the truth." I sighed. "I'm just trying to figure this out."

"It's okay." Zoya grabbed my hand. "I'll help you. And so will Dasha and Sasha, if we can find a way to get them inside the hospital."

"Dasha's here?" I smiled. My dog could cure just about anything.

"Between God, you, me and our *łic'aes*, we can do it."

I prayed she was right.

April 12
Providence Hospital
Anchorage, Alaska
9:01 a.m.

"So . . . how do you feel? I mean, you really had a rampage in there." Zoya's eyes glistened with tears.

"I feel fine. And I'm sorry. To tell you the truth, I don't even remember what I was thinking at the time. Everything just happened. All I really remember is being so angry. And . . ." Cole's worried, kind face popped into my head. I shook the memories away and fiddled with my hands. *Think about something else.* I couldn't look at Zoya; she'd see my doubt.

"It's okay, Andie. Just remember"—she grabbed my cold hands—"I'll always be right beside you, okay?"

"Thanks. You've always been there when I need you. You've been an awesome friend."

"Well, you've been awesome-er. I mean, awesome-*est*."

I laughed. *God, thank You for Zoya.*

"So, what's with that Cole guy? What does he have to do with anything?"

"Well . . ." *Good question.* "I don't know the—"

"Are you, Andie?"

Zoya and I jumped at the sound of a gruff voice, and we turned to look at the end of the bed. A tall man in scrubs stood with his hands clasped in front of him, staring at us as if we'd just pulled all the fire alarms in the building.

Where did you *come from? And what kind of doctor are you?*

He may have been wearing scrubs but I didn't see any badge-type-thing that all of the other staff wore. I stared. My stomach tied up in knots. *Uh, Cole? This would be a good time to come save the day.*

The man's eyes were dark and held an air of authority. If he had been a lady, I was sure his name would be Cruella de Vil.

No, he looked more like the Grinch.

He cleared his throat and asked again. "Are you Andie?"

I looked at him from head to toe, and Zoya squeezed my shaking hand. *Well, who are you little mister appear-out-of-nowhere-I'm-in-charge-and-don't-you-dare-pull-all-the-fire-alarms?* His eyes narrowed.

Go ahead . . . if you can. I'm not scared, Grinch.

The curtain pulled back and Dr. Baker walked through.

As quickly as he had appeared, the Grinch was gone.

"Who was that? And . . . where's the nurse?" Dr. Baker's eyes narrowed and worry etched his face as he clutched his notebook, like he would bang it on the Grinch's head if he ever set foot in the hospital again.

Go Doc Baker!

He turned back to me. "Andie?"

I shook my head. "We don't know who he was."

Zoya's voice chimed in. "Whoever it was, he was *super* creepy!"

I shuddered as I remembered looking into his dark eyes. *God, please tell me he isn't another bad guy trying to kill us.*

Doc walked over and looked toward the exit. "From what I saw he did look a little . . . scary."

I stared at the white curtains again.

"And evil."

COLE

April 12
Providence Hospital
Anchorage, Alaska
9:03 a.m.

Jenna's head snapped up. "Murdered?"

He watched her choke on the word and cast a glance at Anesia. "You mean, Marc's death wasn't an accident?"

Pain.

Her face filled with pain. And *he'd* put it there.

Cole raked his hand through his hair. How much to tell her. Hadn't he done enough already? Looking down at Jenna's expectant face, he saw the tears shimmering on her cheeks. The questions hovering on her lips. She'd trusted him. Fat lotta good it did her.

He moved away from the door and headed to the window. Couldn't bear to look into her eyes. This next part would be hard.

Cole took a deep breath and plunged into the story he'd hoped to never have to tell. "Marc e-mailed me the morning he died. Said we had to meet ASAP. Said his encrypted transmissions had been compromised, so there was no other choice but to give me the information in person." His heart sank in his chest remembering that fateful morning. His friend . . .

Shaking his head, he lifted his chin and continued. "We met at a coffee shop. Marc handed me a piece of paper, but said it was imperative to show me everything. And fast. The paper didn't make sense—some sort of hidden clues in the text, *protect with my heart*—but Marc and I climbed in his vehicle and he said he would explain. Was tired of carrying the burden around. As he gave me the details surrounding the threats against him—against you and Andie—he cried. I've never seen a man cry from his gut like that. Pouring out his regrets, wondering how he ever allowed it to go so far."

Cole stared out the window. Seeing Marc so broken began the thawing of his own icy heart. And now here Cole stood. Trying to fulfill a promise.

A promise he desperately wanted to carry out. But didn't think he could.

"Cole? Please . . ." Jenna choked on a sob. "Please continue."

The pleading in her voice just about did him in. He turned to face her. "He loved you both so much, Jenna. He was worried. Knew what they were capable of. That's when he made me promise. To protect you. Take care of you."

She wiped her face with tissues. Anesia stood with her arm around Jenna's shoulders, a scowl on her face.

"I promised him I would do everything in my power. We'd had it out several weeks prior. When I confronted him about what we were doing, how many lives were at stake, we actually got into a fight." His chuckle sounded sad and raw, even to his own ears. "Marc was a solid, tough man. He could've taken me out, but he stopped mid-swing. His face changed, and he just sat down. Shook his head. And then? Then, he had the gall to bring up his God. About how he knew better. And how I needed that God too."

Bitterness seeped into Cole's heart—and his words. "I asked him why, if his God cared so much about him and his family, had He let Marc venture down on this path? How could this hypothetical great God let his family be in danger? And why couldn't Marc trust Him?" Sarcasm spewed out. "Marc tried to convince me that he alone was responsible for his mistakes. That God gave him free will to do as he pleased. He sat there, a smile on his face, praising his God for forgiving him even though he'd done some really horrific junk."

"Cole—"

"Don't say it, Jenna. I didn't want to listen then, and I definitely don't want to listen to it now. I'm supposed to protect you and I can't do that with some fairy tale in my head—"

At Jenna's gasp, he knew he'd gone too far. But that didn't change things. "I'm sorry. I shouldn't have said that. After watching you and Andie . . . I understand a little better, but . . . never mind. That doesn't matter right now. Anyway, in Marc's car that morning, he talked about God again. And I wanted to run. Marc was scared. But also at peace. Something I'd never seen in anyone. Ever."

He stiffened his spine. Stood at attention. Time to just spit it out. "Marc had just put the car into drive. We were going to your house. He said he wanted to show me everything, call his contact at the FBI so we could meet. But I jumped out of the car. I'm not even sure why. I was angry. I needed time to think, couldn't take the anger churning in my gut. He yelled out the window to me. I told him I forgot something in my truck."

Cole struggled with his next words. *Suck it up, Maddox. She deserves to know the truth.* "I planned on going back, but the other vehicle came out of nowhere. By the time I turned around, it slammed into Marc's car. The explosion threw me off my feet."

He finally faced the woman who had captured his heart, but he could never have. "That bomb was meant for both of us."

CHAPTER TWENTY-FOUR

COLE
April 12
Providence Hospital
Anchorage, Alaska
9:08 a.m.

"Bomb? What are you talking about? Marc was killed by that car hitting his gas tank!" Jenna's voice was broken. Shrill. Angry.

"That's what the police report said, yes. But I was there. I knew. They wanted a quick and easy way to get rid of us."

"But . . . how do you know it wasn't an accident? How do you know it was a bomb?" Her eyes were desperate. She didn't want to believe the truth.

"Trust me. The bomb went off a full four seconds after the car crashed into Marc. It was rigged. It's what they do."

"So they killed him for this . . . this . . . AMI?"

"Yes."

"And it's not a woman?"

"No."

She trembled, tears streaming down her face. He had no idea the torture she'd endured all this time. Thinking her husband unfaithful. Now she dealt with the details of her husband's work all these years. And that he'd come close to betraying his own country.

"Advanced Missile Interceptor. That's what AMI stands for. Only it's not just a—"

"Jenna." Dr. Baker's voice broke into the room. "I've brought Andie back. Only nineteen stitches."

Cole moved away from Jenna's bed as the doctor came up to stand beside her. What would happen when they found out everything? What he'd done? What he'd been capable of doing?

"She lost a lot of blood, but she'll be just fine." The doctor looked around the room at each of the adults. When his gaze came to Cole's, the doctor frowned. "I've adjusted her medications, but let's try to keep her calm, shall we?"

"Thank you, Doctor." Jenna swiped at the tears on her cheeks. "Thanks for everything."

"I'll be back in a little bit." Dr. Baker left the room as the nurses wheeled Andie's bed back into position. Zoya followed.

Andie looked at him with sad eyes. "I'm sorry for trying to hit you, Cole."

His throat locked with emotion. Chloe's face swam in front of his mind. They were so much alike.

"I'm still mad at you, but I'm really sorry."

Cole couldn't stay a second longer. With long, determined strides, he left the room as fast as his legs could carry him.

ANDIE

9:17 a.m.

Cole hadn't said a word to me and I knew why. I did something I'd always feared doing: Taking out my anger on someone I loved. Someone I loved a lot.

A whole lot.

I hurt him in the worst way and knew it. Whether he deserved it or not didn't matter. I just wanted him back.

It's no use moping, Andie. You blew it. Tears welled up inside my eyes as I remembered his shocked expression. We had come a long way in a short time. But I smashed all dreams of fun and joy with my stinkin' temper.

All because of me.

I turned to Mom. She had tears streaming down her face.

"What's wrong?" Was she mad at me too?

Mom patted the bed, then wiped her tear-soggy face. I climbed up beside her, careful to not mess up my new IV.

"Andie?"

"Yes, ma'am?"

"We need to talk."

My heart pounded in my chest. "Mom, I know what I did was wrong, and I'm sorry. I didn't mean to make Cole go away, honest! I was . . . I am just upset, and . . . and confused and I don't know who to trust—"

"Shh. Andie, calm down." Mom's hand wiped my wet cheeks. "That's not what I meant."

"What did you mean?" I sniffed.

"We need to talk about your dad." She tucked me into the crook of her arm and I snuggled up next to her.

"Andie, your dad's death wasn't an accident. He was in this group of bad men. At first they weren't bad. But they . . . lost their way and made some very bad decisions."

Something sparked in my brain. I didn't want to hear this. "Even Daddy?"

Tears slipped from Mom's eyes as she nodded. "But Daddy changed his mind. He decided to turn back and do the right thing, but . . . the bad men killed him. Those same men are the ones that are after us."

As the information sank in, I remembered Cole and Hank fighting, the helicopter, the explosion . . .

So Cole told the truth?

"*North Korea is anxious to get the prototype . . .*"

My eyes widened. *Is* that *what these weird people are after? Some sort of . . . prototype?* Was I supposed to tell Mom about what I heard? That Dad made me promise not to tell anyone?

What would it mean to break my promise? Would it be helpful or harmful? If I kept the promise for my dad, would that make me an accomplice? Would I go to jail? What would Mom think? What would happen to her and Dasha?

Daddy, why did you leave? Didn't you love us? Why did you go into that group of bad men? If you hadn't, you would still be here with me and Mom. You could have turned back to the good side! What's going to happen to Mom?

What would this do to her? What was happening that I couldn't see?

"Andie, what's going on in that head of yours?" Mom nudged me, but I buried my face in her shoulder and cried. I couldn't tell her.

What were you thinking, Daddy? What have you done? I couldn't believe my dad had been one of the bad guys. What had gotten into his head? Had he been a bad guy from the beginning?

I can't believe I have a bad guy for a father. You betrayed us, Daddy. You were my hero, why did you throw everything away? Me and Mom and Dasha . . . and your life!

How many times had he laughed and played with me when he got home from work? How many times had he sat and watched *Little House on the Prairie* with me when I was sick with migraines? How many times had he tickled me, played Barbies with me, comforted me, put Band-Aids on my skinned knees?

He had been my hero.

How could he have done this to us? He betrayed Mom, put my heart into pure torture. Christians were supposed to be the good examples, not the bad ones. Then why go down such a bad path?

But Daddy *had* been a great example. He had prayed for tons and tons of people all the time and truly meant it. He read his Bible every morning with me, he had done devotions with me and taught me why it was important to live for God, fully and completely, he . . .

I gasped. *He betrayed God!*

Did that mean he wasn't in heaven? Had he been pretending? Did God try to get Dad to follow him? Did He think Dad was like Judas? A betrayer?

Tears rolled down my cheeks. I clenched my fists. My chest burned as I realized I'd been holding my breath. I clamped my teeth tight at the untamed anger bubbling higher and higher.

I hate you, Daddy. I never should have trusted you.

COLE

9:30 a.m.

"I need a favor." Cole spoke in hushed tones into the receiver.

His longtime military buddy was quick to respond. "Sure thing, man. Whatcha need?"

"A couple of private bodyguards. Have some valuable items that need protection."

"Clearance?" The code words were understood.

"As high as you can get. FBI will probably be stepping in eventually." *I hope.* Cole didn't know who Marc had contacted, and wasn't ready to trust just anyone. "Get me the best you've got. Guys you can trust."

"I'm on it."

"How long?"

"Gimme a couple hours."

"Don't use my old cell, I'll call with a new number today." Cole slid his hand through his hair. "Don't let anyone know you've heard from me."

"Got it." His friend's voice changed. "Dude, be careful. I saw it on the news."

Cole watched a nurse who'd been scribbling on a sheet of paper at the station. "Thanks, gotta run." He hung up the phone and walked past the nurse, checking her ID as he strode by. Then turned back around. "Can you get me security?"

"Yes, sir." She picked up the phone. "Is there a problem?"

"No, I just need to speak with them, please."

He wouldn't let his guard down again. There were already too many mistakes made. It was his fault.

"Here you are, sir." She offered him the phone.

"This is Major Maddox. I need to speak with the head of your security for the hospital. In person."

JENNA

10:08 a.m.

A short tap on the door put Jenna's senses on high alert. She glanced at Anesia. Her friend hurried to intercept their visitor.

"Mrs. Gray?"

Anesia allowed the security guard to enter.

"Major Maddox has alerted us to your situation. He asked me to guard your door until he returns."

"Okay." Jenna's heart hammered in her chest. "Y-yes. Thank you."

The man stepped back into the hallway and shut the door.

Anesia crossed her arms over her chest as she approached the hospital bed. "He must care for you a great deal."

Jenna's head snapped to attention. "What do you mean?"

"This Cole . . . I've seen how he looks at you. And you him."

"Oh, that. I don't know what to think. Or what to feel."

"He's trying to protect you, that much I can see. He seems honorable. But I sense deep pain in him."

"I believe he *is* honorable. But the circumstances surrounding this . . . this mess . . . have confused me more than once. And I'm scared." She leaned down to kiss Andie's head. Her daughter hadn't spoken since she explained about Marc.

"I must admit this is more than I expected. But don't worry, it'll all work out. Fear can sometimes help us to reach deep inside and find we've got more guts than we thought."

Jenna smiled and shook her head. "You, my friend, make me laugh. Reminds me of camping in the Arrigetch Peaks when those *sos* cubs wandered in to check out our food. You had no fear. Not even when the mama bear came at you."

Anesia chuckled. "Those cubs were precious. I just wanted a closer picture."

"We've been around bear all our lives, but that grizzly put the fear of God in me!"

"See? Exactly."

"Point taken." She eyed her friend. "In all seriousness, thanks for coming."

"You're welcome."

All banter was gone. "Since Marc died . . . well—"

"Hush. I know."

"Auntie Jenna?" Zoya laid a hand on her arm.

"Yes?"

"I get scared every time we get ready for a new race. But Andie always comes over and prays with me, then the fear is gone."

"You know what?" She squeezed her daughter in her arms, and grabbed Zoya's hand. "You're right. Time we handed this over."

COLE

11:01 a.m.

His long legs ate up the corridors of the hospital. Searching for a way to escape his anger and uproar of emotions, he continued to stalk the hallways. Why did he have to go and get attached? His carefully guarded façade had served him quite well all these years. Stupid. Stupid. Stupid.

What he really needed was a good, long run. But he couldn't leave the hospital right now. The girls still needed protection. But could he even face them right now? Andie's face had said it all. He'd broken her trust. Shattered her sweet spirit.

It was all his fault.

And Jenna. She would probably never speak to him again. Not after he'd kept the truth from her all that time. He deserved to be punished. Banished from them. Just rip his heart out now. He could take it. At least then the pain would be bearable.

He wandered for several minutes until his feet brought him to a door with a cross beside it. Before he could argue with himself, he walked into the quiet chapel.

CHAPTER TWENTY-FIVE

COLE
April 12
Providence Hospital
Anchorage, Alaska
11:48 a.m.

The plush carpet absorbed the sound of his steps. Feeling drawn to the front—like a magnet pulled him—Cole strode to the altar. The simple furnishings were draped with a purple tablecloth, flames from candles put off a soft, glowing light. Everything seemed to exude hope. That all would be okay. That blind trust was the answer.

He shook his head. How? He was used to control. Plans. Missions. Planting his hands on his hips, he stared at a statue of Jesus. "Who are You?"

"You need anything, son?"

Cole snapped his attention to the voice behind him.

"Can I help?" A man dressed in slacks and golf shirt approached, a small leather book in his left hand.

Turning his attention back to the statue, he pulled his thoughts together. "I don't think so."

"I'm a chaplain. Scott Murphy." The man nudged Cole's elbow with his hand. "Would you like to talk about it?"

He turned around and gripped the man's hand. What could it hurt? Maybe Andie and Jenna's God had heard his question and sent this guy.

Yeah, right.

Cole sat down and rested his elbows on his knees. The chaplain just sat beside him and waited. Didn't say a word.

Guess I asked for it. He glanced up at the ceiling. If God was orchestrating this, maybe he should pay attention. Maybe. "I've never had much use for God. In fact, I've been pretty mad at Him for a long time."

"All right. So what brought you in here today?"

"A twelve-year-old girl whose faith is so real, I feel like I could reach out and touch it."

The guy laughed. "Don't we wish we all had faith like that."

"I wish it were that easy." Sarcasm came without effort at this point.

"And you think it's not?" The chaplain wasn't accusatory, just to the point.

"I don't know, sir. How can anything be easy?"

"Call me Scott. And that's the beauty of it. It really is that easy. *We* are the ones who make it complicated."

Cole chewed on that one for a few minutes. He often longed for the same hope and joy that Andie portrayed. But it was more comfortable when she'd been mad at him, because then he didn't have to care and he deserved the anger. He didn't deserve hope or joy or love. Not after all he'd done.

"Faith isn't seeing or doing, planning or achieving. It's believing. Plain and simple."

"But I've lost so much, how can I reconcile the fact that God made so many terrible things happen?"

Scott gripped the book with both hands. "You really believe that? That God *made* all the bad things in your life happen? Sounds to me like you want someone to blame."

Irritation surged, but then faded. Okay, so maybe the guy was right. But shouldn't he be allowed to blame someone? "And I'm sure you're going to sit there and tell me that God is all love and happiness? How can I justify that when He took away everyone I loved?"

"If you're so sure about who God is, and what I'm going to say, then why are you here? Why are you so angry?" Scott leaned back in his chair, looking like he was settling in for a casual conversation.

The man's calm exterior rattled Cole. This chaplain wasn't pulling any punches, but he spoke with kindness. And truth. Cole clenched his fists, wanting to run the man over with his anger, but found himself spilling his guts instead. "Because I want what that little girl has, but I can't get past the fact God took my wife and daughter away from me. Even if I deserved that punishment, *they* didn't deserve to die."

"Ah, so now we're getting to the crux of the matter."

"Yeah, God killed my family." He couldn't help the bitterness spewing out of his mouth.

"No. You feel guilty. And to cover up the pain, you're blaming God."

"What?" Cole jerked his head around to the man, barely restraining himself from planting a fist square on the good chaplain's nose.

Scott just sat there, looking calm and collected. "You're contradicting yourself." He leaned forward. "God's an easy target. On one hand, you don't want to believe in Him or admit that there is a Creator, a Higher Power, because then you'd realize there's Someone bigger than yourself. On the other hand, when things go wrong, it's easier to blame it all on Someone you can't see. Someone you're *then* willing to say is all-powerful and all-controlling as long as you can say *He* caused everything bad that happened. 'Cause then, you're not responsible for your actions. In essence, you're saying *no one* is responsible for his or her actions. And that way you don't have to look inside yourself for the *real* source of your pain."

Cole turned away and leaned his arms on the altar. Was that what he'd done? "So you're saying I'm selfish?"

"We all are." Scott sighed. "And we all need a Savior. Even you. Not a god of convenience. A God of truth and love."

Cole wanted to accept what the man was saying, but it was easier to stay angry at God. And himself.

"You'll never have the peace you're so desperately searching for until you trust in Him." The chaplain's BlackBerry chimed. He pulled it out of the holster on his hip and checked the screen. "I'm sorry, son. I need to go." He reached into his back pocket and then handed Cole a card. "Here's my number in case you want to talk."

Cole nodded.

Scott Murphy walked out the door, leaving Cole alone with his thoughts. As he sat back down, he flipped the card over and over in his hands.

No. He couldn't have what Andie and Jenna had. Peace belonged to people like them. Good people. Sweet, loving people. But for him?

Not in a million years.

ANDIE

12:32 p.m.

"Auntie Anesia?" My voice cracked.

God, please help me. Please let Cole forgive me for what I've done. Please help me to forgive myself.

"Yes, *Syats'ae*?"

I smiled. I loved her special name for me. It helped ease my swirly stomach.

I took a deep breath, like that would make all of the tension inside disappear. *Here it goes.* "Will you and Zoya help me find Cole? I have some apologies to make."

That was the hard part. Now I just have to ask him to forgive me, and not cry when he tells me he can never forgive a bad, stubborn, and angry kid like me. Yeah . . . it'll be easy. Piece of cake.

Oh! Who am I kidding?

Zoya grabbed my hand, her gaze shifting to Auntie. "Can we?"

Auntie Anesia turned to Mom.

"Andie . . . are you sure you have enough strength?" Her eyes held worry, but conveyed that she understood.

I sighed. "I really need to see Cole. Will you help me?"

Mom and Auntie shared a look.

"Okay, Andie, but I'm going to get a wheelchair. I don't want you walking around and I'm sure the doctor would agree. I think I know where Cole went. Hopefully we won't be out for long."

"Why don't you take the guard?" Mom gave Auntie another look.

"Don't worry, girl. I'm armed." Auntie winked at me, then turned back to Mom. "Besides, you need him. I have a feeling I know what Andie needs to do. Trust me."

She came back with a wheelchair and helped me get into it. It was fun avoiding the IV pole and trying not to knock it over.

Let the games begin.

As we headed out the door I looked back at Mom. I could tell she was worried about us going out without protection, but then again Auntie Anesia had fought off more than one thug. I bet she still had her Maglite in that humongous purse of hers. She always did. We would be safe. Nobody could get past Auntie Anesia.

Zoya and Auntie seemed to know where they were going.

I didn't.

In fact, I wasn't sure if I really wanted to know.

We passed rooms, rooms, rooms, and more rooms. Doors, doors, doors, and more doors. Lobbies and desks. I was getting more fidgety by the minute. *Will he accept my apology?*

As we walked through a tunnel, we passed two doors. The door of "Turn Around" and the door of "Keep Going." I was leaning toward the door of Turn Around.

Well, I guess he's not here. Time to go back!

"Here we are."

Oh, snap!

Wait . . . what? I stared at the little wooden plate hanging on the wall. "The chapel? You must be thinking of the wrong guy, Cole wouldn't go to the chapel."

Would he?

Auntie nodded. "I saw him walk in here earlier. Let's go."

Go Back? Great idea!

Auntie opened the door and Zoya wheeled me in.

Okay, never mind then.

Someone sat in the front pew. Broad shoulders . . . brown hair. *Cole.*

I tried to swallow back my fear. It didn't work. "Zoya?"

"Yeah?"

"I'm gonna go on alone. Will you guys wait here in the back for me? This will only take . . ." *fifty years.* "A little while. I'll be right back." I wheeled up the center aisle.

Lord, help me!

Cole sat at the end of the pew with his elbows on his knees and his head in his hands. He didn't seem to see me as I scooted up beside him.

"Cole? I'm sorry. Really sorry."

Cole's head jerked up. His eyes settled on me. "Squirt—"

"I didn't mean what I said about you being a monster and stuff. Honest. I'm just . . ." My voice choked. "I'm *so* sorry."

"Andie, it's okay." He shook his head and looked forward. "You had a right to say what you did."

"No I didn't! I—"

"Listen, I'm sorry you had to hear what I said about your dad."

"Mom explained to me what happened."

"I knew she would. But I'm still sorry."

"You shouldn't be the sorry one."

"Yes, Andie. I should."

"No, I should've *never, ever, ever* said and thought those things about you. Cole"—I choked again—"I love you. I'm really sorry for what I did. Please, forgive me." I started fidgeting. *Please . . .*

"Andie, I appreciate all that you've said but . . ."

I stared into his dark brown eyes. What was he not telling me? "But?"

"It's not you I can't forgive. It's me."

LEAPER

April 12
Fairbanks, Alaska
2:30 p.m.

"So, please explain to me how they are all alive and in the hospital, when you told me they were eliminated?" Viper's voice was calm but hatred spilled out.

Leaper clenched and unclenched his fists to calm his racing heart. Why he decided this meeting would be better in person, he wasn't sure. "I thought they were dead."

"Well, obviously, you were wrong."

"Yes, sir."

"Do you have any idea what kind of difficulty this now presents?"

"Yes—"

"The press is having a field day with the 'little girl who feels no pain' and her poor widowed mother. Their deaths were supposed to be a tragic accident!" Viper's fist slammed into the side of a bookcase.

Leaper watched the back of his superior as glass and books tumbled to the floor. The rigid set of the man's shoulders. The sheer power emanating from him. There was no way out.

"You guaranteed once Gray was out of the way you could acquire AMI. You also guaranteed you'd have it in time for our next deadline."

"I'm sorry, sir."

"And when I planned a way to speed up your search—a nice, convenient way to rid ourselves of Gray's family—you botched that as well!"

Leaper stared at his one-time friend. Greed and the hunger for power had tainted him. His eyes were dark, almost lifeless. Was this where he was headed as well?

"Your time's up. So I suggest you go to the hospital and take care of our problems."

"Sir?"

Those cold, dead eyes drilled holes into his. "Kill them. All of them."

JENNA

April 12
Providence Hospital
Anchorage, Alaska
5:22 p.m.

Her heart ached. How could Marc have done all this and she knew nothing about it? Is that why Cole didn't trust her? Did he think she knew all this time?

Jenna shook her head. There wasn't time for those thoughts. Someone wanted them dead and she needed to protect Andie. But how? She didn't even know who was after them. Or what, exactly, they were after. AMI, yes, but what *was* AMI?

Jenna pressed her lips together. She had to find out. She had to understand it all. Because she was starting to think that maybe . . . just maybe . . .

The only way to protect Andie would be to find AMI first.

Leaning her head back, she wondered how to accomplish that feat. Cole would help. He would protect.

No.

Her heart had attached itself to Cole, but she wasn't sure she wanted to trust him right now. And his anger at God had been clear. Jenna knew the only way they'd survive was by God's grace.

Moving her leg, she winced. The pain had lessened, but the tight pull of the stitches began to itch. Her fever had finally receded—which made Doctor Baker as happy as it did her—but she was so tired. And weak.

Flipping through the channels on the TV, she searched for the news—and her jaw dropped as a picture of her family flashed up on the screen. Jenna turned up the volume.

"Mrs. Tikaani-Gray and her daughter are still being treated at Providence Hospital in Anchorage. Authorities released earlier today that the family was returning from a post-op appointment in Philadelphia—

where twelve-year-old Andrea underwent brain decompression surgery a year ago—when their plane crashed into 17,000-foot Sultana. Andrea's story has been followed by Alaskans for several years as the child has a rare condition . . ."

Jenna flipped to another news station. A picture of Andie stared back at her.

"*The media has kept an eye on this 'little girl who feels no pain' ever since learning about her. But even more heartache and tragedy surrounded this family. Even as this little girl underwent brain surgery, her father, Marcus Gray, a highly decorated Army veteran, was killed in a suspicious accident. Authorities are not releasing details, but we have confirmed that the plane's crash in Denali National Park was not an accident. Park rangers and NTSB will continue in their quest for answers. Back to you, Rob.*"

She punched off the television. Suspicious accident? No one ever said Marc's death was anything more than that—an *accident.* Until Cole. So how did the press get hold of that information? Had she trusted—even given her heart—to the wrong man? Again?

What was going on?

"We're back!" Anesia wheeled Andie into the room. Andie looked up, and Jenna couldn't miss the sadness in those blue eyes. Now was probably not the time to ask about her chat with Cole.

"Hi, Mom."

"Hey, there's my girl." She pasted on a smile and held out her arms for a hug. Visions from her past floated through her mind. Marc with Andie on his shoulders. Marc teaching Andie how to ride a bike. Marc gazing into her eyes on their anniversary . . .

Too many sweet memories to just blot out because of her husband's wrongdoing. Jenna fiddled with the blanket on the bed. Hospitals didn't rank high on her list of favorite places, and having to deal with all this junk on top of being here was beginning to drive her mad. "I want to go home."

"Me too, Mom." Her daughter climbed back into her hospital bed, the wrap on her ankle slowing her down as she fiddled with the IV tubing. "How long will we have to stay here?"

"I don't know. But I plan on asking Dr. Baker when he comes by." Jenna forced her voice to be upbeat. "Things will be back to normal before you know it."

Andie began to cry. "No, they won't, Mom. Not ever."

Jenna opened her mouth to disagree, to offer encouragement. But nothing came out. Because when it came right down to it, her daughter was right. Things would never be normal again.

Not until they found AMI—and got it out of their lives.

CHAPTER TWENTY-SIX

COLE

April 12
Providence Hospital
Anchorage, Alaska
5:45 p.m.

Standing outside the half-open door to Jenna and Andie's hospital room, he couldn't help but overhear Andie's words. They were like a kick to his kidneys.

But she was right.

Things would never be the same for the Tikaani-Gray girls.

Cole took a deep breath and prepared his mind for the task ahead. He cared. A lot more than he ever imagined. But now was not the time to think about feelings. Now was the time to focus on keeping them alive.

With a gentle tap on the door, he pushed it open and walked in.

"Hey, Cole." Andie greeted him, tears still glistening on her cheeks.

He closed the door with a soft click. "Hey, Einstein." He nodded at the others. "Jenna, Anesia. Where's Zoya?"

"She's getting me some M&Ms," Andie said. "They cheer me up."

If only M&Ms could cure every other obstacle that stood in their way. "Well, you might just have to share them with me."

The air around him was thick and heavy, like it held the weight of all their troubles.

Jenna fidgeted, but looked him in the eye. "I'm beginning to know that look on your face, Mr. Maddox. You have something you need to say to us, don't you?"

He watched Anesia sit on the bed next to Andie. "Jenna, we need a plan. To be prepared. I've called in a favor from a friend of mine. We'll have additional protection soon, but there's still a lot to be covered."

Jenna nodded. "Okay. What do we need to do?"

Her eyes were guarded . . . So they both were pulling back. Fine. "We need different cell phones. Disposable ones." He turned to Anesia. "Do you think you could handle that? We all need numbers no one knows about. That way we can communicate without worrying about anyone listening in. One for each of us, you"—he nodded at Anesia—"Zoya, Jenna, Andie, and me."

Anesia's dark eyes held his gaze, a new flicker of trust flashed at him. "Sure. I can do that. I assume you want them registered to a different name?"

Cole had underestimated these women. "Yes, that would be safest."

"I've got a P.O. Box I can register as the billing address," Anesia added.

"Good. And you mentioned you have dogs with you?"

"Yes. The girls' huskies. They're very protective."

"Perfect. We'll want them with us at all times once we leave the hospital. Even before, if I can convince the hospital admin."

Jenna raised a hand. "What exactly are you planning to do? Andie and I are both a little incapacitated."

Cole wanted to take her in his arms, to cradle her close and tell her she didn't need to be afraid. Didn't need to worry. About anything. The longing in his gut so intense, he wanted to kiss her breathless. But judging by the expression on her face, such action or words wouldn't be welcomed at the moment. "We've got to find AMI and get it into the right hands. That's the only way you'll ever be safe."

Something flickered in Jenna's eyes. A look of . . . what? Surprise? Agreement?

"What about the people who are after it?"

"They're getting desperate. The fact that they tried to eliminate you proves that. They figured if they got rid of you and no one knew for a while, they could find AMI before the government knew what was happening. Remember, this is all about money. And power."

Anesia hopped off Andie's bed and walked over to Cole. "So that's why I kept finding footprints around Jenna's property?"

Cole tensed. "Did you see anyone?"

"I thought I did, but I wasn't sure. But the dogs got riled up every time we went over there, which tells me someone they didn't recognize was around." Anesia reached for Jenna's hand.

He walked over to the window again. So they'd been at Jenna's house. They'd probably been inside, searched everywhere. But they still hadn't found AMI. So it wasn't in the house . . .

He spoke to the window, not wanting to look at the terrified, but brave faces, watching him. "At least their plan backfired. Not only did we survive, but the media is involved now."

"You're saying that's a good thing?"

At Jenna's question, he turned to face them. "Absolutely. That brings attention to you. If anything happens to you two now, it won't be viewed as an accident. They won't want the heat an investigation would bring."

"So what do we do now?"

Jenna sounded so weary. And frightened. He studied the faces before him. Jenna's eyes pleaded with him. Anesia's held a healthy respect for the danger they were in. Andie's pooled with tears. No kid should ever have to deal with such horrors.

"I told you we were all experts in our fields. We could take on the most difficult and specialized of missions. Leaper was a paratrooper. He took on some of the riskiest jumps I've ever seen. Shadow was trained in infiltration. The guy was invisible; he could appear and disappear without anyone knowing he'd ever been there. Viper, he was a sniper. He'd take out enemies before they knew what hit 'em, Hacker—Marcus—he could do anything with computers."

"What about you, Cole?" Anesia fidgeted with the blanket on Jenna's bed.

"Explosives expert."

"And? What exactly did you blow up?"

He ignored the question. "As the years went on and Viper decided to branch out, he and Marc came up with some brilliant weapons and defense programs. Viper had the vision, Marc had the know-how to make it happen. Eventually, Viper decided it was smarter to sell those weapons, rather than us going out into the field risking our necks for who-knows-what."

Jenna piped up. "Is that when you confronted Marc?"

"No. At that point, I didn't know any of this. We were soldiers. We did as we were told. We still thought we were on the right side. The good guys. It took a lot more to get me to the point where I confronted Marc." He looked into her eyes, longing for her to believe him. To understand him. "Anyway, a lot of other stuff happened and then Marc seemed completely caught up in this new weapon he envisioned. The program and prototype that has now put us all in danger."

"Amy." Anesia and Jenna voiced at the same time.

"AMI—*A-M-I.* It stands for Advanced Missile Interceptor. In testing it had a 99.7 percent accuracy. But what's so unique about AMI is that Marc programmed it to be a weapon as well. The AMI will target an enemy missile to intercept, and then milliseconds before destroying the incoming missile, it can shoot up to three attack missiles to follow the trajectory—the trail—of the enemy missile. That then destroys the missile's point of origin and everything around it."

Jenna gasped. *"That's* what Marc developed?"

"Yes. It was ingenious."

"And it got him killed." Jenna looked down at the blanket on her bed.

"Sounds dangerous to me." They looked at Anesia, and she crossed her arms. "It could be used against the U.S."

So Jenna's friend was as sharp as she was. "Exactly." Cole looked from Jenna to Anesia, and then dared a glance at Andie. "But like I said, Marc was trying to do the right thing at the end. He may have gotten caught up in the ugliness, but in the end, he died trying to make up for what he'd done wrong."

"Cole?" Fear and confusion ruled Andie's face. "Does this have anything to do with North Korea?"

CHAPTER TWENTY-SEVEN

JENNA
April 12
Providence Hospital
Anchorage, Alaska
8:15 p.m.

Did she just hear her daughter correctly? Why on earth would Andie ask about North Korea?

Cole interrupted her thoughts. "Andie, how do you know about that?"

Her eyes glistened, and then tears slid down her cheeks. She bit her lip. "I overheard a conversation a long time ago. I needed Daddy to fix my bike tire, and when I found him he was on the phone. When I asked him about it, he made me promise not to ever tell anyone what I heard."

Jenna's heartbeat raced. Marc had done that to his little girl? She reached across the room toward Andie. "Oh, baby, come here."

Anesia helped her child from the hospital bed and up into Jenna's. Sobs shook Andie's frame and her tears soaked Jenna's gown.

"I'm so sorry." Andie wiped her eyes with the back of her hand. "I'm sorry I kept it from you, and I'm sorry I broke my promise to Daddy. I'm just so sorry . . ."

Jenna placed her hands on either side of Andie's face. "Andrea Nicole, this is not your fault! And don't you blame yourself for any of it. Daddy wasn't right to be doing what he did, and he never should've asked you to promise something like that."

Her daughter just nodded then threw her arms around Jenna.

Zoya and the security guard entered the room just then, bearing a huge bag of M&Ms. Zoya took in the expressions in the room as she glanced from one face to another. Anesia went over and pulled her close.

Just then, Jenna's favorite nurse came in holding little medicine cups. Petite as Jenna, with a smile as big as Alaska. "All right, you two. Here's your evening medication. This round will probably make you sleepy, but Doc says you need sleep anyway." Handing a cup of water to each of her patients, she waited until they took their pills, and then disposed of the trash.

"Thank you, Tammy." Jenna returned the smile. "I can't tell you how much I appreciate everything you've done for us."

"Aw, thanks, hon. You guys are awesome. I'll see ya tomorrow." And with a wave, she was off.

"Cole?" Jenna stroked Andie's hair. "I think we've probably hit our limit for today. The best cure for now is sleep."

He nodded. "You're right. Why don't we all get some rest."

Anesia came over and kissed Jenna on top of her head. "Okay, my friend. Zoya and I will head to our hotel. I'll take care of the cell phones first thing in the morning."

"Mom? Can I just stay here with Andie?"

"Yeah, Auntie Anesia, there's plenty of room in that bed and it would help me feel safer."

Jenna chuckled at the manipulative powers of the two girls and nodded at her friend. The stress of everything completely overwhelmed her body. Andie needed Zoya.

Anesia turned to Cole. "The guard is staying?"

"Yes, ma'am. And so am I."

"Okay then." Anesia gave them a tight smile. "I'll be here as soon as I can in the morning." She turned to kiss her daughter good night, then sent a wave to Jenna and left the room.

Cole pulled the reclining chair closer to the door and hunkered his long frame down into the vinyl cushions.

"Good night, Cole," Jenna whispered. The medicine was already taking effect. Drowsiness swept over her like a warm blanket.

"'Night, Jenna." He fluffed a pillow with his fist.

Andie hugged her once more and then hobbled over to her own bed, climbing in and adjusting her IV tubing to make room for Zoya. Jenna closed her eyes to the sweet sound of the girls' whispering voices. She prayed for rest and healing—and safety.

Several minutes passed and then Cole's soft snores permeated the room. Once that man decided to sleep, he slept. Good grief, if only she could turn off her mind that easily.

Shifting to a more comfortable position, she listened to the girls whisper more good nights to each other. All was quiet for a few seconds, and then Zoya's whisper floated over to Jenna.

"Did you tell them about that guy?"

Jenna frowned. Guy? What guy?

Andie's drowsy reply didn't help. "Um, no. I forgot about it. Prob'ly no big deal. We'll tell 'em tomorrow."

As the girls settled in again, Jenna strained to stay awake so she could hear if they said anything else. But her thoughts began to jumble all together as sleep made its claim on her body. With one last attempt at coherency, she prayed.

Please, Lord. Let it be nothing . . .

ANDIE

April 13
Providence Hospital
Anchorage, Alaska
6:52 a.m.

The sun peeked over the mountains. Pink, orange, and yellow blended together in perfect color harmony. Zoya sat at the end of the bed as we watched the sunrise together.

"It's so pretty." Zoya's quiet whisper was barely audible.

I nodded, unable to speak as the beauty of the sunrise and the pain of my mistakes stabbed my heart.

Zoya turned to me and grabbed my hand. "So, I hope I'm not being weird or anything, but aren't you . . . ya know, mad at your dad and Cole?"

I sighed. *Of course I am.* Tears threatened to escape from my eyes. *Don't dwell on the past, Andie.* I didn't know if I was really mad or just kinda mad. After my episode of exploding thoughts with Dad and exploding actions with Cole, I wasn't quite sure where my emotions stood.

Cole saying that he couldn't forgive himself hurt. It didn't make sense to me why he couldn't.

We were all safe, he'd done his job.

Was he worried about Mom? If so, why? Was Mom getting worse? I glanced over at her bed. She slept soundly. *No, she couldn't be.* The doc said she was doing fine. Dr. Baker would tell me if something was wrong with Mom. He was always honest with us.

I shook my head, trying to rid it of all the confusion. *I apologized to Cole and Daddy. I know I'm forgiven, so why can't I move on?*

God had forgiven me and He loved me. I didn't know if I was capable of forgiving Cole and my dad like God did, but I was determined to try.

Zoya waved her other hand in front of my face. "Helloooo? Anybody home? Did you hear me?"

"Oops, sorry. I was thinking about your question." A heavy sigh escaped. "You know, God forgave us for our sins, so why can't I forgive them?" I looked over at Cole's sleeping, snoring form. "I mean . . . let's just say that Cole was the one who killed Dad, okay? Wouldn't God want me to minister to him and to forgive him so that he would have a chance at eternity? I mean, if I miss the chance to minister to anyone, not just good people, isn't it just like murdering them myself? Because I missed the chance to tell them about Christ, they may not ever hear about Jesus and then have to spend eternity down there." I pointed to the floor. "And, that's the last thing I want. For Cole and *everybody* else."

Zoya thought about what I'd said. "I like the way you think. Besides, the only way other people are going to meet Jesus is if we're willing to show them how amazing He is, right?"

"Right." My heart pounded in my chest. *This doesn't only mean Cole. We need to be an example to everybody.*

"And that means laying down our pride and trusting God to put the people He wants in our path. And to trust them."

My face burned. "All right, I get your point."

Zoya grabbed my hand. "I didn't mean it like that."

"I know. I guess that's just how God speaks through us." *Okay God, I promise to never doubt Your choices again. Please help Cole. And* . . . I gulped and squeezed my eyes shut. *Okay. Please help me to forgive those who killed Daddy. And to minister to them.*

I turned away from the mountains and the sunset with a sigh. "Thanks for sticking with me, Zoya. I don't know what I would do without you. Especially now that we know all the secrets." Well, I hope we know them all.

"Aw, no problem. You're my BFF, I would never leave ya. You know that."

I nodded. "Thanks."

"Now"—Zoya's smile grew—"How about a game of I-Spy?"

CHAPTER TWENTY-EIGHT

JENNA

April 13
Providence Hospital
Anchorage, Alaska
7:27 a.m.

A knock sounded at the door and Dr. Baker walked in.

"Good morning, Jenna."

The man was obviously a morning person. No one should be that chipper this early. "Morning, Doctor."

"Things seem calmer in here today. How are we doing?"

"Yesterday was too long. I'm glad it's over. And I'm tired." Her words were clipped.

"Did you sleep?"

"The first couple of hours, yes. That medicine knocked me out. But after that? Not that great. Especially when people have to keep poking and prodding all night long."

"Ah, so that's why you're grumpy?" The doctor's eyes twinkled.

Cole laughed from across the room.

Jenna crossed her arms over her chest. "I am *not* grumpy."

"Right, Mom." Andie threw in from her bed. "Just like the sky isn't blue."

"Oh, good grief. Just because I'm not a morning person, doesn't mean I'm grumpy." She worked to stretch the kinks out of her shoulders.

Thankfully, the doctor changed the subject. "Don't forget our agreement, Jenna. I'll be bringing in the doctor for the psych consult in a little bit." He patted her arm. "After you eat breakfast. Maybe a little food in your stomach will chase the grumpies away." With that, the doctor moved away with a swift step.

"Oh yeah? Well maybe I just won't agree to your psych consult." She didn't want to be the problem child, but seriously? They were taking this grumpy thing way too far.

Dr. Baker laughed. "Jenna, you forget. I've known you a long time. And if you want me to allow those mangy mutts anywhere near your daughter"—he paused for effect—"for *therapy*, you better be cooperative."

"Dasha!" Andie squirmed in her bed. "Really, Dr. Baker? I can see her?"

"If you can get your mom to cooperate."

"Oh. Good. Grief!" Jenna lifted her pillow from behind her head and smashed it over her face so she could let out a scream. They were all being impossible today.

"All right, all right. I think she's had enough." Cole's teasing voice broke through the muffler of pillow.

Jenna lowered the pillow and frowned.

Dr. Baker walked back over with a sheepish grin on his face. "Sorry, Jenna. Just trying to lighten the mood." Switching back into full doctor mode, the doctor walked over to Andie's bed. "So, let's check you two out this morning. How are you today?"

"Just fine, Dr. Baker." Andie beamed up at him. "Especially if you let me see Dasha."

"Well, now. That's good to hear. I see that your numbers are good, your temp is normal, and your lungs are clear." Pages flipped on the chart as he read through all the notes. The glasses on the end of his nose slid a little further as he looked from mother to daughter. "We need to talk about your ankle. The damage is probably from walking on it when you didn't know it was injured. But that's okay. It will heal." A bony finger pointed at Andie. "But you must keep it wrapped for now, and then you'll have to wear an air cast to keep it stable until it's completely healed. Understood?"

"Yes, sir," Andie replied.

"Now explain to me how it felt."

"Felt?" Andie laughed. "That's a good one, Doc."

"Seriously, Andie. What was it like? Can you describe it? Did you know you were hurt when you fell?"

"Well, when I fell down, it was in the middle of a blizzard and pretty cold. I can't say that I felt anything other than my ankle turning the wrong direction. After that, I noticed it didn't move the same way and seemed to buckle under me, you know, like it wasn't properly attached." Her nervous giggle made the doctor pause.

"Okay. But no pain?"

"I can't really say pain. It was uncomfortable, especially when my boots got tight."

"Can you describe anything else?"

"Um . . . no . . . not really. I'm sorry."

The doctor patted her knee. "That's all right. Thanks for trying, Andie."

His attention swung back to Jenna. "Now you, young lady. You need more rest. The fluids have done you good, as well as the antibiotics. But that infection needs to be completely knocked out of the park before I can allow you to leave."

"When do you think that will be?" At least in Alaska they had doctors who spoke in normal language. Every time they had gone somewhere else for treatment, she'd had to request the doctors to speak in layman's terms. Here, in Anchorage, Dr. Baker was the best. She always knew he would be up front with her.

"Possibly another day or two. We'll just have to see. Your leg was pretty nasty when you arrived. We pulled metal and glass out of it during surgery, so you must realize you were lucky. We'll also need to discuss Andie's physical therapy before you go. We want to make sure that ankle heals as good as new."

"Yes, Doctor."

Another knock sounded at the door and a nurse strode in with their breakfast.

Cole nodded at the petite blonde and grabbed one of the trays, pretending to be chivalrous.

But Jenna knew better. He hadn't allowed them to eat any hospital food. After the nurse scooted out with a giant grin for Cole, and Dr. Baker left with the promise to return shortly, Jenna looked at her handsome protector. "So, you're not going to let us eat, are you?"

His chuckle reverberated in the room. "Nope. I asked Anesia to bring some breakfast when she came. I just don't want to take the risk that anyone else has touched that food."

Andie pulled out the M&Ms. "I'm good. I've got these."

Jenna rolled her eyes. She was hungry. Anesia better hurry.

A moment later, Anesia stepped into the room, white paper bags clutched in her hands. "Who's hungry?"

"Oh, you didn't." Jenna sat up straighter in bed.

"Oh, yes, I did."

The smell wafted across the room and Jenna sighed. "My favorite."

Cole looked just a tad bit puzzled. "What's your favorite?"

Anesia placed a bag in front of Jenna and answered for her. "A Crabby Omelet."

His laughter rang out. "Are you serious?" Turning to Jenna, he added, "How appropriate."

The contents of her bag now safe on her tray, Jenna balled up the bag and threw it at him.

"Here's a Polar Bear Breakfast for Andie." Anesia kissed the top of Andie's head and continued, "Tundra Scramble for Zoya." She kissed the top of Zoya's head, then headed toward Cole. "And for you? Heart Attack on a Plate. Or should I say, in a bag?"

Jenna laughed at Cole's face when Anesia plopped the bag in front of him. "Anesia, you're awesome. Thanks for going to Snow City Café for all this."

"You are most welcome. I called the manager last night and put our order in. You know how crazy-busy that place is. After a little explanation, and reminding him about last time we were there," Anesia laughed, "he said he'd love to help his 'favorite' customer."

It felt so good to laugh along with her friend. Anesia knew her so well. Food from Snow City Café was the best prescription she could have gotten this morning.

Jenna couldn't stay away from the famous café. Let her be within a hundred miles of Anchorage, and she'd make her way there. Last time, she'd bought breakfast for all the sprint-dog racers from Anesia's kennel. She'd spent a small fortune, while sled-dog trucks lined the streets and hundreds of dogs yapped.

She'd had a blast.

Anesia took a deep whiff as she opened her own bag. "I have to wait an hour for the phones, but figured you all needed some food before I run back out."

Cole eyed his food and looked at Anesia's. "So what is yours? It looks a lot like mine."

"Veggie Bypass."

As their laughter continued, Jenna wanted to capture the moment in a bottle. If only this fun, normal moment could continue.

Without thoughts of plane crashes, missiles, or North Korea.

No one after them.

Everyone safe.

But no. That was just a dream. A dream that might never come true.

"Jenna?" Cole had snuck up on her when she wasn't looking. "Aren't you going to eat?"

Pasting a smile on her face, she took a bite. The omelet melted in her mouth and she savored the flavors of avocado, swiss cheese, green onions, and crab. Closing her eyes, she allowed her mind to relax for a moment. Plenty of time to worry about what would happen next.

Cole patted her shoulder. "Good girl."

"I'm not a dog, Cole." The omelet might be yummy, but it didn't keep her from snapping at him.

"I know." He walked away, putting a little distance between them. "Even though you do have a pretty serious bite."

Andie covered her mouth and laughed, almost choking on her food. "Sorry, Mom. You have to admit, that was pretty funny."

"I don't have to admit anything, young lady." She winked at Andie. "Other than the fact that this omelet is super-fantabulous." Jenna wiggled her eyebrows.

Everyone laughed with her, as a knock sounded at the door.

In walked Dr. Baker with a tall, severe woman. "Well now, this looks like fun. Anyone bring me anything?"

The woman beside him frowned and looked at him as if he'd just announced she'd be performing as a clown next. Highly doubtful the woman could even crack a smile.

"I'll share with you, Dr. Baker, if you want." Andie held up her plate of goodies. "I even have M&Ms."

"Well, now, I might just have to take you up on that." The doctor smiled at Andie, then looked to his companion. "May I introduce Dr. Fullerton? She's here for the psych consult."

"Great," Jenna mumbled under her breath. The woman looked like she'd sucked on a few too many lemons.

"Shall we get started?" The woman pushed her glasses up her nose and looked from Jenna to Andie. "I'd like to talk to Andie alone, if you don't mind."

"I *do* mind. You may talk to her here. With me." Jenna gave her a look that she hoped was threatening as she shoved another bite of omelet into her mouth.

The lady doctor looked to Dr. Baker. "This is highly unusual."

Dr. Baker chuckled. "You'll find lots of unusual things here in Alaska, Doctor. Remember, this is unofficial and Jenna has also asked me to stay." He looked at Jenna. "Dr. Fullerton has been in New York the past few years. This is her first week in Anchorage. She likes to do things by the book." He shot her a sympathetic look. "Our normal doctor was unavailable."

"Oh." Jenna kept eating.

The flustered doctor straightened her shoulders. "I don't believe my newness to Alaska has any bearing on this situation, Dr. Baker. Might I ask for the rest of this . . . entourage"—she waved at the others in the room—"to leave?"

Cole stepped forward, his solid arms folded across his chest. "Why?"

Her hero. Jenna offered him a smile. "I see no need for that, Doctor."

"All right." With a huff, the doctor approached Andie with her clipboard. "Since you refuse to cooperate with standard protocol, I can be flexible." She straightened her papers and pulled a pen from the pocket of her doctor's coat. "Only since this is *unofficial*." Sarcasm dripped from her words with the pointed look she shot Dr. Baker.

"Andie, I hear things have been pretty traumatic for you lately?" The doctor's voice was smooth as silk.

It was annoying.

"Yes, ma'am. But I've got God, I'm okay." Andie's face beamed.

"Want to tell me about the incident yesterday?"

"Which one?"

The doctor cleared her throat as stifled chuckles rippled through the room. "I wasn't aware there was more than one."

"There's always incidents with me, Doctor. I'm not normal."

Cole, Anesia, Zoya, and Dr. Baker all laughed out loud.

The psych doctor silenced them with a stern look. "Well, how about you talk to me about losing your temper yesterday—how it felt, what set you off, why you felt the need to attack?"

"I don't feel things like you, so *felt* is not an appropriate word to use in your questioning." Andie's huge smile lit up the room as her response evoked a chuckle from Dr. Baker. She was obviously satisfied with her answer, but the new doctor didn't seem to have a sense of humor.

"All right, Andie. What would be an appropriate word?" One look at the doctor proved that she did *not* find this amusing. *And they thought* I *was grumpy!*

"I don't know. I don't feel things."

"Not even emotions?" The doctor caught on.

"Well, of course I feel emotions."

"So, did you feel angry yesterday?" The smooth as silk tone returned.

"Yes, I did."

"Let's talk about that anger. What was it like?"

"Well, for one thing, it wasn't fun. I found out my dad had done some things I didn't like. And for another thing, I was on steroids. Steroids make me emotional and hostile. That's not normal for me either."

Jenna watched her twelve-year-old and nodded her head. *You tell her, sweetie.*

"So you're telling me, you believe you are fine now?" The doctor pointed her pen at Andie.

"Yes, ma'am."

"No more anger?"

"Not really. Nope."

"Very unusual. This will be a good one for the books."

"I don't ever do things like the books say I should." Another nod.

Dr. Baker chuckled again. "Isn't that the truth."

"Excuse me? Would you care to explain, Doctor?" Protocol lady studied him, pen and paper ready.

"Andie's case has never fit any of the medical books or journals. That's what she means. In essence, we try to predict what will happen next—according to the books—and she normally does the opposite." Dr. Baker looked like he was ready to end this.

Jenna wanted to move things along. "Dr. Baker, is this really necessary? Andie is fine."

A knock sounded at the door. The security guard entered. "Hate to disturb you guys, but we've got a Mr. Carmichael here from the NTSB."

The NTSB? Jenna knew the National Transportation Safety Board investigated any plane accidents, but it surprised her they'd come to see them here. In the hospital. She watched Cole shoot a glance to Dr. Baker.

"You know, I think we're done here." Dr. Baker smiled at Jenna. "Let's not waste the good doctor's time."

Dr. Fullerton grimaced. "That's normally *my* call, Doctor."

He patted the woman's shoulder. "I understand how you feel, Doctor. But this was just a test. Not a full-fledged consult." He took her by the elbow, tugging her toward the door, and winked at Andie. "You understand, don't you?"

"But—but I—"

Jenna waved. "Thank you so much for stopping by, Dr. Fullerton."

"You're welcome." The doctor stammered, shaking hands with everyone as Dr. Baker ushered her out of the room.

The door closed, and the girls began to giggle.

"That was too funny! Auntie Jenna, you should've seen your face."

"Yeah, Mom. Your eyes looked like you were gonna shoot fire at her."

Another knock.

Cole moved to the door and escorted another man and a police officer into the room. "Officer. Sir." He shook hands with the men. "Cole Maddox."

"Matt Carmichael, NTSB."

"Officer Lucas, APD."

The NTSB agent approached her bed. "Mrs. Gray, I need to ask you all a few questions."

CHAPTER TWENTY-NINE

COLE
April 13
Providence Hospital
Anchorage, Alaska
11:14 a.m.

Cole walked to Jenna's side. "What is this about, Mr. Carmichael?"

"Please, call me Matt. The NTSB needs to investigate the crash so the debris can be removed from Denali National Park."

"Of course." Jenna nodded. "What do you need to know?"

"Thank you. Officer Lucas is here because of the media and rumors that are going around. The APD would like to stay informed and help where necessary. It also falls under their jurisdiction since we know your plane took off from Anchorage."

Lucas stood against the wall, watching.

"Mrs. Gray, we don't wish to alarm you, but were you aware that your flight plan had been erased?"

Jenna didn't hesitate. "I was not aware at the time, but I've heard about it since then, yes."

"And your pilot was someone you knew and trusted?"

"Up until that day, yes. He'd been a friend of my late husband, and after Marc passed away, I hired Hank to fly my plane for me until I had my pilot's license."

Cole hovered over Jenna while the NTSB proceeded to grill her about the minutes before the crash. He watched her shoulders slump as she relived the experience.

"I must apologize, ma'am, but some things aren't adding up. We flew over the area and couldn't find the plane."

Jenna peered up at Cole, questions in her eyes.

Cole straightened. "Matt, do you mind if I answer this one?"

"Not at all, be my guest."

"An avalanche covered the crash site after a helicopter shot a missile into the plane."

Both officers' eyes widened.

"That's why you can't find it."

ANDIE

11:25 a.m.

I shoved another M&M in my mouth as the investigators closed their notebooks.

"Thank you for your help, Cole." The NTSB guy shook his hand. "We should be able to find the plane with your coordinates." He turned to Mom. "The Talkeetna rangers will fly us in with a law enforcement ranger. We'll investigate the crash, and then we'll need your help removing the crash from the park."

Mom bit her lip. "Thank you."

As the investigator dudes left the room, Dr. Baker walked in with a smile. Cole leaned in and whispered something in his ear.

What?

"Well, let's check that ankle of yours, Andie." Dr. Baker walked over to me and slipped my sock off.

He glanced at Cole, looking . . . apprehensive. Was he concerned I would have another outburst?

Apparently.

"Dr. Baker, want an M&M?" I used my cute voice and the "innocent look."

A smile softened his face. "Sure."

Once finished, he stood up and shook a finger at me. "*Do not* walk on that ankle unless you use the air cast, understand?"

"Yes, sir. Besides"— I giggled and shifted my gaze to Cole— "I don't think Mr. Bodyguard would let me so much as sneeze without him knowing."

Cole winked. "Don't you know it."

"I should go pick up the cell phones now." Auntie Anesia stood and walked toward the door. "Need anything while I'm gone?"

I held up the almost empty bag of M&Ms. "*Please*?" I turned to Mom and did the puppy-dog pout.

"You finished those already?" Cole's exclamation made me laugh.

"It wasn't just me, Zoya helped too."

"Yeah, Andie couldn't eat a whole bag by herself. Well, not normally." Zoya giggled.

"Girl, nothing about me is normal."

"I know. That's why I love you so much." She gave me a sideways hug.

"The M&Ms love me too." I hugged the bag to my chest and gave a dramatic sigh.

"More like your stomach loves the M&Ms." Cole shifted and lifted his right ankle to rest on his left knee. I could tell he was trying not to smile.

"So . . ." This time it was two against one. Zoya joined me in perfect puppy-dog pout harmony.

"Okay, okay. A *small* bag. Like the ones you buy at the cash register." Mom glanced at Auntie Anesia with a "don't-you-dare-spoil-her" glare.

Like she's ever spoiled me and gotten a big bag of my favorite candy. Oh, wait. She had.

Auntie Anesia smiled and left the room with a wave.

"Let's take a look at those stitches now, Andie." Dr. Baker sat back down on the bed. "Lookin' good. Just don't go crashing into any more machinery."

"Aww. Why not?" I smiled as Dr. Baker gave me "the look." "Okay, I won't."

"Good girl."

Mom smiled. "Thank you so much, Dr. Baker."

"Not a problem, Jenna. I'm just glad you're all okay." He stood. "I guess that's all. I'll come and check on you guys again in a little while." He began to walk out, but stopped and turned around. "Girls, I'm so sorry I forgot, but have you told them about that man?"

"What man?" Mom and Cole spoke simultaneously and turned to me.

"Uh . . ." I peeked at Zoya.

"Andie, what man?" Cole stood up and walked over.

He sat down and grabbed my hand, face stern, eyes worried.

"We . . . well, when I got my stitches done this odd man in scrubs, without a name badge or anything, kinda appeared and—"

"He didn't have a badge?"

Before I could answer Mom, Cole jumped in. "What did he say? What did he do to you?" Cole looked *mean*. I'd never seen him so angry.

"He just asked if I was Andie."

"What did he do?"

"Nothing. That's it. He just asked twice if I was Andie. I'm sorry, I forgot to tell you." Why had I forgotten? My gaze shifted to the blankets on my lap. *Did my not telling them put us in more danger?*

"What happened to him?" Cole put a hand on my shoulder and squeezed.

"Dr. Baker walked in and he just . . . vanished."

JENNA
12:30 p.m.

"What do you mean he just vanished? How does someone vanish?" Jenna pushed herself up in the bed. Bile rose in her throat. She looked to Cole. Someone had been close to her daughter. Close enough to do harm. And she hadn't been there to protect her. "What do we do?"

Cole glanced to the doctor, his jaw twitching. "I thought you said someone would be with the girls the whole time."

Regret weighed heavy on Dr. Baker's features. "There *was* someone with them. A nurse. But when I returned, she was gone."

"Can we question the nurse?" Cole looked ready to pounce.

"Let me see if she's here today. If not, I'll contact her. I'm sure she would do anything she could to help." The doctor left the room in a rush.

Jenna forced herself to breathe normally. The weight of what could have happened settled on her chest. A hospital was supposed to be a safe place. Were they in danger even here? How could that be? She shifted in the bed. They had to leave. But where would they go? Fear gripped her heart and threatened to choke her. She gasped for air.

"Jenna!" Cole was by her side in an instant. "Jenna, don't panic."

She gritted her teeth. "I'm not panicking." Another deep breath. "Not yet." *Hold it together. For Andie.* A tentative smile for her daughter. "It just overwhelmed me there for a minute. The danger. It's so real. So . . . close." She shuddered.

"Mom, we're okay. Dr. Baker came in at just the right time. I know God was watching out for us."

Cole laid a hand on Jenna's shoulder. "Andie, do you think you and Zoya would recognize the man if you saw him again?"

The girls exchanged glances and nodded. "Yeah, I'm sure we could."

"Good. And from now on, you won't be left alone. Period." Cole squeezed Jenna's shoulder and sat on the edge of the bed. His words comforted her—almost as much as his presence.

"I can't believe we're not safe here."

"Jenna, I called in some help yesterday, but it took a while to arrange it. I requested men with top clearance, but they were difficult to find on short notice. They should be here soon."

"Not soon enough," she muttered. From Cole's expression, she could see he agreed.

He shifted his gaze to the girls. "I shouldn't have left the room yesterday and I'm sorry for that. Andie, thanks for coming to find me, but that was dangerous. From now on, I don't want anyone leaving this room without me. A guard will always be stationed outside. We need to leave the hospital. And soon."

Andie shook her head at Cole. "I know you need to keep us safe and all, and it's because you care, but Cole, you really needed to go to the chapel yesterday. I'm glad you did."

"That's beside the point, Andie. Something could've happened to you or your mom. I shouldn't have left."

Andie huffed in a way only tween girls could master. "You're ridiculous, you know that? I know this is heavy-duty, but your heart and soul are on the line here." She crossed her arms and glared at him. "Just admit that you need help."

"Andie, this is not the time for a God-talk—"

"It most certainly *is* time for it! If *ever* there was a time, it's now."

Jenna felt like she was at a tennis match. Back and forth. Back and forth, she watched the words volley between Andie and Cole. Why couldn't she share her faith as easily and with the same genuine love that Andie did anymore? Had Marc's death robbed her of that as well?

Dr. Baker burst into the room. "Jenna, we have a problem." He took a deep breath and glanced at Cole. "The nurse with the girls yesterday in the ER disappeared. The staff didn't realize she was missing until about an hour later. Assuming she left, the last person that saw her said she was white as a sheet racing down the hallway. After a crazy night in the ER, the charge nurse thought she had gone home sick. Then, she didn't show up today for her shift. No one has seen or heard from her since she was with the girls." The doctor's pager went off. He swiped a hand down his jaw. "Please excuse me, I'll be back later."

The doctor's news hung in the air as he left. "Oh my goodness." Would they find her? What if they did something terrible to her? Because of them? Jenna's thoughts ran away with her. "Cole, what do we do?"

Cole hesitated.

Andie responded instead. "We pray. God knows exactly where we are and what's going on."

Cole's jaw clenched. And twitched. He turned to look out the window. No response.

Andie's words pierced Jenna's heart. Her daughter was right. She closed her eyes. *God, forgive me for not trusting wholly in You. Give me that childlike faith again.*

Resolve flooded her veins. No more hiding behind her fears. In the flutter of a breath, her foundation shifted from sinking sand to solid ground. No matter what happened, God was God, and He was faithful.

"Mom?"

Jenna opened her eyes. "You're right, Andie. We need to pray."

ANDIE

12:39 p.m.

"Dear Lord"—with my hands folded on my lap, I started the prayer—"we need Your help. Please make the bad guys get caught and"—I peeked at Cole—"please let this stubborn mule named Cole let Your love take over."

His head shot around from looking out the window. I closed my eyes again and continued before he could deny anything. "Please keep us safe. Amen."

I looked up. Something different shone in Mom's eyes. A new . . . sparkle. Her smile was brighter and bigger. Bigger than it had been since . . . well, since before my dad died.

"Thanks, Andie."

What was going on inside that soft heart of hers? "Not a problem. Any time." I snuggled down under my thin blanket. Chills raced up my spine. *Kinda cold in here.*

The door opened and Auntie walked in with a plastic bag. "I got the cells. Each one is programmed with the others' numbers." She looked at Mom, then stopped. "What did I miss?"

"Well, let me see"—I counted it all off on my fingers—"a great discussion with God that apparently made Mom feel great and made Cole even more stubborn." He grunted. "And a stomach that has been in *desperate* need of M&Ms."

Mom and Auntie laughed.

"What? Don't you know that my tummy could be in grave danger? Without M&Ms, it would . . . would . . ." I frowned. *Ummmm . . .*

Mom crossed her arms. "Would do what? Cease to exist?"

"Don't you know it!"

A knock sounded on the door. A *loud* knock.

Cole stood and walked to the door.

As it opened, my jaw dropped.

Two giants stood in the doorway, their faces cold and stiff as stone. The room seemed to shrink as they accepted Cole's invitation to come in.

They're as big as elephants!

I just stared. A shiver raced up and down my spine. And it wasn't from the cold.

I hope they're on our side.

CHAPTER THIRTY

COLE
April 13
Providence Hospital
Anchorage, Alaska
1:00 p.m.

Finally.

It was about time these guys arrived. And they were huge. Perfect.

Cole turned to the others in the room. The tension in the air was so thick, it felt like a giant curtain closing in on them. He needed to diffuse it. "Jenna, I'd like you to meet Bill and Charles. They're your protection while we get to the bottom of all this."

Jenna leaned back against the pillows, the tense lines in her forehead relaxing. "Thank you." Her voice cracked. "Thank you so much for coming."

"You're welcome, ma'am. Marc was a good friend many years ago." Bill was an imposing figure, thanks to shoulders the size of Texas, but he was as loyal as the day was long. "I'm Bill, by the way." He moved forward, reaching a hand to shake in greeting.

Charles was taller and leaner, but equally formidable. He stepped forward. "Charles, ma'am. Marc and I served together at Richardson."

Jenna smiled. "It's nice to meet you both. Have you known Cole very long?"

Both men looked at him, and he answered. "No. But they can be trusted." And they could definitely intimidate. They towered over his six-foot-three-inch frame.

"Ma'am, if I could interject here." Bill stepped back, hands clasped behind him. "Your husband invited us to an OCF Bible Study when we first met. That's how we got to know one another. We attended until Chuck and I were stationed elsewhere. Marc was a good man." The big man looked down at the floor for a moment, then lifted his eyes to Cole. "We've known of Major Maddox for a long time, but hadn't had the privilege to meet until now."

Anesia stood by her daughter, her brow furrowed. She took a slight step forward. "And you're sure they can be trusted?"

The question was aimed at Cole, but her eyes didn't leave the bodyguards. He understood her protectiveness. Jenna and Andie were family.

Before he could answer Anesia, Charles stepped forward. "Ma'am, you can know this. We will lay down our lives for these ladies, and for you, if necessary."

Anesia studied Charles for a moment, then nodded and cocked her head. "And you're both believers?"

"Yes, ma'am."

"Yes, ma'am."

"Good."

Jenna's soft smile swept over him before she looked to the men again. "Thank you for sacrificing your time for us." She looked back at Cole, capturing him with those dark brown eyes. "So. What's the plan?"

"Either Bill or Charles will be outside your door at all times. You need to make sure you don't talk to anyone other than the people in this room, Dr. Baker, or the nurses we've already cleared." He walked to Jenna's side. "Now, let's learn how to use the phones and keep them charged."

"Any word yet from the FBI?" Charles punched numbers into his phone.

"Not yet. I wish I knew who Marc had talked to, but I put in a call to a contact there first thing this morning." Cole sighed. "Here's hoping they get involved sooner rather than later."

Bill crossed his arms over his expansive chest. "And the local authorities?"

"They're involved, but only on a surface level. They don't know the true situation. We can't risk word getting out about AMI. Last thing we need is black-market dealers after us on top of everything else."

"Agreed." Charles glanced at Jenna and Andie. "We need to get them someplace secure anyway."

Andie raised her hand. "Cole?"

"Yeah, Squirt?"

"Aren't the police the good guys? Don't we *want* their help?"

Cole gauged his response. He wanted to be honest without causing Andie even more alarm. "They are. And if we need their help, we'll call them. But we'll be heading back to North Pole soon, which will be out of their jurisdiction. I've already contacted the authorities there, and the MPs."

Now it was Zoya's turn to raise her hand. "Do you know who that creepy guy was? And do you think he'll come back?"

Cole cast a glance at Bill and Charles before responding. "I have an idea who it was." Understanding dawned on the other men's faces. Good. Message received. They knew Shadow's reputation. He turned back to Andie and her friend. "But don't worry about it. That's why we've got these two goons here to help."

Anesia walked over to Jenna. "I need to go check on the twins and make sure they're not tearing up the sled dog truck. Can I get anyone anything while I'm out?"

"An end to this nightmare?" Jenna shot a nervous smile at Cole.

"Wish I could, girl." Anesia hugged her tight.

Cole turned to the window. If only it *were* the end . . . but he was afraid the nightmare had only just begun.

LEAPER

4:32 p.m.

The wheels of his chair creaked as he rolled in slow motion toward the window. With a flick of his wrist, the blinds closed. He tugged on the drapes next.

Dark. He needed dark.

Twenty years he'd been following Viper's orders. Twenty. Years.

Enough to drive the sanest of men crazy.

It hadn't started out this way. No. He'd been loyal. Patriotic. Full of dreams and aspirations. His own grandmother had taken his hands the day he left to enlist and told him how proud she was of him. That he was serving his country. Keeping other people free.

She'd roll over in her grave if she knew what he'd become. Where lies and deceit, greed and power had taken him.

The force that drove him all those years faded. What a waste.

But none of that mattered now.

The Glock and silencer lay on the coffee table. One more assignment. One more spilling of blood.

And then it would be over.

COLE

5:12 p.m.

The afternoon passed in a blur of activity. Dr. Baker had expressed his worry to Cole about the stress taking a toll on Jenna, that it would hinder her body's ability to heal from the infection. But her strength and recovery shot through the roof, surprising them both. A new calm and serenity had passed over her. When they first met, she'd been strong and independent, protective and caring, but this . . . this was new.

Andie beamed as mother and daughter sat together on the bed.

Cole had to admit it annoyed him just a little. The attraction between him and Jenna was strong. He liked being her protector, being needed. But now, instead of looking to him for everything, she was relying on her God.

He shook his head. Focus. So much to cover. He needed to meet with the guards and brief them. He needed to grill Andie and Jenna about their home and property. They had to find AMI first.

It was their only chance.

Maybe Anesia knew something that could help. Sometimes people didn't even realize what they knew. And what about the dogs? Maybe they could help as well.

If he knew Viper at all, he knew that his former team would be desperate to secure AMI. The only thing working in their favor at this point was the media's interest in the story. But would that keep Viper from finishing what he tried to do on the mountain?

If he was right and it was Shadow who'd come after Andie and Zoya, then Viper's team had already come to the hospital once. They wouldn't hesitate to do it again. But he wasn't convinced it was safe to take them back to North Pole.

There was no way out. Except to find AMI first.

Anesia ran into the room, her breathing labored. She stopped, leaned over, and put her hands on her knees, catching her breath.

"What's wrong?" Jenna leaned forward. "What happened?"

Anesia stood up, grabbing her side. "I just heard from Joe. Someone broke into my house while he was in town getting supplies. The dogs were all in an uproar, the kennel is a mess. Joe has no idea if anything is missing." She sucked in air, straining to get the words out. "The worst part is that Peter had gone to your place while he was in town."

"Oh, no. Is everything okay?"

"We don't know. He can't get hold of Peter."

Jenna's eyes closed and two tears trickled down her cheeks. "It's all my fault. If only I had cooperated when they asked!"

Cole moved to her side. "What do you mean?"

"All those times. The men who said they were with the government. Looking for Marc's research." She hiccupped a sob. "Will more people get hurt because of me?"

"Jenna, listen to me. It's not your fault. And we don't know if anything has happened to Peter." He glanced at Anesia. Their eyes locked. She understood. "We need to get AMI into the right hands, and that will save thousands, hundreds of thousands, possibly even millions of lives."

Jenna grabbed his arm.

He looked back to her beautiful, dark eyes.

With a deep breath, she wiped her face with her other hand. "I'm so sorry. Deep down"— she choked on the words—"deep down, I think I knew. I should've found what Marc was working on and handed it over to the government. It would've kept all this from happening." Her shoulders shook with silent sobs as she buried her face in her hands.

"No. It wouldn't." Cole tugged her hands away from her face so he could look into her eyes. "The guys who claimed they were with the government weren't. If you had done anything differently, you wouldn't be here now, and AMI would be in terrorists' hands. Those men need to be stopped." He sat on the edge of the bed. "Which means we've got to get out of here. Soon."

LEAPER

Providence Hospital
Anchorage, Alaska
9:12 p.m.

Quiet ruled the hospital hallway. The white doctor's coat, too tight in the shoulders and arms, made him sweat like crazy.

Viper planned to get rid of him. He'd made too many mistakes. But maybe . . . he could accomplish this one last thing before that happened.

The timing was perfect. He had to move now.

Maddox and the hulk of a bodyguard were deep in conversation in the waiting room.

His shoe squeaked on the tile floor. The cane and cast thumped and tapped out an accompanying rhythm. Monitors beeped and echoed through the halls. A few whispered conversations drifted over him from rooms with open doors. The stale air smelled like disinfectant.

Pulling at his collar, he made a vain attempt to breathe deep, to steady his pulse. Entirely too warm in this hospital. Especially beneath all his layers. He just wanted it over. Maybe then he could have peace. Something different. Away from all the horrors of the life he'd chosen.

But no.

It would end tonight. There was no escape.

As he walked down the corridor, he noticed a temperature drop. This section of the hallway was definitely colder. That—and the fact that the other bodyguard stood outside a nearby door—confirmed he was where he needed to be.

He reached into his pocket, gripping the Taser C2.

The guard turned at his approaching footsteps. He kept the smile on his face as he pulled the Taser out and pressed the trigger. The two small probes shot into the guard and he collapsed to the floor.

Only thirty seconds to hide him.

Stepping over the huge man, he tied the limp guard's ankles, then his hands, and gagged his mouth. He gripped under the hulk's arms and dragged him into the men's restroom across the hall. Pressing the trigger again, he sent another charge through the man and threw it on top of him.

Sweat poured from his brow now. His leg ached with pain so fierce he thought he might pass out. He shouldn't be walking, but he couldn't very well sneak into the room in a wheelchair.

Slipping from the restroom, he glanced down the hall. His breaths came in huffs. It'd taken all his energy to haul the huge man away from that door. He realized the Taser he'd lifted off the little lady in the parking lot would have his fingerprints on it, but it was all about to be over anyway.

Another glance down the hall. Still quiet.

Once again, he approached the hospital room.

With a clench of his jaw, he reached for the handle and pushed the door open.

ANDIE

Providence Hospital
Anchorage, Alaska
9:12 p.m.

The darkness outside scared me more than I wanted to admit. It was darker out there than my heart had been when I got mad at Cole.

No, I didn't want to think about that . . .

It was cloudy and foggy and I couldn't see the moon or its light or any stars. *Totally* freaky.

Auntie Anesia and Zoya had gone back to the hotel to take care of Dasha and Sasha. I didn't think Auntie wanted to be alone anyway, what with the break-in at home, and the turmoil going on here. But it made it harder to sleep without the comfort of my best friend. I knew God was with me, but that didn't mean I wasn't scared.

Mom slept soundly. I didn't hear anything except her deep breathing and the machines beeping in that annoying *bleep, beep, bleep, beep, bleep, beep*. Why did they have to make the machines so loud? Hadn't they ever heard of the word *sleep*?

Uh, oh. Grumpiness was taking over. Again.

God, You know I'm confuzzled. You know what's going on, but couldn't You give us some answers? I'm still baffled about all of this.

Dad was a Christian, of that I was sure. But then why did he do all of those bad things? Why did he make bad choices? Cole wasn't a Christian, but *he* did the right thing and made the right choices.

What had gone wrong that Dad would go down the dark path?

I didn't watch *Star Wars* very often—it was too much of a boy movie—but my dad was like Darth Vader. Switching to the dark side, but in the end turning back to good. And dying for it.

How could I show Cole that Christians weren't perfect, but that he needed Jesus? How could I show him that someone cared enough to *die* for him? I could understand where Cole came from. Something bad happened to him. He'd never really said what . . . but I knew all the same. Whatever it was, it was bad.

And he blamed God for it.

So how was I supposed to get it through his hard noggin that God cared enough for him to send His Son to die for his life and his eternity? How could I convince him that God loves everybody, no matter what they've done?

I couldn't. Even though I didn't like that answer, I knew it was true. If God wanted to get it through Cole's head that He is always there for us, He'd have to be the One to do it.

A thud sounded outside the door. My heart thumped in my chest as I heard a grunt and then another thud.

I held my breath.

And waited.

Was that the bodyguard?

The door handle moved. Everything blurred into slow motion. My eyes widened and my breaths came in huffs. Was it one of the bad guys? Or worse, was it the Grinch from the stitches room?

Mom didn't seem to be awake. Would we die without a fight? Would he just appear and kill us in no time flat? Then vanish again?

What would Cole do when he found us dead?

The door creaked open. A dark figure stepped from behind the half-opened door and turned around—

"Hank!"

CHAPTER THIRTY-ONE

JENNA
Providence Hospital
Anchorage, Alaska
9:15 p.m.

Andie's voice broke through the barrier of sleep. What had her daughter just said?

Jenna's eyes flew open and she confirmed for herself. The man standing in front of Andie was indeed Hank.

Alive.

Jenna ripped the IV tubes from her arms and leapt from the bed, grabbing the IV pole as a weapon. Where were the guards? Where was Cole?

"I'm not here to hurt you." Hank held his hands up in front of him. "I promise."

Jenna searched the man's eyes. No way she would trust this man again.

"Mom, I think he's telling the truth."

"I don't trust him." All the anger she'd quenched boiled up again. If only she could reach her phone, but she'd placed it under her pillow before she fell asleep. Taking a step back, she leaned against the bed, fumbled with the pillow, and tried to hit the speed dial for Cole.

Hank moved forward and she jerked, dropping the phone. She could only hope that it connected. She moved between Hank and Andie, her leg screaming in protest.

"What did you do to the bodyguard?" Andie squeaked.

"He's fine. But this was the only way to talk to you." The man she'd known all these years looked . . . ashamed? "Look, we don't have much time. I just wanted to tell you what they're planning. You know they want you dead. Viper will do anything to get the prototype for AMI and sell it off. They sent me here to kill you, but they know I won't do it."

Jenna squinted her eyes at him. "How do *we* know that?"

"Because I covered for you on the mountain." His voice was barely above a whisper. "When they came in the helicopter to the site, they pulled me out of the wreckage and I told them I'd taken care of your bodies."

"Why would you do that?" She aimed the pole at him; she wasn't taking any chances. "Especially after you tried to *kill* us in the plane?"

"Because of your daughter."

"What?" Jenna looked down at Andie.

A small smile brightened her twelve-year-old's face. "You *were* listening."

"I still don't see how God could forgive me for all I've done, but seeing the faith of that little girl even in the midst of fear . . ." He stopped. Cleared his throat. "It made me think. Hard. And I've had a lot of time to think the past few days."

Jenna shifted the pole. None of this made sense.

"They'll send someone else." He wiped a hand down his face. "I'm here to help you. And I'm sorry."

"You're forgiven." Andie piped up from her place in bed.

Jenna just shook her head. This man had intended to kill them! How could she trust him, let alone forgive? What if this was all a ruse?

Hank held a hand out to Jenna. "I'm so sorry. They killed Marc. And when you wouldn't give up the information they wanted, they decided to get rid of you as well. Yes, I sabotaged your plane. I'd planned to fly the plane into the Alaska Range and jump out before it crashed. There was a tracking beacon in my parachute so they could locate me. They were hoping your crash would go unnoticed in the wilderness for a long time, which would give them the time they needed to acquire AMI."

Jenna wanted to believe him, she really did. But . . . *Lord, help me! Show me the truth, and help me forgive.*

"What did you do to Cole on the plane?" Andie leaned forward, elbows on her knees.

"I gave him a packet of creamer laced with drugs."

"So you knew he was going to be on the plane? That he would try to save us?" The pieces were coming together. She should've trusted Cole from the beginning.

"Yes. Viper had tracked his movements for a while. What better way to get rid of him than with all of you together?" Hank turned an ear toward the door. "Speaking of Cole, we need him. And we need to get you out of here tonight."

With a small step, Jenna moved closer to Hank. She searched his eyes—and nodded. "What about you?"

"Don't worry about me. About time I made things right."

Andie reached to grab his hand. "God loves you, Hank. Don't doubt that."

"I just can't help but think it's too late for—"

A large figure burst through the door, gun raised. Jenna gasped and moved to shield Andie. The room spun.

Andie screamed, gripping Jenna's waist.

Hank stepped in front of Jenna just as the assailant pulled the trigger.

Thwap! Thwap! Thwap!

Hank grunted, his arms out, shielding them, taking each of the three muffled shots. A silencer. Marc had taught her enough about guns to understand. This guy would kill them all. And just walk away.

Thwap! Hank grunted again, staggering back.

Two more figures flew into the room, tackling the shooter. Bill and Cole. Where was Charles?

As the three men scuffled at the foot of Andie's bed, Hank groaned and fell back onto Jenna. The warmth of his blood soaked into her thin hospital gown as she lowered him to the floor.

Andie slid off the bed beside her, cradling Hank's head.

His weight crushed Jenna into the hard floor.

Gasping for air, Hank gripped Andie's hand. "I'm so . . . sorry . . . so . . . sorry."

Jenna cried. For this man who stepped in front of a bullet for her, for Marc, for all the loss that greed had inspired. "I forgive you, Hank." She sobbed.

Andie put her hands on either side of Hank's face. "You believe in Jesus, don't you, Hank?"

His body trembled. Blood trickled out of his mouth, but he focused on Andie and nodded.

"That's all you have to do. It's a free gift for everyone. I know you've heard us talk about it before, He loves you, He died for you. All you have to do is believe."

"I'm . . . not good . . ." His voice came thin, weak.

Andie wasn't having any of it. "That doesn't matter. 'Believe in the Lord Jesus, and you will be saved.'"

Hank blinked once, twice, then a small smile lifted his lips—and a raspy breath left his body.

"Jenna! Andie! Are you okay?" Cole was there, kneeling in front of them.

Hank lifted a bloody hand to Cole's shirt and grabbed it, pulling Cole's face down. "I'm sorry . . . Cole . . ."

Cole just stared at him, a harsh look on his face.

"Find it . . . before Vi—" Blood gurgled up out of Hank's mouth, choking him.

"Shh, Hank, calm down. It's okay." Jenna tried to soothe him.

"Not until you . . . find . . ."

Cole gripped Hank by the shoulders. "Do you know where AMI is?"

Hank's other hand emerged from his pocket. With one last breath, he thrust something into Cole's hand. "Go . . . the house . . . at the house . . ." He looked at Andie one more time, then went limp.

Tears streamed down Andie's face as she cradled Hank's head in her hands.

"Jenna, are you okay?" Cole's voice broke through the moment.

"Thanks to Hank. We're fine." She wanted to memorize Cole's rugged face, the worry and care etched in it. Even with a bloody nose and what looked to be a busted lip, he looked wonderful.

Cole opened his hand and looked down. "I'm afraid that's where you're wrong." He trembled slightly as he closed his hand over whatever Hank had given him. "You're in far more danger now than I thought. We just got word that the nurse who was with the girls yesterday has been found dead in her apartment."

CHAPTER THIRTY-TWO

COLE
Providence Hospital
Anchorage, Alaska
9:41 p.m.

Marc's words washed over him as he fingered the bloody keychain: "*Protect with my heart.*" What on earth was that supposed to mean? How could Marc's heart protect anyone when he was dead? Cole raked his hand through his hair. He was horrible at riddles. Black and white. That's how he liked it.

Bill rushed into the room, Charles on his heels. "I found him." Bill pointed at Charles. "Shot him with a Taser and tied him up in the restroom."

"You all right?" Cole stood, wiping the blood off his hands with a hospital blanket.

"Yes, sir. I'm sorry. He took me by surprise. I tried to get back here."

Bill patted the other bodyguard on the back. "He was on his knees at the door, trying to open it when I plowed him over."

A uniformed Anchorage Police officer entered the room. "I need to speak with Mr. Maddox."

Cole strode over to the man. "I'm Maddox."

The officer leaned in and lowered his voice. "The shooter is in custody, and we contacted the FBI like Bill asked. Special Agent McAdams will be here shortly."

"Only one agent?" Cole wanted an army to protect his girls.

"Agent McAdams will handle the transport of the family back home. The director is already in North Pole awaiting their arrival."

"And the media?"

"They're camped outside the hospital. We'll give you all a chance to leave before we hold a press conference. We've got officers at the entrance, in the hallway, and two at the door. That, with your men, should be adequate."

Cole nodded. If only he were confident that were true. But the biggest threat was still out there.

The officer continued. "We're arranging for the patients to be moved. This room will have to be taped off. I'll be back in a few minutes." The officer left.

"Cole?" Jenna pulled herself up, glancing down at Andie who hadn't left Hank's still form. "We need to call Anesia and Dr. Baker."

He nodded again, pulling out the cell phone.

"We need clothes. And to get cleaned up." She looked at her daughter again, bottom lip quivering. "I think Andie would do a lot better if Dasha and Zoya were here as well."

Cole pulled her into his arms. Her body trembled and shivered. She'd been quiet, though covered in another man's blood, for what seemed to be an eternity. What he wouldn't do to erase all the pain and heartache she carried. "I'll make sure you're taken care of. I promise."

He held her close as he called the doctor and her friend. His words were brief, but they would be here soon. Right now, he needed this time with Jenna.

She leaned into him, gripping the front of his shirt, and spoke her soft words against his chest. "I heard what Hank said. You need to go, don't you?"

"No." He squeezed her tight. "No. I need to stay with you. I promised to protect you."

"But, Cole. What about—"

He kissed the top of her head. "Don't worry about it. I'll figure it out."

They stood there for several long moments. He couldn't leave them again. Too much had happened and they were in increasing danger. But who else could figure out where Marc hid the program and prototype? And if he didn't find it, Viper would.

The turmoil in his gut was almost more than he could bear. It only got worse when a cold realization hit him: North Korea was only the beginning. Viper wouldn't stop with them.

How many terrorists would he sell it to? How many other countries that were out for American blood . . .

He balled his fists into Jenna's back as the thought took root.

"What did he give you?" She pulled back, looking up into his eyes.

"What?" His thoughts tumbled over one another. Focus. He needed to focus. One problem at a time.

"Hank. What did he give you?"

Reaching into his pocket, he pulled the keychain back out. "This."

She gasped and stumbled back toward the bed. "Where . . . where did he get this?"

"From me."

"From you? How did *you* get it?"

"Marc gave it to me right before he died. Along with the cryptic message."

She gently plucked the keychain from his open palm. "I always wondered what happened to it. It wasn't with Marc's things that the police brought us." The blood stains on her hands matched the stains on the keychain as she turned it over and over with her fingers.

"I'm sorry I didn't tell you about it, Jenna. I wanted to, but then I couldn't find it. Thought something happened to it in the crash."

She nodded, not taking her eyes from the object in her hands. "What was the message again?"

"From Marc?"

"Yeah, something about his heart?"

"Protect with my heart."

"That's it?"

"Yes." He touched her face with his knuckles. "He asked me to promise to take care of you, and I did. Then he handed me the keychain and said that."

Jenna's eyes grew round and she covered her mouth with her hand.

"Jenna? What is it?"

She sat back down on the bed and grabbed his hand with both of hers. "I know . . ."

He frowned. "You know . . . ?"

Her gaze met his. "I know where AMI is."

JENNA

Providence Hospital
Anchorage, Alaska
10:02 p.m.

Of all the crazy things. Why didn't she think of it before?

"Where, Jenna? Where is AMI?" Cole gripped her hands.

She closed her eyes and smiled to herself. It would all be over. Finally. "We have an underground bunker on our property."

"What makes you so sure AMI is there?"

She let out a wry laugh and wiped at the tears forming in her eyes. "The symbol on this keychain?" She pointed to it. "It's carved into the wall in the bunker. That's how it all started."

"How what all started?"

"Let me back up." She squeezed his hand, not letting go. "When we bought the property and built our home, I asked Marc to build a bunker."

"Why?"

"I'm getting to that. Just wait." Jenna blinked back more tears at the memory. "Marc teased me that there weren't tornadoes in Alaska, but I told him we needed to be prepared, in case our country was under attack. I thought for sure they would target our location first because of the missile defense and all the military stationed around us."

Cole's mouth held a firm line, his eyes full of questions.

"I know what you're thinking, Cole Maddox." She smacked his arm. "Poor Jenna. Always coming up with worse-case scenarios and trying to be prepared for everything." She shook her head. "Anyway, I don't know why he went along with it—probably because he always gave in to my silly fears and lists. But he had it built. And when it was done, we went down into it and carved this symbol into the wall." She looked again at the two intertwined hearts, one with an *M*, the other with a *J*. "For my birthday, he had these keychains made. One for him and one for me."

Cole just stared at her.

"Don't you get it? No one else has ever been down in that bunker. Or seen that symbol on the wall."

"So AMI is down there?"

"I'm sure of it."

"If only I knew who Marc contacted at the FBI." Cole rubbed his hand over his face.

"Cole, you need to go."

His gaze hardened. "I'm not making that mistake again."

"You've got to go. We'll be fine." How could she convince this stubborn man?

"No, I promised to protect you."

"What good is protecting us if that technology gets in the wrong hands? We're talking about thousands of lives here, Cole. Hundreds of thousands."

His breath crossed her face as he sighed. "You're not making this easy."

"Cole, you're just going to have to face the fact that you can't protect me the way God can." She leaned closer to him, staring into his eyes.

"And if it's my time to go, I'm ready."

CHAPTER THIRTY-THREE

COLE

April 14
12:06 a.m.

The plane bounced around in the turbulent air.

"Sorry, man." The pilot glanced at him. "The air just doesn't want to smooth out tonight."

"Don't worry about it. Just get me there as soon as possible." Cole tried to ease the tension in his shoulders and neck, but it was no use.

"Understood." The man munched on sunflower seeds, spitting out the shells into a foam cup. "Anesia said it was urgent, and I'd do anything for her."

Anesia had called this guy with Talkeetna Air Taxi. Obviously a longtime friend of hers, the man seemed honest and trustworthy. One phone call from her had the man in a plane in less than twenty minutes, and now they were on the way back to North Pole.

As they flew over the rugged terrain, he let his thoughts drift to Andie and Jenna. Dr. Baker arrived soon after the shooting and helped them change rooms. Just long enough to get cleaned up.

Anesia brought two necessities, Zoya and Dasha, and lent a helping hand getting Jenna and Andie ready to travel. Dr. Baker made sure they had plenty of water and medication for the trip, and said he would rush the discharge papers.

All the details had been covered. But though he knew the FBI was escorting them home, he couldn't stop worrying. Was he right to take them home so soon? What if they were headed into an ambush?

Knowing they had Dasha, helped. The beautiful husky was protective of Andie and Jenna, but he couldn't help feeling that he'd left them alone. Anesia and Zoya had started the drive home since his girls would be leaving Anchorage soon. So what bugged him?

He wasn't there.

With them.

Protecting them.

And if anything happened, he'd never forgive himself.

Forgive.

Why did that word hold such power over him? Why couldn't he let go?

His mind raced back to the chapel. *"I can't forgive myself."*

As though she were sitting there next to him, Andie's words when they were on the side of Sultana drifted through his mind: *"No matter who we are, or what we've done, God loves each one of us."*

Why? Why would God waste a second on him when all he'd done was blame Him? And didn't he have the *right* to blame Him? God hadn't saved Amanda and Chloe. He'd never helped Cole before.

"It's a good thing God doesn't give up on us as easily as we give up on Him."

The clarity of Andie's words pierced his heart like a knife. He had to admit the truth: he'd never given God a chance. Walled up behind his anger and grief, it was easier to blame Him, to give up on Him. Just like the chaplain at the hospital had said, when things went so horribly wrong, Cole didn't have to think twice about blaming God.

Amanda believed in God. Believed in Him right up to the moment she died. Talked to Cole about God all the time. But he refused to listen. And now she was gone. Was that God's punishment for his unbelief? Or just a coincidence? A moment in time that proved the sad state of humanity. The loss of someone dear because of the greed and selfishness of another. The crying out of the world for the need of . . .

A Savior.

The dark night surrounded him as he gazed out the windshield of the airplane. Stars shone brilliantly, the moon reflected in the snow far below him.

Hanging in the air, floating, suspended by this flying piece of metal, Cole faced the facts.

He had faith that this plane would fly.

He had faith that a chair could hold him when he sat in it.

He had faith that his legs could carry him across a room when he walked.

He had faith that the sun would rise and set.

And yet, he refused faith in a Savior. *The* Savior. Deep in his heart, he knew the truth. But his pride had gotten in the way. He didn't want to rely on anyone else. He wanted to be self-sufficient. Not answering to anyone.

But for all his skills, all his strength and determination, he hadn't been able to do the most important thing in his life.

Save his family.

And now . . . here he was again. Someone he loved was in danger, and he was doing all he could to protect them. But would that be enough?

Andie would say no. She'd say nothing we do is ever enough. That God has to do it, or you're lost. That little girl had shown him her faith day in and day out. And he'd begun to crave what she had. She'd been a brilliant mirror to him. Blinding him with his own reflection, and the needs in his soul.

Then Jenna struck the final blow: *"You can't protect me the way God can . . ."*

All that time. He'd promised to protect them. He thought they needed him. He'd been wrong. He was the one with the need.

He stared out at the sky. *Okay, God. You've got my attention. I'm asking for Your help. I can't do this . . . can't keep them safe on my own. I need You. Your help. Help them, Lord. Help . . .* He hesitated, then took the step. *Help me.*

Please.

ANDIE

April 14
Providence Hospital
Anchorage, Alaska
12:24 a.m.

The door swung open and a tall man stepped in.

"Mrs. Gray?" His voice held strength and confidence. He was definitely someone who knew what he was doing.

Mom looked at him, suspicion in her dark eyes. "Yes, that's me. Who are you?"

I looked over at Dr. Baker. He seemed uncertain, too. Who was this guy? And where were the bodyguards?

"Special Agent McAdams, ma'am." He lifted his dark glasses. "I'm here to escort you two ladies home."

The same relief I felt showed on Mom's face. "Oh, thank God."

"The plane is ready for us. We should get moving."

Dasha ran over and sniffed the intruder. Special Agent McAdams looked down at her and smiled. "Nice dog."

Well, if he liked Dasha, he had to be a good guy.

"Is this all you have?"

It was funny watching him try and sidestep Dasha. Her nose was almost attached to his leg. She wouldn't leave him alone. As he walked closer to Mom, she followed.

"Just us, Dasha, and the bodyguards," Mom said with a smile.

Dasha wagged her tail as if she understood we wouldn't leave without her.

Again he looked down at my cute puppy. "Should we sedate her for the flight?"

I started to protest—no one was drugging my dog!—but Mom beat me to it.

"No, she'll be fine. She's a good traveler." Mom gave a firm nod as if the matter was settled.

Special Agent McAdams nodded. "Let's get going."

Dr. Baker helped me get the air cast on my foot as Mom searched for the jacket Auntie had brought when she gave us a change of clothes.

"If that's all, then let's go." Special Agent McAdams moved to hold the door of our room for us. FBI and a gentleman. *Cool.*

Mom glanced around as we walked into the hallway. "Where are Bill and Charles? Our bodyguards?"

Good question. I looked around too. I didn't see them anywhere.

"They're already at the airport. But with your dog, we'll only have room for one of the men."

"Oh."

Only one? I frowned. *We can squish together . . .*

- -

We arrived at a small landing strip in the middle of nowhere and hopped out of the Special Agent's car. This plane was smaller than our Beaver.

Remembering those scary moments when our plane crashed made me shudder. I did *not* want that to happen again. *God protect us, God protect us, God protect us.*

I was glad to see Bill, one of our bodyguards, there. He climbed in before us, then gave the okay.

Special Agent McAdams sat in the front, getting things ready.

My stomach was all tied up in knots, and shivers raced up and down my spine as we buckled up. I really didn't want to fly again.

Bill sat in the front with Special Agent McAdams, who started the plane. Before I knew it—or wanted to—we were rolling down the runway.

God protect us, God protect us, God protect us.

I *really* didn't want to crash.

But even if we did, it couldn't be as bad as last time, could it? We wouldn't be on the side of a mountain, and there would be no ice patches to worry about, no avalanches to avoid, no bad guys chasing us . . .

Oh, wait. There would still be bad guys. Would there always be bad guys?

The plane lifted up into the air and I gripped the sides of my seat. *Don't look, just don't look.*

Mom grabbed my hand and squeezed. Hard.

"It will take awhile to get back to your house, so you might as well get some rest." Bill peeked at us over his shoulder and nodded as if saying, "I'll keep my eye on things."

I hadn't even thought about what time it was, or noticed the darkness, for that matter. Glancing out the window, I saw black clouds hovering near the moon. I put my fingers to the small circle-ish glass and the freezing coldness shot up my hand. I hoped our house would be warm when we got home.

Well, at least my kind of warm.

I couldn't wait to get home and go to sleep on my nice, squishy waterbed. The doctors had said to get a waterbed three years before because they knew it would help control my temp while I sleep. It was *so* comfortable.

And squishy.

Food would be a blessing too.

I couldn't wait to have Mom cook a homemade breakfast again. Omelets and crepes and pancakes. Which one would we have first?

I turned to ask, but she'd already fallen asleep. The infection and all the stuff from last night had done a number on her.

Dasha's head nestled on my lap. She was almost asleep too.

No one to ask what they wanted for breakfast tomorrow.

Harsh.

I leaned my head against Mom's shoulder and sighed. Maybe I could get *a little* sleep. If I could stop thinking about crashes.

And blizzards.

And gun shots.

And blood.

Special Agent McAdams looked back at us, and I pretended I'd fallen asleep. Once I heard him turn back around, I peeked my eyes open. I didn't feel like talking, but since I couldn't sleep, I might as well make sure he didn't do anything cocky. Like shoot the radio.

The special agent kept one hand on the yoke and used the other to pull off his FBI jacket. He couldn't be getting cold, not with the air conditioner so high. What was he doing?

A seam ripped as he tugged at the jacket.

Oh. No wonder he was taking it off. He could barely get it over his huge arms. That was funny. What was an FBI agent doing with a jacket that didn't even fit him?

I wanted to rush up front and help him so that he wouldn't let go of the yoke and make us plummet toward the earth, but he finally got it off. Underneath he wore a plain, white, short-sleeve shirt with a shoulder holster and gun. His arms were like Cole's, with solid muscles and—

I gasped.

It can't be!

I grabbed my cell phone from the pocket of my jacket. We weren't supposed to use phones on airplanes, but I didn't care. Peeking through my eyelashes, I clicked on Cole's name as the special agent put on a heavier jacket. I tried to press the buttons without making them click.

Once I finished typing a text, I sent the message over and over again, praying it would go through.

> Cole HELP! Special agent guy has same tattoo as u, Hank, & Dad!

CHAPTER THIRTY-FOUR

JENNA
April 14
North Pole, Alaska
Tikanni-Gray property along the Chena River
3:47 a.m.

The wheels of the plane had barely stopped when their FBI escort jumped out and pointed a gun at Bill—

Thwap!

Bill slumped onto the seat. Jenna threw her hand over her mouth as Andie gripped her arm tighter.

"Get out of the plane." Agent McAdams held the door open with one hand. In the other was a Glock elongated with a silencer—aimed at her chest.

Jenna shielded her daughter with her own body. *Lord, help us!*

Who was this man? They'd been so close. To home. To safety.

She'd thought it was all over. But she was wrong. This man would probably kill them in their own home.

Dasha growled.

"You're not the FBI, are you?" Andie grilled from behind her.

Brave little Andie.

"No, I'm not." The man's deep chuckle sent chills up Jenna's spine. "How'd you ever guess that?"

"Your eyes." Andie shrank back. "And your tattoo."

"So you know about the tattoo, huh? Somebody must've been faking sleep during the flight." He moved closer, his cold gaze piercing Jenna. "Games are over. Get out of the plane. Now."

Jenna slid off the seat, hands clutching Andie behind her. Dasha growled again and moved forward.

He pointed the gun at Dasha's head.

"*No!*" Andie lunged from behind her, almost knocking Jenna off her feet. "Hike, Dasha! *Hike!*"

Dasha jumped out of the plane and took off running. There'd be no stopping her now.

For a moment the man tracked Dasha with his gun, then brought it back to bear on Jenna. "Would you like to tell me where our friend Mr. Maddox is?"

"He left the hospital before we did."

"Ah, so he's here, isn't he?" The man smirked.

"I . . . I don't know." That was true. She didn't know *where* Cole was at that moment.

"That's all right. I look forward to seeing him again." He winked at her. "Which I'm sure will be soon."

"Don't you dare hurt him!" Andie shouted at the dark stranger.

He halted in his tracks and turned his full attention on her daughter, leaning down so his face was only inches from hers. "Only if he gets in my way." His sneer made Jenna shiver all the way down to her toes.

Jenna pulled Andie away from him.

But Andie stared him down.

Straightening to his full height, he laid the gun on Jenna's shoulder, eyes focused on Andie. "Now. Let's go find AMI, shall we?"

ANDIE
3:50 a.m.

I walked behind Mom hoping, praying that this McAdams dude wouldn't see or hear the phone. My fingers flew across the small keys.

> Watch out, on r way 2 bunkR, Bad guy with us, shot Bill on plane.

I pretended to cower behind Mom as he glared at me over his shoulder. "What's wrong, little girl, scared?"

I pushed my cell deep into my jacket pocket, praying Cole got the text in time.

As we trekked across our property, I wondered what it would feel like to get shot. Would I feel it? Would it be painful? Would I bleed to death or just conk my head and die . . .

Would the bad guys get what they wanted?

How many other people would die?

JENNA
3:53 a.m.

A hundred yards had never felt so far away. Her leg ached. And her heart ached.

As they walked to the bunker, memories rushed in. She could almost see Marc there anxious to show it to her. Pride and delight evident in his eyes . . .

The twelve-inch thick, solid steel door was visible between the two trees that marked the bunker's entrance. The turf covering had been thrown to the side. Someone was already here. *God, if it's Cole, please give him a warning that we're coming . . .*

The fake agent jerked the door open—and Cole was there! He spun, but McAdams was ready for him. He slammed the gun into Cole's left temple, and their protector slumped to the floor.

Cole!

Her heart felt like it stopped. Andie turned, burying her face in Jenna's chest. "Oh, Andie, I'm sure he's okay." She hoped her whispered words were true.

The dark man waved his gun at them. "Get over here. Or you're next."

Each step down into the bunker made her leg send piercing pain signals to her brain. A panel in the wall caught her attention. She'd never seen that before. The panel was open under the carving of their initials. Inside were a computer screen and keyboard.

What are those for?

That awful man jerked them further into the bunker, and Jenna stifled a scream with a hand to her mouth. Another body lay in the corner.

Peter!

"Let's focus, shall we?"

Andie straightened her shoulders, but sidled closer to Jenna's side as her attention snapped back to McAdams.

He turned to them, eyes steely. "How about you tell me the password."

Andie glared at him. "What's the matter, aren't you smart enough to figure it out?"

"Andie, hush!" Jenna couldn't let her daughter antagonize this man. Who knew what he would do to her. But Andie just crossed her arms.

Those glacial eyes glared at them. "I'd watch my words if I were you, little girl."

"I don't know, you seem to have a big enough mouth for both of us."

Jenna jerked Andie by the collar and pulled her outspoken daughter behind her. "That's enough, young lady."

A slow, wicked smile slithered across the man's face. He looked down at Cole . . . and kicked him in the stomach.

Jenna and Andie yelled at the same time. "Stop that!"

He sneered at them, then pointed the gun at Cole's head. "I can do much worse than that, so I suggest you do as I say."

Jenna's stomach turned. This man would kill them all.

ANDIE

3:59 a.m.

Ooo! I wanted to hurt him bad. *How dare you!* But what could I do to a man who had a gun? Pray that God would strike him down with lightning?

Sounded good.

Love your enemies.

Where did *that* voice come from? How could I love the *bad* guy who hurt Cole, held us hostage, and probably killed my dad?

Feel sorry for? Yes!

Love?

No.

"What are the codes?" He was talking to Mom, but kept his creepy gaze on me. He wouldn't hurt Mom, would he?

Mom pulled me behind her. Again. "We don't know."

I gave him another angry look over Mom's shoulder. I really wanted to stick my tongue out at him too.

Better not.

"Oh, really. I have a hard time believing you. Now tell me the codes"— he held the gun up again, and this time it was pointing right between my eyes—"or I'll shoot your daughter." He inclined his head. "It's your choice."

COLE

4:01 a.m.

Cole listened to Viper threaten Jenna and Andie. The throbbing in his head awakened him, but he didn't open his eyes. Yet. Best to let Viper think he was still out cold.

A short beep echoed in the bunker. Must be Viper's phone. He listened as Viper spoke.

"Is that it?" A pause. "Nothing else?"

Time ticked by with the beat of his heart.

"I'll check the house again. I haven't finished setting the charges anyway."

Charges? Great. Viper was going to blow the house and who knows what else.

"Just make sure everything is ready. I'm confident I'll have it soon."

A beep signaled the end of the call. Viper let out a sigh. "Well, now. I'm going to leave you alone with your thoughts a few minutes."

Cole listened to Viper's footsteps. He must be circling them.

"And maybe by the time I get back, you'll remember what the codes are."

He heard a rustle and a quick intake of breath.

"Or your daughter here, will take a little trip with me."

"No! I don't know the codes. Please, don't hurt my daughter!" Jenna's voice shook.

"We'll see."

Footsteps.

Movement up the stairs.

The creak of the outside bunker door.

SLAM!

The sliding of . . . a chain?

Viper was locking them in. Good.

He opened his eyes. "Jenna, Andie, don't say anything, be really quiet."

They both rushed to his side.

"Cole!" Jenna's concern pricked his heart.

Andie tugged on his hands. "Why didn't you hide? I texted you. Tried to warn you—"

"I didn't get any texts. But then, those cheap phones of ours probably wouldn't have reception in here."

Andie touched his face. "I was so worried about you."

"No need, Squirt. Not with my hard head. Now, we don't have a lot of time." He sat, scowling when he felt blood trickle down his face. "Andie, I want you to sit on the stairs and listen at the door. As soon as you hear him coming, let me know."

Her little girl arms around his waist were better than completing any mission he'd ever gone on. "Got it." She spun to the stairs, scrambled up them, and sat near the top.

"Jenna, I need you to think. We've got to figure out Marc's password. We need a nine-digit sequence."

Her dark eyes pooled. "I was so worried . . ." She shook her head. "Protect with my heart. That was the message, right?"

"Yes." His brain flashed back to the plane crash. The locked bag. "Hey, Jenna. What was in your locked laptop bag?"

She frowned at him. "Andie's medical files, why?"

There went that theory. "Just wondering if Marc had left you some other clue."

"Sorry. But I did find that shiny, little black box. It had Marc's initials on it, but it was locked."

"Black box? Viper had one of those . . . he fiddled with it a lot." Thoughts careened through his mind. But if Viper had a black box, why would he need Marc's?

Jenna pulled it out of her pocket. "Here."

He turned it over in his hands. Nothing. "Only his initials." Cole gave it back to Jenna.

"Why don't we focus on the clue he gave you." She began to pace the small room. Back and forth, the limp from her injury very pronounced. "'Protect with my heart.' That doesn't make any sense." She let out a sigh. "But then, Marc was frighteningly good at making up riddles. This won't be easy, Cole." The pacing continued as she stared at the floor, the ceiling, and the carving in the wall. Stopping in her tracks, she reached to her neck and grabbed something. "Wait a minute. Heart. Marc's dogtags. He wore them over his heart." She slipped the chain over her head and studied the engravings.

Cole stepped beside her and looked over her shoulder.

"The only number is his Social Security Number. Marc would never use that. It's too easy."

"Wait." Cole looked from one tag to the other. "Look. The other tag is different."

Her brow furrowed. "But aren't both tags supposed to be the same?"

He studied the numbers. "Marc must've switched them. This tag contains the same numbers as his SSN but in a different order."

Jenna looked toward the door. "How much time do we have?"

"Not long."

"Then, let's try it. I can't think of anything else."

He walked back over to the keyboard, Jenna right beside him. Tapping the space bar, the screen once again came to life. Nine blank boxes were all that filled the screen. He entered the sequence from the different dogtag and hit enter.

The boxes scrolled and flew around the screen, coming back to rest empty in front of him.

SEQUENCE ORDER flashed over the boxes.

"Put them in the correct order this time." Jenna suggested.

Could it really be that easy? He tapped in the appropriate numbers and hit enter again.

This time the boxes completely disappeared.

A cursor flashed and then SQUIRT appeared with eight bubbles underneath.

"There's only eight digits this time." Jenna chewed on her thumbnail and turned to Andie. "You know any special, eight-digit code?"

Andie slowly shook her head.

Jenna turned back to him. "What do we do?"

"I don't know. *Squirt* was his nickname for Andie, right?"

"Yeah."

"Did he have any other nicknames for her? What about her initials? An Athabaskan nickname of some sort?" He shook his head. That was reaching. Too many possibilities.

The beautiful woman beside him grabbed his hand. "We need to pray."

For once, he didn't feel like arguing. "Okay." Holding her hand again sent a jolt up his arm into his skull. This woman turned him inside-out.

"Heavenly Father, we don't know what to do. And we're afraid. We need that code, so many lives are at stake. Please give

Cole the wisdom he needs to finish this mission. And please forgive me where I've failed You. In Jesus' name, Amen."

"Amen." Andie's voice floated from the stairs.

He looked at the kid. Stuck between being a little girl and a teenager, she was all heart. In that moment he remembered his first thoughts of her, *innocence and wisdom. Terrifying combination.* Now wasn't that the truth. That little girl had pried open his heart and wormed her way inside. And he loved her as if she were his own.

Fiddling with her Medic-Alert bracelet, her bottom lip between her teeth, he could almost hear the wheels turning in her brain.

"Why would Dad put *SQUIRT* in there if I don't know what the code is?" She looked at her mom.

"I don't know, sweetie. I don't know."

Andie's eyes grew round. "Unless . . ."

"Unless what?" Cole walked over to her.

Andie's eyes shone in the dim light of the stairwell. Flipping over her bracelet, she showed Cole the back. "Unless he knew I didn't have to *know* the code, just always have it with me."

"That's got to be it!" Jenna grabbed his arm, bouncing on her toes. "Andie never takes off her MedicAlert bracelet, and Marc memorized the number."

Cole went to crouch beside Andie. Sure enough. Her ID number was eight digits. He smacked her cheek with a sloppy kiss and raced back to the keyboard. "Read me those numbers, Einstein. Your name was never more fitting."

His fingers flew over the keys. As soon as his pinky hit enter, the wall slid open, revealing a solid steel door that lifted up from the floor into the ceiling. "Andie, stay there and listen for anyone coming. Jenna, stay outside the door in case this thing closes on me. You'll probably have to start over with the sequences to get me out."

His girls nodded at him.

Ducking to fit through the opening, Cole walked into the small cubicle. Only about eight feet square, the far corners were stacked with boxes of files. On one wall were three computers with labels above each of them. Possibly other programs or weapons he'd been working on. And then to his right were four file boxes labeled AMI, a metal lock box with the same label, and a stack of DVDs.

"Cole!" Andie's loud whisper jerked his attention back. She scooted down the stairs, a finger to her lips, her other arm pointing frantically at the door. "Footsteps . . . coming . . ."

He walked out of the room, and hit enter on the keyboard. Nothing happened.

"How do we get it to close?" Jenna gripped his arm. "We can't let them find it."

"I know, I know." His heart raced. Holding his breath, he couldn't think of anything else to try. The screen was blank. No help. No clues. *God, I could use some—*

Andie was beside him now, tugging on his shirt. "How about typing c-l-o-s-e?"

If anyone understood Marc's labyrinthine mind, it was probably his kid. He shrugged his shoulders and typed in the letters.

The doors closed.

Of course. Why hadn't he thought of that?

They let out a collective sigh and huddled down on the floor.

"What do we do?" Jenna had a death grip on his arm.

"I'm working on that."

Andie scooted closer. "I'll keep praying."

"That'd be great." And he meant it. They were going to need a miracle to get out of this.

The clanking of metal against metal came from the door.

Think.

It creaked and groaned as it opened.

Viper's thousand-dollar shoes appeared on the steps.

God, help us.

"Well, well, well . . . Look who's awake?" Viper chuckled and aimed his gun at Cole. "Have a nice nap, Maddox?"

Before he could respond, a growl erupted behind Viper. A ball of fur attacked the big man's arm.

"Dasha!" Andie jumped up, but Jenna held her back.

Dasha's teeth were around Viper's hand.

This was his chance. Cole tackled Viper and pummeled his face with his fists. Dasha violently shook Viper's hand in her teeth, ripping the gun from Viper's hand, taking part of his trigger finger with it.

His old boss didn't even cry out, just wrapped both hands around Cole's neck and squeezed.

With a knee to the man's groin, Cole spun and flipped him onto his back. Much-needed air flowed through his windpipe. He yelled to the girls. "Get out of here! Now!"

Viper came at him again, plowing him into the cement wall.

CHAPTER THIRTY-FIVE

ANDIE
April 14
North Pole, Alaska
Tikanni-Gray property along the Chena River
4:18 a.m.

Cole took another punch as Mom, Dasha, and I cowered in a corner. *God help Cole, help Cole, please help!*

Cole tackled the guy and grunted. *"Go!"*

Mom shot up and ran, dragging me with her. Dasha followed, nudging my leg and propelling me forward.

We ran-limp-hobbled as fast as we could. I didn't want to leave Cole but couldn't pull against Mom's grip. She kept looking behind us as we ran.

God, please help us!

Mom tried to gain speed, but tripped. Everything moved in slow motion as she fell and screamed in pain. I fell to my knees and tried not to squash her.

Looking down, I saw her leg wound, open and bleeding. Her pant leg had been ripped open and had a hole at least a foot long. My stomach clenched as I realized how bad it was.

"Mom—"

"We have to run!" She grabbed my hand and we started running.

I could tell the more we ran the more her leg hurt. She stumbled, but kept scrambling along.

Dasha barked and growled. Before I could comment, an explosion sounded near the house, knocking us to the ground.

Our home burst into flames and sparks flew everywhere.

Dasha cuddled up against my back, still barking, but this time at the fire all around us. Mom tore her pants and used the cloth to wrap around her leg. She grabbed my hand and stood. We ran for a few feet, but her leg gave away again and we fell back onto the ground.

Smoke filled the air and the sky went black as the fire spread.

We started crawling.

My legs began to burn and the itchy feeling crept onto my back. Mom thrust her water bottle at me.

She still had one? Thank You, Jesus! I sipped it, not knowing how long we would be crawling.

Every time I thought we were getting close to a safe place the fire would move in front of us and we'd have to go around.

Another explosion near the house sent us sprawling to the ground. Were they blowing up everything?

The trees were all on fire and I kept tripping on rocks, bushes, and twigs. I got hotter by the minute and knew it would only be a few seconds before I passed out.

Oh, no . . . Jesus, help me!

I gripped Mom's arm.

The blackness came.

COLE

4:25 a.m.

A third explosion rent the air. Soon, every building on the property would be engulfed. They were surrounded by fire. And his girls were in there . . . somewhere.

How would he find them? Save them?

What if he couldn't save them? What if this was the end? Jenna had said if it was her time, she was ready.

But he wasn't.

Wasn't ready to let go again.

Wasn't ready to lose.

Wasn't ready to die.

Wasn't ready to meet his Maker.

But if this was the end—if he couldn't save them—he still needed to set things straight. Because it didn't have to be the end. If he couldn't be with them here, he wanted to be with them in eternity.

"God, I get it. I need Your help. I'm Yours. Body and soul. Do with me what You will."

A cooling wave of peace rushed throughout his body even as the heat of the flames drew closer. The peace filled him. Took over his senses.

God had heard him. He knew it as sure as he knew anything. And He'd responded with a flooding of strength and joy.

New purpose propelled him forward as he raced into the heart of the fire.

JENNA

4:27 a.m.

"Andie!"

The scream scratched and pierced Jenna's dry throat. She worked to drag them both away from the fire, but it began to close in. Dasha circled them, nudging Andie with her nose. Whining and yapping at her beloved mistress.

The flames licked higher and higher.

Too hot.

What could she do? Nowhere to go. Her water was gone. The fire surrounded them. She fanned her daughter, but fear took hold. What if it was too late? She placed her hand on Andie's forehead. Too hot.

A lone figure jumped through the flames toward them.

Please, God! Let it be Cole. Please. I need help! Please, save my baby!

The figure crouched low, appearing and disappearing in the smoke.

In an instant, Cole was beside her, scooping up Andie with one arm, and grabbing Jenna around the waist with the other. "Hang on!" The roar of the flames grew.

Dragging her leg behind her, she hopped to keep up with Cole as he guided them. Dasha was glued to her side, whimpering and barking at the fire around them. As they came to the wall separating them from the plane, she prayed. How would they make it through?

"We have to run through it," Cole spoke in her ear. "I'll protect Andie as much as I can, so you'll just have to hang on to my arm and run, okay? The plane should be about a hundred yards from here."

He shifted Andie into both arms, curling her up against his body.

All Jenna could do was nod. Her leg was a mess. *God, we need some divine intervention. Please, help us. Please.*

In that instant, a strong wind blew in, and the flames shifted, opening a small gap no larger than two feet. Cole must've seen it too, because he led them straight for it and they ran through. Flames licking at their heels as the wall closed back in and grew higher.

They fell to the ground in a heap about twenty yards from the fire. Dasha barking, dashing back and forth to the plane, panic in her eyes.

Cold water poured over Andie and Jenna as Bill, their bloody bodyguard, dumped out the contents of two water bottles on them.

"Bill! You're alive!" Jenna reached up to hug him.

"Barely." He gasped, pressing a hand to the gunshot wound in his upper chest. "I think the good Lord has plans for me yet." He handed her another bottle of water and let out a groan. "I was so worried about you all when I heard the explosion. Didn't know how long I'd been out. But I think it's time to leave."

"You're right." Cole lifted Andie back into his arms and headed for the plane. Gently laying Andie on the back seat, he grabbed Bill's arm. "Get them outta here. As far away as you can, and get that little girl cooled off."

Jenna poured more water on Andie, and she moaned. "Hey, sweet girl. Wake up."

She opened her eyes. "Mom?"

Dasha licked Andie's face.

"Hey, baby, I'm here."

"So thirsty."

Jenna opened the last water bottle. "Here you go."

As Andie drank, her eyes followed Cole. Jenna looked behind her. Cole wasn't getting in the plane.

She jumped out and yanked at Cole's arm. "We're not leaving without you!"

"Jenna, you have to. AMI is still back there. I can't risk them finding it."

She gripped his waist and tugged him close. Lifting a hand to his head, she pulled his lips down to hers and kissed him with all the emotion locked inside her. God help her, she loved this man.

"Jenna," he spoke against her lips, "I . . . I . . ."

She kissed him again and then pulled back. "I know. Thank you."

His arms wrapped around her in a tight hug and he lifted her into the plane. "We'll talk later. I promise. Now go."

Hot tears streamed down Jenna's face.

He closed the door of the plane and she pressed her hand against the glass. He laid his on the outside. *God, keep him safe. Please.*

The plane began to taxi away. Jenna kept her hand on the window as she watched Cole head back into the fiery abyss. *He needs You, Father.*

As the small plane picked up speed, her heart thundered inside her chest. Would she ever get the chance to tell him that she loved him? She gripped Andie's hands as the plane lifted into the air. Andie lay unconscious again, still flushed from the heat. Jenna prayed there wouldn't be permanent damage, but the heat had been too much, lasted too long. *Oh, God. Please help her. Help us all.*

So much at stake.

Flashing lights drew her attention back to the window. Emergency vehicles swarmed the scene of her property, their red-and-blue lights a welcome sight. Help had finally arrived.

They circled around, watching, and waiting. Her eyes found the bunker, just as Cole's head appeared in the doorway. Cole looked up at the plane and raised his hand to her. *Thank You, God, he's safe.* She placed her hand on the cool window and rested her forehead against it. She couldn't wait to have Cole's strong arms around her again. She brushed Andie's face with her hand. Maybe then, everything would feel righ—

Boom!

Boom! BOOM!

The massive explosions sent a shock wave that hit the plane a second later.

A scream started in the depths of her soul and pushed its way through her lips like a tidal wave. "*Cole!*"

Her voice echoed through the plane.

In her head.

In her ears.

And pierced her heart.

Placing both hands on the glass window of the plane, she searched the rolling cloud of flame and smoke. The barn was gone. The house was gone. The bunker, where she last saw Cole . . . gone.

Engulfed in fire.

Flashing lights formed a perimeter and were the only break in the devastation below. Everything from her life before . . . gone.

Everything she'd been hoping for her future, for her daughter's future.

Gone.

Bill steadied the shaken aircraft and headed in the other direction.

She tore away from the window. There was nothing to see.

Cole was gone.

Sobs shook her body as she clung to Andie's hand. Her daughter moaned again, and she gave her more water. All the while, the if-onlys stampeding through her mind.

If only she'd told him how she truly felt . . .

If only he hadn't gone back . . .

If only . . .

And then a still, small voice.

Greater love has no man than this, that one lay down his life for his friends.

CHAPTER THIRTY-SIX

JENNA
April 15
Fairbanks Memorial Hospital
Fairbanks, Alaska
10:55 a.m.

The familiar beeping awoke her. She blinked the sleep away, rubbing her eyes with her hand. Wow, she was groggy. Her mouth felt filled with cotton.

A glance to her right brought Andie in a hospital bed into view. She looked back down at herself and found she, too, was in a hospital bed.

Hooked up to machines.

Again.

What happened? What day was it?

Cole! Her heart ached. *God, why? Why? Why would You take him away? He needed You so badly . . . and . . . and . . . I loved him!*

She closed her eyes to the pain, wishing she could close her heart to it as well. Tears streamed down her cheeks. It was all her fault. She could've prevented it. She could've done more. She could've saved Cole.

"Ahem." A low and rumbling voice broke through her thoughts.

Opening her eyes, she swiped at her wet cheeks with her hands.

"Mrs. Tikaani-Gray, I'm Special Agent Phillips." The man paused and nodded to another man beside him. "And this is Special Agent Miller. Your husband, Marcus, contacted me at the Bureau. He was a good man, and I'm sorry we lost him. But we've come here to thank you for all you've done to get AMI back into U.S. hands."

The trembling of her lower lip kept her from speaking. She nodded instead.

"We're very sorry for all you've had to endure."

"That man . . . he wasn't an agent, was he?"

He shook his head. "We found Special Agent McAdams dead in his car."

Jenna closed her eyes. "So many people have been lost because of all this . . ."

"There has been some good come out of it. Thanks to your husband contacting us, and to Mr. Maddox's intervention, we've been able to secure the technology and locate the black-market buyers."

Cole. She'd never see him again. Never hear his voice—never feel his arms around her. She turned away. Hugged herself tight as gut-wrenching sobs wracked her frame.

"Mrs. Gray."

She shook her head and waved them off. Pulling her good knee up to her chest, she wrapped her arms around it, and laid her head down, giving in to the torrent of emotion.

"Jenna."

Great. Now she was imagining things. She longed for Cole so much, she heard his voice. Why couldn't they all just leave her alone?

"Mom." Andie's weak voice pursued her. "Mom. It's okay. Please don't cry. I'm all right. Please, Mom. Please. Open your eyes."

Breathe, Jenna. Breathe. Andie needs you. Suck it up. You can do it. Stop crying like a two-year-old.

But it hurt. And she just wanted the pain to go away.

"Consider it pure joy, my brothers, whenever you face trials of many kinds . . ."

Of course. She had to remember *that* verse. Now. Of all times.

"Jenna."

There it was again. Cole's voice. Would the torment never end?

Wait a minute.

Cole's voice.

Her eyes popped open and she lifted her head with a jerk.

"Cole." Tears continued to stream down her face. Her nose ran. Chin quivered. "You're here."

He winked from his wheelchair, his right arm and leg wrapped in bandages, Andie's arms securely around his neck.

"I'm here. And I'm not going away."

COLE

April 15
Fairbanks Memorial Hospital
4:00 p.m.

Cole thought his heart would burst. Never in his life had he been in so much physical pain, but it paled in comparison to the joy flooding his heart.

Thank You, God.

He'd been given a second chance. And he planned to do everything within his power to make it count.

Glancing around the room, he watched Andie play with Dasha on her bed, all smiles and giggles even though thirty-six hours before she'd suffered an intense heat stroke. Talk about miracles.

The FBI agents stood in the corner drinking coffee.

The doctor talked to Jenna.

His girls would have quite a recovery period, but they were his. And they were safe.

A knock sounded at the door, and Dasha barked.

Andie giggled. "That means, 'come in.'"

A woman wheeled Bill into the room. "Hi, guys. How's everyone doin' today?"

"Bill!" Jenna and Andie both exclaimed.

Andie clapped gleefully. "I'm so glad you're okay!"

Bill smiled at them.

"Thank you." More tears streamed down Jenna's face. "Thank you for everything."

"Bill, there's one question, I really want to ask." Her daughter tapped the man's arm.

"All right. I'm ready." The big man winked.

"What does it feel like to get shot?"

The afternoon held one joyful reunion after another. After Bill arrived, Anesia and Zoya returned with new clothes for Andie and Jenna. And M&Ms.

Lots of M&Ms.

Questions flew around the room as everyone put the pieces of the puzzle together.

"Cole, how did you survive the explosions? I watched from the plane, and just knew you were dead." Jenna's voice shook as she fiddled with Marc's little black box.

"Paul," he nodded toward Anesia, "the pilot who flew me up there, noticed the charges when he was leaving. The first explosion took out his plane, so he tried to see what he could do to help. When he spotted me heading back to the bunker, he followed me. Another explosion threw us back, into the bunker. Paul pulled the door shut before the next blast could fry us both. The steel door slammed in the nick of time."

The action of that perfect stranger hit him hard. Like another Stranger who gave everything for him. "He lost his plane in the blast, but he saved our lives. Thankfully, Marc had a wife who was paranoid so he built a bunker that could withstand that kind of blast." He winked at Jenna as the others laughed.

"God knew what He was doing." Cole tried to convey his heart to the woman he loved.

Her eyebrows raised. The *do you believe* question clear in her eyes.

They shared a smile. What he wouldn't give to see that every day. Jenna turned to Bill, her eyes somber. "What happened after we left the plane. I thought . . . I was so sure . . ."

"Well, ma'am. I think that was my own little miracle. I fell forward after the bullet hit me. My blood just drippin' out of me—my life drainin' before my eyes. I closed my eyes and knew my time had come." He took a deep breath. "After Viper took off with you, Dasha appeared in the pilot's seat, nudgin' her way under me. Crazy dog pushed me up and licked my face until I came to. And then, your dog kept pawin' at the door by me. I wasn't coherent enough yet to do anything to help myself, but she kept pushing me toward that door. She came in through the other door that was left open, so I didn't understand why she was so blasted determined to get me to open the door, but thankfully, I didn't argue. I must've fallen out of the plane with her, because I woke up face-down on the ground. Thing was, I landed in mud, and the force of my fall packed the mud into my wound. I have no doubt that saved my life."

Cole nodded. "Slowed the bleeding."

Bill shifted in his chair. "I must have passed out, but when I came to, I managed to get up and pull the first aid kit from the plane and bandage the wound. I was checking for whatever I could use against Viper when I found the water bottles stashed in the back."

"And that's when we arrived." Jenna's whispered voice reflected her wonder. "That's why you had the water bottles ready when Andie needed them."

Cole knew how she felt. Every moment, every thing they faced . . . God had been there. Providing. He'd thought Jenna was so naïve when they were on the mountain. So foolish to trust this imaginary God of hers. But now he knew. She was right.

It wasn't Cole's strength . . . or Bill's, or Charles's . . . that saved them. It was God's. And it was time he let his girls know he didn't just understand that—he believed it.

"Jenna, Andie, I want to tell you both something."

"Would you like to be alone?"

He knew Bill was kidding, but he considered it. It would be easier to just tell the girls . . . but no. He needed to be up-front with them all. "No. Stay. Please. I want you to know something."

Andie beamed, her dimples practically jumping out of her cheeks. "I know what it is." She clapped her hands. "You accepted God's gift, didn't you?"

The prick of tears forced him to blink. "Yes, Andie, I did."

"I knew it. I could see it in your eyes."

Jenna burst into laughing sobs. Her hands shot up to her face, wiping at the tears, but the love and happiness reflected in her eyes made his heart swell with pride.

Ever-quiet Zoya snuck up to his side. "I'm proud of you." She popped another M&M in her mouth.

Anesia hugged him, holding him so tight it hurt. But he didn't care. It felt great.

Bill smacked him on the arm, then extended a hand. "That's great news, brother. Welcome to the family."

Cole took the hand Bill held out to him and shook it. Bill was right. It really was like becoming part of a family.

Bill leaned his elbows on the arms of his wheelchair. "So, what's up next for you, Maddox?"

Cole smiled. God had taken care of everything. "I've been given a second chance. The FBI has asked me to help the military with AMI and all its components. And I have to fill them in on everything Viper and the group did. Any contacts or information I can supply will help them shut down other covert groups. I'll be writing sworn statements until I die."

The guys guffawed. None of them liked paperwork. Cole's wheelchair was between his girls' hospital beds, so he reached for Andie with his bandaged hand, and Jenna with the other. "And"—he met Jenna's eyes—"I've been given a second chance. At love." He turned to Andie. "And at being a dad. If, that is, you two will have m—"

Andie was hugging him before he finished talking. "Will we? You better believe it!"

He wrapped his arms around this precious girl who'd given him so much. "You know, Squirt, from the day I lost my family, I haven't had a safe haven to run to. Didn't have peace . . . didn't have joy. Every mission kept me in the danger zone, relying on myself. Because it hurt too much to care. About anyone." He took a deep breath. "Then you came busting into my life." He touched her damp cheek. "And my heart. You showed me I've only been hurting myself. Thanks, Squirt."

"For what?"

"For telling me like it is. And showing me God's love in a way I couldn't ignore."

"I love you, Cole."

"I love you, too, Einstein."

Andie leaned back, and her smile slid into a frown. "But there is one thing I have to say, Mr. Cole Maddox."

Uh oh. This sounded serious. Was she having second thoughts—

"I'm not *ever* climbing a mountain with you again. Ever." Andie sat back and crossed her arms.

The room erupted in laughter.

Cole clutched his chest with his bandaged hand. "Oh, you've wounded me! Why not?"

"Because you snore." Those cute dimples winked at him from her cheeks. "A lot."

Jenna leaned forward to take Andie's other hand. "We'll just have to get you some earplugs, kiddo."

"Yeah, but what about you, Mom?"

Jenna cocked her head. "Me?"

"Well, if you and Cole are gonna get married, you'll have to listen to him snore every night. Yuck."

Jenna's cheeks went pink, but the smile she directed at Cole was full of mischief. "We'll think of something . . ."

Cole let a slow smile ease onto his face. Indeed they would. "So, is it safe to assume, Jenna, that your answer is *yes,* as well?"

Jenna leaned in and planted a kiss on his lips. He wrapped her in his arms, prolonging the contact, lost in the feel, the gift, of her.

"Come on, you two."

Cole pulled away, but kept his arms around Jenna. No way he was letting go now. Or ever.

Andie made a face at him and rolled her eyes.

Cole grinned. "Get used to it, Squirt. You're gonna be seeing a lot of that."

Andie's grin stretched from ear to ear. "I guess I can deal." She came to join their hug, wrapping her arms around him. "Welcome to the families, Cole." She peeked up at him.

"'Families?'"

"God's . . . and ours."

Cole leaned his forehead against Jenna's. Two families in one day.

It didn't get any better than that.

AUTHOR'S NOTE

Thank you so much for traveling this exciting journey with us. Our characters, Jenna and Andie, mirror a lot of the real-life Kim and Kayla, but not all. It is, after all, a work of fiction.

Research is no important in novel writing. Many thanks go out to all the experts who helped along the way. Any errors are purely our own.

In crafting *No Safe Haven*, we used real-life medical issues that Kayla and other HSAN patients have so that you could understand this fascinating nerve disorder. While Andie has the same rare conditions as Kayla—both HSAN and Chiari—there are still differences. HSAN (some are diagnosed CIPA) is extremely rare, and doctors are constantly learning and making discoveries to help the few dozen patients in the world living with it. But so few people truly understand the intricacies. (Including us! And we live with it every day.)

Through this story, we hope we've given you a glimpse into our special relationship as mother and daughter, what it feels like to be a twelve-year-old who has HSAN, and what it's like to be the mom of a child with a rare disorder. We had a blast writing

No Safe Haven, and hope you'll join us for more of Jenna, Andie, Cole, Zoya, and Anesia in *Race Against Time*—where Zoya is a champion sprint-dog racer.

Please let us know what you think. We love to hear from our readers!

Kim and Kayla

www.kimberleywoodhouse.com
www.kimberleyandkaylawoodhouse.com
www.kaylawoodhouse.com

DISCUSSION QUESTIONS

1. In the beginning of *No Safe Haven*, the flight is going smoothly, life is finally looking up for Jenna and Andie, and then suddenly things turn to disaster. When has your life been interrupted unexpectedly? How did that affect you?

2. Isaiah 26:3 says, "You will keep in perfect peace the mind that is dependent on You, because it is trusting in You." Have you experienced that kind of peace of the Lord? What are some ways to put this verse into practice, especially when life takes unexpected—and difficult—turns?

3. Andie wakes up after the plane crash and discovers she's all alone. Fear threatens to overtake her. When in your life have you felt this alone? How did you move past that feeling?

4. Trust in others is a struggle for the characters of *No Safe Haven*. Do you find it easy to trust people or are you more guarded? How does this affect your ability to trust God?

5. Cole has a hidden past of family pain. When Jenna and Andie start to trust him, that slowly breaks through his wall. What

one event in your life has most impacted you. Does it continue to do so?

6. How can we, as Christians, move beyond the painful parts of our pasts? How do you reach out to people who have deep pain like Cole's?

7. In the beginning, Jenna fights Cole every step of the way—until the avalanche, when she realizes if they'd done things *her* way, they would have been buried. Why does Jenna have such trouble letting someone else—even someone with more experience than she—be in control?

8. If you were stuck on a mountain in a blizzard, what supplies would you like with you? How would you handle the fear and despair that inevitably come with being stuck in a desperate situation?

9. Jenna realizes that her husband hid important information from her and she feels betrayed. How can we, as believers in Christ, handle betrayal from people who are close to us?

10. How can we resolve situations where *we* are the ones who have betrayed others?

11. James 1:2–3 says, "Consider it a great joy, my brothers, whenever you experience various trials, knowing that the testing of your faith produces endurance." How do you apply this verse when encountering trials? What does joy look like in the midst of pain and suffering?

12. While on the mountain, Cole, Jenna, and Andie use humor to relieve some of the tension of their serious situation.

How do you find humor in the hard times in life? Think back on a time where humor relieved the tension in a situation. How did that change your outlook?

13. Andie has to ask Cole for forgiveness after she gets angry at him through a misunderstanding. Why is it so difficult to ask others for forgiveness? Have you ever had to do so? How did you approach the person you wronged? How did this experience change you?

14. Scripture commands us several times to not fear. Is this an easy command for you to obey? Do you tend to worry? How do you turn your fear over to the Lord? Discuss situations where there has been fear and the Lord has intervened.

15. Andie and Jenna have close friends in Anesia and Zoya. Who are your closest friends? What circumstances brought you together? Name qualities that you appreciate most about your closest friends.

16. Toward the end of the book, Hank, who had attempted to kill Andie and Jenna in the beginning, ends up trying to save them. How did you feel about the change in him? Were you angry that he seemed to "get away" with what he'd done? Many times we judge people by the sin in their lives, rather than seeing them with the love of Christ. Think of a time when you thought a person you knew was one way and their behavior ended up surprising you in a positive way.

17. If you had to pinpoint your favorite part of the story, what would it be? Why?

Another Exciting Title by
Kimberley Woodhouse

Woodhouse Family
Welcome Home!
OUR FAMILY'S JOURNEY TO EXTREME JOY

Kimberley
Woodhouse